# The Warrior Queen

This first edition published in 2022 by
Blue Moon Rising Publishing
www.ektaabali.com

ISBN ebook: 978-0-6454650-0-6
Paperback: 978-0-6454650-1-3
Hardcover: 978-0-6454650-2-0
Paperback (Pastel Edition): 978-0-6454650-7-5
Hardcover (Pastel Edition): 978-0-6454650-8-2

Illustrated Cover design by Carly Diep
Hardcover Case by Jessica Lowdell
Maps by Najlakay
Chapter Header by Jessica Lowdell
Book Formatting by E.P. Bali with Vellum

The author acknowledges the Traditional Custodians of the land where this book was written. We acknowledge their connections to land, sea and community. We pay our respects to their Elders past and present and extend that respect to all Aboriginal and Torres Strait Islander Peoples today.

# A NOTE ON THE CONTENT

I care about the mental health of my readers.
This book contains some themes you might want to know about
before you read.
They are listed at www.ektaabali.com / themes

*Please note this novel contains mature themes and is best suited to
audiences ages 18+*

HUMAN REALM

FARLOUGH CITY

SERUS

KAALON

PEACH TREE CITY

SAMPATI CITY

KUSHA

TRAENARA

SHOBNA CITY

WAELAN

BALNOR CITY

QUARTZ

LUMENCIA QUARTZ QUARRY

LOBRATHIA

THE TEMARI FOREST

TEMPLE RUINS

THE SILENT MOUNTAINS

FAE WARRIOR ACADEMY

BLACK COURT

ECLIPSE COURT

OBSIDIAN COURT

REALM OF THE DARK FAE

THE LOTUS SEA

ELLYTHIA

LOTA

THE JUNGLE ACADEMY

# E.P. BALI

# The
# Warrior
# Queen

*This novel is an ode to feminine rage.*
*May our voices be heard, may our feet tread steady, may our swords*
*always be sharp.*

# 1

# SARAYA

The first thing I knew was a torturous burning pain right through my core.

A low, constant vibration rumbled through my back and it took me a moment to realise I was lying down on something that was moving. I blinked up at a leafy green canopy—a sheet stitched out of leaves that shielded me from a bright sun set in a cornflower blue sky. I was enveloped in humid warmth that was at once fresh and comforting, the scent of mint and grass filling my nose.

I knew at once that I was not in either the Human Realm nor the Dark Fae Realm.

I bent my knees and a new onslaught of pain sliced through me, making a gasp escape my throat. Immediately, I made to magically scan my body to detect the problem. But as I turned my consciousness inward, I came up against a wall of empty darkness and it felt just like it had when I'd been forced to wear the demonic magic-stopping shackles. I felt my wrists on reflex and found of course, that I was not wearing any demonic shackles. Agatha's voice swam into my mind. *"You've made the*

1

*midwives lazy."* Imagining my old midwife mentor's finger jabbing at me, I took a deep breath.

I'd have to do it the old fashioned way. Trying to stop the rising panic, I did a physical scan instead. My shoes had been removed, but I felt some old, healing blisters on my feet, not a huge concern. My calves and knees were raw where the skin had been grazed, but that too was nothing major. I palpated my thighs and pelvis with my fingers. They were all intact, only bruised, but—*oh no.*

Buried within my torso was a relentless, deep-rooted burn. My hand flew to my stomach, the midwife in me immediately taking over, palpating each quadrant of my abdomen. The skin itself was fine, and as I made my way around my organs, I ticked each one of them off my list. The pain was unlikely to be my appendix or spleen or liver. Nor my bowel or uterus, which was definitely not pregnant from the last time I'd slept with Drake, I had made precautions for that—

*Drake.*

An involuntary sob tore from my throat, and my hand flew from my stomach to my mouth. I raised my right arm. My magical black mating mark was gone. My skin was bare of the magically inked twisted tree, leaving smooth brown skin behind. Any evidence that Drake had been my mate had vanished... for good.

I was not prepared for this pain. My heart felt like it was being sliced into two by a jagged blade, a vise was around my throat, restricting my air flow. The splitting pain in my chest threatened to overwhelm me and all I could do was keep breathing—to focus on the sole act of pulling air into my lungs. This couldn't be happening. This could *not* be happening to me. Not here, not now.

There would be a permenant mark on my soul that was the sight of Drake's face when I had uttered those heinous words:

*I reject you as my mate.*

The Black Court battle had been devastating *before* the colossal-sized fire wraiths had arrived, and Drake had single-handedly fought them. I had done it for his own good. For *our* own good. He needed to be strong if he was going to survive that fall into the chasm created by the falling wraith.

Survival. That's what this was.

Why did it have to hurt so much?

It wasn't until the vehicle I was on jolted on even ground that I came back to reality. I was *not* this person. Not the type of woman who fell down at the first difficulty. I needed to find out where I was and what happened to my magic. With a concentrated effort, I put up a dam against the flood of grief and raw pain that was Drake's face as he hung from his fingers on the edge of that chasm.

What *had* happened on the battlefield after Drake had fallen into that endless chasm? Magic had torn through me. Wild, as if a dam had been unleashed. Lightning upon lightning had fallen and I had directed it to kill our enemies in battle. I had never used that amount of magic before. I ran my hand over my stomach once again as a dull realisation crawled through me. This pain was not physical in origin at all, but magical. I was magically drained and the last time this had happened to me…was not a time I liked to think about. That memory was something I'd shoved deep inside my being until I couldn't feel it anymore.

Because it had been the first time Glacine had stolen me away into her room to whip me. I don't even remember the actual event, I just recall that afterwards, it took my magic days to return. Every time Glacine whipped me I fell down into that well and every time I crawled back out I got better at it. It just felt like I left a little piece of me down there.

I blinked away the burn in my eyes. Now that I knew what was wrong with me, I needed to understand what was happening around me. I could see that I was on a small, open-fronted wagon. A horse was hitched to it and trudging along just ahead. I squinted at the figure leading the horse. The world was so bright and warm out there that it felt like the beginning of summer. Only it couldn't be—we were supposed to be in the latter half of winter now.

Muttered voices sounded outside the wagon.

"Hello?" I called. My voice emerged hoarse. I had been screaming, I recalled, back when my magic had torn free.

There was a shout and the patter of boots. Abruptly, the wagon stopped.

The first face I saw was pale, baby blue-eyed and raven-haired.

"Blythe?" I choked, scrambling onto my knees with a wince.

"Goddess!" Blythe squealed, immediately climbing into the wagon and lunging for me. I suppressed a groan as my aching bones took the weight of my blubbering friend. "Saraya, it was terrifying, but I'm an even better fighter now and it was all a mess, and then we saw you go all lightning crazy, and Slade and I and Jerali—"

"Slow down," I wheezed, rubbing her back. "Where—"

"Get off her, Blythe," came a low voice. "You'll strangle our queen and then I'll have to hang you for regicide."

I choked once again as Blythe got off me. Jerali Jones climbed up to sit on the edge of the wagon, narrow face grinning. Relief flooded through me, and I reached for my Armsmaster's hand. Jerali grasped it in return. They were alive and well. I was not alone.

Behind my Armsmaster, Lysander and Slade appeared. Slade, a brawny fae warrior with raven dark hair and eyes, and Lysander, the complete opposite, fair with long blond hair and blue eyes. Both fae warriors bore grim expressions on their handsome faces. They'd seen everything from a distance, I vaguely recalled, and had not been able to help Drake either.

Lysander tossed his blond mane and wiggled his fingers at me in greeting. "Welcome to the Solar Fae Realm, Princess." He gestured to the impossibly green trees on either side of the gravel road. "The Black Court portal took us into Blossom Court, but Sky Court is only a day's ride away."

I raised my brows.

"They wanted to go back to Kaalon," Jerali explained, side-eyeing Slade, who glowered and tugged at his shirt collar in an old habit. "But I said that we had to listen to what you were saying as you collapsed."

I nodded. "Thank you. Did you just call me—"

"She did," Blythe nodded firmly. "After you collapsed, King Daxian told us your intentions to take the throne of Lobrathia. And gosh, yes, I'm so glad this is the plan because me and Tembry and Delilah—"

"Tell me everything," I interjected, making to climb out of the wagon. My body felt like crumpled parchment that needed straightening out and without my magic I felt all the more worse. I had also not seen my friends for weeks. "Did you all make it safely to Peach Tree City after the massacre at Havrok's Court? Drake sent a raven, but we didn't get a reply."

Jerali nodded. "I'm sorry about that. We discovered letters were being intercepted by Obsidian Court. We mostly all made it, with some losses. There were more demons at the quarry portal than I'd anticipated, but with Opal's help, we managed."

"And Opal?" I had not seen my tiny ball of coloured fluff in weeks as well and the last time we'd been separated, both her legs had been broken.

"She wanted to come, but I bade her to stay with Delilah, and she agreed."

I knew that Opal took her baby-protecting duties very seriously. "I'm going to take back Quartz with..." *With what?* My own forces were destroyed by the demons, so my plan to take back Lobrathia from them had depended on Drake being Commander of our neighbour—Kaalon's forces. But as I thought on it, I had been able to protect Black Court castle with a shield of lightning and had done it easily. I knew I was capable of more. Arishnie had said in the old days, it would've only taken seven Warrior Midwives to do it.

But there was only one. It was just me. Would it be enough?

I clenched my fists, remembering the feeling of that electricity teeming under my skin, wanting out, wanting to be used. There was a power in me now that no one else had. That was powerful enough to protect an entire city on its own. I just had to wait and heal. And if we found this sword...Goddess knew what I could do with it.

All *I* knew was that the rage and sadness in my heart would not be quelled.

I had been betrayed time and time again by those I loved.

First, my mother kept her secrets from me.

Then my father had lied to and sold me like a brood mare to the Fae King.

Then Glacine had come along and hurt and betrayed my entire Kingdom.

Then I had fought tooth and nail to help the fae widow Xenita Darkcleaver, and she too had betrayed us all in the end.

Now I had done the betraying. I betrayed my—Drake. He was not my mate anymore. I had rejected him. I had said the words, thinking that it would make him powerful enough to beat our enemies. But I could not help but get the feeling that we were worse off for it.

Looking at my friends now, they'd changed immensely since I'd last seen them. Blythe had a fierce look in her eyes that was a magnified version of what she'd always had, but there were deep bags under them now. As if she'd seen and done things she had never dreamed of. Jerali's face was set in a grim, haunted way and there were scars on my Armsmaster's arms that were new. My heart clenched at what we'd all been through over the last few months at Havrok's Court and then at the battle.

But everything I did now, I did to get Lobrathia back. We had to fight against the demon occupation of my lands. And the Reaper. My mother had given me an idea as to how to do it.

"I'm going to take back Lobrathia as Queen," I confirmed. "In the birthing ritual with Xenita Darkcleaver, I saw my mother's spirit. She told me that Sky Court holds the Temari Blade, Umali's ancient weapon. I'm going to use it to get our home back."

They all stared at me with a mixture of wariness and uncertainty marking their faces.

"How?" was all Jerali said.

I looked at my hands, calloused and marked. I could not feel any magic stirring in me, only a burning ache that was making my eyes droop.

Jerali's face eased into a softness I did not often see. "I'm here with you, Saraya."

Blythe looked at our Armsmaster in surprise before clenching the hilt of the sword at her hip and nodding firmly. "You will always have us." She swallowed, glancing back at the two warrior fae. "Mate or not, We are your family. Me and Jerali and

Tembry and baby Delilah. Even Slade and Lysander. *We* are with you. And we will find this blade together."

I shook my head, breathing in sharply through my nose to stop the tears that threatened to spill. I was tired, so tired. But there was more to be done yet. "What did I do to deserve you guys?"

Blythe flung her arms around my neck as the fae made to start back off again. Jerali threw off the wagon covering and Blythe sat with me, breathing in the fresh air and letting the warmth of the Blossom Court sun soothe my bones.

Ordinarily, I would've healed every ailment and injury by now, and it irritated me to no end that I could do nothing. That gaping well of darkness in me was a void I dared not to look at for too long. I just had to have faith that it would come back once I'd rested. I just had to focus on what my mother had told me to do.

How long had I wished that my parents were here to give me advice? To guide me, to simply tell me what to do? And finally, in Xenita's birthing ordeal, I'd had that opportunity. Few were so lucky to speak with the dead and I would cherish those moments forever. I couldn't wait to tell Altara when I saw her next.

My stomach twisted. When *would* I see my sister next? Not before Lobrathia was ours again, I knew that much. It was too dangerous for her to come back—there was a full horde of demons waiting for us there. She was better off in Ellythia away from all of this.

With the impossibly verdant landscape of Blossom Court soothing my eyes, I rested my chin on the wagon's edge and let the slow rumbling movement lull my mind into a sort of doze. The air was sweet and fresh, a mild breeze tickling my skin.

Lysander strolled next to me, in black scaled armour he

must've gotten from Black Court and a savage blade at his hip. His preternaturally handsome face took in every part of our surroundings at once. "It's said the Ellythians and Sky Court royals used to trade," his deep voice rumbled. "I wonder if that's why your mother told you to go there?"

"I didn't know that," I said, surprised. "Perhaps that's why they were chosen to guard the blade?"

Lysander nodded absently, his long blond hair gleaming brilliantly. There was so much I didn't know. So much my mother had not told me. The same was true of the Green Reaper. Our ignorance was a serious problem. If we could just find out more about him, we could have the upper hand.

As I blinked sleepily at Lysander's abnormally handsome face, I remembered where his good looks had landed him. Once, as a courtesan and then again as a concubine at the side of a demon lord in Havrok's Court.

"Are you alright, 'Sander?" I said in a low voice.

He glanced at me, the side of his mouth quirking up in that good natured way he always had. "Always, Princess."

Drake had said that both Lysander and Slade had been through more horrific things than any fae had a right to. And I remembered what we had done for Havrok down in the subterranean realm.

"Drake assassinated a rogue demon lord for Havrok," I said slowly, observing him. "He said you knew him. Lord Gangrene."

Something flickered in those ocean blue eyes. A fleeting shadow. But like the flutter of a butterfly's wings it was gone in an instant.

"Ah. Gangrene," Lysander turned his head toward the sky, his face expressionless. "I remember him. That was just before I met Drake."

I nodded. "Did you know any of them? At Havrok's Court?"

Lysander shrugged nonchalantly. "Mmm. Some were vaguely familiar. When they passed us around we were often drunk or drugged."

Black horror twisted around my gut. Lysander had only been a teenager at the time. "And being down there again?"

The warrior gave me a pointed look. "I'm a fae grown. I was fine, Saraya, really. That Lord of the Feast was almost courteous. No, the real monsters are the dealers. The ones who organise the barter and exchange of orphans in the black markets. *My* dealer, Bonagon Darkray, now *there's* a demon I'd like to exterminate. But I never could find him."

"Drake could never—"

"I asked him not to go on a hunt. *I* want to be fully responsible for his demise. But he's run off to another Demon Court, so it was well out of my way. One day though…" He glanced at me and grinned. "I'm alright, really, Princess. I think you had it much worse."

Havrok and Glacine had humiliated me in front of their court, it was true. But after Drake and I had been married, he'd stopped anything actually awful from happening to me—or Opal for that matter. I rubbed the back of my right hand as if I could scrub away the hollow feeling in my heart.

WE TRAVELLED DOWN THE PATH FOR THE REST OF THE DAY, AND when night came, we made camp in a spacious clearing.

We sat around a crackling fireplace, bowls of soup in hand. Lysander and Slade had been travelling their entire lives, from what I understood of them. And it showed. They were well prepared with food and water and had sourced bedrolls for us to sleep on from a Blossom Court village.

As I sat on one of the logs Lysander had rolled over for us to sit on, my eyes were drawn to Blythe across the campfire.

My friend touched Slade affectionately on the arm, and he leaned reflexively toward her.

Watching the two of them, I felt my brows shoot up as surprise spun through me. I had never seen Slade smile, granted I had only known him a short while, but the way he and Blythe glanced at each other was the same way Drake and I had once side-eyed one another as we got closer. My stomach turned sickly and I looked away from the two of them. Blythe deserved all the happiness in the world, but I couldn't bear looking at them just now.

Lysander shifted on the log next to me. Ever watchful, the fae warrior cast a concerned look at me, hesitating only a moment before covering my hand with his. "I'm here for you, Saraya." His voice was gentle, but I sensed the strain in it. "Even if he's lost to us right now, you still have Slade and me."

I gave him a tiny smile and gripped his broad, long-fingered hand. I could only nod glumly into my soup. There had been a chance that the two fae would despise me for rejecting their friend as my mate, but neither seemed to hold any hate in their heart for me.

Afterwards, when Blythe and Jerali said goodnight, it was just me, Lysander and Slade by the dying fire. Finally, I spoke my dreaded thoughts out loud.

"Do you think he'd survive that fall?" I swallowed the lump in my throat as the image of the abyss swam into my mind. "I couldn't even see the bottom. All I could see was that massive fire wraith gripping onto his ankle."

Lysander briefly squeezed my hand as his gaze searched the

night sky above us. "Drake's tough," he said softly. "More powerful than even I realised. I've never seen someone take on a beast that size like that before. No one has."

"I would've gone in," said Slade with a determined look in his dark eyes. "If we'd gotten there in time, I would've jumped right in. I owe him my life, Princess."

"We both do," Lysander agreed. "He's not like anyone I've ever met. The things we've been through together...I just can't imagine doing this without him."

The backs of my eyes burned. I had not ever met anyone else like him either.

"He told me," Lysander said, avoiding my gaze. "Even before his memories were returned, he knew you would do great things. That you were like no other human or fae he'd ever met."

I pressed my lips together, but I could not stop the tears that fell onto my lap. I couldn't look at them. I just couldn't. I'd rejected their friend, put him in such great danger and he had thought of me so highly. I didn't know if I could ever forgive myself.

"You still have *us*," Slade said through gritted teeth, fighting his own emotions. "And we still have *you*. I saw what you did back there at Black Court. No one has *ever* seen anything like that, Princess. Not since the old days when humans had magic aplenty. There is change coming, and you're going to bring it."

I looked up at him then, at Slade. His perfect fae features held something that other fae males didn't. There was a hardness, a wildness borne of what I knew was a hard, battle-ridden childhood. But beneath all that was a new sort of glow. And his dark eyes were staring at me with a glimmer of resolve and hope. Perhaps his love for Blythe had given him a renewed sense of purpose.

Slade nodded. "He believed in you, Saraya. Even before he knew you. And as his mate—"

"I'm not," I interjected, "not anymore."

"I don't care," Slade said firmly. "I know why you did it. And that makes you a worthy mate. Your mark might be gone, but in my eyes, you're *still* our friend's mate."

"That means we stand by you," Lysander said with a savage smile. "To the end."

# 2
# DRAKE

I sat on the ledge above a fiery chasm, my legs dangling over the deep drop.

When I'd first fallen into the abyss of darkness, my ankle in the grip of a forty-foot tall, lava-skinned fire wraith, we'd fought in mid-air for a solid ten minutes during the free-fall. The massive beast returned each one of my blows—which for any other person would have proven lethal.

It managed to dislocate my jaw with a steaming punch that knocked me sideways, but I'd pushed my jaw back into place and kicked the thing in its burning hot temple.

I lived for this.

For the pain, for the violence, for the primal fight for life and death. The fire wraith was a worthy opponent for me, and even then, I was having the time of my life. Violence was addictive. Especially when one is in pain. Sometimes violence is the *only* thing you can do when you're in the type of pain that could make you go mad.

That is how I survived.

This beast had never known love. I didn't actually know

what went on in its fiery brain, but it wasn't the memory of his mate, her caress, her scent. The way her fingers felt on his skin. The way her lips felt against his. The way she was strong and brave.

The way she could say six words and butcher me in two.

But *I* remembered those things. And it gave the violence in me a way to be unleashed.

Eventually, I saw the abyss was no longer an abyss. A lava-filled chasm flowed beneath us, a glowing orange-yellow, bubbling river that promised death.

The wraith and the temperature of the deep earth might have already burned me into oblivion if it weren't for the magical shield I'd surrounded myself with.

But where were we? Some pit of hell, no doubt, deep in the centre of the earth. Deeper even than the demon lands.

The first fire guardian had already landed beneath us and was swimming, almost camouflaged within the river of glowing lava and melted rock. Steam rose, and I knew this heat should have killed me five times over, shield or not.

Even as the son of a Goddess, I was not completely infallible.

As we were about to land, I flew on top of my fire wraith's head, clinging onto the burning rock that made up its skull. He landed into the river with a powerful splat, lava shooting up around us. I leapt and pummelled through the shots of lava onto the rocky cliff on either side of the river.

I clawed my way up the rock, finger climbing up the sheer face.

The fire wraith bellowed behind me and I knew I only had seconds. I kicked off and in one bound, cleared the final ten meters and careened over the ledge.

A hellsome heat warmed my back and I knew the wraith had jumped after me. Turning and simultaneously bolting backwards, I brought up my forearm just in time, blocking its massive downward punch. The force of it pushed me backwards, my boots grinding against the rocky ground. The smell of burning leather and smoke filled my nose and I breathed it in like it was nectar.

I never anticipated what it would do next.

Having given up defeating me in hand-to-hand combat, the giant beast opened its burning maw. Just as a rocky wall came up behind me, it fell upon me, swallowing me whole.

Vaguely interested by this new experience, I looked around at the raging fire on all sides, threatening to crush me with flaming, rocky teeth. I did the only thing I thought would be interesting at the time. I dived down its throat, head first.

But the beast had no belly. I supposed it got all of its energy by burning up its food in its mouth. The only organ was in its chest compartment—a beating boulder-sized heart enveloped in a vicious blue-white flame.

That colour reminded me of someone else's magic.

I reached out, grabbing its heart in one shaking hand. An ageless, powerful magic kept it pumping. Gritting my teeth as my shield began to falter, I squeezed with all my might. Just as my clothes were singed—vaporised into nothing—its heart shattered.

The beast roared, but all I heard was one soft voice in my head.

*Lightning does not yield.*

The single tear that came from my eye evaporated immediately.

Then the light around me was collapsing and I collapsed with it, falling onto hard ground, naked as the day I was born. Heat dissipated into nothing.

The fire of the wraith burned out with a few sad flickers on the ground, and all that was left was ash and stone. I reached into the mound of ashes and took out its heart, now just a head-sized boulder, tossing it in the air like a ball.

While the first fire wraith had not been easy to kill, the second one had simply swam away down the river of lava and I never saw it again. It was probably headed back to the Court of Flames, where it usually resided. King Flamekeeper would not be happy about losing one of his family guardians. In the back of my mind, I realised that perhaps they weren't made to be killed.

But I didn't care. Politics was of no consequence to me anymore. *Nothing* was of consequence anymore.

So now, I sat at the centre of the earth. Wandering within the raging storm of my mind. A storm that had once been rain, lightning, and thunder. But now, it was a roaring tornado made of fire and blood.

And I let myself spin within it.

MINUTES, MAYBE HOURS LATER, I DIDN'T KNOW OR CARE, SOMETHING crept at the corners of my mind. A being darker than me. Crueller than me.

My attention piqued, I looked at it with emotionless curiosity.

Eyes of green flames. Many seeing eyes. Watching eyes. Leering eyes.

"We are the same, Drakus Silverhand. You and I are both, Niyati, rejected."

I cocked my head to listen. In my mind, there were no words registered, only meaning. It was wrong because, in *his* case, he was the one who had done the rejecting.

It didn't matter.

"You are now, Drakus Fireborn," the voice in the dark said. "Work with me. And I will give you more violence. Work with me, and you will have all the creatures you could want to kill."

He was right. I had become the very monster I was born to be and I enjoyed every second of it.

Words would not emerge from my vocal cords. They were singed, torn, broken along with the shrivelled black coal that was my own heart.

I was a creature of death. Violence was the only thing I wanted. So I nodded and held out my hand.

And the darkness reached out and shook it. "Very good, Drakus. Now, there are a number of people I need you to kill for me."

# 3
# SARAYA

S ky Court was a breathtaking sight. In the Solar Courts, it was always either Summer or Spring, as Lysander explained to us. The sky was always blue, the flowers were always in bloom, and the air always sweet. It was a place that had magic in the very air and even without my own, I knew that tingle on my skin, that buzzing sensation in my nose.

I slept a majority of the way to the palace, a tiredness like no other plaguing me to the core. But during the moments I was awake, the land was such a delight. We spotted winged fae flying in the distance, small colourful specs of light as their wings caught the sun's rays. The fae native to Sky Court were the only species of fae with wings. I was painfully reminded of the time that Drake flew us up to Dacre's tower in Obsidian Palace and wings of shadow and smoke had curled protectively around me. I supposed that was a perk of being the son of a monster Goddess. But Sky Court Fae did not have wings of shadow and smoke. Instead, their wings were a translucent colourful affair like stained glass, more like butterfly's wings, as Lysander fondly put it.

While the earth was full of beautiful flowers, the sky was just as full of the breathtaking. Gigantic birds with colourful feathers flew around us, watching curiously or suspiciously, squawking and chirping with strange sounds. One of them even had feathers with all the colours of a rainbow that reminded me of Opal. The backs of my eyes burned as I imagined her curled up snug next to baby Delilah, watching over her when Tembry was busy. My stomach turned just a little as I wondered what awaited us back in Kaalon and how my second-cousin, Sarone and the other humans, now liberated from their demonic slavery, were doing.

Eventually, we passed a valley full of trees with leaves that were a brilliant halo of purple.

"They call it the Valley of Kings," Lysander said. "This is where every Fae King comes after their coronation to visit with Mother Jacaranda. She tells him a prophecy—something about his reign. Often a warning."

Boy, did I know about the Jacaranda Prophecy ritual.

It was one of these prophecies that had been told to the late Black Court Fae King, Wyxian, that had led him to find me as a bride for Daxian. To find a bride as a sacrifice to protect his realm. I was made to be a sacrifice. Yet all I could feel in my heart was that I had sacrificed Drake instead. Lysander nudged me as if he knew my thoughts had turned somewhere dark. I glanced at him, and his handsome face peered back at me, blue eyes a mirror of the sky.

"We'll be there just after sundown," he murmured as he walked next to the wagon.

I nodded, resting my head back down on the tiny pillow of soft grass he'd made for me.

It was not until dusk had fallen that Blythe's cry woke me up in alarm.

Ahead of us, six tall demon warriors stood in formation, unsheathed blades glinting by the light of the crescent moon.

I scrambled to my feet, just as Slade and Lysander leapt forward to engage them, the ring of their swords being unsheathed resounding in my ears. Jerali Jones ran forward right behind them. I jumped off the wagon, extending my hand out to summon my sword. But not a spark of light came from me.

Groaning in dismay, Blythe ran up to me, her sword unsheathed, eyes wild. She handed me a blade, Black Court military grade, I recognised.

But my core was burning, my legs like jelly as I clumsily stumbled after Blythe to engage the demon warriors. My brows flew up as I watched my old friend strike a demon warrior with a heavy blow, a battle worn snarl on her face. Blythe had been good before, but now? She fought like a seasoned warrior. I suppose she was, now that she'd fought in three large battles.

I barely got my blade up in time to meet an oncoming downswing. Pain shot up my arm, but I gritted my teeth and fought through it. I might not have my magic, but I had still trained with Jerali Jones and at the fae Warrior Academy. This demon— blue skinned and rotund, was like no demon I'd come across before. A completely new species, with oozing orange sweat as I forced him backwards with a flip of the wrist and a clever upward strike. I disarmed him instantly and watched his eyes widen when I plunged the blade into his abdomen and slid it upwards. When I pulled out my blade, his bowel spilled out with a splat, a foul stench filling my nose. Jerali would tut at me — my Armsmaster always said that disembowelling was an unnecessary activity.

I turned to find the others panting, the demons dead on the ground. Jerali was indeed casting me a dark look and I returned a one shoulder shrug.

A cry ran through the air, guttural and familiar. Our heads snapped to the north.

"Is that—" Blythe began.

A whole demon horde was stampeding towards us, battle cries falling heavy on my ears.

"These were scouts!" Jerali swore.

"There's too many!" Slade shouted. "We need to get to Sky Palace!"

"It's a twenty minute sprint," Lysander grunted. "We can make it."

"Make a run for it!" Jerali called to me. "Let's go!"

Seemingly understanding that I needed help, Jerali grabbed me around the bicep and dragged me forward as we ran at full pelt. The fae warriors were clearly slowing their own sprints just for me. Gritting my teeth, I realised I was physically the weakest in the group. Whatever I had done to myself at Black Court had taken a greater toll than I thought possible.

But I had twenty minutes of running to do.

We left the horse and wagon and stumbled our way over the rocky, flat grassy land, sweating and panting. My legs burned a lot quicker than they ought to and I clutched my stomach for support. Every bound of my legs brought a new wave of pain. Jerali cast a worried look at me, knowing full well this was not normal for me. But I grunted at her and pressed on, urging my legs to obey.

I knew we were almost there when Lysander suddenly shot past me, a blur in the dark, heading right into the forest looming ahead of us.

A loud clanging bell resounded through the air, amongst the cries of the demons gaining on us.

Blythe let out a shout of surprise as we stumbled into the

forest after the fae warrior. The bell continued, on and on, as if Lysander was wringing the bell's rope for all it was worth.

"Straight!" Slade shouted from behind me. "The crossing guard should meet us!"

Thoroughly confused, but having no choice, we humans carefully jogged through the forest, following the continued tolling of the bell, seeing with the tiny bit of moonlight streaming through the canopy.

Ahead of us, the now deafening bell abruptly fell silent and Blythe let out a shout.

When Jerali pulled me along into an open area, my jaw dropped open. Despite our situation, my friend was pointing and shouting with glee. And for good reason.

We had reached the edge of a cliff, a sheer drop. But across from us, hanging in mid-air, was a gigantic palace of glittering glass sitting on its own land. I could not help the gasp that escaped from my own throat. I marvelled at one of the most beautiful things I had ever seen. Winged fae flit about the palace, up turrets and spires, moving through the night, pops of colour swirling around in their own patterns. A group of those winged fae were currently flying straight over us. Two broke from the group and zoomed down, while the others continued over us, armour glinting, arrows nocked on bows and ready to fire.

"But how do we get across?" Blythe asked, panicked as I came to stand next to her, looking down at the deep drop. To my surprise, I could see no earth below. It was an infinite drop of air.

As the two fae approached, I saw they were fae females—warriors by the look of the gold armour covering their broad muscled shoulders. One had a whistle and was frantically sounding high pitched notes.

"The Sky Guard," Lysander said to us, indicating that we should move back.

Blythe, Jerali, and I hastened to comply as the two warriors descended upon our side, touching down smoothly on the rocky ledge, wings beating to slow their momentum down.

They wasted no time.

The guards both bowed. "Your Highness," said one to me, unsheathing a blade, "we will summon a crossing for your party."

Something was rapidly moving in the air between us and the glass palace. I squinted, surprised to see two fluffy clouds zooming toward us with purpose.

"Climb aboard," said one of the Sky Guards, "We'll meet you on the other side." They leapt up, wings beating powerfully, propelling them back into the sky.

"By the Goddess!" Blythe exclaimed, flinging up her hand as the strong downwind caught us unprepared.

Just as there came the sound of demons crashing into the forest behind us, the two clouds bumped impatiently onto the edge of the cliff. The sigh of relief that escaped from me was loud to my own ears.

Lysander shooed us onto the clouds as the sounds of battle began not far from us.

Quickly, Blythe hopped onto one cloud and Jerali and I onto the other.

It was like stepping onto cotton wool. But I couldn't bear to stand. Roughly, I sat cross-legged, but Lysander remained on the cliff, surveying the forest.

"Go!" He called, giving my cloud a kick. "Shoo!"

"Wait!" I called as the cloud began to float away from him.

"Slade!" Blythe screamed as her cloud began to move too. "No! Wait!"

Just as we were five strides away from the cliff, the trees shook and out ran Slade, demon blood all down his shirt, a look

24

of such determination on his face that it made my breath stop. But Slade only had eyes for Blythe and he continued running towards the cliff's edge, barked something to Lysander and in a single bound, soared through the air landing smoothly next to Blythe. She grabbed at him and he kissed her fiercely.

Jerali shifted to the side just as I saw Lysander zooming towards us. Hastily, I made room on our cloud for him, and when he landed in a crouch, the cloud didn't shake an inch.

I gave him a dark look, but the fae warrior smirked in return, running a hand through his hair.

"No one knows what lies below," Lysander said casually peering over the edge of our cloud. "Anyone who's fallen or flown down has never returned."

I shivered, goosebumps erupting all over me.

The clouds zoomed us gently across the bottomless divide, the wind beating at our faces. I did everything I could to not look down, knowing I was likely to keel over right then and there.

I had never been a fragile sort of person, but I felt like glass, ready to shatter at the barest touch. This absence of magic was uncomfortable in the worst sort of way.

"What the fuck were those demons doing there?" Jerali growled. "You said they wouldn't come into this realm."

"We were wrong," Lysander muttered shaking his head. "And did you see them? They weren't from Havrok's Court. These were demons from another Court entirely." He swore under his breath.

Sharp fear lanced through my core. "*Another* Court?" I asked. "How—"

Lysander's dark look silenced me. "It means the Reaper is petitioning the other Courts," he took a deep breath. "And they are agreeing to work with him."

I clutched my stomach and squeezed my eyes shut, thankful for Jerali's firm grip still around my bicep. More demons. More numbers for the other side. This lessened our odds significantly.

We got to the other side, the clouds gently bopping into the grassy earth. Jerali, Lysander and Slade lightly leapt off, leaving Blythe and me to stumble forward like toddlers. I took Lysander's offered hand and gratefully climbed back onto solid land.

The lush green lawn in front of the Sky Palace was a flurry of activity as more guards leapt into the sky and flew towards the battle.

Two servants awaited us in dresses of the palest blue and silver, their hair in thick braids close to their heads and their wings tucked tightly back.

"Welcome to Sky Court, Your Highness," said one, curtseying. "Lord Chalamey Springfoot awaits you inside."

I sagged in relief.

Chalamey was the reassuring and wise Dean of the Mountain Academy and had been with us planning for battle at Black Court until he'd returned to his home for safety. He had also been a father figure for Drake.

Smiling, the maids escorted us up the green lawn to the palace entrance, where glass steps were bordered by deep blue and purple flowers. Inside a cool and airy entrance hall, Chalamey Springfoot awaited us upon his black fae hound, Bubble. Chalamey was a pygmy fae, a rare breed of fae from Sky Court no more than three feet tall, with skin as dark as night and a kind smile that lit up my heart.

He wore a purple wrap-around robe and a matching cap perched upon his small head.

"I told you we would meet again, Your Highness," Chalamey said, nudging Bubble forward as a warrior does his noble steed.

26

I smiled tiredly at him. "We didn't expect the demons. And my mother told me to come here..." perhaps it was the grief or the tiredness or the shock of it all, but I could not find my words. I pressed my fingers to my mouth, and Blythe shot over to me, grabbing my hand.

Chalamey nodded knowingly. "I will have the maids escort you to rooms where you may eat and rest and sleep as you please. When you are ready, and when you have rested, we may then talk, Your Highness." he smiled at Slade, Lysander, and Jerali in turn.

Suddenly, I realised how weary I was, with my stomach growling, and feeling like I needed to wash a week's worth of sweat and grime off me. It was only three days worth, I noted, but I felt worse for wear than I ever had. I couldn't have missed my magic more.

Gratefully, we followed the two maids down a maze of corridors until we came to two guest suites, side by side. I was thankful when Blythe kissed Slade on the cheek, then came to me and took my hand, pulling me to follow Jerali into one room, leaving Lysander and Slade to head into the other. There, the maids drew us baths, where we soaked in the steaming water until we were wrinkly and pink with scrubbing. I might have fallen asleep inside the tub if not for Blythe prodding me gently, holding a soft cotton robe and towel out for me. She might have been my maid for a great part of my life, and I suppose a part of her would always feel the need to look after me, but more than a maid, she was my friend. And her eyes did not look upon me with sympathy because she knew that I would not want that. Instead, she shone with compassion. We had been through a lot together and I imagined that there was still a lot more to come.

"Let's go to bed," she said softly.

There were three large beds in the bedchamber and I was

very thankful that we would get cushioned softness instead of hard ground to sleep on. But tonight, I would not have Drake's warmth at my back nor his muscled arm around me, holding me close. Nor his mere presence reassuring me that all would be okay.

Because all was *not* okay. The wariness of the last few days took over me and wiping my eyes, I fell into an uneasy sleep plagued by dreams of fire and smoke, and demons with cobalt skin and gnashing teeth.

I AWOKE TO SOFT VOICES AND THE TREAD OF EVEN SOFTER FEET. Bleary-eyed, I sat up in bed to see our small dining table laden with baked items and fresh fruits, Jerali and Blythe shovelling food into their mouths. Blythe grinned at me, and I could not help but return a grin myself.

Blythe was a beautiful woman. With raven-coloured hair and a dusting of freckles upon her nose, she was earnest but self-assured. I knew why Slade would have found himself drawn to her down in the Demon Court. She also had a particular eye for colour and light, such that her brain worked in a way that was constantly assessing her environment for its potential to be painted. Perhaps it was one of the most charming things about her. Somewhere in my palace, tucked away in a bag I hoped safe and sound though I did not think of the alternative, was a tiny painting she had made of my mother, an exact replica of Blythe's memory of her dancing in the back garden of our palace.

Now that we knew other Demon Courts were involved, was it too grand of a thought to hope that I would take my palace back? Was it too ambitious? Was I mad for even thinking of it?

But then I remembered what Drake had said to me the first time I uttered that thought aloud in a verbal letter to Altara.

My vision turned blurry again. Drake had not been surprised at all. He had said that he would help me. Drake had always been honest. If he had thought, even for a moment, that it could not have been done, he would have told me.

I looked down at my hands, clenching them and relaxing them, looking at the brown lines strewn across my palms. There was a deep-seated power currently lying dormant within me, and I was here for a weapon—possibly the most powerful weapon ever made.

I could do this.

And I would do it for Blythe, Tembry, and baby Delilah. I would do it for my mother and father, and I would do it for Drake. So I swung out of bed, feeling slightly dizzy as I did so, a hand shooting out to grab the corner of the bed to steady myself. I realised that I had not been eating well the last few days. I sat down opposite Blythe and Jerali, and together, we feasted upon Sky Court delicacies—bread as light as air, cakes as fluffy as clouds, fruits of the sweetest kind. And once we leaned back in our chairs stroking full bellies while Jerali strode out the door, Blythe and I then returned to bed and I asked her about what had happened in the Demon Court between her and Slade. She spilled her heart to me about how she'd seen him that first day in the gladiator's arena and how he'd been withdrawn and stony. Over time, she'd coaxed him out of himself and the more time they spent together, the more she found herself falling for the fae warrior who always seemed to know what move his enemy was going to make, and who protected the weaker gladiators by taking blows and dealing them in return. She spoke about him in a breathy voice with a smile I could hear as I lay my head down on the soft Sky Court pillows. And it must have been catchy because just for a moment, before I fell asleep, I allowed a tiny smile to grace my own lips.

When we woke next, the room was dark, and someone had lit lanterns—not the quartz lamps that Blythe and I were used to. No, it was an opalescent wax candle with a real burning flame. I suppose the Solar Fae were too far from the quartz quarry, for as far as I knew, there was never any trade of quartz into this realm. I stared at it for a moment, impossibly bright light flickering, and I shivered as I remembered another flickering light. This time, flames the colour of the brightest green.

For all I knew, the Green Reaper was still on the move, preparing to execute the next part of his strategy. I needed to see Chalamey Springfoot, and he needed to tell me everything he knew.

# 4
# SARAYA

T hat evening our maids returned. In their arms were delicate dresses of sky blue with sweeping necklines trimmed with tiny sparkling gems. Blythe's eyes lit up as the maids held these dresses out for our inspection. I'm sure she had never worn something quite so grand before, and it made my heart happy that she could experience this with me. In that moment, I'm sure it was not only me who missed Tembry just a little, and even little baby Delilah who would have looked so sweet in a tiny gown of the same colour. We shoved aside our worn travelling clothes immediately.

While Jerali was dressed in the Armsmaster's preferred breeches and shirt, Blythe and I both donned our dresses. With the help of our maids, we styled our hair into the thick braided up-do that seemed to be favoured here in Sky Court—among fae who no doubt needed secure hairstyles for braving the winds in their travels through the sky.

Once we were ready, we headed outside to find Lysander and Slade dressed in fine white shirts, blue embroidered vests, and brown trousers that were the Sky Court dress for males.

Lysander beamed at me and swept a bow while I nodded in approval at his attire. But Lysander was a beautiful male, and his taste for fashion so absolute, I doubted that I would ever see him dressed in anything less than something magnificent. Even in the Demon Court, wearing his required attire—or lack of—he had always managed to look perfectly kempt.

Meanwhile, Blythe smiled shyly through her eyelashes at Slade, who graciously took her hand and pressed his lips against it.

We were to meet with the two Queens of Sky Court, or, rather, the High Queen and the Queen-Consort, newly married and eager to meet us for dinner with Chalomey Springfoot. I, too, was eager as I had much to ask of these people regarding whatever they knew about both the Green Reaper and the sole reason that I had come here at my mother's behest—the Temari Blade.

We were led to a private dining hall at the east aspect of the glass palace. Through a set of magnificent frosted glass doors, two guards ushered us into a spectacular golden-painted room. It had a long crystal table and matching plush chairs with low backs clearly made to accommodate fae with wings.

The two queens awaited us on the other side of the room, smiling widely. As we came up to meet them I found my breath hitching at the pure raw beauty of both royal fae.

The first was a blue-haired, cherub-faced beauty with sparkling lavender eyes and wings the colour of the deep sea. She wore an elegant navy blue gown that curved low at the breast. Rosy-cheeked, she beamed at us with straight white teeth and held out her hands to me. She held herself in the manner of a woman who came from a long line of royalty, straight and proud. When I took her hands, I was surprised to find that a magical tingle danced up my arm.

"It is a pleasure to meet you, Princess Saraya, soon-to-be Queen." Her lavender eyes glittered as she appraised me. "My name is Leena Stormwind, I am High Queen of these lands and it is a glorious pleasure to have you in my home. My family have long known the Ellythian queens as friends and confidants."

Stormwind. Perhaps we *would* get along well. It was no wonder that they were chosen as guardians of Umali's blade, their magic complimented ours perfectly.

"The pleasure is mine," I said softly. "Though I am afraid that we do not bring good tidings."

High Queen Leena nodded gravely. "We have much to talk about. Please meet my mate and my wife, Queen Anthi Skytrotter."

I turned to the second fae beauty who shook my hand with both of hers. Her hair was as thick and as curly as mine but coloured a brilliant silver. Shining diamonds decorated the entire curve of both her fae ears and a gown of silken red graced her form. Her eyes were a soft powder blue that matched her wings. It was then that I noticed the marks inked onto the right hands of both Queens.

Mating marks.

My heart squeezed in my chest just a little. Where my own mating mark had been curling branches and leaves, the two queens bore marks that were feathered with thin strokes that depicted fluttering wings and soft clouds. I tore my eyes away from the magical ink and forced a smile onto my face. Wherever Drake was now, I could not afford to wallow in the grief of losing him. I knew it might destroy me. I had a kingdom to think about and an enemy at my doorstep. There was work to be done.

"Are you both Queens?" Blythe blurted out after the remaining introductions were made.

Leena let out a tinkling laugh. "Indeed we are, and happily

so. I inherited the throne from my mother, so technically, I'm High Queen, and my mate is Queen-Consort. Sky Court has long held a matrilineal line of rulers so its considered proper if the ruler's mate is female to name her as queen." She waved a hand and patted her stomach with the other. "But come! Let us talk more at the table. I'm far too hungry!"

"You must forgive the High Queen," Anthi said as we sat down at the long table and were served the first course by blue and silver-clad waiters. "Her hunger gets the better of her after a morning of flying." She looked at us meaningfully as Leena began eating. "We've had to start daily patrols with the demon sightings of late. The tidings from the Dark Fae Courts do not bode well. So I, for one, am quite happy to see Chalamey Spring-foot back in-house."

The pygmy fae beamed at his queen. "Thank you, Your Highness." He turned to me. "I have closed the Mountain Academy, and I do not anticipate opening up anytime soon. You must tell us everything about what ensued once the Reaper arrived at Black Court."

I ate my soup quietly as Lysander and Slade, thankfully, took over and gave a blow-by-blow detail of the battle at Black Court once they arrived. The two queens murmured in sympathy and concern.

"Ordinarily," said Leena. "The Solar Fae and the Dark Fae do not mingle in each other's affairs. However, the demons have breeched the portal for the first time. And—" she leaned forward, "—the matter of the Temari Blade concerns *us* more than anyone else."

My head jerked up, and Leena's eyes flicked to the now ever present High Priestess mark on my forehead— a crescent moon and lotus given to me by Goddess Umali. I nodded. "My mother died many years ago," I explained. "But I accompanied Queen

Xenita in her birth ritual for her sixth child. I wasn't expecting it, but I saw my mother and my father. My mother urged me—" Suddenly, a wave of emotion climbed up my throat, cold and biting. I took a ragged moment to centre myself as the memory of my mother's face swam into my mind's eye. As a ghost, translucent though her face had been, her expression had been urgent. "My mother urged me to come here and find the Temari Blade. She said that I should retrieve it. I'm assuming she meant that it could help me take back my Kingdom from the demons."

Both Queens and Chalamey hung on to every word I spoke, oddly coloured fae eyes boring into mine with a strange intensity that made me break out into a sweat. I searched their gazes. "Does this…make sense to you?"

Leena put her soup spoon down and sat back in her chair. "More than you know, Princess."

But it was Chalamey who spoke next. "The Green Reaper is also a concern to the Solar Courts. It was he, after all, who split the fae into two regions hundreds of years ago."

"Who is *he* exactly?" asked Blythe. "Is he some mad spirit that has come up from hell to destroy us? Or a demon?"

Chalamey shook his head. "Not a demon at all, my child. He was once a fae. He willingly corrupted himself. But it was not until he rejected his own Tyaag that he became truly evil." He looked at me meaningfully, and my stomach twisted violently upon itself. He had rejected his mate as I had rejected mine. I remembered the Reaper's corrupted face, the way his fae ears had been slashed at the tops, and the many eyes he wore on his face.

"But what is a Tyaag?" Blythe asked, sounding the foreign word slowly. "And a Niyati? I keep hearing these strange words."

"They are a cross between Ellythian and fae languages," said

Chalamey patiently. "A Niyati is a person of destiny. A person who creates a turning point in the history of the world. One who is born with great power. But such people can be far too powerful, far too wild and strong. They need a counter-power, a Tyaag, to be bound to them. Their mate, to balance nature lest they get out of control."

"Like the Reaper," Blythe whispered.

Chalamey smiled sadly at her. "Indeed. In rejecting his Tyaag —and he has had more than one—his power runs unchecked."

"I rejected Drake to save him," I said hoarsely. "So he might have a chance at surviving the fire wraiths. I didn't know…"

From the side of my eye, I saw Anthi reach out for Leena's marked hand. "That's the difference," Anthi said, her eyes glistening. "Your intention was pure, Princess. Not self serving."

I looked down at my soup, unable to meet their fae eyes any longer. "I didn't want to," I said. "But his mother told me that it was something I needed to do—that Drake would be the one to save us from the Green Reaper. Only another full-powered Niyati, without their Tyaag, could do it." I was rambling now. I cut myself off and looked up at Chalamey with pleading eyes. "Did I do the right thing? I did, didn't I?"

"But your power also increased." Jerali spoke for the first time. "After Drake fell, you…exploded with a force even the fae have never seen." The Armsmaster nodded at our two fae warriors, both of whom nodded in agreement.

Leena looked sharply at Chalamey, and Anthi was frowning in thought.

"What is it?" I asked.

Chalamey considered me gravely, his purple eyes seeming to darken. "Whatever is done is done, Princess. Drakus will find his own path. He always has. But you did not come here to discuss him."

A pang of guilt shot through me before I shook myself slightly and nodded at the old Dean of Mountain Academy. I knew then why Drake had loved his mentor so. He was sharp as a tack and wiser than anyone I knew. "Right. The Temari Blade will help in this fight anyway. How do I retrieve it?"

Leena wiped her mouth delicately with a silver napkin before she straightened in her chair. Her eyes took on a feverish glint. "The blade will call you. There is really no way we can tell when or how it will come about. Much like the Goddess who created it, the weapon is wild and unpredictable. But fear not. It will sense you are here. You are of the blood."

I nodded slowly, trying to understand this. So I would have to wait here. I didn't like that at all. It was not in me to sit idle while demons were terrorising my people. But I could see no choice in the matter. I would just have to wait.

"Then, in the meantime," I said firmly, "I must find out everything I can about the Green Reaper. Exactly who he is…and who his most recent Tyaag was. If he has weaknesses, I must know."

"There was much arguing at the Council of Solar Fae a few weeks back," Anthi said, throwing herself back in her chair as if the memory was too much to bear. "Flame Court were all for him. Blossom had no idea, as usual, of course…" she rolled her eyes. "And any knowledge of a Niyati was forbidden in the time the Reaper was rampant here. He burned all the texts and killed anyone who knew anything about it. But we *did* learn some new things in amongst the bickering, including the name of his most recent Tyaag."

My ears perked up at that.

"Her name was Clementine Eyesmith," said Leena softly, toying with her golden spoon.

"Ah yes," Anthi said. "They said the ruins of the Eyesmith

Palace still lie in the Court of Light. They were an old, rather famous fae royal family before the eldest son chose a human woman. But they eventually fled the realm."

"All because Clementine, the first born, was promised to the Reaper," Chalamey explained. "They needed a way to leash the rogue Niyati, so a half-human seemed like the perfect sacrifice. A Tyaag must give up their life to stop a Niyati."

I shivered. Just like Wyxian had thought with me, the old fae thought humans could be easily sacrificed for their benefit.

"Not all of us fae think that way, of course," said Anthi gently. "It's an archaic mindset. But didn't they also say one of the Eyesmiths had returned?"

Leena nodded. "A niece—some woman called Glacine is the only one left—"

Both Lysander and Blythe choked on their soup.

"I beg your pardon?" I asked, staring at them in horror.

The three Sky Court fae stared at us back with raised brows. "You know the name?"

"Glacine," I said through a clenched jaw, "was my step-mother. Also married to the late Havrok Scorpax, the demon king."

"And," interjected Slade gruffly, "now being toted around by the Green Reaper. We saw her in his chariot when he appeared for a short amount of time on the battlefield."

*That* news shook me. Of course Glacine had jumped ship to the next powerful person.

"Ah," Anthi said, a knowing look in her eye. "A ladder climber. There's one in every Court."

Ladder climber indeed. She'd gone from king to king as if she were playing musical chairs. But it disturbed me that Havrok had sent her to my family. They'd known that I was Tyaag to

Drake before we did. Is that why she'd whipped me for all those years?

But Chalamey shook his head at Anthi's comment. "Not just that," he said thoughtfully. "She is a direct relative of his old Tyaag. That means he is trying to…"

"Surely not?" cried Anthi in horror, slapping the table. Leena put a placating hand on her mate's forearm.

"Do what?" I asked reproachfully.

Chalamey observed me grimly. "A Tyaag and Niyati often have complementary powers. When they work combined, there are very few who can defeat them. At one time he might have wanted to be a solitary power. But it is clear to me that the Reaper has seen the powers of you and Drake and that he, too, might benefit from a Tyaag. I believe he is trying to make a new, corrupted version of his mate."

# 5
# AGATHA

I'd had enough of these blasted demons.

I hobbled out of the birthing room with the babe in my arms, the child's father hovering behind me like a nervous shadow. Unravelling the babe's wrapping—a blue crocheted piece by the child's grandmother—I went to the front door of their cottage.

When I angrily yanked the door open, two ugly demon warriors waited impatiently on the stoop. The first was picking his nose.

The second brute grunted through his mouthful of yellow canines, "Boy or girl?"

I quickly opened the child's wrap to show him. "Boy," I grumbled.

He grunted again.

"Yeah, yeah, I know. I'll be taking him now."

The giblet-eating creatures hadn't even suspected we were lying about the children's genders until a drunk bragging father let slip about it. Now they checked each babe at birth just to make sure the midwives weren't lying.

While the girls were allowed to reside with their parents, the boys were taken to a nursery they set up to keep the children away from their mother—apparently building an army for their stupid campaign to take over the Human Realm.

We kicked up a fuss at the start—well, the men of the city did, the fathers of the children. But heads were smashed in by the demons, and that stopped any future protest rather abruptly.

Though the parents could do nothing, the midwives could.

We marked each child with identification where the demons would not check—on the soles of their feet. Bertha on Sacks Street had any grandmother who could spare the time, crocheting woollen booties to protect the inked markings so we could slip them on at birth. Date, time, and surname. That was all I would need to match them to their parents after this was over.

Apparently, the brutes only trained the older children, not the infants. They'd left the babes for their female slaves and wet nurses to care for. But it meant they knew nothing about infants and so never frequented the nursery.

We snuck in the new mothers, keeping them there all day and more than half slept there at night. The babies needed to be fed, after all. And the demons wanted to make them strong, so they allowed the 'wet nurses' to come and go as they pleased.

I don't think they understood that human women needed to give birth to produce milk.

Idiots.

I hurried down the main road to the nursery, glancing up at the now ever-dark sky. When they first arrived, it had been night time. But once day came, a strange blanket of unnatural clouds swamped the city meaning that during the day, it looked like twilight and once night came, it was impossibly dark.

Without any moon or sun, our quartz lights had begun to

falter. The demons then began sending out groups of humans to charge the quartz. The first lot ran straight for the border into Kaalon. The idiots hadn't realised that once night fell, the demons would hunt them, out run them, and bring them back kicking and screaming. Then they started keeping their wives hostage and it stopped all attempts to escape.

As I reached the nursery— a building that had once been an aristocrat's house—I passed a group of ten-year-old boys trudging with wooden practice swords in single file. They were being led to the training field on farmer Thompson's land. The boys returned with injuries more often than not. Broken bones were frequent, as well as deaths. These demon captains trained the boys as men and did not care for any perceived weakness. Once Lobrathia's military had been executed, it had not taken the people of the city long to realise this was not a battle we could win.

We tried everything we could think of. But these brutes bashed us down at every turn. They might be dumb, but their instincts were always right in that animalistic way of theirs.

I handed the sleeping newborn babe to Christine, one of my long-serving midwives, deep bags under her eyes from stress. I nodded to Bluebell sitting in the corner of the room for our eight-month-olds. Her twins were growing, and we'd had to trick them into thinking both twins were boys so Bluebell could feed them here together.

As I left the nursery, a commotion by Jeremy's forge made me abruptly change my route.

A demon warrior had a knife angled at Jeremy's throat. The muscled, fifty-year-old man was a blacksmith, one of the best in the city, and had been forging the kings' swords for decades.

I stomped over to them and barked, "You do that, and we've

lost a blacksmith. Then who'll fix those blasted swords you break so often, eh?"

The ugly oaf had the intellect to think about it.

"Ah, get out of my way, you great big lump." I gave him no heed because that's all he was worth. He shifted out of my path just in time, lowering his sword. "That's what I thought," I muttered, yanking Jeremy to his feet—not really because he weighed as much as an ox—and prodded him back into his forge. I picked up the box Jeremy had ready for me and made my way back out.

"I'll have them rectified, Captain!" Jeremy called to the demon. He had an X on his chest and skin the colour of fresh blood. He was the head honcho of the demons—Argoth—and had only appeared a month ago to take charge of the palace with the new demon king. He narrowed his eyes as I passed him, but I ignored the brute and continued on my way before he could say anything.

We had an understanding, Argoth and I. Back when he first arrived, we'd had an altercation over a wet nurse. He was mildly smarter than the rest, so he understood the sway I had on the people and that I was not disposable. I'd also introduced him to blue ganja, and it did not take him long to get addicted to smoking the hand rolls only I could make. He got his ganja, I got my safety, and that was that.

But the ganja was not easy to obtain and I needed a fresh supply before he came looking again. For my part, I needed to smoke it more often these days to keep a sense of calm.

In Madame Yolande's fine institution of sex workers, where many of my clients lived and worked, I handed the Madame a full box of contraceptive potions, and she handed me an identical box in return. This one would be full of the glass bottles emptied of contraceptives but full with my ganja.

It had taken me weeks to find the recipe for the contraceptive. Together with the herbalists and medicine women of the city, we'd toiled day and night until we found a way of reproducing Queen Yasani's potion. The recipe had been locked up in a palace office somewhere, but we'd found it and begun making it beneath Jeremy's forge.

The Madame accepted the box with a grim look on her narrow, pale face. Yolande was a hardened woman in her fifties, but months of these demon scum would wear anyone down. "You keep 'em busy, Yolande," I said to her. "Keep them from causing trouble."

"I *am* Agatha," she grumbled. "But the girls are tired. How long is this going to go on for?"

Our agreement had been simple. The demons would use the city's brothels for free, whenever and however they liked, as long as they kept from harassing the other civilian women. The concept of brothels had been new to them, but they'd taken to it like children in a sweet store. Madame Yolande's girls and the other brothels' girls soldiered on and kept us safe better than any military of ours had. They deserved solid gold medals as far as I was concerned. And I would make sure they would get them too, once these bastards were out of our hair.

I'd had enough of it. To make it worse, our supplies of blue ganja were limited. No one from Waelan Kingdom, where it was grown, could travel here anymore.

In my bones, I knew Saraya was still alive and out there. I'd heard the demons talking about her— about the human princess who flew lightning from her hands like a weapon from the Gods. I didn't know whether it was a figure of speech, but I knew the wariness in their eyes was real. And if these brutish demons held fear in their hearts for her, then I knew she would return to us.

And she had better get here and get rid of these creatures soon. Otherwise, she would get the tongue lashing of a lifetime.

# 6
# SARAYA

I awoke with a start.

We'd been at Sky Court for two days now while I recovered and waited for my magic to return. It would have been difficult if I hadn't been so tired and slept most of the time. But slowly my physical strength returned and I had been able to handle a bout of sparring with Jerali yesterday. Now, in the middle of the night, my body was responding to *something*.

A feeling of otherness swept over me. It was like a sweep of magic but grander and stronger. The life in it was crackling and expectant, like a volcano on the verge of erupting.

Abruptly, I sat up. To my surprise, my ghostly warrior mentor, Arishnie, awaited me at the end of my bed, translucent eyes glistening in the dim light. She was dressed as always in the armour and sword she'd always worn as a living warrior midwife. But the moon was in its waxing phase, not a full moon. She shouldn't have been able to be here.

"Arishnie?" I whispered.

My mentor looked at me with meaning and some emotion in her eyes I could not interpret. "Claim your birthright, Saraya."

My High Priestess mark burned on my forehead and my heart hammered in my ears as I climbed out of bed. "What do you mean?"

Arishnie did not answer. Instead, she turned and walked right through the closed bedchamber door. I had no choice but to follow, marvelling at the way my own magic was rising up in response to the pregnant current in the air. Finally, my power was coming back.

It was dark, but the magic flickering in tiny particles around me made it easy for me to see. Jerali Jones and Blythe were fast asleep in their beds, so quietly, I opened the door and slipped out of our chamber.

In the corridor, my path was lit for me by those particles streaming behind Arishnie.

My skin tingled, my breath hitched. It felt as if I were walking on air.

I followed the speckles of light through the Sky Palace, while around me, fae emerged from their rooms in their nightgowns, and like me, led by the magic, they swept forward, trance-like.

We were all led to the outside of the palace.

Under a blanket of foreign stars, the air was charged with a power that reminded me of my own. Electric, volatile, powerful. It prickled the hairs on my arms and tickled the insides of my nose. It was expectant and watchful.

On the green lawn, half of the palace fae were already gathered, each holding a candle, waiting on either side of the centre path. All was quiet, with only the sigh of breathing, the whisper of satin and silk.

At the end of the path, the two Sky Queens awaited me. High Queen Leena, with a tall ethereal crown atop her navy hair and a flowing gown of white. Next to her, Queen Anthi in a corset of armour over a flowing dress. Their eyes were fevered, their wings reflecting the magical lights. The dense magic made my head swim. But the two Queens beckoned me forward with long, pale fingers.

Gooseflesh erupted all over my skin.

Wearing nothing but my night gown, I walked towards them.

As I passed the observing fae, they whispered in their fae language and the flame of each candle they held turned a bright blue of electric intensity.

Arishnie had disappeared, but Leena was grinning at me now.

Walking towards her under that glittering night sky might have felt like a dream, but everything fell into a too-sharp focus. This was real and sure. Magic seeped out from my skin, my electric power crackling around each one of my limbs. Umali's power, Voltanius House power. I knew in my heart that I had been born for this.

I had known it back in Black Court when I had used lightning to find and destroy Obsidian Court forces. This tangible crackling was not only a part of my father's heritage but a part of being the High Priestess of the Order of Temari. Umali's chosen. The thought made my breath catch with emotion.

I knew I even looked like her a little, barring the midnight blue skin. And I wondered if this was how the Goddess Umali felt whenever she came upon the earth. Like she were in a strange world with strange beings, a feeling of immense power around and inside of her.

When I reached Leena, she held her pale hand out for me, and I reached out and clasped it. Magic shot up my arm, at once familiar and biting.

"From one Queen to another," she began. A shiver fell upon me, and I swallowed. I was not yet a proven queen. I didn't yet feel that I deserved the title. She smiled knowingly at me, her lavender eyes taking on an intense glimmer. "Go dark. Go deep. *That* is the place where things are born. Be guided by your courage."

She was speaking to the midwife in me. And this is something all women inherently knew. Deep and dark within us all was a place we daren't travel too often. I nodded sagely. "Thank you, Your Highness."

She stepped to the side and swept out her other hand, gesturing towards the cliff's edge. "Go now to sacred land, Princess."

I let go of her hand, and my stomach dropped when I saw her meaning. A travelling cloud sat waiting for me at the edge. I swallowed my fear and strode purposefully onto it, not daring to look down at the drop.

I remained standing, even as my legs were shaking. This was definitely not the time to sit. The cloud trundled off, and I wobbled just a little as we flew through the air, away from the Sky Palace and into the dark night.

I took to one knee for stability as we travelled for some length of time I could only imagine at. Time seemed to stand still as I floated, swamped in the sensation of my own returned magic and the feeling of the cool, charged air against my skin. The sky around me took on a blue glow, the clouds high above limned with silver light. A slither of the moon smiled down upon me. As if she knew. As if she approved.

Eventually, through the mist, I spotted lightning flashing high above. Then a gaping maw came into view, and I was reminded of only a few days ago when I accompanied Xenita into the Birth Realm to retrieve her baby. A mountainous land-scape emerged, hanging in mid-air, lightning flashing above the highest peaks. It was so grand and so unexpected, my throat closed over. My hand flew to my chest as I took in what I instinctively knew were ancient mountains, forged thousands of years ago by old Gods not known to me. This was sacred. This was a place few were allowed to enter. I drew in a shaky breath as we got closer and those ancient mountains looked down upon me lit up by flashes of silent lightning, as if they were assessing my worth. I felt dwarfed, I felt small, but not in a bad way. It was humbling to be here. I had been summoned, I had been approved of.

The cloud sailed me right up to the cliff's edge, gently bumping into it, kissing the rock.

Gingerly, I stepped onto the land and looked up into the gaping shadow in the mountain face. I was expected to enter, that much was obvious. The darkness seemed to suck me in and I peered into it, my heart thundering in my ears.

Taking a deep breath, I reached out with my magic, probing into the cave.

I came up against a powerful magical force that made me flinch in surprise. But there was no going back now. It had to be Umali's Blade that was calling me. Now was not the time to baulk.

*Go dark. Go deep.*

Lightning lit up the sky and violent though its nature, it calmed me, somehow. Lightning was where I was home and my magic gave a little spark in response. Taking a deep breath, I squared my shoulders and strode into the darkness. I was engulfed in churning grand magic, the likes of which I had never felt before. Through the pitch-black, I put one foot in front of the other, feeling my magic rise up within me. The foreign magic of this place caressed my own power, searching out for me, studying me.

That power drew me forward, beckoned to me like it found me familiar. With every step, it grew stronger until, eventually, a glimmer of light emerged through the shadows. I could hear only my breath and the sound of my heart beating in my ears, but that glimmer made my heart stutter. It was a shimmering blue, the colour of the ocean, and as I came up to it, a grand cavern came into view. At its centre was a gigantic glowing lake of shimmering blue and green light.

A voice like ancient tides wrapped in silk reverberated around me. *"Who are you?"*

It was distinctly female, though deep, and it swept through me like a storm. I licked my dry lips, but when I spoke, my voice was strong. "I am High Priestess of the Order of Temari, Princess of Ellythia and Voltanius House."

From the centre of the lake, a shadow grew and rose to the surface. A woman arose from the water, her hair the colour of deep earth, her dark skin swirling with silver and blue geometric patterns that glowed with their own light. Her cheekbones were high, her face ethereally beautiful, the tips of her ears pointed. She looked ancient and new at the same time.

I saw her graceful supernatural form and just knew: an ancient half-Ellythian, half-fae.

She emerged perfectly naked from the water and came to stand upon its surface, skin glistening by the light of the lake. In her hands, she held a brilliant, heavy sword that sung a song of terrible power. Its hilt was a blue speckled with gold, silver, and electric blue. Lapis Lazuli, I recognised.

*"Come forth, daughter of lightning."* Her voice echoed all around me though she had not opened her mouth to speak. *"Daughter of the lotus. Daughter of Umali. Niyati to Drakus Fireborn."*

I frowned as I stepped forward into the cool water, absently noting that I stood *on* it and not in it. "I am no longer mate to Drakus," I said softly.

She lifted her chin as I approached her, the water feeling soft and cool like a cloud under my bare feet. *"You may no longer be his mate. But you were born soul-bound to him."*

Something in my heart softened a little. A small piece of relief, I think. In some way, I was still connected to Drake, however imagined the connection was.

And then I was standing before her, and up close, she looked like a thing from another world, her eyes glistening with soft light, her skin like marble, her posture like that of an ancient queen. And when she spoke, her voice was heavy with meaning.

*"The Te'mari Blade is a weapon of destruction. It represents those things which must be unmade to be remade and born anew."*

Born anew. Lobrathia needed to be born anew.

*"Do you accept guardianship of the sword of Te'mari and all that comes with it?"*

I looked down upon the sword in her hands. It was like no sword that I had ever seen before—even the one of my own making. Nothing in my imagination could have conjured *this* weapon. It was a heavy two-handed broadsword. A marbled blue and gold lapis lazuli hilt was shaped like the Goddess Umali herself, dancing, fixed in a vicious, teeth-baring pose. Umali's arms stretched out above her with a skull in either hand, forming the T-bar of the hilt. The blade itself seemed to be made with no material known to humankind or that I had ever seen in my time. It appeared to be made of particles of light condensed into a solid structure that glistened and reflected what was around it. Whatever the sword was capable of, I knew it would do great and terrible things. As High Priestess of the Order of Temari, it was well-suited to me. But I could not help but ask the question.

"Where did the sword come from? Who gave it to you?"

She answered me solemnly, *"Your mother, Yasani Lota of*

*Ellythia. This is your family sword. It was forged by Umali herself and bestowed upon the ancient Queen Ellythia."*

A tiny spark of shock echoed through me. I knew we were descended from an old bloodline in Ellythia, but my mother had never mentioned to me that we were of *the* oldest bloodline descended from the *founding* Queen of Ellythia. She hardly ever spoke of her family in fact. Even her mother, who was still the current Queen of Ellythia. Some wound was there. Regardless, given this information, the sword was rightfully mine to use. So then, why did I feel this nagging sensation? This dark spot at the back of my mind that hesitated in taking this sword in my hands? A sword that was, rightfully mine?

But this ancient guardian seemed to register my hesitation. She asked me again, *"Do you, Saraya Yasani Voltanius accept guardianship of the Te'mari Blade?"*

With this sword, I could do great things. It would help me take back Lobrathia. Regardless of what I thought, I would do my duty.

My mother had held this sword once. Protected me with it after my own birth.

"I accept it."

The guardian raised the sword in the air with both hands. I held out my upturned hands, and she placed the sword gracefully upon them.

Savage, raw power shot through my arms and into my core. It hit me like a bolt of electricity, making me reel from the sheer magnitude of it. Trembling, I took a step back and gritted my teeth, staring down at this blade—the heaviest sword I had ever held in my life. And its weight was welcome.

*"Though you have accepted the Te'mari Blade,"* said the ancient guardian, *"the blade has yet to accept you. You must gain her trust. You must prove to her that you are a worthy bearer. That you are*

*worthy of being Umali's chosen. Of being a true daughter of Ellythia, the first warrior midwife."*

Reeling with this information, I curled my fingers around the hilt, knowing what I was about to ask of it. This blade would indeed get to know me. "I will."

In a flash of light, the blade was now in a matching blue and gold sheath, with golden straps for securing to my back or hip.

A magical gust of air swept around us, whipping up my hair. The guardian of the lake disappeared, and all around the mountain cavern, translucent beings appeared.

I knew who they were immediately.

Hard faces but soft eyes, armoured bodies with hands on the hilts of heavy swords. A glowing moon mark on every forehead.

The old, dead, Warrior Midwives. And there were hundreds of them.

"Saraya," Arishnie's voice had me swinging to my left, towards the entrance to the cavern. Next to her were two faces I had not seen since my first visit to the temple ruins in the Temari forest. Silent Tara and Epelthi. They nodded seriously at me.

"How are you all here?" I said in awe. A hundred eyes were trained upon me, and I felt each and every one with a tingle of fascinating power.

"It's the power of the Temari Blade being in the hands of a High Priestess," Arishnie said calmly.

Warmth blossomed within me, perhaps for the first time in weeks.

Arishnie bent down on one knee, and I had to stop myself from gaping.

As one, each of the Warrior Midwives knelt upon one knee. I clasped the hilt of the Temari Blade in a suddenly sweaty hand.

"We follow the High Priestess of the Order of Temari," Arishnie called out. "We will fight with you against the demons that have taken the Human Realm. You are not alone. Will you lead us?"

The other ghosts murmured in agreement, fierce faces lighting up at the thought of battle once more.

Standing in the center of that glowing lake, I gripped the hilt of the sword and its power stroked my own like oil poured onto fire. "I will," I called to them, thrusting my sword in the air. "I will lead you to destroy those demons and send them back to the depths of hell once and for all!"

The sound of metal scraping sang as swords were unsheathed and thrust into the air.

The Warrior Midwives roared in assent.

# 7
# SARAYA

I rode the cloud back to the palace under the night sky, just me and the Temari Blade strapped to my back under the careful watch of the stars.

My mind clung to the image of Arishnie. There had been a pride burning in her eyes in that cavern. She had been my mentor since the beginning—as I was leaving Lobrathia for the Fae Realm all those months ago when she began training me to become a warrior midwife. Now she and the other warrior midwife spectres had pledged to help me take back Lobrathia from the demon horde.

The wind was cool and soft on my face and the silent moments of contemplation allowed me to finally mentally come to terms with all that had happened in the last few days.

I closed my eyes against the assault of conflicting emotions. I worried about my sister, somewhere in Ellythia, probably worrying about me. Tomorrow, I would send her another letter with the Sky Court doves. Much had happened since my last missive.

But my mind kept returning to Drake.

For over a month, he had been my constant companion—up until a few days ago, and I could not help but feel his absence like a barren hollow in my centre. I traced the skin of the back of my right hand, a new habit I would have to rid myself of. Somewhere incredibly deep inside me, like a fine strand of a spiderweb connecting us both, I *knew* that he was still alive. Initially I had brushed it aside as something I was imagining. Wishful thinking, Jerali might have called it, because how was it possible that I knew for sure? But the Fae-Ellythian guardian had said we were soul-bound. So perhaps though I'd severed the mate bond, maybe I could still feel *some* part of his existence.

Regardless, if he *was* alive after his fall and battle with those fire wraiths, he would hate me. Perhaps he would even want to kill me. Sometimes that happened to lovers whose relationship had turned sour. They ended up hating one another with the same grand passion they had loved each other with.

But I folded those thoughts away because, in reality, I would need a solid focus to win back Lobrathia. I had no idea what power the Temari blade had except that it summoned the ghosts of the Warrior Midwives. And from what the guardian had told me, both the sword and I would have to learn about each other if we were to fight properly. A wrong move with a magical object could prove disastrous. I knew enough about my own magic to realise that.

The cloud deposited me back on the Sky Palace grounds, and all was bare and empty, the wind stirring stray leaves across the lawn. While everyone had gone, they had left their candles inside stained glass lanterns, lighting my path back inside.

The sword felt reassuringly heavy where I'd strapped it to my back and a new found strength had grown in my bones. I held a powerful weapon—perhaps the most powerful known on the continent. Not only that, I had regained my magic and acquired information about the Green Reaper.

Now it was time to leave.

And at this journey's end lay Lobrathia, a prisoner more than ready for release.

THE NEXT MORNING, I WAS AWOKEN BY A GASP AND A SCREAM. Jerali Jones shook me awake, grey eyes wide and trained on my face. "Excuse me, young lady. Do you care to tell us what *this* is?"

Blythe was prancing in front of the Temari Blade, where I'd leaned it against my bedside table. "Oh my Goddess, you vixen, Saraya! We had no idea! How is it here? Tell us everything!"

Bleary-eyed, I sat up in bed. I had snuck back into the room last night and there must have been some magic at play because Jerali Jones, who slept like a cat and usually awoke to *any* noise, had not stirred as I'd quietly climbed back into bed.

"All the fae were there," I said, twisting my back to stretch out the kinks. "There was magic that woke them up, but it was like they were in a trance."

I told them the story from start to finish, and both listened, Blythe gasping at the appropriate moments, her blue eyes shiny, with Jerali as still as stone. The only thing that gave any of my Armsmaster's emotions away were those glimmering steel eyes alight with pride.

"I certainly feel better having this and the ghosts by our side when we go back to Lobrathia," I said quietly as we sat down at our small dining table.

"I'm a little sorry we're leaving," Blythe said after swallowing a pastry whole. "Isn't it lovely here? But it *will* be good to get home."

Jerali was silent and brooding, and I knew that a hundred thoughts stirred behind that pale face. Battle strategy. Execution.

I might not have Drake here commanding my forces, but we didn't need him. There was a whole lot of talent I could still draw upon, and I was proud of that.

The last thing we did before leaving was go to the thatched hut where Sky Palace kept their messenger doves. The young female who was their keeper merrily assisted me in picking one out. I tied my letter to Altara onto her spindly leg and sent her off to Ellythia.

My sister needed to know I was taking Lobrathia back as ruler and that we were still at risk of the Green Reaper coming after us. How I wished I could see her and hold her in my arms. I knew Altara could hold her own, but she was my only blood family left. Uncle Ansel, my father's brother, hadn't been seen in years. He'd always had a penchant for sailing, and we'd just assumed that he'd shirked his princely duties and started a new life elsewhere.

The two queens awaited us in a private drawing-room, with Chalamey seated on an ottoman, his tiny silver wings tittering with excitement when I presented the Temari Blade. Lysander and Slade went still as they all stared at its magnificent hilt and glittering blade. The two queens exchanged an excited grin.

"I am glad to see her back in the hands of her own blood," smiled Leena, lavender eyes hopeful. "It's been far too long!"

I sheathed the sword back into its holder on my back. "I can only hope to be worthy of her." A blade like this had served for centuries, if the stories were true, and wielded by the most powerful Ellythian Queens. Doing it justice would be no easy feat, but I suspected winning back a Kingdom might just do the job.

"I'm sure you will be, Princess," Anthi said, silver wings fluttering a little.

"We will not forget you," Leena said, rising to her feet. "We've never ventured out of our realm, that is not the way of Solar Fae since the Reaper cleaved the Realms into two, but we will be watching."

I smiled. It was a shame. If we could have gone to Ellythia with the help of the Sky Guard, our odds would be significantly better. "I understand the old ways," I took her offered hand and looked both queens in their fae eyes. "The Ellythians will not leave their lands either. You have that in common, it seems."

A glimmer of uncertainty graced Leena's lavender eyes and she exchanged a look with her mate. "Farewell, Saraya. And perhaps we can come for your coronation, at the very least."

My stomach flopped on itself. *My coronation.* Between me and my crown lay an entire war. But I shook that enormous gaping well aside and grasped both queens and Chalamey Springfoot's hands and bade them farewell.

Before we left, we spoke with the now seventeen-year-old Sage and eight-year-old Wren, Daxian's youngest siblings, who had been swept away to Sky Court well before the battle had begun. Both were understandably nervous and teary-eyed, but were putting up a brave front. Sage, with her waist length mahogany curls, and Wren, with his lower lip trembling, held hands as we sat with them in the drawing room. I told them a great deal about their new baby sister and how their eldest brother had still been a proud and strong king when we left Black Court. That seemed to please them. We promised that we would do what we could to find out what had happened.

As they waved us on our way back upon the transport clouds

to the mainland, the Sky Guard flew above us. They'd made sure our path was clear of demons, and would see us half of the way back to the portal. Butterflies piled in my stomach, making my breakfast flop uncomfortably inside of me. The last time I had seen Sage and Wren, had been in their carriage just after my engagement to Daxian. Back then, Sage had been the one to do the reassuring and explaining, as I'd known nothing about the fae at all. How the tides had turned. Back then, we never would have guessed what awaited us all.

Jerali Jones was forever watching me now, even from the side of the eye, and I knew what my new General was thinking. How on earth were we going to do this?

But I had one trick up my sleeve yet, courtesy of Arishnie. I just had to hope the women I chose had the guts to follow through. Sarone's green eyes flashed before me, fierce and brave, a mirror of my own. Blood would be shed. Both demon and human alike, I had no doubt about that. No matter how good any of us were at fighting, no matter how clever or brave, there was a whole city of demons just waiting for us to strike.

THE RETURN JOURNEY FROM SKY COURT TO THE INTER-REALM portal felt a lot shorter than the journey there. With my injuries healed and not needing a cart to travel on, we made for good time.

We waved the Sky Guard goodbye at the halfway point and continued on to cross the tree portal back into the Dark Fae Realm. The Black Court ferns towered over us, the cool, dry wind brushing our faces. But as I stepped through the forest, a prickling in the back of my neck gave me pause. I glanced at

Lysander, who was frowning up at the dark-leafed trees, and Slade, who was standing stock-still, eyes darting around the shadows. I sniffed the fresh air, frowning as I caught wind of something vaguely familiar.

While Blythe was chattering away, searching through her backpack for food, Jerali Jones noticed our unease immediately. The Armsmaster's fair brows raised in a silent question.

I swallowed and shook my head. Now was not the time to talk. If someone or *something* was watching us, we needed to keep moving.

Slade led the way through the forest, and we followed, Lysander hovering protectively beside me. With Drake not here, I think he felt some sort of obligation to be my protector against our possible adversaries. The Dark Fae Realm was now the property of the Reaper—four out of five courts: one was decimated, and three had sworn allegiance to him. Only Black Court still stood as far as we knew.

A part of me wished we could turn westward and see what had become of Black Court. Daxian would have followed my instructions to keep the lightning shield protecting the palace, but what of the remaining enemy soldiers? I had managed to dispatch many in my lightning rage after Drake fell, but there would have been some Eclipse Court warriors left, as well as their king. But we could not spare the time when we needed to head for the eastern mountain pass. As it was, the Black Court lands were eerily quiet and desolate in a barren way. I had travelled through here before with Drake, and there had been more General woodland activity, more *life* in the air. But now, it felt like everything had retreated and gone into hiding. Nature itself was holding its breath, waiting to see what would become of us.

It was with this in mind that we set up camp at the border of the Black Grove. Slade said that the Black Widow's domain was a place any fae with sense avoided. But Drake's mother was familiar with not only me but also Slade and Lysander, and they were comfortable with the idea of us sleeping there. We set our bedrolls up around a low smokeless campfire, wary of any Midnight or Eclipse Court militia that might be patrolling.

Perhaps it was being so close to Drake's home—Slade and Lysander made no mention of the tree house, barely a half an hour from here, for which I was thankful—my mind went to a dark place. The thought of the tree house and being there, without Drake in it was too much to bear. It was these thoughts that made it so that I could not, for the life of me, find sleep. I tossed and turned until Lysander took second watch just after midnight. Eventually, I got up and followed him out, rubbing the goosebumps out of my arms.

I joined the blond fae on a flat rock as he took out a wooden pipe of Sky Court origin, stamping down some type of herb into the bowl of it.

"You feel it too, huh?" he murmured without looking at me.

I stilled, observing the forest around us. "It's too quiet."

Lysander breathed deeply. "Something stirs in these lands, and it's not the Black Widow or fae soldiers."

"You don't think Black Court has been taken, do you?" I asked nervously. We had worked so hard to hold the palace at the time and I hated to think that all of our efforts had been in vain. But none of the doves that had left from Sky Court for Black Court had returned.

"All I know," Lysander said, too casually inhaling on his pipe, "is that we are being watched."

I clenched my fists. I knew it. I had known it the moment we had entered the Dark Fae Realm. But who was it? The Reaper, or one of his servants?

The mountain passes were all watched by the enemy. We

knew they would be. Chalamey had given Slade and Lysander instructions on a secret entrance through the mountains, one that only certain members of the Academy knew about. It was our only hope of getting to the Human Realm safely. But we'd *never* anticipated this *watched* feeling.

Something was clawing at Lysander's mind. I knew it by the way his eyes moved in thought. He knew something and didn't want to tell me. That made me all the more worried.

Lysander got up to relieve himself, carefully treading to the side of our camp where we'd set up the latrine.

As I sat there alone, I reached out with my magical mind, tentatively searching the surrounding darkness. Silver ferns hung limply, wild flowers stood still on their stalks, the cold night air smelled of dry earth, leaf litter, and…something tickled the insides of my nose. Something powerful and predatory. Something dark and watchful. It was drawing me in…pulling me towards the darkness like a hook on a line, away from Lysander and the others, urging me to go *into* the dark—

Abruptly, I rose. A familiar scent brushed my nose. Earthen and distinctly male. A male whose scent I'd known from sleeping next to him for weeks on end, chained by the neck to his wrist. I could not breathe. I did not want to breathe.

"Drake?" I whispered into the dark.

How? It couldn't be. But that scent, at once comforting and intoxicating was real. And it was here. My insides became a furnace. I opened my mouth to say his name again, but my voice would not come. My face crumpled as dark emotion took me over like a tide at midnight. I searched the darkness, hoping that a tall muscular figure would emerge from the shadows. Hoping beyond hope that I could run into his warm arms and tell him that I…that I what? That I wanted forgiveness? That I was sorry and that I would never do it again? Because what was done, was done. I had done something that was at once necessary and unforgivable. My heart raged in a fevered storm and my hands involuntary let out a spark. I jumped, despite myself. Brought back to reality, I panted and breathed in the frigid night air. The scent was gone.

Lysander's dancer's tread sounded behind me, the smell of smoke filling my nose.

"Saraya? Are you alright?" His voice held a timbre of worry, but not alarm. Lysander was never alarmed by anything. I couldn't tell him, he'd think I was mad. *I* thought I was mad.

"I'm going to bed," I said and immediately hastened past his tall figure to our sleeping area, climbed into my bedroll, and pulled my blanket tightly over me.

# 8
# DRAKE

The world was a different place than I remembered.

I remembered that *things* used to be solid.

But everything around me now existed in balls made of colours that danced or attacked each other.

All I could hear was the thumping of blood through hearts and the swoosh of breath into lungs.

All I could smell was fear, jealousy, love, grief, anxiety.

They were connected, the colours and the sounds and smells, I knew that much. I also knew that my instinct was to squeeze those beating hearts until they exploded.

But the darkness that was leading me advised me not to. He said it would be messy. And so I refrained, letting the beats and smells surround me instead and learned about them.

The place the darkness led me to was full of heavy colours. No twinkling lights, only shifting, oozing clouds of blue and orange and green so dark they could have been black. The colours were looking at me and the darkness as we moved through this place. Whispers followed, words I couldn't be bothered to decipher. The darkness told me to obtain new clothes, and they were given to me when I beckoned with my fingers. The colours blanched at my approach, hurrying to reply and obey. Wherever I went, the smell of fear followed me. Colours trembled and turned grey.

That is the way it should be.

I put pants on my legs and a shirt on my torso. This was normal, the darkness said. This was needed. I obliged, but I didn't really care.

Then a new scent wafted toward me on the breeze, and I stopped in my tracks.

It was at once familiar and foreign. I knew I had to follow it. This was important. In the fiery tornado of my mind, this was a beacon of light. I hunted for its source.

I came to a stop where bright colours bounced sleepily. But these were little colours. Colours with four legs, not two like the rest.

The clouds parted in my mind, and I was able to see what was in front of me. A shop, it was called. A shop with cages of tiny balls of fur. But they did not hold the scent I was looking for — *that* was inside. I leapt over the stall and went into the shadows in the back.

Someone tried to stop me, but I pushed them away—no one got to disturb me while I was hunting. From out of the shadows came a minuscule growling. There was a cage, and there was my mark.

The little ball of black fluff was angry and snarling, backing away into the corner of its metal cage. Tiny teeth marks peppered the iron bars. I found a strange smile creeping at the corners of my mouth.

Ignoring the protests and jabberings of the creature who owned the stall, I opened the cage, reached in and wrapped my

E.P. BALI

fingers firmly around the creature sitting alone, pressed against the corner. Alone like me.

He bit my hand.

Now *that* was interesting

But pain barely registered in my consciousness now. So I let him bite me again, tiny teeth marking my skin, drawing blood.

"Fluffy," I said. But it came out as a heathen grating sound. Like a rock over gravel.

I realised the shopkeeper was talking and I concentrated to make out the words.

"Yes, yes, very fluffy." He nervously rubbed his hands together. "It is rabid, My Lord. Uncontrollable. It needs to be put down." In his darting eyes and sharp smell, I knew his thoughts —that he was going to kill it. I looked back down at the ball of inky black fur as the male spoke hurriedly. But I did not care about what he was saying and held the scrambling ball close to my chest.

I was feeling the rapidly beating heart, the silken strands of fur, the tiny squeaks and growls. And then the thing lifted its head and looked at me. Its irises were black of every shade—not that eyes other than mine could register that. It blinked once then twice. And between those blinks I saw him and he saw me. And we knew each other as the same. Discarded again and again. Vicious, unyielding, unbroken. We came to an unspoken understanding.

He reminded me of someone, but I could not put my finger on it through the storm of my mind. But I knew one thing.

No one was killing this Fluffy.

With my magic, I spoke to Fluffy, telling him I would not kill him. But if he behaved, he could come with me. He could even bite some people if he wanted to.

Fluffy blinked those big eyes and slowly nodded his black head.

I reached into my pocket and pulled out a fistful of gold kruzos, and tossed them on the table. Someone had given them to me, but I couldn't remember who. I might've even just taken them. As the shopkeeper scrambled to collect the coin, I turned from him and strode back into the market, settling the creature on my shoulder. It didn't like sitting there, but I didn't give him a choice. It made me feel…something I could not properly place, but it was my warm inside my chest, where my heart had once been whole.

THE DARK BEING I'D SHAKEN HANDS WITH BROUGHT ME TO A PLACE of shadows, where smoke and wind coiled as if they were looking for prey.

From the shadows, three beings came to meet us. Their essence was of the earth, of natural plant-like things, but also dark—not as dark as me, but still, their colours were heavy.

One smelled like the deepest parts of the night.

One smelled like the shadow of the full moon.

One smelled like ancient volcanic rock.

I concentrated, trying to understand what the dark being was saying.

*"Three kings lost me a battle,"* the dark presence said. *"Tell me, why should I let such weakness keep their thrones?"*

There were high pitched noises that sounded like pleas, but nothing that sounded important. Fluffy began growling from my shoulder. I think he knew what was coming.

*"Kill the Dark Fae Kings, Drakus,"* the voice hissed in my ear. *"We need fresh blood on their thrones."*

Something sparked in my memory. A whisper of a voice that said these people were familiar to me. But I was no longer interested in the old voices that lay in the back of my mind like long dead ghosts.

The kings were saying things, but I could not understand their words. I only understood one language now. I moved, and blood spilled. I moved, and bones splintered. I moved, and three souls violently departed from this world.

Fluffy licked something off my face.

*"Very good, Drakus. And now I want you to kill one more. Hunt the woman who smells like the sea in a storm. Like lightning made human."*

I nodded eagerly. That sounded interesting. Fluffy and I wanted a hunt. *Needed it* like a beast needs water.

FLUFFY WAS GROWLING ALL THE TIME.

So I put him down my shirt to shut him up. Eventually, he went quiet, sleeping with little snores.

I needed to concentrate for the hunt. Searching this vast land that smelled of moist earth and old blood had taken a little time.

One day, I felt it. Lightning made into a feminine form. A familiar power drew me in like a warm caress. I followed it across the land, my mouth watering, my heart thumping.

The scent led me to a purple ball of light. It was fire bright and sparkling in a mesmerising way. I stared at it for hours, mesmerised by the way it twinkled like the night sky, sometimes crackling like lightning falling. It was beautiful, and I had never seen anything like it before. Why did the dark master want it dead?

No...I *had* seen this before. But where? I squeezed my eyes shut and searched the crevices of my mind for a memory of it. Where had I seen it before? But all that search yielded was a headache. I shook it out and continued my watch. Fluffy wanted to stare at it too.

I wanted it. I wanted to know its name, what it was thinking about. What its purpose was moving across the Fae Realm so swiftly. I could help it find what it was looking for.

I shook my head.

What would that sparkling light want with my darkness? I might only hinder it. There were other colours with it, helping it along. I growled in jealousy. Fluffy growled with me.

Then my purple ball of light was moving again.

So I followed—only at a distance because I didn't want to scare it.

My little purple ball moved far and headed for a group of rocky peaks that I remembered were called mountains.

A group of beings who smelled like earthen shadows were collected in the space between the mountains.

But I wanted to see where the little ball of purple was going, and those things were in the way.

There were many of them, but they felt small to me.

I needed the kill, I was starting to get irritable, and Fluffy knew it too, growling unhappily. I cheerfully exterminated them all. This is where I belonged, this is what I was born to do.

The purple ball and the other colours, vaguely familiar, went right through the mountains.

Fascinated, I eagerly followed.

# 9
# SARAYA

We continued our travels the next day, using the small amounts of magic Lysander and Slade had to camouflage us with our surroundings.

Watching their faint green magic at work, I was reminded of my sister Altara. She had magic like this. As a magical empath, she could take on her surroundings at will. Her surroundings also included other people—specifically, the ailments of other people. Where I could heal *others*, she could *take on* the ailments or injuries of others into her own body and heal it from there. She couldn't heal them directly. My mother had strict rules for her to follow that were in some ways, more stringent than her rules for me. Altara could do serious damage to herself if she took on more than she could handle. Magic was strange like that. It had manifested in a strange way in both of us. I wondered if she was happy in the Ellythian Jungle School, what she was doing there, what friends she had made to replace my companionship. We had been together for so long, sought comfort in one another for all of our lives, that being without her for these past many months would have felt strange if I hadn't been distracted by so many terrible goings-on.

I shivered against the chill Black Court wind, rubbing my arms. Now Jerali was looking behind us with a frown, rubbing the back of that lean neck. Whatever I had felt yesterday had been a whisper of Drake, I knew it like I knew my own heartbeat. But I dare not voice my thoughts out loud. Whatever this was, if it was him, or some other predator, that prickling feeling of being watched followed us all the way to the base of the Silent Mountains.

It was around midday when a distinctly magical wind stirred the air, making Lysander, Slade, and I stop in our tracks. Jerali Jones and Blythe stared at us in alarm. It smelled like black twisted pine and a cold, ancient wood. Before I could warn them, the Black Widow emerged into existence before us, the willowy silver shape of her wobbling just a little before she solidified.

Even out of her dark Grove and in bright day light, her appearance was terrifying and slightly alluring. All-black eyes set in a cold, beautiful fae-shaped face, silver hair hanging in a thick braid down her chest. A thin silver dress rippled in the wind, her potent magic striking me like a wintery blast.

She ignored the others and spoke directly to me. "Drakus will not acknowledge me, but I sense him lurking in the shadows at the corner of things. It is *he* who hunts you."

My heart dropped into my chest, a weighted coal. My hand flew to my stomach as I attempted to reel in the wave of emotion. It had been him. I had been right. "Drake is alive?" I breathed. By the Goddess, it was a miracle.

The Black Widow gave me a droll look. "Did you really think a meagre fall would kill him?"

I didn't bother telling her that this 'meagre fall' was a seemingly endless chasm accompanied by two palace-sized fire wraiths that were intent on killing him. Blythe's panicked voice bought me back to reality.

"*Drakus Silverhand* is hunting us?" Her voice was slightly shrill. "What in the Goddess' name does that mean? He wants to kill us?" She looked wildly around at Slade and Lysander for an answer. But both fae warriors were standing as if they were hewn out of stone, as no doubt disbelief and shock coursed through them as it did me.

But I knew all of us had the same thought. Drake only hunted things he wanted to kill.

And he always caught his mark.

"He is *more* than he was before," the Black Widow said, a wicked gleam in her all-black eyes. "His rejection has turned him into something I could only have guessed at. His power is incredible, but whether he can be reasoned with is a different story."

I had done this to him. My heart clenched. With this evolution, even the five of us together would be no match for him. The Temari Blade still sat on my back, reminding me that I *did* have some power. But if it came to using it on Drake, could I? *Would* I? Drake and I had joked that we had never actually fought one another in single combat. But the thought of landing a killing blow to his body made me want to vomit. The Goddess stood before me, her silver dress flapping violently in the air, her gaze predatory on me. Just like her son's would be. I was not above asking for advice. "What should I do?"

She bared her teeth in a way that made me want to recoil. "Let him."

With that, she was gone.

Blythe groaned behind me as my heart leapt into my throat. "Who's side is she on?"

"She's a helpful one, isn't she?" Jerali Jones said, eyes trained on the spot the Goddess had vanished. Oddly, my General's eyes shone hungrily, as if with the challenge of a good fight. I didn't have time to warn Jerali against pursuing a supernatural creature for a chance at a good battle. And anyway, chances were, none of us humans would ever be returning to the fae lands once we'd returned to our native realm.

"She's on her own side," Slade growled. "Like all of her…type."

"I can't believe I just met an actual Goddess, and she turned out to be like that!" Blythe exclaimed. "Useless!"

Lysander hissed at her to quiet. Slade put a warning hand on her arm. "Careful, love. She'll be watching us."

I was surprised to see Blythe nodding as she obeyed the broad warrior. She asked him, "So what do we do now? Run?"

"That'll only provoke him to give chase," Lysander said quietly. "No, we move slowly, casually back to Kaalon."

"He's likely to follow all the way there," I warned. "Do you think he actually wants to kill us?"

Lysander rubbed his chin, casting a casual eye around. I did the same, wondering how far away Drake actually was and if he was watching us right now. The thought made goosebumps pucker all over my skin. In reality, it was very likely he wanted to kill *me*, and by Lysander's look of sympathy and warning, he thought the same. The memory of his eyes—the way they'd changed when I'd rejected him as my mate. They'd glittered with a fell red light that made my heart tremble with guilt and fear.

In whatever monstrous state he was in now, it would be worse than what I'd seen be unleashed before. I'd been able to bring him out of his monstrous reveries when I was with him. But I had been his mate then.

And now, I was the mate who had rejected him. He would bear no love for me. Only hate. And human reasoning might very well be beyond him.

"Let's go," I said, giving the trees a final look. "We keep our pace. We do not hurry. Our plans have not changed. And if he presents himself, then…well, we'll deal with him."

The fae warriors nodded. Slade added, "And we do night watch in pairs from now on."

THE MOUNTAIN PASS WAS GOING TO BE OUR BIGGEST CHALLENGE. WE predicted that the Green Reaper would not want anyone passing through, so they had every reason to attack us.

Two days later, as we came to the foot of the mountains and began seeking out Chalamey's hidden entrance, I stopped everyone with a sharp, "Halt!"

Lysander and Slade looked back at me with deep frowns. We were supposed to be trying to be quiet. But I had been vigilant, using my magical sight to scope out what was ahead of us. I had done the very same thing on my way to the Mountain Academy. I had been by myself back then and did not want to come across any fae unawares. How things had changed since then.

But it meant that I was well practised at scoping out the path ahead for bodies.

What I had not expected was for those bodies to be dead.

I swallowed. "We don't need to take the underground path," I said, holding Slade and Lysander's eyes in turn. "I think…" I took a deep breath because if I was right…if what I was recognising was true, then I wasn't sure what I would do. "I think someone has been here before us."

Slade searched my gaze questioningly.

My heart rate was through the roof. I clasped my hands in front of me and continued up the mountain path, right into the pass into the Human Realm.

Silently, the others followed.

Lysander must have smelled the blood because he shot in front of me, quickly followed by Slade. When we came upon them, Blythe gasped, and Jerali went as still as stone.

Before us were a whole company of massacred guards. Bodies scattered into the dirt, heads at crooked angles, rib cages crushed where hearts had been pulled out. On every breast was the red crescent sigil of Eclipse Court.

I had seen this before.

Lysander turned to look at me, his nostrils flaring, blue eyes flashing.

Blythe turned and retched into a bush. Slade shot over to her immediately, but she righted herself, recovering quickly. She'd seen this before too.

I said it first. "Drake."

Jerali squatted down to assess one of the bodies. Part of its rib cage was missing, right over his heart. "It's him, alright. I've never seen anyone else take a heart from a man in this manner."

Slade laughed humourlessly, then looked up and around the mountainous walls, searching. I followed his gaze. Blue sky, saffron and sable coloured rock, small green bushes, the metallic tang of blood in the air.

But I knew if Drake wanted us to see him, he would show himself.

"They're fresh," said Jerali, straightening. My General's fair face was grim. "He was here minutes ago."

I shivered, my heart pounding. He was so close I could have seen him if we'd arrived only moments earlier. Seen his face…

and those all black and red glittering eyes. A thousand emotions stormed through me, my head spinning until Slade's deep rumble brought me back to where we were.

"Can you feel him?" Slade asked me. "Can you feel him here?"

"I don't think so," I said. It was more of an inkling, a prickling at the back of my neck. "But I can't be sure."

"We should go," Blythe said, folding her arms around herself.

"There's no point staying," I sighed miserably. "Let's get out of here."

From there, it took us one week to get to the capital of Kaalon, Peach Tree City. And every step of the way, I knew in my bones and in my spirit that Drake was following us, like a predator stalking prey.

# 10

# SARAYA

W e arrived in Kaalon in the dead of night, a cold wind at our backs.

The city lay silent and eerie, just as it had the last time Drake and I had come upon it with the demons. That felt like so long ago now. Drake and I had spoken into each other's minds the entire way and I missed the intimacy of it, the ease of speaking to someone directly into their consciousness. And now, I dare not search out his mind for communication. He felt swathed in darkness, at once terribly far and terribly close.

"This is powerful magic, even for us," Lysander said as we strode past the city gates, our footsteps echoing. "I couldn't believe it the first time we came here."

"Be on your guard," Jerali warned. "There could still be demons from Quartz trying to figure it out."

After Drake had killed the Demon King, Havrok, I'd taken Drake to the Fae Realm while Slade, Lysander, Jerali, and Blythe, who'd also been trapped down there with us, released all of Havrok's human slaves and gladiators and had taken them, as I'd advised, to Peach Tree City. I'd known that King Osring, in his kindness, would take them in as refugees until I could get Lobrathia back.

The illusion that lay over this Kingdom was emergency magic from the old days when all humans had magical ability. Although Osring had no magic, the knowledge of using his blood to activate it had been passed down. His entire city became cloaked in an illusion, leaving an empty mirror city to confuse the enemy. It was the perfect defence because it made it look like everyone had simply left Peach Tree City when they were all here, just *underneath*, living their lives normally.

When we'd gone to war with the Green Reaper at Black Court, we'd called for help from Osring. Lysander and Slade had arrived on the day of battle with a human army to help. There had been many human losses that day, I was sure of it, though we'd had to leave before we found out exactly how many.

"Oh, I can't wait to see Tembry and Delilah," Blythe whispered. "It feels like we've been gone ages!"

"Sh!" Jerali warned.

I gave my friend a smile. I, too, was keen to see what had become of everyone after we'd left Havrok's Court. My helpers at the Demon Court, the teenagers Tarangi and Flora, as well as my newly found second cousin from my mother's Ellythian side, Sarone.

Grumbling under her breath, Blythe and I followed the others into the dark of the city. The fae warriors remembered the path fairly easily as we came up to the city square and then down a wide street. It was the same path to the house Tembry had led me and Drake through to the real city.

"Last time Tem came to us," I whispered. "Osring had some sort of magical way to see who was walking around the illusion side of the city."

Jerali nodded. "I've seen it in the military offices. It looks like a painting of a map only the people move inside of it."

Peering down the line of houses, I magically scoped the inside and, finding no trespasser in our way, nodded to Lysander. The fae warrior opened the door, and we all slipped into the shadowy darkness. He led them to the other side, right to the back door. But this door would not budge.

My blood ran cold.

"What's wrong?" Jerali asked.

But Slade had leapt outside.

"It's just me, It's just me!" cried a female voice. A familiar warble had me crying out.

We all rushed outside again, and I roughly pushed past Slade to see a Tembry with Opal sitting on her shoulder, peering through my friend's red hair.

"Tem!" Blythe cried.

I rushed forward, Blythe close behind me. Opal leapt off Tembry's shoulder, crooning loudly. "Oh, Ope!" I sobbed, squashing her against my cheek where she licked my tears away, making happy lumzen sounds. "I missed you!" I pulled her away so I could look at her, patting the soft fur of her head, her rainbow-coloured irises glowing with happiness as she took me in.

Opal was a lumzen, a fae illusion-making creature. She was about the size of a large kitten now, still a juvenile by the standards of her slow-growing species, but still a little bigger than when I'd last seen her on the day we escaped from the Demon Court, well over a month ago. She had soft rainbow-coloured fur, a precious, round body and a long tail, like a cat. She was incredibly intelligent and had helped us out of many tight situations.

I looked from Opal to Tembry, who was sobbing into Blythe's

shoulder. I went over and joined them. Opal scrambled onto her favourite place, my shoulder, and I put my arms around my friends.

We stood there for a moment, crying quietly. Relief pounded through me with each heartbeat, like a summer wind only sweeter. Tembry let go of Blythe and put her arms around my neck, hugging me tight.

"I'm so glad you're all okay," she whispered. "When you sent word about the war, and the boys went off—" She looked up at Lysander and, to my surprise, went to hug him too, followed by Slade.

The fae warriors shifted as Tembry turned back to me, and I could tell they were taken aback by Tembry's emotion. I hid a smile by kissing Opal on the cheek.

"Let's get inside, hey?" Tembry said, suddenly wiping her cheeks and taking charge, stomping down the street.

I grinned at Blythe. Just as we'd changed, Tembry had too. It was the type of difference I saw in women who returned to me with their second pregnancy. Motherhood changes women on a soul-deep level, and for those with the eyes to see it, it's a beautiful thing.

Tembry led us into another house in the street adjacent, explaining that the entrance to the real Peach Tree City changed every week as a security measure.

As with my last fateful visit, she led us out a back door, and we found ourselves on a bustling, cobblestoned street, where the tavern was in full business tonight.

Where also stood, waiting for us, a full contingent of Osring's royal guard, an orange tree sigil on their chests. Every single one of them also wore a black mourning band around their bicep.

Lysander and Slade went up to meet them, shaking hands and talking in low voices. Probably, I thought darkly, inquiring about the men they'd lost during the battle of Black Court. My stomach churned. How many *had* we lost? How many more would we lose by the end?

An idea had been stalking around my brain ever since Arishnie had instructed me the night before that awful battle. I learned a great many things that night—things that I fully intended to put into place.

I realised I was being watched and turned to find Jerali eying me with those sharp grey eyes. As my new war General, Jerali would be a key part of my plan to get Lobrathia back.

The guards escorted us, not to the out-of-the-way townhouse like last time, but straight up to the palace. Lysander and Slade went into a meeting with the captains of the human guard, while Tembry eagerly took Blythe to see Delilah. Jerali Jones and I were taken into a first-floor room where the King and Prince of Kaalon, Uncle Osring and Adlain, were consulting papers at the long table, their advisors warily watching on.

My adopted uncle was thin and wiry, with a shock of white hair. He was dressed in a black doublet and pants, a black mourning band around his wrist. Adlain was in his late twenties, had always been studious, and was the spitting image of his wiry father.

"Uncle!" I cried, surging forward.

Wearily, King Osring stood, looking as fragile as ever. He wobbled on his cane, and a pang of sorrow struck me. He saw me glance down at the mourning band, a braided black twine, and nodded sadly.

"The queen passed two weeks ago. She was always poorly. We never thought she'd last as long as she did."

"I'm so sorry, Uncle," I whispered, placing my hand over his. "I wish it had happened in different times."

"I heard about your father, my dear," he said softly, his dark eyes kind. "I am very sorry. In his prime, Eldon was a marvel. A good man."

I could only nod, not able to say what I felt. I had seen both my parents during my time in the Astral Realm with Queen Xenita during her fae birthing ritual. We had spoken, and it was a time I would treasure in my heart forever. Osring was now the closest thing I had to a father. And he knew it, as he smiled at me.

"I intend to take Lobrathia back as Queen," I said softly. "I only need to—"

"Now, now," Osring said sharply. "We must not be hasty with our strategy, Saraya."

My mouth snapped shut, and I was forced to step aside as a captain of his guard shifted impatiently.

"Speaking of the times," Osring said, taking a deep breath that moved his narrow shoulders. "Queen Helene is here. She arrived from Waelan two days ago. King Omni insists on setting up his militia in Serus and has sent a contingent along with his General."

I frowned. "Does the Traenaran King think you will lose Kaalon?"

Osring gripped his cane with a white knuckled fist and his lips thinned in disapproval. "He thinks our hiding in the illusion means that we have given up the city. That we plan to stay here forevermore."

I eyed my adopted uncle, suddenly very aware that, for the first time, Osring was not really my family. A lot had changed between my spending childhood summers here and now, with a demon horde at his doorstep. Staying here, hidden in this illusion, was convenient. They were safe. It would never be breached. And Osring was old, his reign stood tenuously. I could see Adlain eyeing his father with hawk-like eyes. He was concerned.

"And you, Adlain?" I asked. "What do you think about the Traenaran strategy?"

Adlain set his jaw. "They're smart. A conservative choice is wise considering what has become of Quartz." He scoffed. "It's unsalvageable."

Fire surged through my veins, but Osring tutted. "Queen Helene does not think so, and nor do I. Come, we are expected to meet with our allies. They will be happy to see you, Saraya."

Something dark roiled in me at Adlain's words. He did not think Lobrathia was *salvageable*. I couldn't believe he'd given up on us so easily. "I'm surprised at you, Adlain. I would have thought our alliance meant something to you."

His head snapped towards me and he stammered before replying. "Of course, Saraya. I only meant that the case is rather dire. It would be a massacre to head in unawares." Then he frowned at me, looking closely at my face. I stared back at him. "Oh, you do not know." He scratched the back of his neck. "We sent half our forces to Black Court, Saraya. Barely ten returned."

I blanched at his words, horror shooting into my core.

Adlain scoffed at me. "You think human forces have any chance against fae? By the Gods, Saraya, you really can't be that naive, the demons are much the same."

I blinked in shock at Adlain, Jerali Jones bristling like a tiger by my side as he walked past us down the corridor. Opal crooned softly in my ear. He had no idea, none at all. He was bitter about the loss of his forces and had every right to be. My magic sparked a little at the jibe and I followed after them, a heat in me, beginning to simmer.

But if I thought this disagreement was anything of note, I was sincerely mistaken.

When we entered the meeting chamber, loud voices abruptly stopped. It was a brightly quartz-lit room with a long mahogany table that could seat ten. Queen Helene, a robust woman with a sharp eye and an evern sharper tongue had her hands on her hips, thin, custom made plate armour covering her torso. Her deep red hair was braided securely back in a fashionable but practical style. Opposite her sat a dark-skinned Traenaran man with war General's stars on his breast and large hands clasped firmly in front of him. As I walked in he was shaking his head in dismay.

"Saraya!" Helene cried, rushing towards me and pulling me into her substantial bosom. "My dear, we have been worried. I am so sorry about dear Eldon! My! Don't you look a bit peaky. Sit, sit!"

"Your Highness," the Traenaran General strode forward to kiss my hand as Helene prodded me into one of the chairs. He was a tall, broad-shouldered man with a tiny scar through his brow and the demeanour of someone used to being in charge. "I am General Tarjin of the Traenaran forces. We are glad to see Voltanius House still lives."

I murmured my thanks, not entirely sure if I meant it.

"We have been preparing to take back Lobrathia while we awaited your return," Helene said firmly as everyone took their seat, Jerali sitting right next to me.

"But I'm afraid we cannot decide on the strategy," interjected General Tarjin, his face stony. "I will not have my men going in to a demon city unprepared."

Anger spiked in me and I hastily clenched my fists as a spark of electricity flashed from my finger tips. *Demon City*. Lobrathia was still a human city as far as I was concerned.

I forced my face into a smooth courtier's mask my mother

had been drilling into me since childhood. I needed them on my side, I had to convince them we could save Quartz.

"That is understandable," I said carefully. "However, I was planning a stealth attack—"

"Nonsense!" said Helene, thumping her fist on the table, making it vibrate. "We will take it back with an army of full force, with both of us combined—"

"I will *not*," said Adlain, shocked, "be charging into Lobrathia. They will see us from miles away."

"I have—" I began.

But I was swiftly interrupted by General Tarjin. "Prince Adlain is correct. There is no point at all. No point! The demons are ruthless. We cannot possibly…"

Helene interjected once again but I was no longer listening.

The noise was crowding my brain, falling upon me, a cacophony of arguments piling on top of each other. Osring had practically dismissed me when I declared my intention to take back my Kingdom as Queen. That meant he didn't think I could do it—perhaps he thought my father's brother, my uncle, would miraculously return from his voyage and claim it back? But my real uncle had never wanted the throne. We'd not even heard from him in years. And now, it was clear to me none of these royals would listen to a thing I was saying. They still thought me a girl, unproven. Untested. And even if they didn't think that, none of them were willing to risk their men for me. This realisation stabbed at my chest like a paring knife.

Opal must have sensed my roiling emotions because she nuzzled into my neck

As I sat there, my power surged, wanting release. Wanting blood. The Temari Blade was still on my back, a heavy presence that could deal a heavy blow. Arishnie's round face swam in my vision.

I didn't need Kaalon. I didn't need the Traenaran forces. Nor Waelan's military.

It didn't matter that they would not stand by me. I only needed seven of us.

"Excuse me," I said quietly. But I do not think anyone noticed as I stood and exited the room, Jerali Jones close behind me. My General eyed me knowingly and murmured, "What are you planning, Saraya?"

I gestured for Jerali to follow me away from the ears of the guards at the door and out to the courtyard, where there would be no prying ears.

"They don't know what they're doing," I said softly, containing the rising anger within me, hot and spiking like a mace. "They have no idea what they're up against and what to do. They bicker while my people are being subjected to Goddess knows what. I'm done with talking. Done."

Opal crooned in interest as Jerali nodded. "We don't have men, Saraya. The numbers—"

Jerali was interrupted by two loud girly squeals. We both turned to see two teenage girls bolting into the courtyard.

"Your Highness! Your Highness!"

Two familiar faces that pulled at my heart—Tarangi, an Ellythian girl, and Flora, a mainland girl, both of whom I'd met as slaves in Harvrok's Court, ran towards me, their faces screwed up into glorious smiles.

They ran straight into my arms, both of them crying. Kissing each of them on their heads, one light and one dark, I laughed. "I've missed you two!"

"I can't believe you're finally here!" Flora wailed.

Tarangi pulled the other girl off me, and Flora settled instead for clinging on to her Ellythian friend. Both girls had spent a lot of time with me, first helping me dress as a bride and then in the other ridiculous clothing the demon king had us wear all the time.

"You should see what we've been up to!" Tarangi said excitedly, wiping a tear from her eye. "When Jerali Jones got us out, we came here and started going to school and learning trades! Flora is an excellent seamstress."

Flora nodded, twirling her fair hair in her fingers. "I made you a dress," she whispered, looking at me with wide watery eyes. "To wear for your coronation."

"And I'm training to be a midwife," Tarangi said shyly, looking at her sandalled feet. "Just like you."

The backs of my eyes burned. They were clean, clothed well, and planning for their future. I could not have hoped for more. "That's amazing Tarangi. And thank you, Flora, that's wonderful. Although, I do actually need to get Lobrathia back first. We're planning for it now."

Tarangi nodded seriously. "What can we do to help?"

I grinned at her and turned to Jerali. "I only need seven." I met my General's eye with a steely gaze to make Jerali understand that this was something I would not budge on. "One hour before dawn, gather Blythe and then my cousin Sarone and get her to collect the three best Ellythian fighters that she trusts with her life. Then meet me by the lake in the first peach field with travelling horses just before dawn."

Jerali frowned. "Saraya, I—"

"I know how it sounds, Jerali. But I have a plan. I'll explain everything. Just…trust me."

Jerali stared at me for a long, long moment. Then those grey eyes solidified to hardened steel. "Yes, my queen."

My heart skipped a beat at that. If I could pull this off, I would be a worthy queen. And if I couldn't, well, that wasn't an option. I pushed that heinous thought out of my mind.

"Tarangi," I looked back at the teenagers. "Take Jerali to Sarone. And can you find some tourmaline shackles? There must be a set lying around here somewhere."

Tarangi nodded eagerly. "We took so many off when we came here. I'll find one."

"Then go," I commanded the two girls. "I don't want to waste time."

Jerali Jones bowed at me and gestured for the two girls to lead the way. They both scrambled to comply. Jerali was not a person you kept waiting.

Heat flooded my chest and face, spreading into every pore of my skin. I raised my hand, and a finger of electricity jumped out, curling around my fingers.

Opal warbled in surprise from where she'd settled back down on my shoulder.

I felt jittery and charged, like a heavy cloud before a storm. I couldn't have been more ready.

We were finally going to take back Lobrathia.

It was time for the storm to return home.

## 11

# SARAYA

I t was still dark when Opal and I met Jerali at the first field. I held a saddle bag, stocked with Quartz crystals I'd smuggled from the Kaalon reserves and the Temari Blade strapped securely to my back. My entire body was tingling in anticipation with the knowledge of what I was going to do tonight, and what needed to be done in the days after. Though the night held winter's chill, a rabid flame had caught alight within me. And it burned strong with all the rage and malice of women who wanted revenge. Opal sat silent and sentinel on my shoulder, twitching to every sound, paying keen attention.

"Courage, Ope," I murmured. "You'll need to be brave to survive this. We all will."

She crooned in agreement.

The air smelled faintly of sweet peaches and the fertiliser the farmers used to keep their trees robust through the winter. Kaalon's peaches were not the sort found anywhere else, and I swore they held some magic in them.

Shadows moved ahead of me and I made out seven horses with bulging saddlebags tied in a line under a slither of a moon

—Umali's basket moon. The five women stood next to the horses, Blythe, Jerali, and the Ellythians, shivering slightly from the chill. The demonic subterranean kingdom was not at all cold, it bore a musty humidity to it and although it was cold, I imagined the fresh air was very welcome to them.

Where Jerali and Blythe were fair of skin, Sarone and the rest of the Ellythians had skin a darker brown than mine. They were full-blooded Ellythians, with bodies that were both curved and muscled. They'd all tied or braided their thick and curling black hair, just like mine, and I knew on their palms they bore the marks of callouses they'd earned as children. Ellythian girls were taught to fight from childhood. It was their way and I knew it would serve us tonight.

"Your Highness," Sarone said softly, coming forward to embrace me fiercely. My newly found second cousin was in her mid-twenties, with a strong, fighting body and her eyes, the family green, were alight. "It is good to see you alive and well. Jerali Jones said you were taking back Lobrathia."

"We are family, Sarone," I chided, "you will call me by my first name." I surveyed the six of them, including the three newcomers. "And that's right. *We* are taking back Lobrathia. Did you bring the shackles?"

Metal clinked, and Sarone held out a pair of black tourmaline shackles many of us had worn around our wrists down in the demon palace. It had been specifically made to suppress magic. This one had been broken at both cuffs. But Opal would fix that for me.

"Once we have control over the harbour," I said, stroking Opal on my shoulder, "I will send those of you who want to return, back to Ellythia. This is also what we are fighting for."

"Then we will win," hissed one of the Ellythian women. She

was short and stocky, clenching her fists and looking me in the eye.

I smiled without humour.

"But where are the rest?" Blythe asked, her eyes wide. "We need more men, surely?"

I shook my head and squared my shoulders. "Today, I will be inducting you all into the Order of Temari. My power will work through you. We only need seven of us to take back Quartz."

Recognising the name immediately, the Ellythians murmured in surprise.

"That weapon you carry," breathed a second Ellythian woman— slight of frame and no older than eighteen, "It looks…"

"Magical?" I finished. I unsheathed Umali's blade from my back. It sparkled with its own light, glittering and resplendent in the dark. Despite its brightness, it gave off a dense and heavy energy. My body tingled in response, excitement flowing through my arteries. Every eye before me widened.

"Holy Mother," Sarone whispered. "We all saw Saraya's power back at Havrok's palace," she said to the others. "Umali is behind us. We can do this."

After I relayed the foundations of my plan to them, Jerali and the other women nodded in understanding. The air became a buzz, as if it were charged up. I knew that the Ellythians, who had their magic unlike the mainlanders, were likely contributing to that.

"You freed us, Princess," the tallest Ellythian, said to me. "We owe you a life debt. And we owe it to the other Ellythians to do this. I will give my life for this cause."

Whether it was Umali's basket moon or the excitement of the coming battle, electricity surged in me, shooting around my body and lighting up the faces of the six women before me.

Opal and Blythe gasped, Jerali grinned. The Ellythians nodded as if this confirmed their decision was right.

I nodded back. "Then let us begin."

How I missed my sister. If she were here, she would have brought out her bow and fought alongside me. She was a perfect shot, and I could have sincerely used her help. But as it stood, she was not here, and these warriors were worthy in their own right.

I would induct them into the Order of Temari with my blood. Sarone introduced the Ellythians to me. Hemali, the short, well-muscled woman had been forging weapons with her father before she was taken by the demons. Uma, the tall, wiry woman had been in Ellythia's armed forces. Lastly, Elya, the smallest of the group, had been training as a healer. None were midwives but it was not midwives I needed tonight.

It was warriors.

And each one had been trained to fight since childhood.

As Umali's moon smiled her savage smile, I inducted them the way Arishnie had instructed me in Black Court.

With each one bent on one knee, I pricked my thumb on the edge of the Blade of Temari.

I whispered, "With my blood, I summon the spirit of Umali."

A wild and vicious wind whipped up. Magic spun through the air, encircling our group. My heart leapt into my chest as a haze of shadows began manifesting in a circle around us. Opal shivered on my shoulder, and all stilled as the shadows solidified into one hundred armed female figures standing boldly. My breath caught in my throat.

"Dear Goddess," Sarone whispered. The others murmured in awe.

"The Warrior Midwives have come again," Arishnie came forward, her moon-like face eyeing me fiercely.

I swallowed my nerves down as one hundred pairs of warrior midwife eyes fell upon me. Their gazes were fierce, their hands clenching their weapons, their ghostly armour glinting under the moonlight. My High Priestess' mark burned like a brand and my arms crackled with electricity as blood dripped from my thumb. After so many decades they had returned to follow me, and I was here to lead them.

I clenched my teeth against the tide of emotion and looked at my six companions. Letting my voice carry through the wild night, I called out, "We are the sword in the night. The protectors of human potential. The shields against all that is evil. Do you accept this pledge?"

"We accept this pledge," they said in unison.

Turning first to Jerali Jones, I took a deep breath and marked my second-in-command's forehead with the blood. While Jerali did not identify as female, to the Order of Temari, the matter of gender had never mattered. Midwife meant "with- woman", after all, not that you had to *be* a woman.

"Jerali Jones, with my blood, I ordain you."

I moved to Blythe kneeling next to Jerali. When she looked up at me, her blue eyes were brimming with tears.

"Blythe Swanson, I ordain you."

Then came the four Ellythians turned warriors once again. They each gave me their full name, and I anointed each with my blood of my thumb.

"Sarone Lota, with my blood, I ordain you."

"Elya Harranpul, with my blood, I ordain you."

"Hemali Durgash, with my blood, I ordain you."

"Uma Saffran, with my blood, I ordain you."

Then for good measure, I took Opal in my hand and anointed her forehead too. "Opal Voltanius, with my blood, I ordain you."

She crooned seriously, and I placed her back on my shoulder.

I stepped back and looked at them all, a bloody thumbprint drying on each forehead. I felt my magic flowing into each one as a river splits into multiple paths. It was a shining, burning force and I felt them in my veins like anger made manifest. I was not the only one who was angry at being taken away from my home. "Six new acolytes of the Order of Temari. You now bear the strength and speed of our order. Goddes be with us all."

As I watched, the blood on their forehead absorbed into their skin and in its place a purple light in the shape of a crescent moon began to glow.

Behind me, Arishnie took up a roar that shook my bones, "The Order of Temari lives again!"

One hundred Warrior Midwives thrust their swords in the air and roared, "The Order of Temari lives again!"

Their voices resounded in my heart, their rage pooled in my clenched fists. And through the night, my entire body crackled and flashed with white hot lightning.

At dawn, we rode for Quartz.

BY THE SECOND DAY, WE HAD CROSSED THE SWIFT RIVER DIVIDING Kaalon and Lobrathia and headed for the quarry. My plan would take place in three stages, and securing the quartz quarry was the first.

Being daytime, the demons had taken shelter, leaving the entire quarry vacant. It was this very trait of theirs—the inability to handle sunlight—that I would exploit.

I handed Blythe the saddle bag of quartz rocks I had taken from Osring's stock. All seven of us rode around the circumference of the quarry. When each stone was dropped at the cardinal points, I initiated a lightning shield.

The electricity flew out of me, eager and jumping, brighter even than the sunlight. I directed it with a surprised but steady hand into a column that surged upwards like a needle.

Once the four pillars of lightning were set, I concentrated on joining them together. Fingers of electricity searched outwards and they grabbed onto each other, creating a sheet of protection around the entire quarry.

No one would be able to get in, and any demons coming through the portal at the base would be trapped. The quartz we'd dropped would ensure the shield stayed up for hours.

After that was done, I shook the tingle out of my hands, and we headed for the city. The jolting, surging feeling inside of me never went away. The battle at Black Court had opened something within me— perhaps not the battle, rather the rejecting of Drake had made my power surge and release through some gate I would not perceive. Before, my lightning fizzed, *now* it surged with an alarming intensity that did frighten me a little. I wouldn't admit it to anyone, but this sheer power I had was for destruction. Great destruction. When Drake's mother had explained the Niyati and Tyaag dynamic between Drake and me, I'd assumed that the Niyati was supposed to have the destructive force. But apparently I assumed wrong because even though I was the Tyaag, my power seemed equally destructive.

As dusk fell we made it to the outskirts of the city. Soon, it would be time to do possibly the riskiest thing I'd ever done.

We approached from the south, at Jerali's suggestion, where we would get a view of the city from the forest a little way from the main gate.

But what we found when we came to the city surprised even my hardened General.

A black shadow lay across the city— so dense and murky that it would block out all sunlight.

"So that's how they're doing it," Sarone muttered. "I wondered how they intended to take over when they couldn't bear the sun."

"They're literally going to envelop the entire realm in darkness!" Hemali said angrily, making her horse prance under her.

"But how do they have this much power?" Blythe asked. "It must take a lot of magic to do this."

"The Reaper," Sarone said through clenched teeth. "He's a Niyati who's rejected his mate. The most powerful being on the continent."

My fists tightened around the reins of the mare I rode. Drake was a Niyati as well. His mother had said his power would grow with a rejection from his mate. So *was* the Reaper still the most powerful? Until the rogue Drake showed himself, we wouldn't know. I wondered if he was here, watching me now. But I eyed that dark cloud over my city, assessing it and observing the way it shifted heavily.

As the sun set, the quartz lights of the city twinkled to life, a multicoloured array of jewels dotting the city's windows, doors, as well as the palace towers. We were the home of the quartz crystal, and not for a solid one hundred years had a human used the city's quartz for magic.

"Wow," breathed Sarone.

"I'd almost forgotten how beautiful our city is," Blythe said.

We camped there for the night, hidden under a bubble of Opal's magic. An hour before dawn, it was time.

Opal crooned in awe from my shoulder. "Are you ready, Ope?"

She warbled a keen 'yes,' and I nodded in reply.

We all gathered in a circle. I unstrapped the Temari Blade

from my back and held it out to Sarone with both hands. It only felt right to give it to her. She was my kinswoman, after all. The Blade belonged to her as much as it did to me.

But the young woman blanched, her beautiful eyes going wide. "Are…are you sure?"

"It's just for a short time. The right to wield it is in our blood. It's as much yours as it is mine. It's only right you keep it for me for the moment, Sarone."

She nodded, taking the blade reverently and strapping it to her own back.

Then I looked around at the five women and Jerali, closed my eyes and held out my right hand. A brilliant white light burst forth through my eyelids and a weight fell into my fist. I caught it, and when I opened my eyes, in my hand was a sword with a silver hilt and a white-hot blade crackling with electricity. I took a quartz bracelet from the bundle from Kaalon I'd been keeping in my pants pocket, pressed the tip of the sword against it and with a concentrated effort, energetically pushed the sword into the bracelet. The jewellery glowed in my hand. It was the last thing Arishnie had taught me. In ancient times, during old wars against the dark fae, the High Priestess of the Order of Temari had done the very same thing for the human soldiers.

I passed the bracelet to Jerali, who took it with an excited grin. "I might not be able to teach you how to do this," I said, "but I can do it for you. Even for you two without magic, the sword will come out when you want it."

Closing my eyes, I manifested another sword of the same and handed it to Blythe. Four more times, I manifested lightning swords and handed them to the Ellythian warriors.

Now, they too were armed with the power of lightning.

Sarone was grinning with all of her teeth, as if she were ready to skewer a demon right then and there. With her own magic helping her, she would be a vicious opponent.

It was just as well. We needed a generous upper hand.

I knew the Warrior Midwives would be waiting in the Astral Realm, ready for the right moment. I took out the tourmaline shackles, and Jerali held them for me while I slipped my hands in through the narrow gap that had been cut into it when they'd been cut off one of the slaves. I turned them around so the gaps were not visible, and at my request, Opal's magic fell over it, hiding the cut-off portion completely.

Leaving the others behind, Jerali, Sarone, and I strode out into the night.

## 12
# SARAYA

Opal, now sitting on Jerali's shoulder, hid herself in a shimmer of rainbow glitter. Her magic then fell over my two companions and masked them both in a convincing illusion that made them look like hulking crimson-skinned demon warriors. Just like the ones who'd escorted us to Kaalon on that mission to assassinate Osring. I assessed Opal's work and praised her finesse. She'd been down in the demon lands with us long enough to know the look of these demons perfectly. Even this close to both of them, I was convinced of the likeness, right down to the matte black armour.

"Dear Goddess!" Sarone hissed, looking down at her male demon-sized, wrinkled hand. "I'd never thought I'd see the day."

Jerali choked a laugh.

I swear my General was having a good time. Some things never changed, I supposed. Jerali was bred for this and I think, in some ways, so was I.

We headed out towards the gate and I looked up at my city. Umali's approving smile sat low in the western sky. I had done

E.P. BALI

this before— come into Lobrathia under an enemy's control. But last time, that enemy had been the fae—with Drake as their leader.

A pang of grief shot through me.

I could feel him. Really feel this presence as a tingling, prowling magic at the corner of my eye. I felt him on the back of my neck as if he were standing behind me. By some new and strange magic, he was existing in the shadows, just out of sight but not out of my perception. I wondered for the hundredth time when he would show himself.

I think it was these thoughts that made my magic broil inside of me. But I had to keep it under control. I needed to keep up the appearance of being a prisoner.

By the time we got to the gate, demon warriors were gathering on the battlements, looking down upon us and pointing. A guttural shout came from above.

"Halt! What've you got there?"

All three of us and no doubt Opal, looked up. With the yellow quartz lanterns glowing in their faces, the hulking demon guards staring down at us looked more monstrous than they ever had. Deep shadows cast under their eyes and flat noses, serrated teeth appeared enlarged and wolfish.

It was Jerali's time to perform. My General put on the deepest gravelling voice, "We've captured the Princess!"

"Which princess?" came the answering rasp.

"Idiots," hissed Sarone on my left.

I, naturally, had only to be myself, so I scowled furiously up at the leering row of yellow eyes. "I am Princess Saraya Yasani Voltanius of Lobrathia!" I shouted. "I want to see the creature that calls himself king of this place!"

As the demons began shouting excitedly at one another, Jerali gave me a rough shove and said loudly, "Quiet!"

"Let them in!" the captain on the battlements roared above the din.

The doors to the city groaned open as the demons turned the mechanism from above. The last time I had come through these doors, it was Slade who had greeted me, and I had been under my Sam Sourbottom disguise, full beard and all.

"Let me do the talking," whispered Sarone.

Jerali grunted.

An X-marked captain with two other guards greeted us on the ground on the other side, demons craning their necks from all sides to try and get a look at me. Where previously they had born Havrok Scorpax's black scorpion insignia on their chests, now they bore a yellow disc.

Not a disc, I realised with a pang of horror. A *coin*.

I knew at once which demon lord had run here and taken ownership of Quartz after Havrok's death.

The captain barked, "What division are you?"

Sarone, having lived with these demons for the better part of five years, gave an excellent impression of a demon guard. She lowered her voice into a rough growl and gave the name of a division I wasn't familiar with.

"I thought you were all dead," the captain growled.

"Just injured," Sarone growled back angrily, rubbing her stomach as if an old wound sat there, newly healed.

The captain took this as an acceptable response because he waved his hand as if he didn't care and stepped up to me.

I glared back at him. Jerali grabbed my face and turned it left and right for his inspection.

"It's the princess, see, we checked," Jerali barked angrily.

"Oh, I remember her," the captain whispered.

It wasn't until he had stepped into the light that I recognised him as Captain Argoth, the vicious leader of the warriors from

Havrok's Court. I almost swung a punch at him before I remembered my place and clenched my fists tight. Argoth had been our main escort everywhere. He'd also taken great happiness in slugging me across the face at Glacine's behest.

I fully intended to return the favour.

Argoth suddenly tilted his head back and laughed in that guttural choking way demons had. "You thought you got away, eh? Well—" He struck me on the chin, and I did nothing to stop him. I was thrown sideways by the force of it, biting back a cry, pain blossoming across my jaw. Jerali Jones hastily caught me.

But this time, I could block the pain out with my magic. Instantly, I turned off the pain receptors in my jaw and I went numb—but not too quickly, lest it looked suspicious. As Jerali pushed me back upright, I kept my eyes down as if I was in pain.

"Let's see what the king has to say," Argoth jeered. "I'm sure now that your mate is dead, he'll take great pleasure in bedding you. Perhaps he'll let us all have a turn afterwards."

My heart leapt into my throat as anger bubbled dangerously in my blood. Next to me, Sarone stiffened and I felt the raw anger emanating from her with a palpable heat.

Jerali growled low, but I wasn't sure if that was a warning to Sarone or in response to Argoth.

If I didn't have my magic—if I really had been captured—it would have been a disaster because I knew that the person on the demon throne now was the Lord of Gold, Braxus. Now *King* Braxus. He had been obsessed with Ellythians down in the Demon Court. Both Sarone and I knew what he would have done to me if he'd been given the chance. He'd made his wishes clear. But with Drake by my side, as my husband, I'd had nothing to really fear from him.

But Drake was not here.

The demons jeered at us, and we were escorted down to the main city street and up to the palace.

I took in a shuddering breath, ignored the leering stares and lewd comments and steeled myself for what was to come.

Sarone and Jerali each made a show of taking me roughly by my arms and marched me forward. Argoth led the way and quickly word spread and the demons—both the huge muscled warrior breeds and the pathetic lower breeds, lined the streets. They pointed and laughed at me, dragging their thumbs across their throats as if I were a villain in some play being escorted to the chopping block.

But I couldn't care less.

Because we were being led down the cobblestoned streets and tall stone buildings of my childhood home. My throat closed up as it hit me like a tidal wave. This was my home.

I had prowled through the city as a midwife for years. I knew it inside and out. But the difference between *before* and now stood out clearly.

The sight of it crawling with leering, jeering demons scuttling up walls, prowling down lanes as if they owned the place was a harsher sight than I had been prepared for. The city was filthy, rubbish littered in all corners, horse dung littering the streets, and the *smell*: like rotting eggs and rancid meat— as if they'd left the remnants of their food just lying around for weeks on end.

The smell of it stuck to me like oil and surpassed the urge to retch.

My poor poor home.

Unlike Drake's invasion of the capital, in which he instituted a lockdown on the population, the demons let the humans roam around under a watchful guard. The place was so full of demons I was almost sure I was back in the subterranean Demon Realm, back in Xengistas, which I'd been to on a mission with Drake. The taverns were open and full to the brim. I even spotted a bard singing under the eye of a demon warrior, a blade angled at his throat.

Because the demons were leering at me, it meant that the human population saw me as clear as day too.

In amongst the jeers, there were also whispers, which quickly turned into desperate shouts.

"Princess Saraya," they murmured.

"They've caught the princess!"

"Saraya! Where have you been?"

"She's alive!"

My heart clenched impossibly tight. They had all assumed me dead. I returned the looks of each and every human who stared at me. With every step my rage grew. With every breath my lightning begged to run free. With every bound of my aching heart I wanted to plunge my sword deep into Lord Braxus.

My anger grew and my breathing turned haggard as I held my surging magic under a tight rein.

It was not until we were almost at the palace drive that I saw a familiar face.

She had lost weight under her patchwork cardigan and looked more ancient than ever. But those blue eyes were as piercing as they'd always been. It was her, my midwifery teacher, Agatha.

She was coming out of a noble's double storied manse when she froze on the doorstep. She went impossibly white, staring at me as if I were a spectre. I wanted to rush to her, to tell her I wasn't dead. To ask her what had happened here since I'd been gone.

To say sorry.

Xenita Darkcleaver's voice echoed in my head. *That's all the dead ever want. Forgiveness.*

And I was not dead. I would fix this.

So, I held her gaze with my own resolve and gave her a firm and sure nod. After a breath, she nodded back. The sight of her, haggard and pale, almost sent my rage into overdrive. I wondered what she'd been through. What they'd put her through.

As I was led up the palace, a full horde of demons collected behind us, keen to see the fun, no doubt. My palace, my family's home for hundreds of years, stood tall and grand as it ever had, but a shadow had befallen it, making it look heavy and weathered. I didn't hold back the scowl that twisted my face.

The palace doors had been replaced with makeshift wooden ones, and I remembered they'd used a battering ram to try and get inside when we'd shut the doors. I cringed inwardly at the state of my home. Inside the entrance hall, the marble tiles were chipped, and the paintings were crooked and stained with old blood. Next to me, Jerali exhaled a sad breath.

Argoth led us into the throne room. The long red carpet had been torn in multiple places and had stains on it that I didn't want to look too closely at. But at its end stood the throne of Lobrathia. A gilded chair with fine scrollwork, bold strokes of lightning and embedded with the highest grade of rare blue quartz. My father had once sat upon it, and it was not he who sat smugly upon it now. As Argoth led us right up to the base of the red carpeted stairs that led up to the dais the throne sat upon, my vision turned the same crimson colour.

Braxus sat on my father's throne, his large fists on either armrest. He was a tall creature with sallow skin and a barrel-like belly covered in his signature loops of gold necklaces, rings, and bracelets. Beady yellow eyes stared at me with a palpable excitement, his sickly skin shining with droplets of sweat. He was practically bouncing in his seat. And I knew what he was think-ing. *Finally, I get my chance.*

Next to me, Sarone's grip tightened around my bicep and she trembled so slightly I might have missed it. How she was controlling herself was beyond me. She'd spent half a decade down there with him seeing exactly how he treated the Ellythian women. She had more of a reason to hate him than I did.

How many people had sat on this throne since my father had? First Wyxian, now Braxus. None of them belonged there. Usurpers. The throne deserved someone who would serve the people well. Who cared about their welfare. Who cared about peace and justice.

Braxus' eyes took me in greedily. But unlike at the Demon Court, I wore no revealing clothing showing no flesh for him to ogle at.

He stood, spreading his arms out wide. "I wanted you to see me on the Quartz throne, my lovely Saraya," Braxus said, panting a little as he sauntered down the throne steps. "You would look so pretty on my knee, don't you think?"

I clenched my fists just in time, as a spark flew from my fingers. *Free me,* it urged. *Unleash me.*

"No," I said shortly to Braxus. "I don't think so."

A tall, male figure emerged from the shadows behind the so called king.

My heart skipped a foul beat as I recognised that shape and form. Bile rose up my throat. I clenched my fists so tightly the circulation to them ceased.

The hawkish man waiting by the throne with a sheaf of parchment was Oxley. As if he'd never run away. As if he'd never betrayed my entire family. My father's old advisor. No— he had really been *Glacine's* advisor. He must've come back here while Drake and I were down in the Demon Court, fighting for our lives. He'd been a part of it the whole time, just another servant of the Reaper. Every step of the way, he'd been there contributing to my family's demise. We had been so blind.

The words flew from my throat in an animalistic snarl and my voice trembled with barely controlled rage. "Always playing second fiddle, aren't we, Oxley?"

He scowled at me in response, his wide shoulders stiffening. He knew it was true. We'd never seen eye to eye, and after her death, he'd undone all my mother's hard work in the city. It had all been by design. The Reaper's design. Oxley must be a demon breed too.

I had waited long enough. From the fae occupation of my lands, to my imprisonment in the Demon Court. The lotus is patient, but eventually, the storm must come. Lightning must strike.

I could feel the Temari Blade hidden on Sarone's shoulder next to me. Could feel its strength, its will to destroy. Its will to rebuild.

*Umali, give me strength.*

*Lightning does not yield.* I have never yielded. I never would.

As Braxus stood next to Oxley, both men staring down at me —Braxus, greedily and Oxley with distaste. But just as Braxus began to speak, something caught my eye, and I looked at his yellowed, bejewelled hands as he gestured with them.

"Your mate is long gone," Braxus said happily. "So it appears you are a widow, free to claim."

But I didn't care what he was saying. My eye was fixed on his hand—where a familiar fat gold ring sat on his finger. A ring with a plain black rearing dragon.

I stopped breathing. *Drake.* That was Drake's ring.

And I would hack it off Braxus' finger.

Recovering quickly, I cracked my neck. "Just answer me one

question." Braxus abruptly frowned at me. Every demon in the throne room was staring at us, listening keenly. I felt Jerali shift position ever so slightly next to me. My voice was light, direct, calm, though my body was roiling with a mighty rage. "Oxley, did you, or did you not, participate in the poisoning of one or both of my mother or father?"

Oxley's mouth twisted, his narrow nostrils flaring before he said two words. "I did."

Everything around me fell away into darkness. That was all I needed to hear. Rage spun through me like a ferocious tornado, unleashed from the dark.

In a sequence of moves that were a blur to even me, I dropped the tourmaline shackles and they clunked to the ground.

I tore out of my companions' grips, simultaneously summoning my astral blade. It came to life with a flash.

Oxley didn't even get the chance to scream.

I leapt towards him and beheaded him in one swing.

Landing in a crouch, I watched his head hit the ground and roll towards the demon guards. I snarled like a rabid beast. Braxus screamed, his eyes feverishly huge.

The guards stared in shock for a full second before jumping into action. Braxus turned and ran for it.

Then it was chaos.

But both Jerali and Sarone were ready. Opal dissolved her illusion around them.

Sarone threw me the Temari blade and I snatched it out of the air, strapping it to my back while I covered myself in a protective bubble of lightning. My two warriors, now with purple glowing crescent moons on their foreheads, pulled out their lightning swords from their bracelets and launched themselves at the demon guards.

Jerali was a beauty to behold. My General fought like a dancer, every move calculated, cunning, precise. No energy was wasted and the result was devastating.

Sarone fought like a lioness, all snarling teeth, powerful downward blows that made me shudder.

The enemy were blasted back to death with every swing of those lightning infused swords. With those magical weapons, they each had more power than everyone in the room combined. No one would be able to touch them as long as they kept moving.

Meanwhile, I ran back outside the palace, demons shrieking in my wake. Braxus would have to wait for a moment. With my shield around me, any demon that attempted to come close was instantly shocked and thrown backwards. It was enough electricity to stop a beating heart in its tracks, and while I was within it, I could do anything I wanted. I raised my hands, drawing on that crackling power that begged to be unleashed with full force, I sprinted around the circumference of the palace, throwing out sheets of protective lightning as I did. Demons were blasted back with high pitched screams, the smell of singed hair and skin filling my nose like perfume.

Leaving Sarone and Jerali to take control of the palace, I arrived back the entrance and looked out at the city.

As I stood on the hill of my palace, I lowered my lightning shield and drew the Temari Blade from its sheath.

Powerful magic roiled and surged through my arms and out of my head so powerfully I staggered back a step. It was like I could *feel* their rage.

From within the night, the ghosts of one hundred Warrior Midwives emerged, and their swords flashed in the darkness as if they were made of solid steel.

# 13

# DRAKE

I had been chasing the colours for days.

My purple ball was intoxicating to watch. During the day, Fluffy and I hunted with vigour, and during the night we watched, eyes half open as the purple lights danced and flickered and sang to us. The Dark Master was right. She smelled like the sea in storm, raging, powerful, dancing the tempest's dance.

We followed her to a city that smelled sweet and tart. I had been there before, but the memory was tucked so deep I couldn't bring it out to look at it.

Then, in the dark of night, something strange happened.

My purple ball of light was pulling magic, summoning it out of the ether like a Goddess. *Was* she a Goddess? I would have to find out because she was certainly drawing on powers in colours and smells that I had not ever seen before.

There was a deep purple cloud that followed her now, across the Human Realm into the west. And it pulsed with promise of murder. Excitedly, Fluffy and I growled and bristled, eager to see what violence was in store for us. What show we would get to see.

They stopped at a place that had once been bright. But now, a dark shadow lay over it, suffocating the life out of the colours instead. Dirty, pungent, rotting.

But through it all, laced through the stone walls, the bumpy roads, and even through the other moving colours was the purple light. It shone from every crevice, from every corner, lighting it up like a hope, a memory.

Something inside of me heated up. Like a warm blanket on a cold night. Like a dry cave in a storm.

Disgusted, I pushed the warmth away. There was murder in the air and the darting shapes drew on my need to hunt. On my need to kill. To play the game of life and death.

So I entered the city and hunted darker colours. The greys, the browns, the blacks. Their essence was violence, death and decay, and I was drawn to them like a bear to honey, ready to dominate them. I was hungry and ready to eat.

When I was killing, I could see the shapes of the colours a little better. Could see the bodies attached to those colours. They were flailing about and making noises as I killed them, but it only served to excite me more. So I went faster and faster, shredding and punching, striking and blowing.

It felt incredible.

In amongst it all, a light pierced the night of my mind, and I saw the world properly for the first time in weeks.

I blinked, reality blinding me with its strange appearance. My ears were assaulted with an orchestra of shrieking and screaming, demonic howls of pain. My nose smelled life's blood, demon ichor and sweat.

Upon a hill, in front of a gigantic gilded palace I had seen before, stood my purple ball of light.

Except she was no longer a sphere of colour.

She was a human woman.

It felt like something out of a dream. She was lightning taken shape, a storm made into a human, sheer power turned into a woman.

Something distinctly foreign crept through my veins, and I considered it with a frown. I didn't like it. It was prickling and hurting. Like a blade scraping against my vessels. I pushed it away. Humane emotions were not good. They were stupid and useless and stopped me from doing what I was made for.

Except as much as I craved violence, I also craved my purple ball. Shaking myself thoroughly, to which Fluffy let out a mewl of protest, I looked back at the city with the shadow on top of it.

I wanted to taste blood, to feel death in my hands, so I continued my extermination of the creatures I remembered were called demons.

But as I broke necks and ripped out hearts, my gaze was inextricably drawn to the palace my mark had run into. My hunting instincts kicked in, and excitedly, I headed towards the palace. I would go, I thought, I would go and see what she looked like up close.

Making my way up to the golden building, I exterminated each vermin that I passed. Some were more displeased about dying than others, but it didn't matter in the end. I was death in physical form. There was no possible way they could fight against me, even with the numbers they were trying to surround me with.

They might have been brave or stupid, I wasn't sure, but they were clumsy, their weapons weak, their blows like infants and I tore them a part like pieces of bread. Then a bigger one came up to me, gnashing his teeth, his colours a sickly black. I knew his face well we had spent time together. A name came up from the back of my mind. *Argoth.*

I reached into his body and tore out his spine. It came away in one piece and I tossed it over my shoulder, his body falling with a satisfying thump. Better. I felt much better. Fluffy cackled from my shoulder. I continued on.

I found my purple woman in the shadow of the palace. She was searching for something, her green eyes darting this way and that.

She was hunting. Now, I was even more excited. Following her on the hunt, I sniffed, trying to guess what my little pet was trying to chase. Her scent was intoxicating, the generous curve of her body so familiar and alluring. Every particle of her being drew me in, pulling me towards her—

Then it hit me like an axe to the skull.

The purple light was just like me. More than that, she bore a part of me. A part I had willingly given her.

And this was the woman the Green Reaper had instructed me to murder.

## 14

# SARAYA

I found Sarone and Braxus in a drawing-room through an open servants' door. Clearly, the old demon lord had tried to escape through the servants' tunnels.

My cousin had Braxus on his knees with his back to her front, his hair bunched up in her fist, pulling his head painfully backwards. Her eyes were alight with a feral satisfaction. "Look what I found, Cousin!" she panted, angling her sword against his neck.

"Well, well," I said, stalking forward, a tigress stalking prey.

"Let me go!" Braxus snarled. Drake's ring flashed on his finger as he tried to reach for Sarone's hands.

"Lord Braxus," I drawled. "You are being held by Lady Sarone Lota of the Ellythian Isle and you are addressing the Queen of Lobrathia. I would choose my next words wisely."

"My queen, I want him dead," Sarone snarled. "For what he has done to countless Ellythian girls, I want his heart's blood warming my hands."

"And so you shall, Lady Sarone," I returned her animalistic grin.

"I should have taken you when I had the chance," Braxus spat, his body dripping with sweat as his chest heaved. "I should have—

I didn't let him finish. With a swear, I unsheathed the Temari Blade and swung down upon his neck as Sarone stepped back. Braxus closed his eyes and screamed—

Abruptly, my downswing was stopped. It was as if a magical hand halted the blade just before it touched Braxus' skin. Confused, I pushed against the invisible wall, but the sword would not move forward.

Braxus seemed to realise something was wrong because he opened his eyes, took one look at the stilled blade by his neck and scrambled towards the door.

Sarone screeched and leapt after him, plunging her sword into his back, skewering his lungs and heart. They both fell to the ground, Braxus letting out a gurgling whimper.

But all I could do was stare at the ancient magical sword in my hand, Umali's fierce face screaming at me from the hilt. My heart beat irregularly.

It had stopped me from killing Braxus. But why? The first time I had gone to use it—to enact justice by killing this evil demon lord, it blocked me.

Disturbed, I had no choice but to sheathe the blade upon my back. The warrior midwife ghosts were still out in the city, killing any demon they found, so that part of the sword's power was not an issue. Sarone clambered to her feet, eyeing me warily. Her eyes darted to the Temari Blade on my back.

"Let's go, Cousin," she said, wiping her forehead on her sleeve. "We can figure it out later."

I shook myself. Of course, she was right. There was still much to be done. I could use my regular astral sword in the meantime.

I summoned my usual blade and, leaning down, cleaved

Braxus' ring finger from his hand, pulled Drake's ring off and tossed the finger back down. Pocketing the ring, Sarone and I strode out without looking back.

We returned to the entrance hall to find a blood splatted Jerali Jones pulling a regular sword from a demon's torso. The lightning sword was back inside its bracelet. The bodies of possibly fifty demon warriors littered the floor. Jerali bared teeth at us in satisfaction and turn to sprint right out of the palace.

Sarone and I followed.

The city was chaos. Screams resounded in my ears like an awful cacophony of death. A civilian human man darted past us as we passed through the gap in my lightning shield around the palace. He had a demon warrior's sword in his hands and was pursuing a lesser demon— the slithering, long limbed variety— who was running for his life.

From our vantage point high on the hill above the city, I could see my Order of Temari initiates, Hemali, Uma, Elya, and Blythe lighting up the night with flashes from their lightning swords. Groups of spectral blue bodies were flitting about the city, chasing, executing, slaying. The Warrior Midwives were out in full force and it was a glorious thing.

It brought a smile to my face as Sarone and Jerali ran into the city to join the fray, lightning swords drawn and ready.

But I cast my eyes upwards. The dawn sun was surely clearing the horizon by now and this dark shadow roiling sickly above us was obscuring any view of it.

Light. We needed light.

Surrounding myself in a protective lightning shield I raised my hands towards the sky. My magic leapt keenly from me, and I blasted it towards the shadow-blanket. I felt the electricity come up against a solid wall of dark magic. Gritting my teeth, I amped up the voltage, increasing the intensity of the flow until I felt the darkness yield to me. Sheer power flowed through my hands, fixing me in place and I swear, nothing on heaven or earth had the power to move me with that strength erupting from my core like a latent volcano being born anew.

The dark ceiling cracked like glass. A palpable splitting resounded in my ears and a crack appeared. Fine, like a spider's string at first, then it widened under the pressure I applied to it. I had no doubt in my mind that this was the Reaper's magic. No one else's. And here I was crashing right through it.

Because lightning does not yield. And here on the doorstep to my ancestral home, the Reaper would learn those words too.

Dawn light spilled through the crack in the darkness. I smiled with satisfaction and continued my assault, directing it outwards. More cracks began to appear, first slowly then rapidly expanding. I pulsed the lightning east, then west, until the cracks scattered and joined one another, creating larger fissures in the skin of the dark clouds. They pulsed violently as if they knew their time was coming to an end. Then all at once, the clouds shattered into a million pieces, dissolving into nothing allowing golden light to burst forth upon the city. I squinted up at a clear sky, columns of golden beams spreading from the dawn sun rising up in the east.

And in the far distance, flowing to my ears like a song I had waited my entire life to hear, was the sound of people cheering.

AFTER WHAT FELT LIKE BARELY ANY TIME—BUT WAS REALLY A FEW hours, my Temari initiates returned to the palace and we gathered in the entrance hall. All were flushed and sweaty, their purple crescent moons fading from their foreheads now the fight was done. Hemali and Ella both bore scratches to their faces and backs where they hadn't been quick enough to see an attack coming up behind them. Uma was the only injured one, with a broken sword arm, but Sarone had quickly healed it straight.

"We got all of the warriors," Hemali said, a manic gleam in her brown eyes. "The civilians started helping with the lesser demons…but I could have sworn…" The Ellythian warrior looked behind us, out at the city beyond my lightning shield. "Something was helping us."

My breath hitched. "Helping us," I repeated lamely. I shook my head. "Impossible. Who would it have been?" Perhaps Tarangi had given Lysander and Slade my message early, and they'd arrived already?

But Uma shrugged her wide shoulders and flipped her braid as if she did this every day. "Anyway, the civilians were helping as well, with whatever they could find. There's a midwife demanding to—"

"Where is she?" a crackling, hoarse voice demanded angrily. "Where is Saraya?"

The crowd of civilian men hastily parted, and standing there, with her patchwork cardigan stained with demon blood, her grey hair askew, was an ancient face I'd known and loved.

The tsunami of emotion caught me unawares, "Agatha!" I choked, covering my mouth.

Agatha stomped up to me, her eyes blazing and before I could do anything, she pulled me into a violent embrace. "Oh, you silly, silly girl," she wheezed. "You silly—" Her shoulders heaved, and I realised she was crying. I had never seen Agatha show any emotion, and she'd never ever embraced me before. Startled, all I could was grip her back.

"Oh, Agatha, you have no idea…" I sobbed into her grey

hair, the smell of blue ganja filling my nose. It smelled of her, and that meant I was home.

"I'm really home," I choked out. "We're really back."

She pushed me away, wiping her eyes on her knitted sleeve. Her stern blue eyes looked me up and down. "You've gained muscle," she remarked. "And your magic is tickling me."

I let out a laugh, wiping my nose on my sleeve.

"We have much to discuss," she said, looking around, eyeing Jerali, Sarone and the others, taking them all in with that efficient way of hers. "There are problems."

"I'm sure there are," I sighed. "What's first?" I gestured to Jerali, who barked for someone to find parchment and quill.

"I was marking the children as they were born," Agatha grumbled, leading me out. "But the demons were collecting the boys. They were trying to build an army."

Ice shot through me. "So you can match them all back?"

"Of course I can," she muttered. "But I'll need help to keep it all in line."

"Right. Well, we need to reunite the infants as a priority." I called for Hemali and Elya and instructed them to follow Agatha's orders. The girls left with my midwife mentor, and as I looked out at the carnage of my home, I knew there was a lot more work for us to do. I turned to Jerali. "Have someone send a pigeon to Kaalon and Traenara. Tell them we've taken Quartz back with me as regent and that we're starting the clean up process."

A FEW HOURS LATER, I WAS HAULING A DEMON BODY OFF THE palace stairs when Slade and Lysander rode up the drive, their painfully handsome fae faces white and Lysander's green magic on their heels.

"You had all the fun without us!" Lysander roared in outrage, waving his fist at me. "How could you?"

I cast him a wry look as they dismounted their horses. "I knew you'd come as soon as you got my note. And besides, there's still a lot to do."

"I'll say," muttered Slade, looking around at all the dead demon bodies scattered about the palace front lawn. "Where do you want the mass grave?"

"Farmer Thompson's land," said Jerali. "He won't mind."

The fae warriors nodded.

"He was here," Slade said, nostrils flaring.

"What?" I said sharply, straightening to stare at the brawny fae.

Slade rumbled, his dark eyes expertly searching the palace entrance hall.

Lysander winced. "Even if his scent wasn't all over this place, no one could miss the demon hearts and heads strewn all over the streets."

My heart pounded irregularly as I whipped my head around. "Do you think he's still here?" My voice was slightly shrill and I quickly coughed to clear it.

"I would say so," Slade said, eyeing me with a warning. "You need a permanent guard, Princess."

"On it," said Jerali fiercely. Somehow I don't think my General's bloodlust was satiated quite yet.

I blew out a breath to try and calm myself down. We wouldn't have gotten all the demons—there was a possibility many were hiding against the dawn. Hemali and Uma were currently conducting a search of the city to weed them all out.

And then we would have to scour the outlying land outside the city walls.

Slade suddenly shot behind me, and I whirled around to see him shoot up the stairs and scoop up a blood-splattered Blythe. She held her lightning sword out of the way and squealed in a way that brought a smile to my face, followed by a dull blow to the gut. I clutched my stomach and turned away from them, eyeing the city instead. Where *was* he? Had he been watching us this whole time?

"Was he helping us?" I asked Lysander. "His mother said he wouldn't be thinking properly, but between the mountain pass and this, it looks like he was trying to help."

The blond fae exhaled slowly, eyeing me like he knew I was thinking wishfully. "Honestly? I think he just likes to kill things. It's in his nature. He probably was hunting you, saw some opponents, and took the opportunity."

Something dark settled in my stomach. I could not forget the fact that he was likely hunting me as his mother had cautioned. If I came upon him—if he cornered me, I would have to defend myself against him. The thought made me sick to my stomach. But it only reminded me that the Temari Blade still strapped to my back would not work for me. Hastily, I unbuckled it.

"Something's wrong with it," I said softly. "I tried to kill Braxus, and it stopped me."

"Magical weapons are temperamental," Lysander said, leaning down to eye it suspiciously. "Like the Goddess it hails from, I guess."

I made an unhappy noise before shaking thoughts of the Blade from my mind. My fae warriors arriving also reminded me of the other fae. "Send word to Black Court as well, Jerali, that we've claimed back Lobrathia. If they need refuge, we will accept them. There's a chance Eclipse and Midnight Courts have them captured."

Jerali looked at me incredulously. "At a time like this you want fae refugees here? We need time to salvage the city."

I eyed my General evenly. "I know, Jerali. Take a tally of the dead, of the living. Funerals will need to be arranged. I'll go and take inventory. We need to know how many fighting men we have. How much quartz as well."

Jerali and Lysander quietly exchanged a look and I knew my General was not happy.

"We might have won this battle, Jerali Jones," I said. "But the Green Reaper is still coming. *War* is still coming."

Jerali's grey eyes lit up, and I was too tired to smile. Lysander looked between us incredulously.

"You humans are strange people," he muttered before heading back outside.

SOMETIME BEFORE DAWN, A LARGE GROUP OF US SAT IN THE KITCHEN, eating freshly baked bread made from some flour and yeast we'd salvaged from the underground winter stores the demons hadn't gotten into yet. Five of my fighting Temari initiates and Lysander shovelled their faces with food. Blythe and Slade had disappeared. Likely into a bedroom, I thought wryly, but it was a pocket of happiness in the bone-deep weariness we all had.

I ushered the palace maids in—who the demons had been keeping to cook and clean—so they could take their fill of what we could find to eat. A few of them cried in my arms when we found them in the kitchen, cowering inside the ice room. They were all skinny, with deep bags under their eyes, and I knew what they'd been through. We had a lot to rectify, and I promised them the demons were not coming back—even showing the bodies to placate the hysterical ones. They needed to see that they were safe now, that their assailants were properly dead and could never harm them again. Uma and some civilian helpers had found small groups of them hiding in the city and dispatched them quickly.

Jerali never seemed to tire, combing through long lists of names they'd been collecting as they'd scoured the streets. Everything needed to be accounted for before we could move on.

"Everyone find a bed somewhere," I said, clapping my hands half-heartedly. "Bathe if you can and sleep. Meet back here in the afternoon."

As everyone cleared off, Jerali glanced up at me, "Sarone? Accompany Her Majesty. She's not to be left alone. I'm not sleeping just yet. I want to head out again."

Sarone glanced at me, her green eyes saying what we dare not, in front of the maids. If Drake did come upon us, I wasn't sure if Sarone or anyone could do really anything, as fierce as my initiates were.

Nonetheless, it *was* better if I had company, so I took my cousin to my old bedroom, recently inspected and cleared of random debris by Lysander and the maids.

The Temari Blade found a resting place against my bedside table while Sarone and I hastily bathed, one at a time, each slipped on one of my old nightgowns and fell into bed. I lay there for a moment, holding Drake's ring in my hand, turning it around and around. We'd done it. By ourselves, coupled with ancient magic made for killing demons, we'd followed through. I'd kept my promise and killed my father's enemies. When I last lay in this room, my childhood bedroom, I had never imagined that I would return to it, after being married, having killed my father's advisor. I'd known Oxley for five years and shoving a blade through his neck was a slight shock to my system. But in that moment of lightning rage, I had not cared for anything except avenging my father. I hoped he was proud of me.

It should have been weird sleeping next to Sarone, whom I hadn't known that long. But whether it was pure tiredness or a kinship borne of a bloody battle, we both fell asleep quickly.

# 1 5
# SARAYA

The morning was full of meetings. I had gone down to the city first, with the intention of speaking with the people of the city and hearing directly from them what needed to be done. I met with Bluebell, the last birth I had been supposed to attend before I left with the fae all those months ago. She and her husband Charlie brought me her babies, now smiling and giggling.

"Saraya," Bluebell breathed, looking me up and down with her large, sweet eyes. She was only a girl of eighteen now, but a mother to twins whom she'd given birth to on the very night before my leaving for the Fae Realm. Glacine, my stepmother at the time, had her guards physically restrain me from leaving the palace to go to her aid. Since Bluebell's last birth had ended in a stillborn babe, it was imperative that I was there for her.

Instead, I'd been locked in my room. Anger bubbled in me anew as the memory returned, that wound re-opening. Though I'd failed to help Bluebell, her two babies had been born healthy and she herself had been fine despite blood loss. There'd been murder in my heart for Glacine back then, as well as for her guards Havlem and Yarnat—all of whom I'd seen working in the demon court. I had no restrictions on my movements now, but the threat of the Reaper was still there. Under my watch, I would let no harm come to the citizens of Quartz.

"Are you alright, Bluey?" I asked her, tickling her little girl, Destiny, on the tummy.

Bluebell beamed up at me. "We're all fine, thanks to you. They both breastfeed and I'm fully healed. Agatha was keeping a close eye on us."

Charlie, her young husband, bounced his baby boy on his hip.

The little boy, Luxon, Lucky for short, had been confiscated by the demons and sent to the manor they'd set up as a nursery for the baby boys. I knew they had been trying to mimic the set-up they had in Havrok's palace, where baby boys and girls were raised away from their mothers for the sole purpose of a certain career. Now that they were all reunited, the citizens of Quartz were weary but happy. Once they met the four other Temari initiates that they didn't already know, Sarone and the others were welcomed with open arms. They'd seen us fight for them, and it meant more to them than anything else.

"How's the bakery?" I asked.

Charlie shook his head worriedly, "No wheat, Princess. The demons were hungry, they drained us of everything we had. Even after they started rationing the food it was difficult."

There were issues aplenty. Food being the main one. I wrote to Kaalon, knowing that Osring and the other regents might be a little upset at me for acting without permission, but I also knew they would help us until we got back on our feet. We still had a whole quartz quarry to trade for peaches and wheat while our own crops were nursed back to health.

I spoke with farmer Thompson, who, as it tuned out, was *not* actually happy with the mass demon grave we'd put on his lands. So I promised him recompense after the threat of the Green Reaper was dealt with and began a new grave outside of the city. After he was appeased, I made it my mission to speak to the other tradespeople in Quartz and each one offered to help in their own way.

After a long morning, Sarone and I headed back to the palace for a bite to eat.

"Sarone, I've arranged an account with the seamstress. Now that we're back inside, go and see her to arrange for your clothes."

My cousin was an incredibly attractive woman so it was no wonder to any of us that Havrok had chosen her as his most favoured concubine. Her skin was rich brown, her figure long with a substantial bosom and long lashes framed eyes for a man to lose himself in. But also, she was taller than me and narrower in the waist. She needed more appropriate shirts and trousers for fighting. I wasn't *exactly* being misleading about my intentions, but importantly, the trip would keep her busy for some time.

Her beautiful face lit up as she unstrapped her sword belt. "Goddess! I am sick of these men's hand-me-downs. I'll be right back!"

I probably shouldn't have done it, but something inside of me craved time alone. Just a short while without someone breathing down my neck, asking me a question, or watching me. I wanted to feel the quiet of solitude, and I needed to hear myself think.

I pulled out my old saddlebag from inside my closet. Naturally, the demons had not been interested in clothing and had not done much disturbing of my wardrobes other than throwing the material around the room. But Blythe, in all her blessed foresight, had hidden my bags deep inside a loose board in my cupboard before she'd run out of the palace with Jerali, that night of the demon invasion. I couldn't believe my eyes when she proudly crawled out of my wardrobe with it. There were several things I held dear in there. First, Blythe's tiny portrait of my mother, which I set on my bedside table, then my mother's lotus anklet, which Blythe had a twin of. I secured it to my ankle immediately, wanting to feel closer to my parents now that I was back home. Lastly came my amazing purple travelling cloak, which Blythe and our nursemaid, Geravie, had made for my nineteenth birthday. I fastened it on right away, feeling as if I had my sister with me in spirit now too.

So with Opal riding around on Jerali's shoulder, I headed to a familiar place. A place that reminded me of both my mother, my sister, *and* Drake.

The air was crisp and chilly since we were still coming to the end of winter, and I huddled into my cloak. The smell of my mother's flowers perfumed the air as I swept past the garden beds running around the perimeter of the palace. Luckily for us, the demons had not trampled their mangy boots over the garden beds. Above, it was completely overcast, the sky a sea of white.

There had been a time when clouds were something I looked for, because it meant that Drake was nearby.

A pang of sadness struck me, and crossing my arms against that biting wound, I strode quickly across the palace's back lawn and into the thicket of pine trees where my mother's ritual pond was.

Dry leaves and twigs crunched under my Sky Court boots. I had travelled all the way to Kaalon and then back home and had not had two minutes alone to think about all we'd done. We'd gone all that way there for a blade that would not work for me and I could barely look Sarone in the eye for the sympathy I saw etched there. Perhaps the sword belonged to another—Sarone was of the same blood. She could very well take it as her own, I supposed.

But the thought grated in my mind like a dagger scraping against my brain. My mother would be so disappointed. The urgency and hope in her eyes in the birthing realm would be stuck in my mind forever.

The pond was pristine in the still air, making a mirror of the leafless branches above it. Crouching down to run a finger on its surface, I smiled, thinking of the last time we'd all been here, and Drake had stood watch, protecting me, Blythe, and Altara's maid Lucy, during my bridal ritual. The ripples in the water shifted, and I frowned, peering at the surface.

I saw his reflection first.

I jumped up, my heart pounding. Drakus Silverhand stood, still as a predator, on the other side of the pond.

At well over six feet tall and broad with muscle like all he did was heavy physical activity, he was an imposing sight that usually made any nearby male tense where he stood. Though he appeared rough from weeks in the wilderness, he was still the most handsome creature I had ever seen. My heart clenched as I took a moment to take him in, and as I did, a steady heat spread under my skin.

His all-black eyes twinkled with those eerie red lights I'd seen appear when I'd said those heinous words. He watched me with an intensity that made every particle of my being stand to attention. My body reacted to him on reflex, as if it had been waiting for him for a hundred years. I was unable to tear my eyes off him, he had me completely in his hold.

He'd clearly washed at some stage, though I knew if he'd been following us, he'd been travelling rough. His dark hair was clean though a bit unkempt, a slight scruff on his square jaw.

E.P. BALI

He'd dressed in a black shirt and trousers that looked worn from weeks of hard use.

He'd always had the posture and swagger of a warrior who knew he could easily take any man or creature on, but now… now he was stalking toward me around the lake, like a beast made into a man, more prowl than stalk. An animalistic aura surrounded him now, making him seem bigger, stronger, more imposing than he ever had. I had to steady my breathing.

"Drake," I breathed, turning to watch him walk towards me from around the pond. Every instinct in me was screaming to run up to him and my wrap my arms around his neck, but as if my body also knew his violent and predatory nature, I was stuck to the spot.

He paused a little distance away, his head cocked a subtle fraction as if he'd not expected me to use his name. "I am here to kill you."

I stopped breathing as his voice swept over me, goosebumps erupting on every inch of skin. Oh, dear Goddess, his voice was a guttural rasp more animal than human. So he *did* wish death upon me. I had been right after all. If it weren't for the slight note of uncertainty in his voice, I would have been worried. But as it stood, I knew I could hold my own against him, even in this new, terrible form of his. I blew out a steady exhale, readying myself for anything, and kept my voice casual, "Is that so?"

A pause as he observed me with a needlepoint detail, then he nodded slowly, just once.

I took a careful step forward, thrusting my chin in the air. I was no prey. I, too, hunted in the night. "Well, there's a problem with that. I am your wife. You are my husband. *You* swore a vow."

A crease formed between his brows.

"I…," he looked at me, confusion all over his handsome face, "I can see it. The magic of the vow between us."

Goddess, that voice curled up my spine. I had missed him so much. I just wanted his arms around me, to have him hold me close and safe. But I did not think that the Drake I knew was here. So I urged him, trying to find out who he was now. What he was truly capable of. "And?"

"It's telling me that you severed our bond."

My heart dropped into my stomach, as pain opened like a mortal wound, fresh and bright. But I had borne that guilt for weeks. I had fought with that pain. I had won back my kingdom with that pain slicing my heart in two. He was right, I had done that. That poisonous burn would always be mine. I could only whisper, "You would be dead if I had not."

He took one step toward me. "Instead, I died a different sort of death."

I flinched as if he'd struck me. "Drake, I—"

"Do not call me by that name." His words weere like a nail in a coffin.

My entire body became ice. Instead of physical blows, he was lunging at me with verbal weapons. It was fair. I deserved that. But I would not let him get the better of me. I never had before, why start now? I squared my shoulders. "What do you want me to call you then?"

He stepped forward. "Monster." Another step. "Killer." Another step. "Beast. Any of those."

My breath caught in my throat as he came up to me, close enough to smell. His scent had always been earthen, woody, and now it was laced with a something sharp like a warning. "Then *you* may call me, Your Highness. This is my land. I am queen of it. And as far as I see, you are trespassing."

He cocked his head in that familiar way of his, and the urge to move toward him got the better of me. Stepping forward, I should have been alarmed at the raw power I felt from him, instead, I was satisfied to feel his heat.

His nostrils flared, and I knew he was scenting me.

"Is my scent familiar, Drake?" I asked softly, tilting my chin up to look at him. I knew what he would smell. Desire. "Tell me what you smell," I whispered.

"You," he growled, red lights glowing dangerously.

I smiled back at those fell twinkling lights, though it pained me to see the mark of my rejection. I had liked the old silver stars better. "What else?" I pushed. We were close enough to kiss. I wanted to touch him. I remembered the way his lips had felt against mine the first time we kissed. I had been on top of him in Havrok's drawing-room, putting on a show. Straddling him in that revealing dress, the desire had gotten the better of us.

He made a sound low in his throat, leaning down just a little.

"You're very handsome, Drake," I whispered, tracing my left index finger down his chest. "I don't think I've ever told you that."

He inhaled sharply. Then stiffened.

We both glanced down at the knife I had in my right hand, its tip pressed against his heart. "You did say you were here to kill me, did you not?"

He covered my hand with his large one, and the hot physical contact was so jarring that I gasped. My magic leapt to attention as his magic rose up, inspecting me.

"Do it," he rasped. "Rid me of my pain."

I felt my face crumple under the agony I felt in his voice. Heat shot through my wrist as my magic leapt up, twirling around my body in a wondrous storm. Desire pooled between my legs. I closed my eyes for half a breath.

With a swiftness only the son of a Goddess could muster,

Drake yanked the knife out of my hand, spun me around, and pressed the dagger to my throat, his other arm holding me close to him. My rear was planted right into his groin, and all I could think of was the memory of how he had once felt inside of me. How much like heaven it had felt. How much like home he was to me.

His breath seared the skin of my neck as he gritted out, "Do you want to hear me call you *My Queen* before I use this?"

I felt every part of him pressed against me with a glorious intensity and could not help but close my eyes and enjoy the feel of his hard strength. "I missed you, Drake," I whispered, not caring about the note of desperation that came with it.

Even with a knife pressed against me, I would have spread my legs for him right there. I knew my desire was spiralling through the air and straight into his nose. I let it build up in me, imagined the first time we'd made love in that glowing lake, the way he'd growled and plunged himself inside of me and how moans of pleasure had escaped from my own mouth. I needed him with an intensity that I'd never thought was possible—that I knew I would never find again. Drake had been my mate. My family. My everything. I'd gone and ruined it, but if there was a single chance to have him again, even like this, I would take it.

Drake growled, a mixture of lust and frustration ripping through his voice, and before I knew it, he'd dropped us to the ground, twisting me around to face him. On my back, pinning my hips to the ground with his, he curled my fingers around the dagger and held it to his own neck.

"Do it, Saraya."

# 16
# DRAKE

Her name on my lips felt like something out of a dream. She was a beacon through the dense fog of my mind, and now with a buzzing clarity, every particle of my body wanted her. To possess her, to be inside of her.

With my hips pressed against hers, I felt her heat like a furnace, beckoning me in from a cold and lonely night.

"Take me, Drake," she whispered, her voice like wind chimes in a summer breeze. "Take me right here."

That voice untethered something in me, shooting straight for my manhood. The way she said my name like it was a prayer, precious and sweet. I screwed my eyes shut against the desire, trying to control the rabid lust now pouring through me, demanding to take her. Her softness called to me like a siren. Her curved hips begged to be touched, to be devoured. Her breasts against my chest made me want to hold her close and never let her go. I wanted to taste her all over, to sink my aching manhood into her warmth—

"I *need* you, Drake."

I came undone.

As if it weren't in my control, my hands were removing her pants even before my mind could register what was happening. Gods, it felt right, it felt pure, it felt like the one thing I needed in this forsaken world. She removed her shirt and then tugged at mine.

"I want to feel you against me, Drake."

A back corner of my mind was warning me, telling me I was being seduced. But I didn't fucking care. I *wanted* to be seduced. I wanted this woman more than anything, more than life itself, and I would kill anyone or anything who got in the way of that.

We were naked in an instant, skin against skin, her heat soaking into me, my manhood pressed against her wet sex.

She sighed happily, and I felt like it was the only sound in the world. She was so wet with desire that the head of my cock jerked when it came against her, rock-solid and ready to take her hard and fast. Claim her like the monster I was.

"Oh, Drake," she moaned, wiggling her hips, her fingers clawing at my back, pulling me closer.

Fuck.

This woman could do no wrong. I positioned myself at the entrance to her core. She was dripping freely onto me now. It felt like I had been waiting for this moment but had not realised it. What was wrong with me? Why could I not remember anything from *before*?

I eased myself into her, enjoying every inch of her heat on the way in.

She let out a feminine noise of satisfaction, bringing her legs up around me, ready for me to fill her up. I put my hand around her throat and devoured her lips, sucking and exploring every inch of her softness. She opened her mouth eagerly, allowing me in and I growled at the way she felt, meeting me and wanting me just as much as I did her.

I pulled back, panting with the force of my desire, and looked into her eyes. They were searching mine with a desperation I was not familiar with. They were a brilliant magical green that spoke of great power. But I knew they were eyes that I had looked into many times before. I wracked my brain, trying to remember how I knew her, how I'd been inside this woman before. I knew her scent like the back of my hand, knew it as if it were marked on my very soul.

"Come back to me, Drake," her whisper was filled with need. "I love you. I've always loved you."

Something ignited in the storm of my mind.

An alarming heat spread through me, soft and sensitive. I surged backwards, shocked. An involuntary hand flew to my chest, and I frowned. That poison I had taken into my body from *before* was coiling in me in its usual, vile manner, so it wasn't anything to do with that...

"Drake, what's wrong?" the queen leaned on her elbows, looking at me. Gods, she was a glorious figure, Goddess-like, naked on the forest floor. I knew in all the realms of the universe, there would be no one like her. The slopes and valleys of her body were something that deserved to be revelled in, savoured, and worshipped. And I wanted to be the *only* one to do that.

But I could not. Something was telling me that I. Could. Not. I had been told to kill this woman. To put a knife between her ribs. He had told me only I could do it. A gaping divide stood between us.

"I..." But something was happening deep inside of me. I felt like I was going to explode, this feeling in my chest spreading through me like...like...

*No.*

All I wanted to do was kill. But here, with her skin against mine, my mind was changing, my very being changing into something different. I turned away from her, my heart bleeding with a wound I could not decipher. I forced the words out, "I have to go." I flung out a hand, and my clothes flew to me.

"Drake!"

Her voice was a knife to my gut, but I had to go. I had to leave this place. There was a beehive in my mind. I could not hear myself think. I turned away from her, and it was as if someone twisted that knife already in my gut. I forced my feet to move through the forest with all the power I had. Every step I took brought me away from her, her scent lessening on the wind, the cold of a world without her darkening my vision.

I roughly retrieved Fluffy from the hollow he was sleeping in and pushing myself into the seam of reality and into the ether, I left the land the queen called home. My eyes were burning. My cock was burning. My heart was burning. Why the fuck was I burning?

I settled with Fluffy in a copse of trees, far, far away from the lightning city that bore the queen's magic all around it, when a shadowy finger poked me.

The Reaper was calling.

But my mood was murderous, vicious and sour. He was not Havrok and did not control me. No one could.

So I went anywhere but near him. And anywhere but near her.

But my raging mind could *only* think of her. Of the language of her eyes, the call of her body, the meaning in her voice. There was a meaning between us and an ancient magic drawing us together.

A magic that wanted me to kill everything between me and her.

But I had shaken hands with the Reaper. We had an agreement.

# 17
# SARAYA

I'd just pulled my pants back on when a series of snapping twigs sent me summoning my astral blade. I whirled around, only to see Blythe stomping through the undergrowth, an accusing half-smile on her face. I dissolved my blade back into thin air.

"I'm not going to say that I saw you…" she said. "But I saw you. What's going on? Is he back now? Why did he look so scary? Is it the—"

"Go get Jerali," I said numbly, not looking at her in the eye. "And the fae. We have a problem."

"But—"

"He won't come back for at least a little while," I said quickly, pulling my cloak back on. "Go, Blythe. Now."

Thankfully, she obliged. I just needed a moment to process what had happened. It had been a whirlwind of emotions and desire…

I had spent hours obsessing over what I'd say when I saw him return for the first time. But all of the prepared speeches and declarations of love had fallen by the wayside the moment I'd seen him. It was too much, and those red lights too raw.

I placed a hand over my heart to try and steady myself. Back when we'd first been wed in the Demon Court, I'd kept telling myself that it had been the magic pulling us together. That it had always been the mate bond creating the magical desire between us, making it not real.

But upon my rejection of him in Black Court, that bond had been severed. I'd *felt* the contract between our fathers dissolve in a tangible way. So now, there was no bond magic dragging us together. What on earth was this ecstatic, insane sense of longing that I was feeling?

*I love you.*

The words had dropped from my lips like a kiss, sweet and innocent.

And utterly true. Dear Goddess, I was actually in love with him. I looked at my right hand, where his mark, the twisted black tree, had been etched on me the first time we consummated our relationship. A part of me had hoped the mark would return if we had sex again. But here my hand was, the skin devoid of any marking at all.

Meanwhile, he'd said, "I've been told to kill you." It had not been of his own desire. Drake had been *instructed* to kill me.

But by whom?

Ice chilled my spine, shooting up like a spear. Who was the one person that needed me dead? I needed to talk to Jerali.

"Saraya."

That voice froze me in my boots—as it always had. It was not Jerali, not Blythe, not Slade. Holy mother Goddess. No. Not here, not now. It was impossible.

Slowly, I unstuck my mind from its panic and turned around.

Slumped against a tree, with one arm bracing herself against the bark, was Glacine. She was white as snow, a pained grimace on her angular features. "I need your help."

Her other hand was clutching her abdomen like she was injured, but I could see no blood or obvious surface-level ailment. I noted that the black scorpion tattoo on the side of her neck, Havrok's marking, looked like it had been magically cut off her skin, leaving a raw red imprint. Against her white neck, it still stuck out like a brand.

She was clearly unwell in some way. Even so, it made me sick to my stomach to move towards her. So I stood my ground and forced the words out through gritted teeth."What happened to you?"

Her eyes glistened, and she too, spoke through clenched teeth, "He's done this to me. I'm trying to get away from him, but he won't…There's no escaping him. He's too powerful. But this—" She gestured down to her stomach. "Just look and see. I'm in so much pain."

I raised my brows. She meant the Green Reaper. Jerali had described the battle at Black Court in great detail to me once they'd arrived with the Kaalon forces. Glacine had come with the Reaper, stood in his chariot by his side. But I also could not forget what Chalamey Springfoot had told me.

*He means to make another Tyaag.*

"You want me to look inside of you?" I asked, confused. Never, in my wildest imagination, had I ever anticipated *helping* Glacine. She'd always seemed so untouchable, so put together, so confident. Nothing untoward ever seemed to happen to her. I'd never seen her remotely unwell. Perhaps she never showed it, but it meant seeing her hobbling, grimacing in pain was a raw blow.

"I'm *pregnant*, Saraya," Glacine said through red lips. "He's gotten me *pregnant.*"

I reeled with shock, taking an actual step back. "He can do that?" I asked lamely. In my mind, malevolent beings like the Reaper were destructive forces. How could they procreate? I suppose it had worked the regular way, like for everyone else.

"Yes," Glacine hissed angrily. With her eyes narrowed on me in distaste, she returned to the Glacine I knew. The one who hated me, hated *us all* enough to kill both my parents.

My old stepmother groaned and slid to the ground, her face twisted in pain, clasping her lower stomach. The midwife in me kicked into gear, listing all the things in my mind it could be.

Miscarriage, infection, abruption, ectopic pregnancy…

But this woman had *killed* my mother, murdered her in cold blood and then gloated about it afterwards. I had every right to walk away from her and leave her to her pain. It was my right to kill her, as I'd vowed before my father's lifeless body.

Except I was a midwife. In my blood and in my bones, I had been born to be a midwife.

*When will you get it, Drake? My priority is to pregnant women. Each and every time.*

Those words had come out of my mouth to Drake because they were true.

Every cell in my bones was screaming at me to stick a knife through her heart. To be rid of her vile poisonous personality once and for all. This woman had caused so much pain, so much death. She deserved to die.

But I was a midwife. I had always been a midwife first and everything else second. My vow was to protect women. And here a woman sat, in need.

Despite my heart raging at me not to, I strode forward and crouched by Glacine's side.

I surveyed the trees ahead of us as I did, knowing that Blythe would send the fae warriors and Jerali Jones straight to me. They should be here at any second. Perhaps I could get her inside if it was a problem I could fix. It was terribly cold out here.

Sighing, I murmured, "Do I have your permission to look inside your womb and surrounding organs?"

She gritted her teeth and gave me a curt nod. It was a little reassuring that she disliked the idea of me helping her as much as I did.

Not liking the fact that I had to close my eyes while being this close to her, I set my jaw and did it anyway.

Whatever magical defences she had on herself, she dropped completely, because my mind reached her uterus without trouble. I did a basic scan, something I had done hundreds of times on equally as many women.

It was a strange thing. Whatever we all looked like on the outside, every woman looked the same on the inside. Sure there were individual differences within normal organs, but most of the time, they hardly made a difference. If her grandfather was fae, then Glacine was one quarter-fae, according to the Sky Court Queens—I wondered if that meant she would have to go through the birthing ritual like I did with Xenita Darkcleaver.

I worked sequentially as I always did, first checking her upper vagina for any abnormalities, like a tumour, then up to her cervix for the same. But all her organs were smooth, pink and healthy. Glacine was in her early forties, so an abnormality with a first pregnancy was something I needed to be watchful for. Had she been pregnant before?

As the question was about to leave my mouth, I swept through her uterus and saw no pregnancy at all. Instead, thin scars lined the endometrium—the inside lining. And looking deeper, the scars went into her myometrium—the muscle layer. I grimaced. Someone had performed a termination on Glacine. Multiple ones, by the look of her many scars, and brutally so. That was a shame. It meant an embryo would not be likely to take up home here, not without magical help.

But Glacine sounded so sure she was pregnant. Frowning, I cast my mind upwards and looked at her left fallopian tube and ovary, all normal, and then her right fallopian tube.

I froze.

Stretching the first third of her fallopian tube was a growth— a sac of fluid with a large clump of cells that looked like a bunch of grapes. It looked to be a few weeks along in growth— although it was hard to tell without a growing embryo—and was pushing against both sides of the tube, causing inflamma- tion. It was rare, but it was both a molar pregnancy *and* an ectopic pregnancy.

"How did you know you were pregnant?" I asked, circling round to check her ovary for good measure.

"The Reaper told me."

Interesting. Why would he plan for Glacine to get pregnant?

"Have you been pregnant before?"

"All terminated."

That confirmed the cause of scars, though it looked like it wasn't done by a professional. It also explained why the egg implanted where it did and also perhaps why an embryo had not successfully developed.

"Okay. Well, it's a molar pregnancy but also an ectopic pregnancy."

"What is that?" she asked dully.

"It's where the egg has implanted into your fallopian tube but also didn't create an embryo."

"I don't know what any of that means."

I opened my eyes and looked at her suspiciously. "You were in charge of Havrok's breeding program, and you don't know a thing about the anatomy of the reproductive tract?"

She threw me a look of deep loathing. "I never had someone train me, Saraya," she hissed. "I wasn't taught these things as a child."

I sighed, then explained to her in the way I would have if she were a civilian of my city under my care. "The growing seed is only as big as a marble right now," I indicated with my fingers, "And for some reason, has decided to not grow into a baby, more like a tumour. But the second problem is that it's taken root before it got to your womb—inside the tube that connects where the eggs are released to the womb. Does that make sense?"

She nodded stiffly. "That's why it hurts."

I nodded. "Because the tube isn't meant to expand."

She clutched her abdomen, panting a little. "So, what do I do?"

"I'll need to detach it. Your body should then treat it like a miscarriage."

She spoke through gritted teeth, "Do it."

I bit my lip. The egg had taken root within her, obtaining her blood supply, infiltrating the organ just as an embryo would have.

"It'll hurt, Glacine."

Her blue eyes bore into mine with such loathing I wanted to get away from her. Then she closed them, grimacing as another wave of pain wracked through her slender frame.

Without assistance, if she didn't miscarry on her own, her fallopian tube would rupture, causing fluid and blood to fill her abdomen. If I didn't intervene, she would die if someone else didn't heal her with their own magic.

"Please, Saraya. I need it done."

I have never heard those words come from her mouth, and I had never imagined they ever would have. I assumed this meant she was no longer siding with the Reaper. After we were done here, I'd have to take her as my prisoner for questioning. Perhaps she would know of the Reaper's plans and we sure could use more information. I sighed, "Alright."

It was quick, lucky for Glacine, as I only had to detach the feeler-like cells that were forming a minuscule placenta digging into her fallopian tube.

"It's done," I said after a few minutes, doing another sweep to make sure I hadn't missed anything. "It'll pass through naturally, now."

"I was watching you down in the Demon Realm, Saraya," Glacine said softly.

"What?" I asked absently, double-checking my work, leaving something behind increased the chances of infection.

"And the one thing I learned was that you always left your defensive wall down when you were working magic with birthing women."

I jerked back, making to open my eyes and finding that I couldn't.

A great shadowy void opened up before me and grabbed my mind in a painful, vice-like grip. I cried out in panic, scrambling backwards and falling painfully onto my bottom into the dirt.

"You always were weak, Saraya," came Glacine's voice from far away. "The same type of weakness your parents had. They couldn't even see their enemy in front of them."

I lashed out against the shadow that held my mind, but it held firm. I cried out in pain.

"Compassion is an admirable trait," I shot back into the dark. "I will *not* be ashamed for it."

"No?" she gloated. "Even if it gets you and your entire city slaughtered?"

I shut my mouth.

There was nothing I could do to stop it as that mental grip held my mind like steel pincers and pulled me down, down, down.

# 18
# SARAYA

I knew exactly what was happening because it had happened to me before—when the Green Reaper had sucked me into the astral plane before Havrok's Court had dissolved into blood and death.

While my body thumped down to collapse on the cold forest floor, my mind was travelling, being forcibly taken to a place of someone else's choosing. I spun in darkness, trying to pull the pieces of my mind together and force my defensive walls back up. But he was already inside my psychic castle walls, I could feel him, the Green Reaper, and try as I might, I could not force him out.

The sheer power overwhelmed me. It reminded me of Drake's power. The way it was dominant, overwhelming, violent.

But where Drake's presence in my mind was softer within its overwhelm, the Reaper's presence was anything but. It felt like he'd shoved a hand down my throat and was ready to pull my heart out.

It went against everything that had been ingrained in me, but

I finally accepted I could do nothing and gave in, allowing the tide to take me. Drown me.

Unable to do anything, I chose to be alert to what was going on. If this was an attack, I wanted to be ready.

When my vision opened up and my astral body landed at its destination, I was sitting down on something soft in a gilded, brightly lit room.

I blinked as my eyes adjusted to the light and found myself sitting at the head of a lavish dinner table in a grand dining room.

To my great shock, six others sat at the table with me, and they were all tall and broad fae males except one.

Sitting to my right was Daxian, perfectly kingly in a regal black shirt and vest, with his matching eyepatch making his other eye look even more turquoise. He somehow looked both carefree and alert at the same time, sitting with a casual posture though his one eye was sharp on me.

To my left was Prince Adlain of Kaalon, pushing his glasses up his long nose and his brown eyes darting nervously around the room.

The rest of the faces staring grimly back at me I knew from my time at Mountain Academy: the other four Crown Princes of the Dark Fae Realm. All were dressed as if for a regal ball, in fine shirts and embroidered vests.

Skelton, the Prince of Twilight Court, brown-skinned and dark-haired, with hollows of grief under his eyes. Ashwood, the Prince of Midnight, pale with brown hair and a dour expression. Naxon, the Prince of the traitorous Eclipse Court, a dirty fighter with cropped blond hair and finally, Prince Fern of Obsidian Court, who had once taught me an excellent manoeuvre to trick your enemy during a sword fight. He was brawny and would've been utterly handsome like the rest if not for his nose, which had been broken multiple times and never healed straight—by his own choice.

"Queen Saraya," Daxian said, bowing in his seat, "we were hoping you would not turn up."

"*Queen*," Naxon shot, blue eyes narrowed on me with an attitude that suggested he thought me nothing but the dirt on his shoe. "Has she been coronated?"

"*She*?" I asked lightly. "That is no way to address a Princess when your question is directed at her, *Your Highness*."

Naxon's sharp fae features reddened. "Or should I be calling you Sam Sourbottom?"

I gave him a droll look, "Everyone else is already past it, Naxon, and no one at Black Court had a problem."

"Well, perhaps I do!" he said banging his fist on the table. "It was a dark deception if you ask me."

"A dark deception would be coming to Black Court as an enemy of war," I shot back.

As Sam Sourbottom, they'd all been rather kind to me. I wasn't a threat, small by fae male standards and most had thought me illiterate. The poor country boy who needed some help to get through classes.

"Be quiet, Nax," Daxian rumbled, staring the Eclipse Court Prince down.

Daxian, being the only one of us actually coronated, outranked us all. Naxon clearly remembered this, enemy or not, and sat back in his seat, though his stormy face remained.

"Why are we all here?" I asked, glancing at Adlain. "First time astral travelling, cousin?"

"*Cousin?*" Fern squinted between Adlain and me.

"In name, only," I said smoothly. "In the Human Realm, we royals rather like each other."

Fern raised his brows but said nothing.

"I suppose the Reaper brought us all here?" asked Adlain nervously.

"Yes, human Prince," said Naxon haughtily, "the Reaper, our lord and saviour, is hosting a meeting of the rulers of the realms."

"Then why are you here?" I asked, surprised. "Shouldn't it be the kings?"

Everyone went still.

"She doesn't know," muttered Fern to Daxian.

"It was only recent," said Daxian so softly I had to lean forward to hear him. His blue eye fixed me like a weapon. "By your mate's hand, the kings of the other three courts are all dead."

Drake had killed them? My heart beat unevenly as I registered what he was saying.

I stared around at the table, stopping on Prince Skelton, who was the only one staring, dejected, down at the gold plate in front of him. My heart squeezed. Twilight Court had been our only hope back when the others, Midnight, Obsidian, and Eclipse, had all sided with the Reaper. Black Court had stood alone, and when Drake and I arrived there to help, our cause had seemed dire. Then Skelton had rode in the night before the battle, telling us that the entire court had been wiped out by the Reaper's army—the other Courts.

I glared around at Fern, Naxon and Ashwood, heat rising in my face. I looked at Daxian, who was still looking at me with his one eye.

"How can you sit there?" I hissed, standing up.

It was then that I realised I wasn't wearing my normal clothes. Somewhere between the forest and here, my clothes had been changed into a blush pink gown of ballroom calibre. It was off the shoulder, pinching in at my waist and flaring out grandly.

The Reaper had dressed me for a royal ball for some bizarre reason. But I pushed that to the back of my mind as the princes stared at me. Prince Skelton's dejected face spurred me on.

I glared at Naxon. "Skelton has lost his *entire* family because of you siding with the Reaper." I looked to Prince Ashwood. "You *could* have sided with us." Midnight Court had been the deciding Court. Their partnership with one side or the other determined who won the battle. There were only five Dark Fae Courts.

"It was not my choice, Princess!" Ashwood said, actually looking distressed. "I was there, in the battle. Naxon—" he shot the prince a hateful look, "—wasn't even there. But I fought. I saw what happened."

"And then you *ran*," sneered Fern, looking down his nose as Ashwood.

"Commander Drakus *told* me to go!" Ashwood muttered into his hands.

I bit back my surprise. Drake had told the enemy's son to leave the battle. No doubt they'd met on the battlefield at the time. The thought warmed my wounded heart.

"Ashwood was smart," shot Daxian. They all went quiet. "If he hadn't left, he'd be dead."

Daxian, on the other hand had charged right into battle with his head held high, looking almost certain death right in the face.

"There's no honour in fleeing a battle!" Fern retorted.

"There's no honour in siding with a dictator!" I hissed.

Fern harrumphed and slumped back into his chair. "This is pointless. We're fighting our fathers' battles."

I sat back down in my chair, the wide skirt of the ballgown rustling, and exchanged a look with Daxian. "How did you end up here?"

He sighed as if he was very disappointed with himself. "Your lightning shield burnt out a week ago, although we've been left alone since. But Reaper got to me through my mother. She fell for his manipulations. She meant well and was trying to make up to me for the fire wraiths, but...well, here I am."

"I fell for Glacine's manipulations," I murmured. But shaking my head, I knew that if I went back in time, I wouldn't have acted differently. Glacine was a woman who needed my midwifery expertise. Denying her could never be an option. And here it became my downfall.

"My father was also manipulated," said Ashwood softly. "He didn't even want a bloody war—"

"Then let us not go to war." The voice that echoed around us was unmistakable. Cold and deep. Malevolent. Adlain jumped in his seat while the fae stiffened.

A set of double doors on the other side of the gilded room swung open, and an imposing figure walked through. Except it was not the black-cloaked, green fire-clad being I'd been expecting.

This fae male looked like a king.

He was about as tall as Drake and tanned with an athletic, muscled body. Thick black curls sat atop a chiselled face, aquiline nose and piercing eyes that swirled in different shades of green.

The others were as taken aback as I was and we all watched the Green Reaper swagger in, his attire, like all of ours, suited to a ball. He wore knee-length shiny black boots, trousers and a fine white shirt and vest—green to match his eyes.

*What* in the Goddess' name was he doing?

He stood behind the remaining seat right at the end of the table—directly opposite me, those magically swirling eyes skewering me to my seat.

Never taking his eyes off mine, he regally sat down. My heart pumped erratically from the sheer power that swamped me. It was such a dark malevolent force that it felt like someone was pressing on my chest, trying to crush me. I knew it for what it was. He was showing us exactly how much power he had over us. Exactly how defenceless we were.

"Imperial Highness," he smiled at me with perfectly straight white teeth, "that is how you address an emperor, is it not?"

It was, but I would die before I called him that. "Don't know, sorry," I said smoothly. "There is no emperor on our continent."

Whatever this game was, I'd played it before in Havrok's Court, and I think I knew how it went. It would go pleasantly until he tired of the ruse.

"Wine!" he called out, his voice striking me like a drum.

Rich red liquor appeared in the golden chalices at each place setting. The Reaper held his own up. "A toast!" he sang in a melodic voice, "To Crown Princess Saraya, for successfully taking back the seat of Lobrathia…for now."

Bristling, I had no intention of tasting the wine but unbidden by me, my hand was forcibly thrust out, and my fingers curled around the stem of the chalice. The others were forced to do the same. Under Daxian's eyepatch, his jaw clenched.

The chalice was forced to my mouth by my own hand, and I had no choice but to part my lips and let the liquid be tipped in.

This level of control over us should have been impossible. My skin crawled as any autonomy over my body was easily taken from me.

The wine was incredibly sweet and fresh on my tongue, but it was still bitter to swallow. The power over my hand suddenly disappeared, and I quickly set the chalice down.

The Reaper was staring at me, his magical swirling eyes missing nothing about my form and face. I suppressed the urge to shiver. Daxian looked between the Reaper and me. Abruptly, the Reaper turned to Adlain, sitting still as a deer, adjacent to me. I almost sagged from the weight of his gaze lifting off me.

"How goes Peach Tree City, Prince Adlain?" he asked conversationally. "Your city is rather fascinating to me."

I stiffened. *Did he know about the illusion?* But the threat was clear to Adlain because he paled.

"There's not much to say," Adlain, recovering quickly to his credit.

The Reaper gave a knowing, terribly handsome smirk. It was a painful beauty, his face almost difficult to look at for too long.

"The forces of Eclipse Court are ready, Your Imperial Highness," Naxon piped up. "Ready to go."

Twat! I could've broken his nose right there.

"Excellent," was all the Reaper said, barely glancing at the blond Fae Prince.

"And what have you been up to, Princess?" the Reaper asked me. "Busy, playing regent?"

"Interesting you ask," I piped. "I healed your partner, Glacine Eyesmith, of an ectopic pregnancy. Awful condition. Exceptionally painful. Also, unnecessary." I gave him a pointed look. "You could have requested a meeting with me. I would've come."

I was *not* going to let him get the better of me.

"Fascinating," he shook his head as if marvelling at me. But his voice was laced with mockery."A princess who is also a midwife. What a treat for the people."

"I wouldn't quite put it that way," I said coldly."It is necessary and important work." I gave my best courtier's smile and leaned forward as if I were telling a great joke. "But to try and convince a room full of men of that? I may have my work cut out for me."

His smile twitched as if he wanted to sneer but stopped

himself just in time. *There it is*, a breaking of the facade. The princes and Daxian shifted uncomfortably.

The Reaper abruptly stood. "Come, my Ellythian Princess." His predatory eyes were stuck on my face like a pair of daggers. "I'd quite like to talk with you."

# 19
# JERALI JONES

I was sitting in the meeting room, pouring over a map of Lobrathia with Slade and Lysander, when Blythe burst into the room as if a pride of lions were on her tail.

"Jerali, Slade! It's Drake!" She shrieked.

"What?" Slade leapt to his feet with a speed only the fae could muster. Lysander was voluntarily slower, warily dragging himself to standing. I remained in my seat.

"Where?" Slade asked, his voice commanding.

"I...well..." Blythe blushed. "I saw the two of them in a compromising position—"

I swore and got to my feet as Lysander groaned. No need to elaborate, really.

*"Where is she, Blythe?"* I pressed, reaching for my sword belt.

"Queen Yasani's pond."

We all shot out the door, the fae warriors naturally speeding ahead.

By the time I reached the back palace steps, Slade and Lysander were disappearing into the forest.

As Blythe and I sprinted across the grass, my mind raced.

Drakus Silverhand was a force to be reckoned with, and Lysander had been quite explicit when he told me that none of us should be engaging in battle with him if we were wise.

I had not yet met a foe I couldn't defeat, and the thought of it intrigued me. Enough that if I *were* to face him in single combat, I would engage him quite happily. It wouldn't be a fair match, granted, with his magic and apparently God-like power, but it couldn't hurt to dream about. Seeing him take on those fire wraiths at Black Court had been a once-in-a-lifetime experience. A battle like that would be whispered in taverns for centuries to come. I could only wish for a match of equal footing such as that!

But on the other hand, if he *were* putting Saraya's life in danger, I would thrust myself between my queen and him and gladly die in combat. No problem.

I owed Saraya and Yasani that much.

When I burst through the line of trees, what I saw made my blood run cold. Blythe screamed and leapt towards Saraya.

Our Queen Apparent was lying on the ground on her back, her body limp, eyes closed in an ashen face. Slade had a finger on her neck as if he were checking her pulse while Lysander was crouched, sniffing her face.

I had to ask it, "Is she—"

"She's alive," Lysander muttered. Then he looked up at the sky, squinting around us. "But her astral body is away."

"What does that mean?" I demanded while Blythe patted Saraya's face, trying to get some reaction, I think.

"Her astral body is like her spirit," Lysander sighed. "She can leave her body and travel through the air, go wherever she wants. But I don't know why she would leave her body in the cold here like this. It could only mean…"

"It's *him*," snarled Slade, standing up.

"Drakus?" I asked, my hand never leaving my sword hilt.

Slade turned and kicked a stone angrily into the forest.

"The Reaper," answered Lysander.

"Get her inside," I ordered. "It's too cold, and Drakus could still be about."

Lysander was obeying me as if I were his General these days. He obediently hauled Saraya into his arms as effortlessly if she were a newborn babe.

"Blythe, go and get her warm," I instructed quickly. "Slade and I are going to scout the area."

Blythe nodded, glancing worriedly at Slade, who was now angrily prowling into the forest like a bull ready to charge. I hurried after him. We would need to stay together if there was a chance of coming across Drakus Silverhand.

In the gladiators dungeons of the Demon Realm, I had spent the better part of the month listening to stories about the famed monster-fae commander and his exploits. He was a legend in those parts, and the story of how he'd rescued Slade had turned into a bedtime story the gladiators told over slop in our cells. He was feared and respected and that was *before* his real powers had been unleashed.

"He's not going to be here, General," Slade grufffed. I think military titles were something that comforted him—he revelled in structure and I was more than happy with that mindset. "I can't sense him at all."

"So we don't think he was involved in Saraya's...astral travel? But he was here. Why did he run?"

"Something clearly happened between them. It was likely he got confused about it and ran. The rejection is a severing of the magic binding them. But if they're still attracted to one another, perhaps their bond was stronger than the magic? Blah! I don't know." He angrily chopped a stray branch with his sword. "Gods, I just want him back to normal."

"So you think the Reaper has taken Saraya's spirit?"

"Yes."

"How do we get it back?"

"We don't."

I had always appreciated Slade's straightforward manner. "Why?"

"Because it's up to her, now. She has to free herself."

As we rounded the forest, sticks crunching underfoot, the air clear of that eerie feeling that came when Drake was watching us, I blew an exasperated sigh. "Well fuck. So we just wait?"

The fae warrior grunted irritably.

Naturally, we found nothing of note in the forest. Not even tracks showing us where Drake had gone. It was like a phantom, coming and going without trace and it made me shiver to think a being was powerful enough to do that.

When we got back to the palace, I was heading to Saraya's suites to see how she was when Lysander strode from the opposite direction—from the entrance hall. Opal was on his shoulder, chattering manically, her eyes wide, her paws gesturing. She leapt onto my shoulder.

I frowned at them both. Lysander needed to be guarding our queen. But the blond fae warrior glowered at me in an uncharacteristic seriousness. "There's another problem," he said darkly. "Go and see."

Abruptly I turned and headed towards the entrance hall, Opal making nervous noises in my ear.

I heard them before I saw them. Women were wailing.

When I strode down the palace steps, I could see a mob of people at the palace gates. But unlike any protest I'd seen before, most of them were women. Women with…

*Dear Goddess Almighty.*

They were all holding children. Infants, specifically, young

161

babies less than a year old. Sarone and Elya were there, trying to calm the women down. Sarone had her eyes closed, her hands over a baby's tiny head as if she were magically looking inside of it like Saraya could.

As I hurried to them, a petite young woman held twin babes in her arms. A boy and girl, both of their heads lolling on her shoulder. "Where is the princess?" she sobbed, tearing running down her red cheeks. "I beg of you, call Saraya. Say Bluebell needs her!"

"Princess!" a man cried from the back.

They were all carrying apparently sleeping babes in their arms. But with *this* amount of noise, surely the babies would have been awoken.

A chill ran down my spine.

Sarone turned to look at me, her face grey, her expression filled with dread. She opened her mouth, but words did not come out.

An elderly woman pushed to the front of the crowd even in their distressed state, the people parted respectfully for her.

I recognised her as Saraya's old midwife teacher, Agatha. We had helped her to reunite these very babes with their parents yesterday. She fixed me with a beady blue eye. "The infants," she rasped. "The infants of the city will not wake up."

Opal wailed.

## 20

# SARAYA

To my extreme disappointment, the Green Reaper had stood from his seat on the other side of the table and was now stalking over to me. My magic prickled uncomfortably at his approach. Malevolence dripped from him like a dark, oily poison, suffocating everything around it and I had every desire to sprint away from here as fast as I could.

Daxian let out a slow exhale from my right as the Reaper stood next to him, offering me a hand.

"Allow me, Princess," the Reaper said. "Let us all go through to the ballroom."

I looked at the Reaper's hand, large and unmarked. I didn't want to touch him, didn't want his hand on mine. But what choice did I have, really? He could make us do whatever he liked—that display with the wine had proved that. He was just so much more powerful than any one of us.

So though it made me want to punch his face, I stood and placed my hand in his. The Reaper flashed me a brilliant, handsome smile and led me down the table, the skin of my palm heating up uncomfortably. Adlain and the fae had no choice but to push back their chairs and follow.

He led us through the set of double doors he'd arrived through, which turned out led into a grand ballroom, complete with a quartz chandelier and ready waiting courtiers, dressed in the finest silks and tule. A string quartet struck up a waltz on a dais in the corner.

It appeared the Reaper had constructed this place just for this occasion.

"Dance with me, Princess." Though his voice was low and melodic, his magic grated against my skin like a serrated knife. I wanted to scream. Revulsion poured through me at the feel of his dry skin against my mine.

The word 'never' wouldn't leave my mouth, try as I might to make my tongue work. The Reaper's influence made my arms fling outwards, and he stepped right into them. He put one hand on my waist and the other in my right hand.

Behind me, the four Fae Princes and Daxian were also forced towards one of the Reaper's courtiers each and led into a waltz.

Whatever the Reaper looked like physically at the moment, he still smelled the same. It was what I realised was the odour of burning, rotting flesh. Scowling, I refused to look at him and instead turned my head and looked past our joined hands as we waltzed. He allowed me that, at least.

I had not attended a ball since before my mother's death, but all royals were trained in such dances from childhood. I knew the steps with my eyes closed, and so did the Fae Princes. I spied Daxian, still sprightly on his feet despite his missing eye, leading a red-gowned beauty just in front of me. He cast me a worried look, a tic in his jaw pulsing.

The Reaper's venomous voice brought my attention right back to him.

"We are the same, you and I," he murmured, his eyes burning the skin of my cheek.

"I rather doubt that."

"We have both rejected our mates."

That stung like a brand. I said nothing, only pursed my lips against the nausea now overwhelming me.

"Your little display at Black Court caused quite a stir," his voice was casual. "I believe my Obsidian forces are decimated. You've destroyed an entire court."

The knowledge struck me like the clang of a cold bell. Frowning, I considered what I remembered of what had happened when I'd lost control after Drake had fallen into the earth. I knew that I'd sought out Obsidian Court and specifically targeted their forces. But I had not realised that I'd killed *all* of them. *Decimated*, the Reaper said. *I'd destroyed an entire court.* But I'd been within my rights—they had all come to kill us. Literally destroy us. I had a worthy cause.

But still, that knowledge curdled in my stomach. What did that make me then? A mass murderer?

I looked at him then, right in those sickly, swirling eyes. "This war of yours is destroying the fae people," I said. "Is that what you want?"

His face remained blank. "I neither care for the fae, the humans, nor the demons, or any other creature in between. What I want is power over the land."

"But why?" I asked incredulously. "Just take one portion of the land and rule it as your Kingdom. People have been doing that for millennia. Why do you need *all* the land? Is that not the reason you split the fae realm into two? So you could rule over the dark side?"

The Reaper smirked at me as if I were a stupid child. "I cleaved the fae lands into two because they were easier to control as divided people. And they needed to be controlled by someone who was worthy to do so."

I frowned at that, because I'd recognised it for what it was. I'd been studying the ways of conquerers from my childhood political studies. He wanted control. And division was the perfect way to do that. Standing together, the fae were too powerful. But split them in half and isolate them....then he had a chance of taking them over one by one. He had the Dark Fae Realm now and had decided to move against the Human Realm. By why not the Solar Fae Realm next? My mind rapidly moved to our visit to Sky Court. How the Sky Guard lived and trained under the two queens. Were they too powerful for the Reaper to move against just yet? The realisation spun through me, making me dizzy.

The Reaper was studying me closely and I came back to the room, shaking myself out of that thought. I would need to bring this up with my fae warriors when I returned to the palace.

The Reaper suddenly said, "You never wondered why I chose Drake's mother's tree as my resting spot?"

No, actually, I hadn't.

"She had a fae name, once," he continued casually. "What was it now, ah yes, Lily Silverfoot."

The name struck a familiar chord in me and I frowned.

"Ah, familiar? She and Fern the First, our little Fern's ancestor, killed the troublesome Niyati, Oberry the Gruesome. She seduced Oberry, and together she and Fern double-daggered him."

Holy mother Goddess. *Every man I lie with dies.* The Black Widow was Lily Silverfoot.

Drake had told me the fae bedtime story about the first rulers slaying Oberry the monster to save the Kingdom.

"She and Fern the first—they were the first Fae King and Queen. Naturally, that made them the first Tyaag and Niyati."

Surprise rang through me, though I suppose it made sense. Niyati were creatures of destiny, beings upon which the turning points of the world happened. It seemed natural that they would be the first rulers.

Drake's mother was the first Tyaag, and she'd been turned into…*that*. What she was now, a dark creature with the power of a Goddess.

"So…" I thought rapidly. "Which fae God is Fern the first?"

"Ah, there it is." His green eyes pulsed.

My mouth twisted in distaste. "I don't understand."

"How does a Tyaag or a Niyati become a living God?"

My step faltered in the waltz, but the Reaper kept me moving with his magic. My insides froze.

"This part of the story is not often told," he murmured. "Lily was concerned with power. She rejected Fern the First as her mate and, in doing so, became the Goddess of the Black Grove you see today."

I couldn't breathe as I registered this.

"Making sense yet?" The Reaper's voice was dangerously low.

I swallowed the lump in my throat. The Black Widow's form came into my mind's eye, those all-black eyes, that silver skin… dangerous, powerful, but also cruel, cunning and wild. I looked up at the Reaper. His power bore the same cadence—that same dark, oily, crooked energy. They were entirely self-serving, their claim to power twisting them both.

Or perhaps it took a twisted person to claim that type of power.

And *I* had just committed the mass murder of Obsidian Court.

Then what of Drake? The Black Widow had wanted me to reject her son. Why? *Why condemn him to the awful fate of her mate?*

The Reaper was watching me so closely that I clenched my jaw and came back to myself. I could not let him create doubt in my mind. I was strong and always did what was right. I would never succumb to that darkness.

But I had.

I had rejected Drake.

*And then I had gone on to destroy an entire Fae Court.*

The Reaper squeezed my hand gently and I twitched so violently that I thought I was about to keel over onto the marble tile. But I didn't, he held me in a prison of his magical grip and said, "For so long, we've thought that rejecting your mate leads to greater power. But I have come to realise that a Niyati and Tyaag are more powerful together. And so, I wish for you to become *my* Tyaag. My partner in crime. My queen."

I was so shocked I stared at him. Right in his green, swirling, hungry eyes, I stared at him. Suddenly his hand squeezing mine, his other hand warm at my waist made sense. Bile rose up my throat.

That's why he wanted to see what I could do, back in Havrok's Court. He'd freed me and allowed us to freely overrun the demon palace. It had all been to see what I could do. To see if I would be a worthy partner.

This is why he had made himself handsome—except I already knew what his vile form truly was.

"Never," I hissed in disgust.

How could he even think I'd give in just like that?

But a smile spread across his lips like a whip. "Yes, see, I suspected you might be of that opinion. So I took the liberty…"

He glanced in front of us. We'd come to the side of the ballroom where another set of doors swung open under his magic, and we waltzed right into it, coming to a stop.

Quite suddenly, my lungs were devoid of air.

Before me were fifty odd small cradles set in neat rows. And in each one was a sleeping baby, all less than a year old.

"You didn't think I'd let you keep the Quartz quarry?" He said looking out at the cradles. "The biggest asset on the entire continent?" He laughed low in his throat, as if I were some little girl he pitied. He turned to me suddenly, the darkness bloating around him like a cloud made of decaying flesh. "If you deny me, Saraya," he hissed. "I will have to kill these children. It's quite simple. I've made the choice for you. No need to trouble yourself."

I whirled around to face him, a storm brewing in my mind, rage filling my veins. "So!" I said fiercely. "From what I understand, you've failed in your take over of the Human Realm, so you've come to me for help? Is that right?" He said nothing, just stared at me with that God-awful smirk. "And you want to blackmail me into doing it?"

He cast an eye back over the infants and right in that moment I wanted to plunge a dagger through his throat.

"I know full well your weakness for pregnant folk and newborns," his voice was living poison. "I know full well that you will give yourself to me to save these infants. All you need to do is pledge yourself to me, and they will be saved. Alive and well to go back to their parents. Who are, right now, extremely distressed. Calling for you, in fact."

My veins turned to ice, the anger in me lapsing into cold, hard fear.

He held up a parchment, written in magical ink, an eerie mirror to my contract to marry Drake.

I couldn't move as the Reaper's dark cloud pressed on me,

like a giant hand squeezing me tight.

"Pledge yourself to me," the Reaper pressed, "and I will spare the infants. Do not, and I will destroy them."

I wanted Drake. I wanted to be held by him, safe in his arms, to feel his reassuring voice in my ear, telling me that it would all be alright. That we would work together to fix this. To tell me of all the ways we would destroy the Reaper.

The astral bodies of the newborns squirmed in their cradles. One of them let out a wail, calling for her mother. I had no choice. I had no choice. What other choice was there? I turned to look at him in those awful green eyes. "I'm going to tell you something, Reaper, and I want you to hear me, very carefully."

His eyes glowed. He thought he was winning. "I'm listening, Princess."

"There is a special place in hell for those who take advantage of the kindness of others."

His lips pressed into a straight line. I'd told the Kraasputin this same thing back in the Mountain Academy, and I meant it. Cruel beings would pay for their crimes in one way or another.

But the Reaper only smirked. "You've not accounted for one thing."

"And what is that?"

"I *am* hell." He grabbed my arm with pincer-like fingers and, surprised by the pain it caused me, I gasped as our surroundings dissolved into nothing. But if this was my astral body, how was he causing me pain?

But I could barely think about it because when we reappeared, the world expanded, and we emerged into a room full of people I knew. With a jarring terror, my heart dropped into my stomach.

"W-what is this?" I stammered.

Red quartz light lit up the room, drawn velvet curtains, a red ottoman. Glacine stood with her back to me. Kneeling on the floor were Marissa and Tenna, Glacine's maids. Between them was a teenager, no more than thirteen. Her dress had been pulled apart at the back, exposing smooth brown skin devoid of any mark.

"This is a memory," the Reaper said goadingly.

This was Glacine's old suite in Quartz palace. This was the first day she had whipped me.

The Reaper's fingers were still pinching painfully into my arm.

"Remember this?" he asked.

I clenched my jaw against the sudden fear rising up my spine. I looked so young, and even then, right at the beginning, I had been immobilised.

This was a memory my brain would not let me remember. Wouldn't let me recall. My mother had just died and been replaced— I had still been grieving. I frowned at the scene as Glacine brought out her whip, and Tenna looked up lovingly at my stepmother, her fingers tight around my bicep, holding me in place.

But it didn't look like she should have worried because I was like a block of ice, frozen. I hadn't fought. I never fought. The one time in my life that I did not have it in me to fight.

"You don't remember," the Reaper said in amazement.

I glanced at him sharply, and he was appraising me closely, his green eyes fixed on me, cat-like.

"I suppose I had no reason to want to remember it," I muttered. The lights, this angle, it was too much. When Glacine bought the whip down for the first time, I closed my eyes. To my great shame, I still flinched.

The Reaper was silent, and I knew he was watching me. It was a sorry weakness that I couldn't watch this. But the sound of the whip striking again had me clenching and re-clenching my jaw. If I could have stopped her, would I? Could I?

I opened my eyes to find the Reaper's eyes bright on my face, his lips curved with enjoyment. I recoiled from him, but his fingers were still fixed around my forearm.

Looking back at the scene, I stared at my back.

Three strikes. Three marks.

Three marks that would never properly heal. But *this* time, I did notice what I never had as a teenager. Glacine's red quartz necklace and earrings glowed brilliantly. She had been taking my magic. Taking it for her own use, doing Goddess knew what. Probably working on that potion for my father. I sighed. I did remember that after this, my magic had disappeared for a few days. It had never happened before the event, nor had it happened after...until Black Court. Something stirred in the depths of my being...something clawing, biting, scratching. I shoved that feeling down into the well of grief and shame inside of me. I didn't have time for weakness.

"What is the point of this Reaper?" I snapped at him.

But the Reaper never flinched, merely stared at my body like he was ready to devour me. "There is a weak girl who could not save herself. Nor her parents. Nor all those children the demons had been collecting magic from."

The room dissolved, and we reappeared in the same room, but things had changed. The palace was older, and so was the girl kneeling over the ottoman. I was as old as I am now, nineteen. But on this day, I had turned around and spoken back.

The Reaper and I watched the altercation. I ran out through the servant's door, and the room erupted into chaos as Marissa ran out the door to get Havelm and Yarnat to come after me.

But my shoulders sagged where I stood because I remembered what was coming next.

My hunched figure returned through the servant's door, and silently I knelt down, pulled my dress open, and laid across the ottoman. My back was a toxic symphony of six years of pain for all to see.

The room was silent, but Glacine's smile was louder than any scream I could have given her. It made my stomach twist into a thousand knots to see this. To remember my defeat.

"There is a girl," whispered the Reaper, "who could do nothing." He pulled on my arm as the scene faded away, his magic pulling us into darkness one again. His eyes bore into mine. "You have great power in you, and I want to show you how to use it. I can help you."

"I know how to use my power!" I shot back. "As you saw at Black Court. I believe you lost that *particular* battle."

The Reaper's smile was knife-sharp on his handsome face. "There is more for you to learn, Princess. You might have explored Voltanius House lightning. But you have not come close to your Ellythian power."

"I've been using my Ellythian power since I was a child," I said, finally yanking my arm out of his grasp.

"That power you revealed after Drakus fell into the chasm was but a hint of your true essence. You have more to show yet. Let me help you find it."

"I don't need your help!" I raked my eyes up and down his body, letting him know exactly what I thought of his offer of partnership. But to my great dismay, he was completely unfazed. It was then that I suddenly realised how old he was. He had been there when the Realms were whole and that meant *hundreds* of years.

"Then why have you not been able to heal your wounds?" He shoved me hard, and completely unprepared, I fell backwards into the dark.

# 21
# SARAYA

Someone caught me roughly, and when I opened my eyes, it was into a single blue turquoise eye that I stared.

Daxian hauled me upwards as if I weighed no more than a child. "Are you alright, Saraya?"

I straightened the skirt of the ridiculous pink ballgown, trying not to look shaken from what I'd just seen. We had been returned to the ballroom, the other fae and Adlain glumly looking about. "Yes, thank you."

"He's fucking with us," Daxian murmured, tugging on the band of his eyepatch as if it bothered him. "He knows exactly what he's doing. He wants us to argue. He wants to unsettle us. We can't let him win."

"Well, that doesn't explain why Naxon is here," I pointed out to the angry blond fae. "He's in love with the Reaper. Why does the Reaper need to toy with him?"

But Daxian wasn't looking at me. He was frowning at something over my shoulder.

I whirled around.

It was Glacine. Gagged and bound to a chair. Her dark hair askew, glowering at us.

Daxian strode forward with purpose.

"Don't untie her!" I cried.

He turned around and raised his brows at me.

I cleared my throat. "Just the gag, for the moment."

Daxian slowly turned toward Glacine and obliged, untying the gag from behind her head. As it came away, it left pink impressions on her alabaster skin.

She scowled at me, but as she opened her mouth, the Reaper's voice rung around us. "What will you do, Saraya? Will you kill her? She deserves it after all she's done to your mother. Your father. She was responsible for both of their deaths."

I scowled into the air. "I do not need to be reminded, Reaper." Turning to face Glacine, I said, "Why are you here?"

She thrust her chin into the air, and even tied with rounds of rope, her dark hair plastered to her head, her black dress crumpled, she still managed to look noble. In fairness, she was descended from Light Court royalty. "I suppose he's done with me."

I shook my head as I really looked at her face for the first time. We had never spoken about *anything* openly like this, and it felt like a poison was being released from me as I got to say, "No. You're planning something. You're always one step ahead of everyone else."

"One step ahead of the Reaper?" Glacine scoffed. "You think *anyone* could be one step ahead of the him?"

"Do you know what?" I said. "If anyone could be, it would be you."

She looked at me incredulously. Daxian looked warily between us both and I knew he was trying to piece this all together. But the image of this woman whipping me for the first time had been burned into my retinas. I might have not remembered it, but I was sure *she* would.

"No, it's true," I nodded, deciding this was right. "You're conniving enough. Self-serving enough. He would never suspect that someone else could be just as cunning as him. What do you have planned?"

Her mouth twisted as she cast me a droll look. "Even if I had a plan, why would I tell you?"

"You'll tell me one thing," I said firmly, pointing at her. "Were you actually stealing my magic when you were flogging me all those times?"

She pushed her chin out stubbornly. "I was. I needed it."

I hated myself for the the way my voice caught as I said quietly, "You didn't feel bad doing that to a child?"

"You were hardly a child." She actually rolled her eyes. "You were pubescent. And no, I didn't feel anything. There is only power. And you have to take it before someone takes it from you."

So that's all she saw about this situation. "I pity you."

"Pity yourself," she spat. "That you could never save your parents. That your parents never saved you. That you cannot save yourself. You have lost, Saraya, on all fronts. He has you completely. You are done."

"The game is never done," I muttered. "Until storm comes." I turned away from her, unable to look at that cold, unforgiving face a second longer. "Lightning does not yield."

"And yet," came that calm, cold voice. "You yielded to me. Your entire family *yielded to me*."

That was a mace to my heart. And its tines cut deep. I froze, my vision going red as electricity rumbled through me. Sparks flashed out of my fingers and I squeezed my eyes shut. She deserved to die. She deserved a slow, painful death. But as that fevered darkness of pure anger enclosed around me, the Reaper's voice struck up a chord in my ears. *You destroyed an entire court.*

Is that what I was now? A destroyer of people?

Daxian, who had been clearly observing both of us very carefully, saw that I was done with the conversation. "So where is the Reaper's Tyaag?" he asked. "The one he rejected—what was her name?"

"He's had a few," Glacine muttered. "In an attempt to subdue him. But the last was Clementine Eyesmith, my missing aunt, who is dead, for all I know or care. Coward."

"But the Eyesmiths all fled this world decades ago," Daxian pointed out. "To run from the Reaper, right?"

"I was born in another world, yes. But once I found out I had fae blood, I was curious. I wanted to see what I could do with it. So I found a portal and came back here."

I was mulling in the dark corner of the astral room, wondering what to make of the information she was giving us. This was the first time I'd seen her in a compromising position and not be able to wheedle her way out of it. It was satisfying to see her caught out and there was one thing I had not ever forgotten.

I had made a vow to my father to kill her.

Turning around to look upon her again, I realised that each time I'd envisioned slitting her throat through Havrok's tattoo—which was now only a faint red mark—it had been with her standing, ready to fight against me.

I was not one to kick a woman when she was down, and the midwife in me knew she was likely still miscarrying from the ectopic-molar pregnancy. There were too many objects barring my way. Perhaps I was a murderer of an entire Fae Court, but I still had my honour.

If I were to kill her, it would be in single combat.

Glacine let out an unimpressed sound in the back of her throat and I realised I had been staring at her. And I think she knew exactly what I was thinking. "Even if you killed me," she sneered, "my mark will always be on you. I'll live on, in a way. Through you." She nodded at me as if indicating my back.

My blood boiled. Goddess, this woman knew no bounds.

"Be as angry as you like," Glacine smirked. "Doesn't change the fact that you've never been able to heal those scars." Her words stuck me like a blow to the gut as she lowered her voice to a soft, gloating sneer. "Oh yes, I noticed."

Daxian looked sharply at me. Shame crept through my core, acidic and biting. She was right. And further, the Temari Blade, my mother's blade, would not work for me. It, too, was ashamed, no doubt.

Daxian abruptly strode up to me and blocked my view of Glacine. "This is what he does," he murmured, and I was forced to look up at his one eye. "He finds your wounds and opens them up. You can't let him get to you through her, Saraya. You cannot."

"And what of *you?*" Glacine sneered. "The one-eyed boy king of Black Court? You needed a human woman to save your palace. I thought the fae could heal a small thing like a missing eye, no?"

Daxian's jaw clenched, but he did not turn around, instead looking down at me with that brilliant turquoise eye. I remembered how he'd been on the eve of the battle at Black Court. He'd been ready to die for his family, for his people. He'd been brave and strong. But I also could not forget the Daxian of the Academy. I *knew* he could be cruel. He'd been cruel to me as both Saraya and Sam Sourbottom.

I had actually wondered the same thing about his eye. The

fae seemed to be masters at all sorts of magics, and yet they'd not been able to save it or replace it.

"Mind your manners, Glacine," I shot back. "You are speaking to a king."

It was a barb meant to poke at her family for running away from their throne. She might have been a princess had the Eyesmiths stayed in the Court of Light.

But Glacine only scoffed behind Daxian's back, and the Fae King's lips twitched just a little.

"You're right, Lady Glacine," Daxian said, turning around to address her. "They didn't save my eye. But by all rights, I shouldn't be alive. Interestingly, none of the healers quite understood how I was still living with an axe lodged in my face." He shrugged nonchalantly. "So I figured, once they got it out and I was fine, an eye was a very small price to pay."

I raised my brows at that, squinting at Daxian's skull with new interest. He should be dead! Fae or not. Had the axe left any other permanent changes to his brain that I didn't know about? But before I could ask him if I could peek at his cerebrum out of professional interest, the room went dark.

An invisible hand gripped my astral body, and once again my feet left the floor and I was tossed into the dark.

## 22
# DRAKE

Fluffy and I sat high in the branches of a stickly tree staring at the city intently. Well *I* was. Fluffy for his part had caught a pigeon. He'd leapt up and snatched it right out of a tree by its neck. I petted him proudly as he devoured the thing, feathers and all. He was still a juvenile for his species, but he was strong and fierce.

It also made a good distraction from what I was avoiding thinking…and feeling.

My little purple ball of crackling light was…mine. She was mine, she had been mine all this time, and I'd shoved that knowledge away.

I clenched my fists angrily. Seeing her had brought out memories covered by the storm right to the fore front of my mind. Her magic had reached into the dark corners of my mind and yanked those things out. Her mere presence had been powerful enough to do that to me. Just being near her made my mind clear. I wanted to find her again, feel the way my name sounded on her lips.

Drake.

That was me.

And her name was Saraya. She had been my mate. We were soul-bound and without each other, we were not whole. I knew that now. Why I felt like killing so badly when I wasn't around her. I had this urge to destroy things, pull them down, force them into submission. I wanted to bind the world in my fists and crush it.

Fuck.

I needed her or I would die. And that death would be crunching, annihilating, consuming. I had to hold her in my arms again, feel her skin on mine and bury my nose in her sweet hair. That scent—cinnamon and fresh air and light made deadly.

Leaping from our tree, I landed on the hard winter ground. Already, the thought of being near her parted the storm clouds of my mind. It meant that I could see that the knife that had been plunged between us. That *she* had plunged between us. I needed to address this, too.

So I headed back to the golden palace on the hill, standing queen-like and proud over the city she now ruled.

Warmth spread through me as I strode out of the forest, Fluffy quickly catching up, growling in annoyance. I realised the warmth was pride. My mate was Queen. My manhood twitched again. It missed her too.

I'd just made it through the city gates when I heard it.

Pain—dark starbursts of colours.

Not physical pain, but the cloud and colours it created were the same, maybe worse. It was agony and disaster and naturally, I was drawn to it. Following the colours, I eagerly filtered through them, studying the way they moved and smelled. But there was no murder and violence like I'd expected.

Tiny creatures, sort of like Fluffy. But they were pale colours. Paler than they should be.

Something had happened to the little creatures.

Creatures that were not like me. They were innocent. They were good. Something had snatched them out. Stolen them. Was going to hurt them.

I growled, and Fluffy did the same from my shoulder.

In the space between worlds, colours shifted like balls being thrown up in the air. A game was being played, I realised excitedly. A game of death and violence.

And there was one player missing.

# 23
# SARAYA

When we all reappeared, we were roughly dropped onto the marble tile. I just managed to get my feet under me and land upright, but Adlain was not so lucky. The Fae Princes all landed with heavy thuds and Fern grabbed a white-faced Adlain and roughly pulled him up to standing.

The Reaper's laugh resounded all around us before he announced in a deep voice, "Look who has arrived!"

In a flash, Glacine and the Reaper reappeared, standing adjacent to us, both smirking with delight. I bristled because her being bound in that chair had clearly been a ruse.

But my anger abruptly disappeared, replaced by shooting heat.

Because Drake stood in front of me, an imposing beast who seemed to make the ballroom look smaller. The lights flickered slightly, and he surveyed the Reaper's astral ballroom like a beast on a hunt. His nostrils flared, and I knew he was scenting everyone in the room.

I swallowed the lump in my throat. Why was he here? Was I right about the Reaper sending him to kill me after all?

"This is your enemy, Drake," taunted the Reaper, gesturing to me. "The mate who rejected you. The cause of your pain."

Drake's all black eyes settled on me and did not move. I felt his gaze like a heavy weight on my shoulders. Yet again, I wanted to run to him. Our interaction in the woods had left me wanting, and I felt that desire rise up again. My fingers twitched, begging to touch him.

Then the Reaper said something that made my blood run cold. "*Kill her.*"

Drake cocked his head in that way of his, and my heart clenched. I had been right. The Reaper had taken advantage of Drake's bestial state and, just like Havrok, had been using him for his bidding. Except this time, no one should have been able to control him. There was no controlling rune, and Drake was a powerful Niyati, just like the Reaper—a person of destiny. So Drake must have been acting of his own accord when he'd killed the three fae kings.

Those twinkling red lights in his eyes promised violence, just as they promised a sort of inhumane bestial consciousness. I could see his mind was a storm—worse than when Havrok had unbound him in the Demon Court.

But I remembered one thing. Everyone had thought Drake would be uncontrolled in that form, and yet he'd listened to me. And again, by my mother's lake, he'd responded to me—to my magic and my touch. Perhaps I could communicate like that with him again.

Two swords appeared between us in the air flying outwards. I caught mine by the hilt on pure reflex. Thank the Goddess Arishnie had sent me to the Fae Academy for training. Although Jerali had been training me since childhood, the fae had added just that extra touch to my skillset.

Drake had caught the second blade and stilled, in that predatory way of his—as if he were assessing me, thinking in whatever way beasts assessed their prey.

But he did not move.

I glanced back at Daxian and the Princes all of whom were watching Drake with a mix of awe and terror. Daxian's pupil was completely dilated, enveloping his blue iris.

But the Reaper had stepped up to me. "It seems you are in need of an incentive. If you do not fight him," he said with meaning, "I will kill these two infants." He indicated two cradles that had suddenly appeared between him and Glacine. The babies were less than a year old, sitting and blinking around in confusion. I recognised them right away, making rage tear through me. "You are familiar with these twins, Saraya, is that correct?"

Destiny and Lucky. Bluebell's children. That stuck a knife where it hurt most. The Reaper knew everything—I had almost failed these two children before.

I had no choice.

By all the Goddesses who existed, I would enjoy sticking a dagger into the heart of the Reaper. I cast him a look, and he grinned savagely in return. But it also told me something else— he'd chosen to blackmail *me*. That meant the Reaper could not control Drake.

Drake, for his part, was still unmoving. Whether he was confused by our previous altercation or whether he recognised me as his mate, I could not tell. But I knew by the way he limply held his sword that he wasn't going to attack. He was just staring at me. I suppressed a shiver.

I would have to force his hand. Looking down at my ridiculous pink ballgown, I frowned. But it mattered not, even dressed in all the length of tule in the word, I could still best most people. So I assumed my fighting stance, feeling Drake watching my every minute movement. Raising my sword, I charged toward him.

Drake brought up his sword at the last minute.

I cast him a dark look, parried and swung, stepping right. Then in a move Fern had taught me back at the Academy, I forced Drake to engage his left, less dominant side.

Something twitched in Drake's face, and the red lights in his all-black eyes shut off. My heart leapt. It was recognition—Drake had been coming to the Mountain Academy to test the senior students. He knew all of their moves. Fighting with me was jogging his memory. If I could just persist, he might remember himself like he had begun to in the forest.

But Drake had no 'less dominant' side because he moved into the offensive, throwing his sword into his left hand and stepping toward me in a bright downward swing.

I blocked it. But the angle made pain shoot up my wrist. It wasn't until then that I realised how strong Drake really was.

Swinging around, I attacked in a flurry of short blows—the sword was so light that I was super fast. Drake met me evenly each time, never breaking a sweat, almost toying with me. We disengaged, stepping back to circle one another. Heat flushed through me as I watched those all-black eyes somehow glow with excitement. He was enjoying this.

That bastard.

So I lunged again, levelling up my strength, beating down upon him with heavy blows that took all of my body and more than a little of my magic. We were Niyati and Tyaag, how could we not use magic against each other? I pushed him harder and harder, until he had no choice but to step backwards and his face became serious. Satisfaction swept through me.

And then Drake turned on the offensive.

Power buzzed through the air, snapping and crackling, and I

realised that it was not his, it was mine. My power was defending me as he pushed me, and I had to step back as he delivered those lethal blows to my face and torso. I began panting with the strain, my muscles engaging completely. I'd never actually fought anyone with this level of strength or raw confidence behind their blows. And I knew he wasn't giving me his full force.

Not Jerali Jones, not Daxian nor Fern, nor any of the demons I'd come up against had this sort of wild strength. I was suddenly painfully aware that Drake had been quite easily removing hearts from people's chests during any sort of melee. He could do the same to me at any time. But I knew he wouldn't. His eyes were curious and considering, his lips parted in thought and perhaps...desire?

I felt my magic rising up in a coil, meeting his. It was engaging and caressing Drake in the most seductive way. A frown spread across his brows and his blows lessened in strength as we returned to a toying spar. Suppressing a satisfied grin, I let my magic have free rein to respond to him in a way that only happened during the times we were intimate. As we engaged in half-hearted blows, my magic enveloped him, stroked his neck, his lip,s and the large biceps I liked to hold onto as we made love. To my great pleasure, I felt his skin through my magic as if I'd stroked him with my own fingers.

As we circled each other, I let my desire for him move the magic lower, down his torso, caressing the hard planes of his abdomen and the V that led down into his manhood. I couldn't help the coy smile that curved my lips as Drake's swing faltered.

I used that moment to launch my next flurry of attacks, unleashing a little electricity into my blade as I did. He met me just in time, his lips curving in to a smile. White-hot sparks flew into the air and we separated. The Princes hissed from somewhere far behind me, but I could not care less about who was in the room at that moment.

Drake cocked his head.

"Surprised, Drake?" I asked, my voice low and seductive. "We always did joke about fighting one another."

"You are strong," he rasped, a deep frown creasing his forehead.

"She," said the Reaper meaningfully, "is a Tyaag who had rejected her mate. Naturally, she is extremely powerful. By natural law, even more powerful than the Niyati she has rejected."

My heart clenched as something sick wound its way through me. If that were true, then I *could* actually win this fight. I remembered Drake's mother—a Tyaag who'd rejected her mate and become a Goddess, dark and powerful. Would I look the same after hundreds of years? But that would mean Drake would never come back to me. I would be alone in the world without him, watching the tides of the world turn. Alone.

Pain tore through me so unexpectedly with this thought that I jerked. But Drake had noticed and his magic reached out for me. Alarmed, I watched as his sword reached for me too and I swung mine up on reflex.

His expression was curious as he forced me to move with him, running his sword down the length of mine, metal scraping against metal. I allowed my sparks to flow freely. His face lit up as he looked at my tiny flashes of lightning. He smiled, and it took my breath away.

We circled each other, his magic reaching out for me, this time, tickling my sides. I jumped a little at his magical touch. It was as if his fingers were really on me. I glared at him.

But he didn't care. He stroked the skin of my outer thigh, and I gave him a dark look. He was going to give as much as he got.

So I allowed my magic at him in full force, and it rushed to him, caressing down to his groin—but he got to me first, and his magic gently caressed the apex of my thighs. My magic stuttered as Drake fingered me gently. I panted, and not from physical strain.

*Goddess*, even his magical touch was alluring. Pleasure tingled through my core, and I allowed the desire to take me over. His magic worked its way around my thighs, caressing, coercing, spreading down the delicate skin of my inner lips.

I saw Drake lick his own lips. Oddly, he was sweating now. I suppressed a moan as his fingers moved into me, and I had to clutch my sword in a painful grip.

Daxian swore behind us, but I didn't care. My magic moved over Drake, and before I knew it, I had his manhood in my magical grasp, and I sucked in a breath as I felt him bulging against his pants, rock hard beneath my grip.

Drake exhaled heavily, his sword continuing to caress mine. Now it was like he'd formed a V with his fingers and was stroking on either side of my clitoris, and the slick wetness of me was aiding him. I swallowed and ran a magical finger over the tip of his manhood. I suddenly wondered what it would be like to have it in my mouth, sucking on its impossibly hard length. I felt a frown over my own face as I let my magic mimic what my lips would do, sucking gently on the tip of him.

Drake let out a heavy exhale, and I grinned at his response— and then he plunged his magical fingers deep into me, and I almost dropped my sword, gasping. I swear everything around me fell away as he finger fucked me, and I felt myself dripping onto his magical fingers. I couldn't concentrate at all now, but I *needed* him to remember who I was, who we were and why we were all here.

So between gasps, I gripped his manhood and, with my

magical mouth, put the whole thing inside and sucked his length.

Drake grunted and lunged at me, but he'd dropped his sword to the floor and instead of attacking me, pulled me towards him with strong arms, pressing my torso against his. His other hand fisted my hair, pulling my head back so he could look into my eyes.

All I saw were black eyes, frowning down at me.

"Saraya," he breathed slowly, as if testing my name out. My heart swelled with joy. He remembered my name! As our bodies were fixed together, I felt every inch of his hardness, his manhood pressed against my groin, our magics caressed and swam around us, toying with each other, entangling and dancing—

And then I saw we *were* surrounded by a field of darkness. I couldn't see anyone, not a single person. We were alone in an endless void.

Startled, I tried to turn and look, but Drake held my hair firm in his grip, as if he were trying to read everything about me through my face and eyes.

"Drake, where is everyone?" I breathed.

"I pushed them out," he rasped, glancing around then back at me like he didn't really care about our surroundings.

Drake had pushed the Reaper out—overpowered the Reaper's magic. I gaped at him. "How the hell did you do that?"

"It doesn't matter," he breathed. He leaned down to brush his lips against mine, and I moaned. I wanted him so badly, so awfully. "Drake," I whispered against his lips. "We need to think. I'm suspecting that whatever he does to us here, will happen to my real body. He hurt me before. I felt the pain—"

Our reality shook as if someone were literally punching it.

Drake growled, looking up at the shadowy reality he'd created and frowned at it.

"He hurt you?" he rasped, clutching me tighter.

But our shadowy haven was cracking open like an egg. The world shook again and something tore through it like it was made of parchment.

Light burst in, and the Reaper's palace walls appeared again. From the side of my eye, I could make out the returned forms of Glacine, Daxian, and the Princes, the Reaper standing with his eyes narrowed at us.

Drake's hold on me never faltered. Instead of reacting to the Reaper returning, he leaned down and shoved his lips against mine, hungrily pushing his tongue inside my mouth as if he wanted to devour me whole.

I was so caught unawares that I yanked away.

"Bastard!" I choked out, hitting him on the chest.

His eyes suddenly cleared, the black fading away, the hazel irises returned. "I am, though, aren't I?" he asked.

# 24
# DRAKE

The question sprung from my mouth reflexively—like my mind was grasping onto bits of information about itself. Trying to get a hold of my humanity.

"Drake...I..."

But I remembered now. I *was* a bastard. My father had never claimed me as his. I had been his commander, not his son, and it was a barb that pinched at my soul time and time again.

Bastard was the name for what I really was. I understood it now.

The room suddenly became clear. The walls stood out in stark contrast to the bodies within them. Now not colours, but real living people.

Daxian, my half-brother, I remembered, and Prince Adlain, a human from the Kaalon Kingdom. Next to them were...Naxon, Ashwood, and Fern. The three princes whose fathers I had killed.

Murdered in cold blood. That explained the glares I was getting.

But it was the woman standing before me whom I only had eyes for.

Her magic was lovingly caressing me, but her emerald eyes, which had been fierce and annoyed a second ago, were filled with something I was not used to seeing. It was an emotion that made my chest clench painfully.

"Drake, I'm sorry I didn't mean…"

Gods, her voice soothed the wild beast in me. It untangled the mess of vines and branches that was my mind and straightened them out. It was at once bizarre and alluring. I wanted to take her now, thrust myself inside of her and hear her scream my name with pleasure.

I was vaguely aware of someone blasting an attack on the secondary protective shield I had around me and my mate—

My heart leapt. My mate. She had once been my mate. She had rejected me, but why? Why had she done it?

A memory was burned into the back of my mind. It had been covered by that mess of vines, but her voice swept them aside and showed it to me.

I held her tighter as the vision of me falling into a chasm, her hand outstretched towards me.

*"I reject you as my mate."*

Then I'd changed. And the only thing remaining in my field of vision was her eyes. Not the colour of her actual eyes but the colour of her very being. Wild and powerful, like no one I'd ever known.

She'd wanted to protect me.

Another blast to my shield, but this time, it shattered.

I growled in irritation. This was important. Why was the dark force interrupting me? I was an idiot to shake hands with him, but he'd tricked me. I'd not been myself at the time. I had been wild. Truly wild.

Abruptly, I let my mate go and turned to look at my real opponent. My real enemy.

I had shaken hands with him. But a contract with a monster like me was moot. I could not be bound by anything.

Not even by the Green Reaper.

Impossibly fast, I lunged for him and was at his side before anyone even knew what was happening. I shoved my hand through his chest, breaking skin and bones and connective tissue, yanking out—

Nothing.

I frowned as the Reaper staggered backwards a few paces. I stared at my empty hand.

My mate moved forward to get a better look. The Reaper's chest cavity was empty. Only a shadowy darkness lay within. No heart, no organs at all. My stomach turned.

The Reaper moved back.

I didn't even feel the magic building in the air before the Reaper launched a gigantic magical assault at me, vile green magic charging through the air like a rampaging ox.

"No!" Saraya screamed. Just as I turned to stop her, she leapt in front of me.

## 25
## SARAYA

As soon as I felt the power collecting outside the Reaper and realised he was about to launch an attack and at whom, I created a lightning shield around my body and flung myself in front of Drake. The blow hit me with a brain-rattling force. Before I fell to the ground, the Reaper's snide voice filled my brain.

*"Three days, Saraya, to make your decision. Or you will be burying hundreds of your city's infants."*

My entire body burst into an electric hurricane of pain.

Something stabbed at my right hand. I was going to go mad, so I shut off the entirety of the pain receptors in my body and set about looking at the damage. My mother had drilled the progression of saving a life into me and my sister from childhood.

My airway was intact, air could get into my lungs.

But my lungs, I was wheezing now, I couldn't breathe—I couldn't get air into the lower lobes. I rapidly reconstructed the passageways in my lungs and the crushed portions of air sacs—

the alveoli— and quickly enough, my wheezing stopped as they inflated back to capacity.

But my heart was bleeding. Literally, the chambers of my heart had been crushed, my aorta was not receiving any blood to pump into my body. Blood was filling my chest cavity.

If I didn't fix this within seconds, I would be dead. I concentrated with an intensity I'd never used before and focused on the fastest reconstruction I'd ever done. I blocked off the bleeding parts of my heart, rapidly rebuilding the lacerated walls, funnelling blood back into my left ventricle so I could pump blood to my brain and not faint. Now my heart was healed, I became aware of deep voices talking around me.

"I can't heal her," someone rasped. "Help her, Daxian, please—"

"I'm here, Drake. Hold her still. Skelton! Come here. Move away, Naxon."

"Well fuck," someone else grumbled, Fern, I thought. "I'll fix her leg. Get out of my way, Nax."

"I've got him," growled Ashwood. Naxon gave a stifled cry.

I was internally bleeding from a number of places, blood pooling in the various compartments of my abdomen. I couldn't get to them fast enough. But just when I started to panic, a flood of green and gold magic flew into me like rivulets of magical ribbons. They sealed off the bleeding arteries, healed the laceration to my liver, the multiple portions of squashed bowel and reconstructed my crushed ribs and femurs. My heart beat regained a steady rhythm as my blood pressure normalised.

As I healed and my brain got a steady flow of oxygen, my thoughts became less muddled. Goddess, fae magic was a marvel to behold. They didn't even have to think about it. The magic just healed of its own accord. That had been a close one.

Something splashed on my face, just a droplet, but it was

enough to make me frown. I blinked my eyes open, and realised I was in someone's lap and a large hand was clutching mine.

The first thing I saw were hazel eyes. I would know that face anywhere.

"Saraya?" Drake breathed. His eyes glistened, and the veins in his neck bulged. They were nice veins too.

"Dear God," Daxian groaned. He was kneeling next to Drake, his hands on my bare torso. Someone had ripped the bodice of my dress open. Drake growled, and suddenly, I was covered with a blanket.

"You asked me what I looked like under my dress once, remember?" I said groggily.

Drake gave an animalistic snarl that had Daxian scooting away from him, holding his hands up. "Really, Saraya?" he said, exasperated. "I didn't save your life just to have Drake take mine."

"Sorry," I mumbled, trying to sit up, but my magic was tired, and my pain flooded back to me. I gasped and fell back into Drake's lap. His strong arms held me still. For the first time in months, I felt safe.

"Why did you do that, Saraya?" he rasped, stroking my cheek. "Why did you—"

"I didn't want you to die," I whispered, blinking up at him. "Because it's all my fault. If you don't want to be near me, I understand. Just call Jerali—"

"We are soul-bound, Saraya," his voice broke. "Do you not understand? I *need* you, heart and body and soul. I cannot be apart from you. I will always find you. Wherever you are—in heaven or on earth or in hell—I will always know where you are. I will always come for you and kill whatever stands in your way. So that you may do what you were born to do."

I frowned up at him. "And what is that?"

His eyes burned with a bestial gleam that took my breath away. "To do good. You are the sword in the night. The protector of human potential. The shield against all that is evil. Is that not your oath?"

I could not speak. I could not move. I was stuck in time. He remembered my warrior midwife oath. All I could do was stare at him as he continued on like a man who had been waiting all his life to say this to me.

"I will protect you so that you may hold your oath and protect others. *That* is the way this works. *That* is how much I love you. And if you do not want me, then I will live with that. I will die knowing that, in some way, my darkness has helped the world through you. Do as you wish, but I will *not* leave you."

He finished, breathing heavily, staring at me with those bright hazel eyes. How I'd missed the expression in them. And right now they were filled with a God like level of knowing and determination.

"As inspiring as this all is," said Daxian ruefully, "we *do* need to get out of here."

I finally looked at the others.

Daxian, Skelton, and Fern were wiping blood—my blood— off their hands. Adlain was cradling his head, his shoulders shaking, on my other side.

Skelton was wiping an eye, Ashwood looked a little pale, and Naxon—well, Naxon had been bound with magical ropes and was glaring at me.

"Help me up, Drake," I groaned. "I need to see if the children are okay." Drake stood, bringing me up with him and holding me close. "Adlain, I expect your army to come to my aid. The Reaper has given me a three day ultimatum."

The Crown Prince of Kaalon nodded lamely, getting to his feet. "What ultimatum?"

"He wants me to join him," I said darkly. "Or he will destroy Quartz and take over the human realm. He needs a Tyaag to do it."

Everyone in the room stilled as they took this in.

"What will you do?" Daxian asked softly.

I levelled him with a fierce look. "Lightning does not yield, Fae King. And neither do I."

The corners of his mouth twitched and he nodded solemnly. "Then we prepare for war." He looked at the other Princes. "All of us."

"There's much to do," I agreed. Looking up at Drake, he looked back at me, his eyes soft. "How do we go back to our bodies?"

He nodded, "I've got it." Scooping me possessively into his arms, he gave the Princes and Daxian a nod.

I felt a little stupid being carried, but I didn't think it would be a good idea to stand just now.

"Hold on, everyone," Drake rasped.

I got one last look at Daxian's one eye before everything went dark, and Drake tossed us back to the Physical Realm.

# 26
# DRAKE

N ow that Saraya was in my arms once again, her warmth and her scent brought back everything I had forgotten while being in the mind-haze that was the wild monster.

My consciousness was once again clear and whole.

Through the ether, I sought out my physical body, where I'd left it in the forest outside of Lobrathia, put myself back into it, and then carried Saraya back to her physical body. Fluffy would just have to come find me by himself.

When we emerged into her room at the palace, I laid her astral body back into her physical one. I recognised Sarone, sitting guard by the bed and the Ellythian warrior jumped out of her chair, immediately drawing her sword.

"It's me," I said, holding my hands up in surrender. "I'm of sane mind, Sarone."

Saraya's second-cousin looked from my clear eyes then to my right hand, Saraya's right hand, and raised her brows. Her shoulders sagged a fraction and she exhaled with relief. "I'll go and tell the others."

As she rushed out of the room, Saraya woke up with a grumble. I immediately sat down next to her. Every follicle in my body rose to attention at her physical body being so close to mine. It had always been like that for me, from the very first day that I'd laid eyes on her inside the entrance hall of this very palace. I was so attuned to every aspect of her body, it almost felt like my own. My mate looked up at me with her beautiful face and sleepily blinked.

"Are we home, Drake?" She whispered.

I smiled at her, my mate, my wife...my Tyaag. A grating unease crept through me, followed by anger. She'd *jumped* in front of me to save my life. I'd been about to make a counter-blast when I felt her leaping in front of me. There'd been no time to push her out the Reaper's way and the sensation of her being blasted into my arms would haunt me for the rest of my life.

She'd flung out a lightning shield, so it was lucky I'd flung up my own shield to save both my own skin and the princes from the electricity she'd let off as she was struck. While the Reaper's connection with the infants and us had been broken, I'd *felt* her bones break, *felt* her body bursting open. That's when I realised the Reaper had stolen away more than her astral body. He was more powerful than I'd thought, but then again, so was Saraya.

With a power I'd always marvelled at, she saved her own body just before Daxian and the princes helped her. How a dying person had the sheer focus and will power to repair their own severed coronary arteries was beyond me.

I would never tire of marvelling at my mate.

Grinning, I said, "Look at your hand, wife."

She held up her right hand, staring at the palm, before flipping it over and gasping loudly. "Oh, my Goddess! Oh, my Goddess!" She covered her mouth as she began sobbing and I had to show her my own hand.

E.P. BALI

Our mating marks had returned. But they were different now.

Hers, the old gnarled tree, now with flames wrapped around the branches and trunk. Mine, a crescent moon and lotus but now it was laced with lightning.

"How?" she sobbed grabbing my hand to inspect it.

Pulling her gently into my arms, I kissed her all over her face as she wept, hot tears running down those beautiful cheeks.

"You gave your life for mine," I said against her sweet-smelling hair. "It's the only thing that can reinstate a rejected bond."

She reached for my face, pulling me down to crush her lips against mine. I held her close to me, careful of the injuries she'd just been healed from. But my mate was hungry, her lips devouring mine. I smiled against her mouth and pulled back to growl against her ear. "I believe we were in the middle of something before the Reaper came."

She let out a wet laugh and buried her face in my neck.

My heart swelled to the size of the sun and I thought it might burst right out of my chest. I fully intended to give my wife a rabid lovemaking and perhaps, if she were ready for it, to let the monster in me take over for a bit. But she was still injured from jumping in front of me. I fully intended to punish her for *that* too.

"The others will be wanting to see you," I sighed, adjusting my manhood so it wouldn't be so obvious through my pants. "Let's go see them."

She sniffed, and hand in hand, we made our way out of her room into the palace.

There was a shout from down the corridor.

Lysander was standing there, white as a sheet, his mouth agape. Slade came up behind him, the look on his face stormy.

They thought I was still of the bestial mind, so I gave them a cheery wave.

Lysander let out a choked laugh. "Drakus Silverhand you right royal bastard!" Slade shouted angrily.

Both of my sergeants sprinted towards us.

I wisely stepped away from Saraya as Lysander and Slade both barrelled into me, knocking the three of us down to the cold marble.

Slade punched my shoulder, and Lysander gave me a kiss on the tip of my ear, swearing loudly and rolling off me. Thoroughly winded but not caring, I rolled over and laughed, pushing Slade off me.

"Gods, you're as ugly as you've ever been, Drake!" Slade grumbled, jumping to his feet. "I can't believe you did that to us."

It was fair. More than fair, really.

"I'm sorry." I got to my feet and gave them both an apologetic look.

"No, you're not," Lysander said, crossing his arms and squinting at me. "You're a piece of shit, walking around as if you've got the biggest cock in the continent."

"I probably do," I said reasonably.

Slade snarled and lunged for me, trying to get me in a headlock, but I twisted out of his reach with a cackle.

"You sound like a bloody monster, too!" Slade grumbled.

I'd have to tell them both about how I'd singed my vocal cords deep under the earth later. We had other things to worry about.

"What happened?" Lysander's voice suddenly became softer. He'd noticed Saraya, standing with a hand across her stomach.

"The Reaper," Saraya said softly, cracking her back. "He got me good, 'Sander."

I moved straight over to her, putting an arm around her waist. "She got a direct hit. Lucky Dax was there."

"Daxian?" choked Lysander. "Well fuck me, Jerali is going to be pissed."

The four of us continued down the corridor, my fae warriors giving me the tongue lashing I deserved, until Jerali Jones came striding around the corner. The Armsmaster took one look at us and levelled angry grey eyes upon me.

I held up my hands once again, lest the feared Armsmaster tried to kill me. "I'm sane of mind, Armsmaster. I'm no threat to my wife."

Jerali got no chance to reply as Blythe, screaming, came running at full pelt, followed by the Ellythian warriors.

"Saraya!" she screamed, her eyes wild.

"Watch out, Blythe, I'm sore," Saraya said quickly, reaching out a hand for her friend. The two women gently hugged. Oddly, through a remnant ability from my bestial state, I saw a spark of sky blue colour that connected her to Slade.

I turned to my sergeant, brows raised. The linking of colours was familiar to me from when I'd followed the group across the Fae Realm.

But it came together now.

Slade grinned savagely at me, and I slapped him on the back in congratulations. From Sarone's shoulder, someone gave a choked warble.

"Opal!" I said, grinning.

The little lumzen wailed as she leapt for me, I caught her and she proceeded to lick me all over the face. I grabbed her and stuck a kiss on her head. "It's alright. I'm back now." She warbled and leapt for Saraya's shoulder, worriedly sniffing all around her face and neck.

"We have no time to delay," Saraya said, breathing a little

heavily. I watched her with concern and I knew she was still in pain from the blow. "The Reaper will be back, and I need to see if the children are safe."

"You need to rest," I warned. "You just broke half your body."

Opal gasped loudly as the others stared at Saraya.

Jerali sent two of the warriors into the city to check on the infants the Reaper had astrally kidnapped. Only then did Saraya calm down a little.

"I'll fill everyone in, and then I'm going to go lie down. But —" she gave me a look, "—he said three days. I don't think he was joking about that."

"Three days," grumbled Jerali. "We're not nearly ready."

"We'll manage," I said firmly.

The Armsmaster looked at us fae one at a time before nodding, seemingly having an understanding with my sergeants. They'd spent a lot of time together in Kaalon, I remembered, while Saraya and I were in the Dark Fae Realm. That was a good thing. We needed to trust each other if we were going to win this war.

After our meeting, in which we told everyone what had happened in the Reaper's astral ballroom, Saraya led me back to her rooms. Two of the Ellythians, Hemali and Uma, came back to tell us the infants of the city had awoken. But Saraya cast me a look I read only too well. The first time had merely been a warning— a show of exactly how much power he had over us and he would just as easily do it again. We needed to prepare for the return assault. He knew our weaknesses now, knew them intimately.

It was an odd thing being back in the palace in such different circumstances. Had I imagined myself buried deep inside her during my time here as an invader? Yes, of course, she was the most beautiful thing I'd ever seen. I'd been infatuated with her even when I hadn't known she was my mate. But I'd never actually thought she'd been leading me back to her room by the hand, a coy smile playing on her lips.

She walked gingerly, so my wild ravaging of her body and soul would have to wait until a little later. But I could *not* wait to have my hands on her skin, devouring her soft curves, sucking on her innermost wet heat...

I was rock solid before she stepped into her room. Kicking the door shut, I strode towards my wife, took her sweet face in my hands, and crushed her lips with mine.

She moaned at my touch, stoking the raging fire in me. I pulled away and looked into her magical emerald eyes, hooded deliciously with desire.

"I missed you so much, Saraya," I whispered. "I'm going to fuck you senseless."

She smiled up at me and pulled her shirt off. Dark blue bruises were scattered all over her torso—what was left over after Daxian and Fern's healing.

None of them were especially proficient healers. As Princes, they always had royal healers on hand to do it for them. They never would have had to step in and actually heal someone else. I had been too concerned at the time to express my surprise when Daxian healed her so easily.

Perhaps the little bastards were repenting for their father's sins.

THE WARRIOR QUEEN

But I knew one thing for sure, the Reaper would pay for what he'd done. He wanted Saraya for himself.

Unbidden, a possessive growl escaped my throat and I realised I was staring at Saraya's naked torso as she stroked me under my shirt. Her fingers sent shivers over my skin. I impatiently yanked off my shirt and pulled her towards me, unable to handle any distance between us. My soul yearned to care for her every need, to protect her, to possess her. In the recesses of my being, a low voice rumbled, *mine.*

My mind cleared and I tugged her towards the thankfully large bed. I paused suddenly, staring at the purple coverings.

"I remember these," I breathed.

Saraya was tugging her pants off when she looked up at me in confusion. "From when you were here, you mean?"

"No," I reached down and touched the velvety soft covering. "Sometimes, in my tree house, as I was falling asleep, I would get a glimpse of you in your bed. I remembered being happy that you were safe and cosy, like me."

Saraya smiled at me as, very naked, she climbed atop her bed and proceeded to crawl to the middle. I growled at the sight of her luscious curves, my cock twitching, and immediately yanked off my pants and pursued her.

Gods, she took my breath away. I paused to look upon her, sprawled like a Goddess herself, her thick hair haloing a precious face that I could stare at for hours on end.

"Gods, you're a sight, Saraya Voltanius," I whispered.

She reached for me, and I melted towards her, surprised to find tears welling in her emerald eyes. "I'm so sorry, Drake," she whispered against my lips. "I'm sorry for—"

"Don't even say it," I breathed. "I don't ever want you to feel bad for it." She spread her legs for me, and I sunk between them, relishing in her heat. I was so ready to pound her into oblivion.

"If you hadn't done it, Saraya, I would be dead. There were fire wraiths down there. No fae could've survived that."

A tear trickled down her face. "I know, but oh—"

I'd positioned myself and sunk my fully hard cock into her supple, wet warmth. Her heat encompassed me, making me whole and my soul growled in appreciation and recognition. Pressing my lips against hers, I filled her completely. She groaned with that sweet feminine sound of hers, urging me on, a call to arms. I would do anything to hear her moan all night long, to pleasure her for hours until she was sweaty and spent. The time for that would come later. For now, I made love to her gently.

"I love you, Drake," she pleaded, her eyes telling me that she desperately needed me to know.

"I know, my love," I groaned, thrusting into her core. "I love you more than life itself."

She'd saved me multiple times now. My fierce, fierce mate. Now it was my turn.

I ravished her body, devouring her nipples, one at a time. Her feminine sounds of pleasure unlocked something within me and I groaned as she shivered and bucked under me. She ground her hips against mine and I practically vibrated with pleasure. Deeper still I pursued her, until suddenly sparks flew from her fingers, stinging my skin.

But the pain only served to excite me and I rumbled with pleasure, the air becoming charged with her magic. I remembered our magic twining around each other as we fought in the Reaper's ballroom. How she'd taken my manhood in her magical mouth and how I'd felt her inner folds with my fingers. Saraya arched her back and cried my name as she came, contracting around my cock. She rode the tide of her climax, shuddering under me.

Throughly pleased, the wound in my chest that had been our time apart sealed together and I fucked her sweet core until my vision narrowed down and all I could see was her and the way she was inextricably mine and mine alone. How our souls had been fused together before we'd been born. I wanted to give her everything. The world, the Reaper, whatever she wanted, it would be my sole responsibility and pleasure to give to her. Her supple body shook under me, her breasts bouncing as I rode the wave of my own pleasure, fuelled by the way she was looking at me.

As if I were her everything.

I climaxed, groaning into her neck and thrusting until she was full of my seed. I kissed her tenderly and she clutched me as if I was the only person in her world. The monster in me needed more of her yet, but he would have to wait. So instead, I pulled her safe into my arms, buried my nose in her hair, and just let the sound of her sweet breath fill my ears.

# 2 7
# SARAYA

I could have stayed in bed with Drake all day. I knew he was holding back to save my poor body from the beating it had just had, but the feeling of us being together was everything I had never known that I wanted. By ourselves, each of us was powerful, but together? I doubted there was anything that could stop us. His mere presence by my side sparked my magic alight, spurred it on, stoked the lightning burning within me. The after glow of our love-making stayed with me long after we left our bed.

That evening, Drake took the fae and Ellythian warriors on a scouting trip about the city when Jerali found me. I was still a bit tender and didn't think I'd make a good riding companion just then.

I was surprised to see that Jerali was not going on the scouting trip. For the first time that I'd known my war General, Jerali looked disturbed, a slight tension in those grey eyes. We huddled in a corner away from the maids who were trying to get a blood stain out of the entrance hall carpet. "While you were gone, we found something in the dungeons," Jerali said.

"What is it?"

"I don't know how to best…I think you should come see."

With nerves bubbling in me, I followed Jerali to the long stairs that led down into the dungeons.

"It is a demon?" I asked, my heart thumping. I hated surprises.

"No, I don't think so."

I didn't like this at all. "Fae then?"

"Definitely not…actually, I don't know. I haven't had the chance to ask our fae."

Jittery on my feet, the darkness of the dungeons encased us as we left the long stone staircase. The last time I'd been here, it was to escape out of my own palace, where Drake had kept me captive to await Wyxian and Daxian's return so that I could be married.

I cringed at the memory. How things had changed—Daxian even more so.

When we got into the depths of the dungeon, orange and yellow quartz lights illuminating our way, Jerali took me to the darkest corridor right at the back.

"The demons must have caught it," Jerali whispered. "We found a couple of demon rogues in here. They had some sort of punishment system for their own trouble-makers, but we had to put all of them down. Some of them, I swear, were rabid."

As we came to the end of the shadowy corridor, my skin began to crawl. My fingers itched, begging to summon lightning —my own magic knew that a predator was lurking. There was a smell of burning—not burning flesh like the Reaper's smell, more like the smell of a campfire.

Jerali gestured to a cell just up ahead, and before I could stop myself, I strode boldly forward.

*I am a Warrior Midwife. The dark is my companion.*

The creature stood tall at the back of the cell—as if he were a nightmare waiting for me. He was barely a shadow inside an old black cloak and the only thing I could see of him were the fiery orbs he had for eyes. This was a creature I had thought I would never see again.

I kept my voice light. "Well met, Kraasputin. You're far away from the Mountain Academy forest."

Jerali Jones cast me a surprised look. But the Kraasputin, by the upward lilt in his voice, was more than pleased to see me.

"Princessssssss," he said in a raspy, breathy ancient voice. "I'm pleassssssed to see you not tied to a tree."

"Queen Apparent," I corrected shortly. I felt like I needed an upper hand. This was a creature who always gained the upper hand on others. But here he was, *my* prisoner now. I wondered how the demons had caught him.

"Indeeeeeed. You have not had your coronation."

"Correct, but I am ruler of this land nonetheless."

"Oh, not your father's brother?

I frowned. "No, we do not know where he is. He abandoned us for the sea long ago."

"He is dead, Your Highness."

I froze as if he'd slapped me. "I beg your pardon?"

"You will find out soon enough."

I pursed my lips. If he was right, it meant I had literally no immediate family except Altara left. I put a lid on my emotions. "How is it that you've come to know so much?"

The Kraasputin cocked his head to the side. "I barter in the precious, Your Highness. We've spoken about thisssss before." Those fiery eyes dipped down to my abdomen, to, I suspected, my ovaries. It was a strange and disturbing preference, but that's what he'd tried to take from me when Daxian had tied me to a tree in the middle of the night. But the tables were turned now.

"Prisoners do not barter."

"Fae creaturessssss do."

He was far too old and far too smart. I didn't think I could outsmart him at his own game. That was Drake's thing. This was a hand that Drake could very well have won. Alas, he was not here.

"Last time, you told me that my stepmother was not human. Thank you. I think it prepared me for what happened afterwards."

The Kraasputin stilled. "Are you thanking me, Princesssssss?"

"I am. My mother raised me to be polite when I could."

He observed me, orange flames licking the air from their deep sockets. To my surprise he stepped forward and lowered his hood. I had to violently suppress the urge to step backwards. I kept my face smooth as I observed the Kraasputin's real form for the first time. He was bald and his skin was shiny and red—a thing from the darkest depths of hell. His face was smooth and that of a fae, with high cheekbones and finely curved ears. I made an effort to control my breathing, feeling Jerali Jones go still next to me. Through his lipless mouth he smiled at me. "Ah, we are two of the sssssame kind, Saraya."

I did flinched then. "What on earth do you mean?" I asked incredulously, looking at his monstrous face. That was twice a monster had said that to me on the same day.

"Time will tell." He sounded sad.

"Were you fae once?" I asked gently, looking at his pointed ears.

"Fae and Niyati."

My brows shot up as surprise spun through me. "I beg your pardon?" I whispered.

"They called me Fern. Fern the firsssst, I believe. That is why

213

I came to the Mountain Academy to find you, the first time you came close to the Fae Realm. Our kind are simply drawn to one another. Drawn to....love, hate...obsess. Oppose."

My heart dropped into my nether regions and I stared at him, shocked in the most un-queenly like way. "You're joking?"

"Never," he sighed as if something heavy was weighing him down. "But it matters not, now. Far too much time and space exist between then and now. There are new forces in the game and I...am no longer consequential. You have replaced me now. And Drakus Fireborn replaces his mother. But what will become of either of you, time will tell."

Oh dear Goddess. This was the Black Widow's first husband. This was the first Niyati, the first king of the fae and he wandered around the continent like a dark wraith, terrorizing and stealing body parts for his own pleasure. I mentally swore in every way I knew. Where Drake's mother became a dark goddess, the rejected Fern had become...this. The Reaper had become his own sort of monster. Were we all just monsters fighting a war against each other? Is that what I was destined to be as well?

But Fern—the Kraasputin—pulled back up his hood and stepped back into the shadows, his flaming eyes flickering slowly as if he were grieving. The weight of his presence lightened a little and I found I could breath a little easier.

Until he said, "A question burnsssss in your heart."

I *did* have a question. One that no one had the answer to. Perhaps I could make this work for us after all. "Indeed," I said slowly. "I want to know why the Temari Blade won't work for me. No one knows why."

Those flames flickered. "Hmmmm. A good question, Your Highness. And what will I get in return for anssssssswering it?"

He wanted something precious. Precious knowledge he

would no doubt use to sell later. He had done so with the information I'd given him last time. That's how Wyxian had found out a golem had gone to their palace in my stead. But he wanted precious knowledge. What could I part with? I wracked my brain.

"I will give you something," Jerali Jones said, suddenly stepping forward. "If it's precious information you are after."

The Kraasputin moved forward as well, interested now. I blinked at Jerali. What could my General possibly—

"A forbidden tale lies in your heart, Jerali Jonessssss," the Kraasputin hissed. "Ooh, this is fair recompense, fair indeed."

Jerali glanced at me warily before stepping forward to the Kraasputin. I stared at the fae creature, wondering if his being here had been some sinister plan of his all along.

"Well," said Jerali. "Deep in the Lotus Sea, between Ellythia and Sky Court lies a hidden place." My heart stopped cold. "A forbidden place, where you can enter but never leave. I was born and raised there."

The Krassputin hissed excitedly. "Sky Court knows about thisssss, do they not?"

"I believe they do," Jerali nodded. "They trade. The Ellythians also know of it. Yasani Lota rescued me on her ship when she saw my raft. To my knowledge, I am the only one who has ever escaped."

This knowledge resounded in my ears. I had always assumed Jerali had come from Waelan. My Armsmaster's accent was common. Nothing stuck out as obviously foreign, exactly.

"Will that suffice?" Jerali narrowed those steel eyes at the Kraasputin while I could not help the sinking feeling consuming me.

But eyes of flame licked and glowed happily. "Yessss. That will suffice, Jerali Jonessssss."

He turned those little fires to look at me. "The Temari Blade represents female rage," he breathed. "The most honest emotion in existence. It will not work for you because you are not honest. You have been lying."

"I have not!" I retorted, stepping up to the bars, "I'm one of the most honest people you'll meet!"

"Is that so? Though you have killed the demons on the outside, you still have one on the inside. One you have been ignoring. One demon you have been telling yourself to ignore. What darkness lurks deep in that well inside of you? What is that gap you cannot breach? That one wound you cannot heal? What has a hold on you, Saraya, Princess Midwife of Lobrathia?"

The green heat of shame rose up within me, choking me, bringing tears to my eyes. I swallowed it down even as the wounds on my back ached. Glacine's cold gaze flashed in my mind's eye.

"Ah, you know," the Kraasputin hissed.

Numbing the old scars on my back had become habit for me. I did it so often I didn't even notice I was doing it. But I felt them now in a stark and violent reality—that every time my step-mother had struck me, it had wounded a deep part of me that I feared would never be healed. Every time she'd struck me and I climbed out of that well of darkness, a tiny part of me remained inside.

Drake might have gotten rid of the clouds hovering over him, but one dark cloud had always hung over me—was still hanging over me. And it would not let me see the stars.

"I would cut them out if I could," I choked. Jerali stepped protectively towards me.

"This is not a wound that needs to be debrided, Midwife, and you know it."

"I do not know how to heal them," I breathed, shaking my head. "I climbed out of the darkness each time, I cannot go looking back within it."

"Then the sword will never honour you," he said simply, stepping further back into the shadows, his eyes burning brighter. "And your stepmother holds you forevermore."

*Even if you kill me, I will live on, in you.*

A black curl of horror wound its way through my chest. There was something in those wounds. She had been drawing magic during my whipping. What darkness lay in there?

I clenched my teeth. "I do not know how to do it."

The Kraasputin hissed. "Not many do."

I clenched my fists. Everything counted on this blade. My mother had bade me to retrieve it. I needed my full power to defeat the Reaper, I knew that much. I was ashamed at the note of desperation that entered my voice, "Tell me how. Please."

"Get rid of this wound, Midwife, and you will be unbound, as your mate became unbound. Tyaag power is a binding force. This knowledge lies only with a Tyaag."

I knew what was coming. The only other living Tyaag was—

"The Black Widow, Lily Silverfoot." The Kraasputin spat with disgust. He held out his shackles with a clank. He'd given the name of his old wife, the mate who rejected him.

I abruptly turned and strode out without another word. My stride never faltered until I reached the entrance hall. I needed air. I needed to see the sky. Something dark was lurking in me. Something that wanted to get out.

The Kraasputin knew it.

Glacine knew it.

And the Green Reaper knew it.

Something dark shot past me and darted out of the palace. Fern the First, the first king of the fae was free once again. But the way he seemed—was he really free at all? I wondered what trouble he would cause with the secret information Jerali Jones had given him.

"I don't understand," I muttered to Jerali when my General came to stand beside me. "What use is the Temari Blade if the Reaper can't be killed? Why would my mother ask me to retrieve it so desperately? There has to be more to it than just summoning the Warrior Midwives."

"It was protected by that entity in Sky Court," Jerali said. "It has to be powerful. What other powers does it have?"

"And!" I spun around and appraised my General. "How come you never told me about being raised in a..." I tried to remember how it had been worded, "...a world between Ellythia and Sky Court? Under the water! Were they fae?"

Jerali gave me a wry smile. "I had no reason to speak on it and your mother advised me against it."

"Why? I should like to think it's my business if there's a Kingdom so close to Lobrathia! And an awful one by the sounds of it, if none can leave."

Jerali sighed. "I do not expect to see those beings ever again. They do not leave their domain. They can't."

"I'm surprised the Kraasputin didn't know about it."

Jerali nodded. "We have bigger problems to worry about, Saraya. Or rather, you do."

Something sharp stabbed at my chest. I had to admit, the Temari Blade was the strongest physical weapon we had. Not being able to use it was a problem. If it could even incapacitate the Reaper so we could figure out how to kill him...

*I will always live on, in you.*

The shiver that came over me was violent and Jerali glanced at me with a frown. I had been turning the pain of my back off since I was thirteen. The thought of delving into it instead of away made my stomach churn.

The Kraasputin had just told me that my uncle was dead. I would wait until we knew for sure if news was coming, as he'd suggested. But to my knowledge, this fae monster had never been wrong. My last living adult relative was dead.

That meant I was officially first in line for the throne of Lobrathia. There was no denying it now. No one could dispute it.

If my mother were here, I would have gone to her for advice. But she'd given me the last advice she was able to, and that had been to get the Temari Blade.

I had no choice, the way I saw it.

I would have to see the only other Tyaag in existence, the Black Widow.

# 28
# DRAKE

Razor, the old bastard, found me in Quartz. He travelled, after picking up his saddlebags, from Daxian's palace—where he'd run after the Black Court battle—and followed my scent all the way here. He trotted right through the city gates, nipping at anyone who dared approach the monstrous black zekar stallion, and right up to the palace entrance. The commotion from the palace ostlers was big enough to draw me out and see what was going on.

*Found you,* he'd said after grumpily dropping the saddlebags at my feet. *Even though your scent has changed. I couldn't have you riding these sorry excuses for zekar.*

He tossed his head in the direction of the stables where Silentfoot, Saraya's mare, and the other palace horses were stabled. I'd apologised for leaving him, but I knew he was still angry at me.

So it was atop him, bareback, that I led our party out of the palace.

The Ellythians, Lysander, and Slade, along with Blythe, followed me on a patrol about the city. I wanted to see exactly what defences we had and what physical strategy the Reaper might use against us.

Lysander smirked knowingly at me because we'd done this before.

It had been the first time I'd met Saraya. Wyxian had instructed us to attend Daxian's engagement to her—the thought made me grip Razor's mane aggressively.

*Watch it*, he snarled at me.

*Sorry, old friend. Mate bond and all.*

Razor snorted.

All that time ago, Wyxian's—my father's—contingency plan, in the event of the humans refusing the marriage to Daxian, had been to invade the city and wed Saraya by force. So, naturally, I had scoped out the place with Lysander and Slade in preparation for it. Because I'd invaded the city myself, I think I had a good indication of how to protect it.

Physically, we had it down if Kaalon forces came—and I had written to Daxian and Ashwood to prod about their forces. From the way Daxian and the others had appeared in the Reaper's Realm, if they could come, I knew they would. The only problem was time. Normally the journey from the Dark Fae Realm to Quartz was more than a week long. They would need a lot of fae magic to hurry them here. We only had three days, after all.

But the Reaper would not only be attacking us physically. The astral capture of the infants had proven that. He would attack us astrally too. And how much astral protection could we have? We had no mages.

And no real plan to kill or capture the Reaper.

I could never forget how I'd reached into his chest, and nothing had been in there. He was beyond anything we'd ever come across.

I had been hoping the Temari Blade could be used as a

weapon against him. But from how Saraya had explained it to me, she could not use it as she'd hoped. And the only possible weapon that would work against the Reaper—the Darkmaul Dagger—was missing.

We reached the quarry an hour later and rested the horses and Razor. Saraya's lightning shield was still burning strong, plunging straight into the dusk sky. Nothing would be able to get through. Not unless the Reaper blasted the thing directly.

"Havrok's Court is destroyed," Blythe said, shielding her eyes as we looked up at the cackling light. "The demon warriors were all massacred—there were hardly any left by the time we got out. We killed even more at the portal. And then we arrived here, and we executed the whole lot of them."

"Some got away," Slade admitted. "Maybe fifty. But they are not the concern, Blythe."

"Then who?"

"There are other Demon Courts in the Subterranean Realm. Other demon kings the Reaper will hold sway upon."

Blythe paled as she stared at us all. "Like the ones we saw in Sky Court. I'd not seen those types of demons in Havrok's Court. They were...green and icky looking."

I glanced at the Ellythian warriors, who were not surprised by the information. They had been down there long enough to know how the Demon Kingdoms worked. Havrok's Kingdom was just one of many under the earth.

"Just like how Lobrathia is just one Kingdom in the Human Realm," explained Slade in the softest voice I'd ever heard him use on a person.

Lysander caught my eye and grinned knowingly. I smirked back. Blythe had brought out the softer side to Slade. A side that I knew had lain hidden deep beneath the rough exterior and I enjoyed seeing that.

"And how much quartz do we have left?" I asked.

"We're using it all up to fuel the lightning shield around the quarry," Sarone said. "I don't know how much is left. Jerali has written to the other Kingdoms for stock."

Jerali Jones was proving to be a worthy General. That was good. We had a good team. But would it be enough?

"The Reaper will bring the others, Drake," Slade said. "I know it."

"I'll write to the fae again," I said. "Including the Solar Courts. Things have changed due to the Reaper paying us all a visit in the Astral Realm. It might very well mean that we have friends now."

"You think Midnight and Eclipse Courts will come?" Lysander asked.

I remembered Naxon's curled-up face. "Eclipse is still loyal to the Reaper. But Daxian will come, and Ashwood might have some heart left."

"All we can do is ask," Blythe said reasonably.

Ellythians were a different breed of human. They were more similar to the fae than our Lobrathian humans. As for Blythe... well, she'd been around us long enough that I considered her and Jerali basically our kind. They'd suffered in the demon lands, same as the rest of us. It was this thought that made me comfortable enough to share my thoughts with the entirety of the group.

"We still have the problem of the Reaper stealing the infants," I said, glancing at Sarone meaningfully, her green eyes blazed at the memory of it. "We don't have the psychic strength to prevent another assault like that."

Sarone cast a glance at the other Ellythians. "See, I think we actually might."

"How do you mean?" I asked.

"The Temari Blade isn't just a physical weapon," tiny Elya said seriously. "See, we have all these stories about it in Ellythia."

"Yeah, why's it so legendary anyway?" Blythe asked, leaning against Slade. The warrior reflexively put his arm around her.

Sarone cleared her throat. "When the first humans arrived in Ellythia in their ships, they landed safely about the shore. But that night, the people were plagued by nightmares. Except these awful visions not only assaulted their minds but their bodies. When they were attacked in their dreams, their real bodies were also attacked. It wasn't until the children began bearing wounds that they got desperate.

"A humble priestess called Ellythia prayed to her Goddess Umali. And through the dark, a weapon appeared."

"The Sword of Temari!" Blythe said excitedly.

Sarone smiled fondly at her. "Yes, Blythe. Since they were already skilled swords-people, Ellythia already knew how to fight with the sword. But when she took hold of the Blade, she took on the form of a wild woman. Except she didn't strike any of the demons. Instead, she plunged the sword into the earth, and a wave of magic spread over their camp.

The attacks were stopped, and the invisible demons were pushed off the land onto the sea. They could not wage their assault that day or any day after."

I listened to Sarone with rapt attention. "Then this is it. The Blade is our defence."

"I believe it will be. I also believe that Saraya is the only one who can wield it. I might be of the blood, but it spoke to her. It chose her."

The rest of us nodded in agreement.

"From what you told us," Hemali said, her dark eyes

assessing me. "The Reaper wants to take our queen for his own. He wants to use her power as his Tyaag."

I was about to reply when Sarone interjected. "We cannot let him near her, Drake," she said earnestly. "Honestly, she *cannot* be allowed near him. If he uses her…we're all gone." Sarone looked at me, chewing on her lip as if something was on her mind, but she dare not say it.

Nodding, I gestured to them to mount our horses. "I won't let it happen," I growled to her. "Not while I'm alive."

WE WERE ROUNDING THE SOUTHERN END OF THE CITY, NEAR THE forest, when a yowl cut through the night. Something black hurtled towards me through the grass. Razor tried to stomp on it as it came up to us.

"Stop!" I called.

Fluffy leapt onto Razor's forequarters and scrambled up to me, warbling angry nonsense.

*Kill it! Kill it!* Razor cried.

"What is that!" Blythe exclaimed, wheeling her mare towards me.

Fluffy bit me angrily on my thumb but I ignored that and patted him affectionately on the head. I held him up for everyone to see. "Fluffy is a lumzen, like Opal."

Fluffy bared his teeth at the group.

"He's nothing like Opal!" Sarone scoffed. "He's rabid!"

"He's had a hard life," I said gently. "But he'll be a sweetie pie given the chance. I wanted Opal to have a friend."

The women surrounded me to peer at Fluffy.

"He's black, though," Blythe said, coming closer to squint at him. "He's got none of that lumzen rainbow." She reached into her pocket and pulled out a tiny sweet. Breaking a piece off, she offered it to Fluffy in her fingers.

Fluffy curiously leaned forward, sniffing suspiciously at it.

"Oh, come on," Blythe cooed, "Opal loves these. She's a friend of mine too." I suddenly realised why Slade loved this woman. I cast my friend a smirk, but his dark eyes were fixed hungrily on Blythe.

Fluffy, with the gentlest manner I'd seen of him, blinked up at Blythe and slowly put his teeth around the white and red sweet, prised it from her fingers and chewed on it thoughtfully.

"Mmmm!" he cooed in wonder.

Blythe let out a happy laugh. Slade blanched a little, and I knew where all his blood flow was probably headed.

Avoiding eye contact with Lysander lest I let out a snort, I said, "He can't do what Opal does. I actually don't think he can. I think someone did something to him, and it went away."

"Poor fellow," Lysander cooed.

Blythe clasped her hands under her chin and stared at Fluffy longingly.

I didn't know if Lysander was talking about Slade or Fluffy, but I nodded all the same. Opal needed protection just as Saraya did. Opal was not a fighting animal as fierce as she wanted to be. Her nature was sweet. I think that's why in my bestial state, I had wanted Fluffy. Not only because he reminded me of Opal, but because if war was coming, someone needed to look after her too.

# 29
## SARAYA

My warriors returned from their journey around the city as night fell, and I met them in the dining room.

"I'm starving!" Slade announced, striding into the room behind Blythe and immediately making for the table. They grinned at me, and I watched the Ellythians walk in, followed by Lysander and Drake bringing up the rear with a saddlebag.

I would never tire of seeing him walk through the door, a smile lighting his face as he saw me already sitting at the table. I couldn't help but match his expression as he strode over to me, dropped his bag to the floor and kissed me on the lips. Everyone averted their eyes, only interested in the roast dinner in front of them.

Food had to be rationed, but we had enough until aid from Kaalon arrived. Hunger was something that could decimate a Kingdom during wartime. Jerali had been careful to remind me of that.

Opal, on my shoulder, suddenly let out a warble of curiosity, patting me on the ear to get my attention. Drake released me and reached down as something dark scrambled up his leg.

"Saraya, Opal, meet Fluffy." He held a ball of black fur in his hand.

"That's a lumzen!" I said in wonder, reaching out to stroke its tiny head. Opal craned her neck to stare at the creature as it leaned into my hand, closing its wide, dark eyes. The lumzen was all black, with black irises that seemed to swirl, but his body was exactly the same as Opal's—like a kitten but rounder in the belly, with pointed ears and a long tail. He was a little older than her too—I could tell because he was bigger—but still a juvenile.

"You called him Fluffy?" I asked, amused as I remembered Drake's name for Opal in the Demon Court had been the same.

Drake rubbed the back of his neck. "I found him in a demon market, they were going to put him down, but I saved him. I didn't understand why I was doing it, I just knew I had to."

My heart squeezed as I smiled at him. "He reminded you of Opal, you were looking for something familiar." I had saved Opal in a similar way when we first met.

He nodded. "Except Fluffy is the opposite of Opal. He's grumpy most of the time." Fluffy lifted a paw and swatted at Drake.

Opal let out a warble of protest, and Fluffy immediately dropped his paw, staring at Opal open-mouthed as if he'd fallen in love right on the spot.

"Here, you two go play," I said, lifting them both and putting them on the floor. Opal scampered into a corner, and Fluffy followed. They proceeded to sit down opposite one another and stare into each other's faces. Opal lifted a paw and touched Fluffy on the nose. Fluffy closed his eyes, patiently keeping still for her inspection.

I angled my chair so I could keep an eye on them.

"He can't do any illusions that I know of," said Drake, the

corner of his mouth quirking up as we watched them. "I'm not sure if he has other abilities."

"We'll find out as he grows older, perhaps."

We began eating, Drake methodically shovelling bread and chicken into his mouth until his plate was empty. Then he took my hand. "Sarone told us an interesting story about the Temari Blade. I'll get her to tell you about it after dinner. But she thinks we can use it to defend the city from the Reaper's astral or psychic attacks."

My mouth dropped open. I quickly closed it and considered his words. If that was true, then perhaps we *could* work against him. There was only one problem. Nervously, I licked my lips. "I can't get it to work for me, Drake," I said in a low voice. "But while you were gone, Jerali led me to see the Kraasputin in the dungeons."

Drake almost dropped his fork. "*What?*" He turned to stare at Jerali on the other side of the room.

"It's alright," I said hastily. "Jerali gave him something he wanted, but in exchange, he told me two things. The first is that he is actually Fern the First."

Drake's hazel eyes searched mine. "You're….he said that?"

I nodded. "I couldn't believe it either."

Drake sat back in his chair and ran a large hand through his dark brown hair. "He's not one to lie. Fuck."

"And the other thing he said was, that I needed to…" what *did* I need to do? Look at my wounds, magically go *into* them like I could with the rest of my body? I shook myself. I couldn't let weakness ruin me. "He told me I have to speak to a Tyaag to help me with it. Then the sword will listen to me."

Drake nodded. "I think it's about time we spoke to my mother. But look what Razor brought back with him—" he leaned down and yanked the saddle bag open, pulling out a familiar, long black box.

"That's Dacre's box!" I said. "Right? The one you took from his tower when we went to—"

"To find the Darkmaul Dagger to capture the Reaper with, yes." He pointed to the letters engraved on it. *E.H.* "My mother wanted this. That's why she sent us there. It's hers, right? If she really is Lily Silverfoot like the Reaper said she is. She must've wanted it returned to her."

The Darkmaul Dagger was supposedly two daggers wielded by two people—specifically Lily Silverfoot and Fern the First—when they killed Oberry. And thanks to the Reaper, we now knew that Lily Silverfoot was actually Drake's mother. The first Queen of the Fae was a Tyaag who had turned into a dark Goddess when she rejected her mate.

"Alright, what's the quickest way to see her?"

BACK IN OUR ROOM, DRAKE, WITH HIS MOTHER'S BOX IN HAND, AND I, lay down on our bed while I led him into our astral bodies. We'd done this before together when we'd left Havrok's Court on his stupid mission to assassinate Osring and take over Kaalon. Instead, Umali had taken the chance to ordain me as High Priestess of the Order of Temari.

In our transparent, blue-grey bodies, we ascended into the ceiling, shooting right above the palace and into the night. With no moon in the sky it was terribly dark and once we left the quartz-bright city and flew south of Lobrathia, I had barely any light to see by. I took Drake's hand, and together with his perfect monstrous night vision, we flew into the night, and he took us straight to the Silent Mountains. In our astral forms, we flew high and fast, and in no time at all, we passed the Temari forest, past the mountains, separating the Fae and Human Realms, and headed right into Black Court.

From there, it was only a matter of minutes before we were flying into Drake's childhood home, the Black Grove.

Naturally, Drake's mother was waiting for us.

In a place that was all darkness, the Black Widow's tree stood in the centre of a clearing, a mirror of Drake's tattoos. Her tree stood sentinel—black bark, sinister curved branches that stabbed at the sky with silver tips.

The Black Widow herself, Lily Silverfoot, stood regally, as queen of her domain, willowy with her silver skin and hair.

"Greetings, Mother," Drake said, a little stiffly, I thought, compared to the last time we were here. Perhaps he felt a little blindsided by her. She'd hidden her previous identity from him, after all.

"Good evening, my son." Her voice stirred the air as the cold wind does. "And my daughter-in-law."

"Good evening, Mother-in-law," I replied smoothly. "It seems we have more similarities than loving your son."

She stilled, observing me in an unnerving way with her all-black eyes. "Speak your meaning, High Priestess."

"The Reaper told us of your heritage as Lily Silverfoot." I gestured to Drake, who held the box of the Darkmaul Dagger.

"You knew Dacre would show it to me," Drake said, darkly. "I'm guessing you wanted it returned."

His mother smiled. "Ah, my own son knows me well. Pass it over, my love."

"There's no dagger in it," I said. "Dacre told us it's been lost."

"And Chalamey told me that you actually needed two

daggers," Drake added. "Like when you used it on Oberry— one for you and one for Fern the First."

The Black Widow stroked the box as if it were a favourite pet. "Indeed. But what is more important about this box is who it belonged to after it left my hands."

I frowned at her and gestured to the initials carved on the top. "What does EH stand for?"

She smiled at me, her many white incisors now visible. "Eye-smith House."

My heart beat irregularly. That box belonged to Glacine's family.

The Black Widow held up a finger, opened the box and plunged her hand aggressively inside it. Silver light burst forth, sparking angrily. She pulled her hand as if she had retrieved something from within it and flung it to the side.

A spectre of an elderly woman appeared, wildly looking around. Though she looked old, possibly in her late seventies with silver hair and lined, pale skin, her form was lithe and sprightly, her movements quick like a much younger person. A purple scarf was tied around her neck that seemed to twitch of its own accord, and she wore long trousers and a shirt. Startled, I stared at her. But she recovered quickly, crossed her arms and stared at us with intelligent, blue eyes. "I'm assuming if old Lily Silverfoot is summoning me, that it's something important."

I raised my brows at the old woman's frankness— and her knowledge of who the Black Widow was.

"Tell the children your name," the Black Widow asked, not unthreateningly.

The woman merely blinked at the Goddess. "Well, I'm Professor Clementine Eyesmith." She spoke matter-of-factly and glanced at Drake and me, her eyes sliding down our clothing. "That means I'm an academic—studied a lot at school."

I nodded that I understood. She had a strange way of speaking, an odd lilt in her accent. Though I couldn't see her surroundings, it was clear as day her upbringing was from another world completely.

Drake's mother hissed, "And who are you to the Green Reaper, Clementine Eyesmith?"

Clementine stilled, and her eyes shifted around the Grove, assessing, calculating. I knew at once that this woman was not something to mess with. Though she looked human, there was a sharp sense of power to her. "I am the Green Reaper's Tyaag. And I'm happily safe at Chrysalis School in case he comes looking for me. You can shove *that* in his God-forsaken face. Ha!" She cackled. "Or lack of one! And then, well? Who are you?" She looked at Drake and me.

"Nice to meet you, Lady Eyesmith," I said, quickly, before the Black Widow could ruin it for us with sharp words. "We need all the information we can get. I am Saraya Voltanius, and I am Crown Princess of Lobrathia, which is in the Human Realm north of the Fae Realms."

Clementine nodded. "I am familiar with the continent on which you live. I made a point of it, since I was born here. Tell me what the old bastard is up too."

In any other situation, I might have been amused. Instead, I was slightly disturbed by her nonchalance as I explained our predicament. "The Reaper is coming after me and my Kingdom in two days. He wants me as his Tyaag, but I am already mate and Tyaag to Drakus Silverhand—" I reached out and grasped Drake's hand. "So we want to be able to defeat him when he comes for us."

Clementine nodded slowly, glancing at Drake's fae ears and then at mine, and seemed to put things together quickly. "Well,

Princess, if you'd like to know it straight from the horse's mouth, you should sit down."

Hesitantly, we obliged, sitting down on the ground because, in our astral forms, we'd probably go straight through the rocks surrounding the Grove. Clementine also sat cross-legged.

She spoke in the easy, confident manner of a teacher giving a lecture to students. "So, my parents were King and Queen of the Court of Summer, as it used to be called before the separation. I think you have a new name for it now. The old King of Spring Court was given his prophecy at his coronation—that his son would be a Niyati. A creature of destiny. A destructive turning point for the world.

"He was told the same story I'm assuming your parents were told," she gestured at Drake, "they would need to pledge someone as a Tyaag before her birth to keep the balance. But in those days, everyone knew what that meant—danger and possible death for that child—and none would pledge a firstborn daughter.

"So, the prince was born and, as expected, grew up and caused great strife within the realm. The kings and queens got together, and they begged each other to pledge a daughter. Fae can be selfish, and none would pledge their own daughter, not even to save the entire Fae Realm.

"Finally, the Queen of Summer—the only human in the room—relented. She would do it, she said. For the good of all, she would do it. The Fae Summer King agreed, but only if each court paid them a hefty fee in recompense. It would only be fair.

"And so I was born, and my parents heard the Prince of Spring—now called the Reaper after he slashed his fae ears and corrupted himself—was coming for me. I was a threat, the only person who could bind him, control him. And so they did what any parents in that situation would do. They fled. Except, they fled that realm, out of this world completely.

"The Green Reaper was powerful enough that he could find a portal and easily cross worlds, so their only hope was in a hidden place, a dimension that would elude him.

"And so we left the name of Summer behind and took my mother's maiden name: Eyesmith. Her family were human mages from Kaalon."

"But he found you, didn't he?" I asked, knowing that he'd rejected her somehow.

"Indeed," Clementine said with a twist of the mouth. "He had to be clever about it. But he found me in my dreams. He was handsome and powerful, and my parents never told me about what I had been destined to be. They never thought the Reaper would actually find me. But they had pledged me as a Tyaag and, in doing so, made *me* powerful too.

"I met him every night in the Astral Realm, and he seduced me. I fell in love with him and thought he loved me in return. I taught him things he should never have known. My mother's people were brutal eye mages and taught me their craft. I became so skilled at magic, so good at study, I was the youngest Professor at our magical university. But love is blind. And one day, he stole me away and, under the Holy Jacarandas, rejected me as his mate.

"I thought my heart was splitting in two. The pain was so great. I had thought he had brought me to this beautiful place to propose to me.

"But I had been raised to suffer pain, and I had grown to know powerful friends. I returned to my home, desolate but determined because now I could see his real intentions.

"I wish I could say I wanted to kill him for destroying so many lives in this world, but my reasons were entirely selfish. I wanted to kill him for what he had done to me. For what greater evil is there than to make someone love you and then stomp on their heart for your own gain?

"War broke out at Chrysalis, at my school. The Reaper came with others of his kind from the other worlds— beings so powerful that none could stand against them. I began a spell that would blast us all away from the war and put everyone, including the Reaper, to sleep. He came back here to heal, and I spent the next fifty years astrally searching the many worlds for a way to kill him, and other evil beings if I could. A way to kill a Niyati."

I couldn't believe what I was hearing, that there were others like him and that this woman had searched for so long to end him. "And did you find it? The way to kill him?"

She smiled at me sadly. "Oh, I did. A Tyaag must kill him, and they must die together. It is a soul bond. The Reaper is tied to my soul—mate or not—and through my hand and my death, he will die." She shook her head ruefully. "I will not lose my life for that creature. I will not."

I blew out a long breath. "That is fair." I nodded. "More than fair."

"But we may still trap him. And that is why the daggers would have worked."

"Where is it?" the Black Widow asked, her eyes sparkling. "Where are the daggers, both of them?"

Clementine shook her head. "The Reaper destroyed them."

The Black Widow hissed and threw her arms up in the air, power angrily cracking from them.

My heart sank. No wonder he was so confident. But Clementine glanced at the Black Widow. "However, another set can be made."

The Black Widow snorted, "Impossible."

Clementine made a noise to say that she disagreed. "She says that because the daggers are made from the bones of a Tyaag."

The Black Widow crossed her arms. "If I hadn't rejected Fern, the process would have killed me."

"You rejected him," I said in wonder as the Kraasputin's face flashed before my eyes, "and yet he still came with you to kill Oberry."

"He was a lovesick fool." The Black Widow was staring at me with hungry eyes.

My skin crawled as I glanced at Drake.

*My bones*, I thought. Tyaag means sacrifice. They would have used my bones to bind Drake if he got out of hand. How could I part with two of my bones? Maybe a couple of fingers? No, that wouldn't be enough to make a whole dagger. The bones would have to be bigger. I looked down at my forearm, frowning.

But Drake's sharp voice roused me from my thoughts, anger emanating from him like a blacksmith's furnace. "You are not giving your bones for *anything*, Saraya."

I sighed, "Drake, if it's needed—"

"Listen," Drake said quickly, looking at the two women before us. "The real reason we came here was to ask for advice about Saraya's wounds. Something is in them. The Kraasputin said she needed to talk to a Tyaag about it."

The Black Widow narrowed her eyes at me, but it was Clementine who spoke. "Turn around, Princess, if you will."

Slightly stunned by this strange and casually powerful woman, I obliged.

"If you don't mind…" Clementine said.

Drake came by my side in an instant, and I looked up at him, grateful. Lifting the back of my shirt, I bared my skin for the Black Widow and Clementine Eyesmith.

But my wounds were met with silence.

"There is something in there," Clementine said with fascination, as if she were squinting at a rather interesting specimen. "But what is it?"

"That's what I need to know," I said. "I need to heal my wounds, or the Temari Blade will not find me honourable and will not work for me."

"A wound that you cannot heal? Hm, my dear, you must charge right in there! Take the bull by the horns!"

But then the Black Widow's voice came low like dry, snapping branches. "What are you afraid of, Saraya?"

I lowered my shirt and whirled around, clenching my teeth. "My stepmother. She began whipping me at thirteen, right after my mother's death. I was grieving, I was hurt, and she hurt me more and was doing magic at the time."

Clementine tutted. "Evil knows no bounds. I hope you kill her. Saraya, my niece."

I stared at her, but the older lady only nodded. "I will not tolerate that behaviour from a family member of mine. But her death is owed to you, not me and my sister is long dead."

A sudden and intense burning struck my eyes.

*I will always live on, in you.*

"I can't release the hold she has on me," I whispered. "It is like...it is like she has her hand on me...all the time..."

"This is quite strange though," Clementine said wonderingly. She hesitated. "She has bound you. In the way a Tyaag might bind a Niyati's power. How odd indeed!" She grumbled under her breath then hissed, "You must sever the bonds. Right away. Just as you are bonded to your mate, you are bonded to your enemy. Cut it. Cut it apart."

Realisation struck me like a slap to the face. Glacine had been using magic each time she whipped me. She'd known to bind me down. She'd been doing it since I was a child. Then the

Reaper had come to tell me he could help me find my true power. They'd been planning this for over half a decade. Anger tore through me and I clenched my fists violently.

Through gritted teeth, I asked, "How do I do it?"

"Go into your wound," commanded the Black Widow. "Delve inside and cut the bonds Glacine Eyesmith has placed upon you."

Drake put his hand on my shoulder, and I realised I was shaking. "We will do it together, Saraya," he murmured.

"No," Clementine said in a low voice. "She must do it alone."

# 30
# SARAYA

At dawn the next morning, I woke up with a dark feeling consuming me. We only had one day left before the Reaper would return.

And if I did not agree to his terms—become his Tyaag, his partner, then I had no doubt that he would decimate my Kingdom in every way he could, including the children. His goal was to take over the entire continent, after all.

Seeing Clementine Eyesmith last night and hearing her story was enough to make anyone feel sick. But from that meeting, two things had been made clear.

We needed the protection of the Temari Blade, and we needed the Darkmaul Daggers. Drake and I quickly decided that we would figure out the protection of the city first.

I would have to do it alone, but that did not mean that I could not have people nearby. In the old days, the Warrior Midwives worked together and having my initiates around me somehow made what I had to do easier.

Opal warbled sleepily from my shoulder as Drake followed

me out into the palace. I had the Temari Blade strapped to my back for good measure and Drake's ring in my pocket.

When I had showed it to him this morning, his eyes widened.

"I cut it off, Braxus' finger," I said, holding it tightly.

Drake's large hand covered my own, folding my fingers around the ring. "That's my girl," he said proudly.

Not wanting to make a big deal of what we were about to do, I quietly went to each of my initiate's rooms—except Slade was in Blythe's room, so naturally, he wanted to come too. Lysander, forever hearing everything and anything, leapt out of his room, not wanting to miss out.

For some reason, I felt the need to go to my mother's lake. This was going to be difficult and I needed all the help I could get. My mother had told me that she would be watching over me and I had to believe that—I *had* to if I was going to get through this.

We reached the clearing to the right of the pond and cleared away the leaves for us to sit down. We sat in a circle. Me, Blythe, Jerali Jones, Sarone, Elya, Hemali, and Uma. Drake, Lysander, and Slade protectively hovered around us, far enough that I could not hear their fae feet moving, but I could still *feel* them watching. I lay the Temari Blade on my lap and reached out my hands on either side of me.

From my right, Jerali Jones grasped my right hand, and Sarone grasped my left. The girls and Jerali all held hands, linking us as a group.

"I know I have to do this by myself," I said, "But if you can just be there to…watch. So I know that I'm not—" I let out a low exhale, and the girls and Jerali nodded.

"We won't let you be alone," Blythe said with a firm nod. "Don't worry."

I smiled fondly at her before taking a deep breath and closing my eyes. With the most reluctance I'd ever felt, I dove into my own body. I started slow because I wanted to work my way towards my back. My intestines, my lungs, and my heart were all thankfully normal, as expected, so I headed into the back cavity of my abdomen.

I felt the darkness like a shadowy cloud. As I came through to the other side, it was almost like coming up against a hazy wall. A shadow stood long and broad in front of me. Letting my defences down, I allowed my new initiates in so they could see what I saw.

"Whoa!" exclaimed Blythe. Elya and Hemali let out their own gasps of surprise.

Jerali shushed them. "It's an actual wall, isn't it?"

"It's not solid, though," whispered Sarone. "It just feels like it is."

"Right," I nodded.

The dark shadow looming before me pulsed and roiled in such a sickly fashion that I felt like I was going to vomit.

"No going back now," said Jerali. "Come on, Saraya."

I swallowed against the sudden dryness of my throat and pressed myself into the shadows.

Nausea pummelled through me, followed by an acidic burn. I bit back a cry, pressing forward, forward, forward. Sarone's hand gripped me tightly from my left, and Jerali Jones did not flinch as I pressed my fingernails into the General's skin.

Darkness surrounded me, pushing in on me, wanting to devour me.

"Go!" Sarone cried. "Go, Saraya!"

Realising my physical reaction, I tried to calm myself down, lowered my head and barged through before I could stop myself. I was shaking now, vibrating with adrenaline and fear.

Voices whispered around me, and the darkness did not let up.

"Are we in?" Blythe whispered.

I squinted at my surroundings, trying to make out where I was. But the shadowy maw had no end, and a prickling feeling was creeping all over my skin.

The nausea was constant, the terror pressing on my brain.

*It's okay,* I said to myself. *It's okay. She cannot hurt you.*

Somehow, I knew Drake was hovering behind me. I didn't want to let him down, so I urged myself further.

I was vaguely aware of the slashing of my skin around me. Pieces of skin that wanted to mend but could not. They were being held back. A gaping well lay at the centre of me.

Down in that well of infinite darkness was the agony of seven years of flogging.

Something stirred.

A figure shifted, a wild power, the scent of raw, invading, erupting energy—eyes that crackled with black lightning blinked back at me.

Someone screamed, and I realised the sound was coming from my own throat.

I rushed back out for all I was worth. Scrambling to regain control, my body literally lunged backwards and I fell right into Drake's arms, the Temari Blade thumping onto the earth.

"What was it?" Blythe cried, her face pale, blue eyes so wide that the whites were visible all the way around. "No, really, Saraya, what the hell was it?"

"I—I don't know," I gasped, wildly looking around, my chest heavy, adrenaline coursing through me like a burning storm. "Dear Goddess, I don't know!" I took a breath. "I'm sorry," I whispered to Sarone, her green eyes steady and silent on me.

"I'm so sorry," I looked up at Drake. I had failed. I'd doomed us all.

But he only pulled me into his strong arms and whispered into my ear. "I love you, Saraya. Never forget it."

But I did not miss the way my Ellythian warriors exchanged glances.

Shaken, I made my slow way back to the palace, only to find Sarone and Elya by my side. The others had split up to go about their day— Drake and the fae warriors had gone off together somewhere while the other Ellythians joined Jerali Jones on a trip into the city.

Elya was a petite girl of eighteen, which meant she was the fastest of all the Elythians. She had also been apprenticing as a healer when she was taken by the demons and then put straight to work as a midwife in Havrok's birthing rooms. I had her working with Agatha in her spare time. The city always needed more midwives.

But she was currently exchanging a glance with Sarone and we all made the unspoken decision to get me back into my room. I needed a place of safety—a means to get away from the terrible danger I had just felt.

"Cousin," Sarone said seriously, as I led them inside my suite. "Tell me what you saw down there."

"You saw it too," I frowned at my hands as I sat down.

"You need to say it out loud," she urged. "So that I know you understood it."

"You know something," I said accusingly. "I saw the way you looked at Hemali. Elya looked like she was going to cry."

Elya grinned at me. "Your Majesty, with respect, you're mistaking my excitement for fear."

"Why on earth would you be excited?"

Sarone sat down next to me, her eyes alight. "Our family,

Saraya, we have always been known for our great power. But it's as if yours lies within you, trapped. This is something different from being a Tyaag."

"We might not have been to Ellythia for years," Elya said softly, "but we all know the stories like the backs of our hands. These things we can't forget."

"Which stories?" I asked lamely.

"Legends about our own family," Sarone said. "Like the one about the Temari Blade and the first Queen, Ellythia."

Shame crept through me. I knew about the first queen, but I'd never guessed that the blade in the story was the Temari Blade. "My mother only told me a few Ellythian stories," I said softly. "But I've forgotten them. Her focus was always on my training, midwifery studies, and on getting me to make my defences impenetrable."

"It's alright," Sarone said kindly. "I'm here to tell you the important parts. But you're avoiding this. Tell me exactly what you saw."

I took a deep breath. "It was a woman. A woman with navy skin laced with lightning, eyes like glowing orbs, wild hair, crouched in a corner, staring at me fiercely. She was terrifying."

"Umali chosen," Sarone said. She and Elya exchanged a glance.

Alarmed, I looked between them, "What on earth is it? What does it mean?"

"How many years did you say Glacine whipped you for?" Sarone tapped her chin.

"Well, almost seven if you count the whipping she gave me in the Demon Court. Is this thing evil?"

"Evil?" Elya choked. "Your Majesty, the seat of your power lies there."

Sarone shook her head ruefully. "Glacine knew exactly what

she was doing—guided no doubt by the Reaper who'd been studying you. Tell me, what was the one thing your mother drilled into you from childhood? Which skill?"

"My defensive shields. It was a game, but she played it with me until I was impenetrable."

She nodded. "And then Glacine began whipping you, and you took all that pain and shoved it right down. Shoved it deeper and deeper so that seven years later, your true power was buried so deeply that even you couldn't reach it. It was clever. The Reaper knew exactly what to do. Glacine helped it along."

"I know Glacine was using magic during my whipping. Collecting my pain for her own use." I cringed at the memory of her red quartz jewellery lighting up. "But my true power is already here, for all to see."

Sarone shook her head. "Our mothers' line is unique. The Ellythian Queens were known for their power. But what was it? When they needed real power against an enemy, something came out of them. It's like…they evolved into a *creature* of power, like a Goddess but in a human. Your mother taught you to control it so that it would not come out before it was time. Before you really needed it."

"It's the Tyaag aspect," Elya said excitedly. "She knew that your Ellythian blood made you powerful, but as a Tyaag as well? She knew your path would lead to a strong force. She knew you needed control until it was time to reveal it. She just never anticipated Glacine knowing about it and trying to push it down to where you couldn't reach it anymore."

It was all confirming what Clementine had told me last night, as well as the Reaper's offer to 'help me' unleash my power. "So Glacine…really the Reaper, knew about my Ellythian powers and tried to take it away from me."

"Couldn't take it away," Sarone muttered. "No one can take

that away from you—but they knew a way to make it so you'd never find it."

"Bastards," Elya said, clenching her fists. "That's why they had to kill your mother when you were young. So she would never reveal it to you."

"So all this basically means," I said, turning this information over in my head, "that I have to go back in there and free her."

But the face of that creature, that sheer raw fierceness, the terror she brought out in me reminded me of the pure destructive power I knew I was capable of. The power that had destroyed all of Obsidian Court. A power that I now needed to unleash in full force. I had never known terror like what I'd just experienced and the feeling of it was permanently marked on my being.

## 31
## DRAKE

My warriors and I walked into the dining room where Saraya, Jerali, and the Ellythians were looking over a map of the city. Both lumzen were sitting on Saraya—one on either shoulder. I'd taken Slade and Lysander to inspect the area east of the city—where we would likely meet our enemies once they arrived. It was an open field, well suited to a thousand strong demon horde arriving through the quarry portal, which was really the only way they could come through to the world above.

But we'd no sooner sat down than we jumped back out of our seats, the humans staring at us in alarm.

In the far distance, less than a quarter of an hour's ride from the city, came the sound of a fae warhorn.

I glanced sharply at Lysander and Slade. "Daxian's here," I announced.

Saraya gaped at me, "How do you know?"

I tapped my fae ears as Lysander and Slade rushed back out the door and nodded to Jerali Jones. "Let's go to meet them."

Saraya made to follow me to the entrance hall, but Sarone

reached for her. "We need to keep trying, Sara," she urged. "There's not much time left."

My mate sighed in resignation, watching Hemali, Uma, and Blythe eagerly leave with Jerali Jones out of the front door. I caught her eye and took her hand. "Sarone is right. I'll meet the fae and see how many they've brought with them. The Kaalon forces will hopefully arrive too. You should rest, then try again. We've got this under control."

She nodded a little glumly, and handed me an excited, chattering Opal, while Fluffy leapt onto my shoulder from hers. The three of us watched her leave with Sarone and Elya. My mate was tired. I knew that by the slope of her shoulders, the slight pallor to her skin. She was shaken by what she'd seen in her wounds, and I should be with her, comforting her and urging her on. She was strong, but even the strongest warriors needed rest and she'd barely had one between taking back Lobrathia with only seven warriors at her side and being kidnapped by the Reaper. In amongst all that, she was finally coming to terms with the wounds on her back. Wounds like that don't just heal in one day.

Irritated I couldn't be by her side, I strode through the entrance hall and out to the stables after the rest. Sarone was a capable woman and a good friend to Saraya. She was older and had grown up in Ellythia, meaning she could teach Saraya things no one else could. The Ellythians were secretive people, only venturing out of their islands to trade rice, cotton, and silk. But that was it. They hardly ever communicated with the main continent, as far as I knew. That meant there were things about Saraya's family that even she did not know. Everything about Ellythia she'd known through her mother, but how much had her mother told her?

That story about the Temari Blade had been news to Saraya.

These myths and legends were important, the fae knew that, but the humans of Lobrathia were not accustomed to myth becoming reality.

This was why I was sure it was Daxian who had come. When we'd been taken by the Reaper, my half-brother had given me a look. And I did not think he would leave Saraya and me on our own. As for the other Fae Courts? I could only hope at least one of them would realise the errors of their fathers' ways. Even if it was me that had killed them.

So it was with great haste that we all saddled our horses. It took a moment for Razor to come to me because he refused to be stabled with the others. I had to whistle for him in a special tune and wait for him to canter to me from where he was grazing east of the castle on Farmer Thompson's lands. Honestly, I think he could still smell the mass grave Lysander had made for burning the demons and liked to loiter there. He was as bloodthirsty a zekar as they came. Perhaps that was why we loved one another so much.

We rode through the city, and eventually, even the humans could hear the baritone of the Black Court warhorns. The people of the city were frightened, but seeing Jerali Jones and the Ellythians calmed them immediately. I don't know what they thought when they saw me—as I'd been the second last person to invade their city—but from their pursed lips and stares, I think they had a begrudging acceptance of me. Honestly, that was fair. But they would come to love me eventually.

The physical city itself had borne the heavy abuse by the demons. As in all demon cities, lesser demons cared little for infrastructure and trashed the place as they pleased. But when I had come upon Quartz in my bestial form for the first time, just two days ago, I could see a change more than that.

Rather, it wasn't that the city had changed, it was that I could now see something that was not visible to anyone else. Saraya's magic was everywhere. It was not obvious, to my monstrous eyes, not out in the open so much— but her magic existed in the dark of things. In the crevices between buildings, in the cracks lining the walls. And here and there, as I looked upon women and children in the street, her mark shone faintly on them too. I was reminded once again, that Saraya had dedicated her life to these people since she was a child. Her magic was laced within the city like she was literally a part of it. I had never come across something like that before. She'd been using her magic on the childbearing women of this city almost her whole life. The beast in me couldn't fathom that level of selflessness, but my fae heart shone with awe and pride for my mate.

By the time our group arrived at the city gates, the city guards were a flurry of anxiety. Quartz had barely any military left, as the demons had decimated the entire force, so we'd had to put a para-military guard made of civilians to man the gates. Luckily the civilians, even the women, were *more* than happy for a compulsory conscription, as organised by Jerali Jones. After being suppressed by the ruthless demons, they wanted to fight. They had been powerless and now wanted no more of it. It wasn't ideal, and to be honest, I was a little more than annoyed at King Osring that he had not sent their forces to us by now.

The captain of the gate, a portly older man, flagged us down.

"General Jones, look at 'em!" he cried, pointing out the gate. "The bastards are setting up camp!"

"Looks like they're here to help, Wolsely," Jerali said, slapping the broad man on the back. He was quite a bit older than the previous captain, in his early sixties, but importantly, the younger men listened to him. "It's Drake's lot." Jerali jerked a thumb back at me. I nodded at the human captain. He nodded back.

Sure enough, when we trotted through the city gates, it was a sea of Black Court standards, flags with a Black Dragon on a gold field. Black-clad fae soldiers were dismounting their horses and beginning a familiar routine of setting down camp.

They would put up the king's tent first.

A rotund fae with a long length of black hair tied up in a bun at the crown of his head was trotting towards us on a chestnut mare.

I recognised Briar Nightclaw immediately. Saraya would be happy to see her friend from her time at the Mountain Academy alive and well after the Black Court battle. I was honestly surprised he was still up and kicking as he had about the same ability to fight as a fae five-year-old. He was thoroughly on my bad side however, having seen Saraya naked one time by accident. When he saw me, his eyes widened just a fraction before he controlled his features and came to a stop before us, bowing in his saddle.

"I've come to deliver a message!' he said, breathing heavily. "Although I had intended to come up to the palace." He looked up at the city with interest—this was his first time out of the Fae Realm, and Briar was the academic sort. No doubt he just wanted to jump into the city and note down the differences.

"Saraya is a little caught up," I said. "Thank you for coming to our aid."

Briar bowed again. "The king will see you now if you'll be so kind as to follow me."

We did so, and as we rode through the beginnings of the army camp, I was surprised and very pleased to see Midnight Court colours—a gold phoenix on a black field as well as an entire horde of bloodthirsty Midnight bred zekar. It looked like Prince Ashwood had decided to help after all.

The king's tent, an almighty black affair that spanned thirty feet, made my heart ring just a little. It was my father's old tent. Now I supposed everything was Daxian's, though it was hard not to see my father in all of his possessions.

We dismounted, and I beckoned Jerali Jones to join me. Blythe, Hemali, and Uma stared around in wonder at the fae camp and my sergeants took our reins.

When we walked in after Briar, I was surprised to see that Daxian was talking to Skelton, the brown-skinned fae from the decimated Twilight Court. Jerali and I bowed.

"Thanks for coming, Dax. Prince Skel."

The both nodded and Daxian gave me a humourless smile. "I knew you were coming," he said.

I raised my brows. "Really, how?"

He glanced at Jerali Jones before tapping his eyepatch. "Something happened to me when those demons lodged that axe into my head. It came on slowly, and I didn't bother telling anyone, but I can see *through* things now."

I frowned, but Jerali answered. "Is that how you healed Saraya so easily?"

He looked closely at our General, then nodded. "Indeed. And how could I not come here after what happened with the Reaper? Both Ashwood and Fern insisted, and their father's old councillors coronated them just yesterday. After what Saraya did at Black Court...well, I owe her. We all do."

"And Naxon?" I asked.

Skelton shook his head, and I noticed a band of black ink—a mourning tattoo on his forearm. "Naxon is dead to me, as far as I'm concerned," he said with fire in his eyes. "I'm glad you killed them, Commander Drakus, those old kings. They deserved to die for what they did to my family."

I nodded sincerely. "The others might not see it that way."

"You'd be surprised," Daxian said. "Fern is here, with the

253

small company of warriors he has left from Obsidian Court. He wants this to be put to an end just as much as you."

"The Reaper will be here tomorrow," Jerali said.

"That's why we came here with all our magic on our heels," Daxian said. "And we have something important to tell you about Saraya. You'd better sit down."

Frowning, Jerali Jones and I sat down on the two chairs Briar pulled up for us. Daxian leaned on his desk.

"I couldn't tell you up in the Astral Realm because the Reaper would have heard everything, and I don't actually think he knows this. But Briar is the one who found out about it."

Briar, who had been standing behind me this entire time, nervously stepped forward, clasping his hands together. "Well, it was Dean Chalamey that sent us a messenger from Sky Court. He told me to check our Ledger of Prophecies. I know they're forbidden, but he said he was curious about the prophecy about you and Saraya." He avoided my gaze then, I could have smiled at the poor fae.

"Go on, Briar," I said gently, trying to show him I meant no harm.

He gulped, then nodded. "I went through the Ledger of Prophecies— they document the prophecies given to the kings from the Mother Jacaranda tree after their coronation," he said for Jerali's benefit. "So I actually saw that the prophecy given to King Wyxian was written… a little oddly."

That got my attention. I leaned forward in my chair. Curiously, Jerali Jones sat next to me as still as any predator scenting prey.

"Once Briar told me," said Daxian. "I knew we had to confirm this straight away. I hadn't been planning on going just yet, but I decided it was important. So I went to the Jacaranda Tree on the pretext of hearing my own coronation prophecy. I asked her for clarification on the prophecy that she gave my father."

Jerali Jones was uncharacteristically clutching their chair as Daxian and Briar exchanged a look before the new King said, "And do you know what she told me?"

"What?"

Daxian grinned and shook his head. "I mean, you're so powerful on your own, right? But we were so stupid. We were so fucking stupid, Drake." Daxian tilted his head back and let out a laugh. "You're not the Niyati, Drake. Saraya is. You're the Tyaag. *You* are meant to balance *her* power. No one ever thought for a moment that a woman could be a Niyati."

Every cell in my body sat to attention as I looked from my General to Daxian. Even my magic rose up like a weapon on reflex. "What the fuck do you mean, Dax?" I said. "What exactly was the prophecy?"

"She told me exactly what she said, and you can see why Father got confused.

*Your first-born son will be a creature of great power.*

*A Niyati must be bound to Tyaag, lest the continent be laid to waste.*

"You were the Tyaag, and as the binding power to *her*, you wanted to seek her out at all costs. Nature wanted to be balanced, and *you were* the balancing force. That's why you were always drawn to seek her. Niyatis are not drawn to their mates. They are drawn to their power and their destiny. *You* roamed around, just looking for her."

But they said that Tyaag meant sacrifice. Like sacrificing myself for her, wanting to protect her at my own expense. "Fuck."

"Fuck is right."

"I knew something was up," Jerali Jones stood up and began

pacing the tent. "Two things, Drakus Silverhand." Lobrathia's General held up one finger. "First, you didn't see her at Black Court," Jerali nodded at Daxian. "We all saw her power was phenomenal. It felt more like *she* was the destructive force. It makes sense now."

Daxian nodded. "None of us have ever seen anything like it."

"Second," Jerali said. "It was something the Kraasputin said that made me suspicious. He said to Saraya "you and I are the same." And Fern the First was a Niyati. He knew!"

I stared at them. A male Tyaag. Who would have thought? I didn't even think that my own mother knew. Her intention had been to birth a Niyati to destroy the Reaper. Little did she know that when Wyxian chose Saraya to wed his first-born, he was actually pledging a Tyaag. It was possibly the greatest joke ever played on my father.

But did the Reaper know?

He'd been working on binding Saraya's power down this whole time. They'd done it in secret, unlike with my bindings. But he wanted Saraya as his Tyaag. He didn't know either. This was possibly the first time the Krassputin has ever *not* sold information. I wonder why he'd kept it to himself.

"This changes everything," I said, glancing at Jerali Jones.

"Why? What difference does it make?" Daxian said sharply.

"Because," I said, looking at the fae meaningfully. "The Reaper can only be bound by the bones of a Tyaag."

WE HAD ONE DAY LEFT TO PREPARE FOR THE REAPER, AND I WOULD be damned if I let him do any harm to Saraya or this city.

Lysander and Slade flanked me as we headed to the northern aspect of the forest behind the castle.

For what I had to do, I could not be disturbed.

We needed daggers made of bones to hold the Reaper, and Clementine Eyesmith had said that only a dagger made of a Tyaag would do.

And here I was.

When we found a place that was far away enough that no one would come across us, I took out my mother's keepsake box from my bag.

"How'd she do it?" I muttered to myself, opening the box up. Inside was soft black velvet, a perfect case for storing a rare dagger that could be split into two parts. Lysander and Slade watched warily on, but they knew me too well to bother giving me caution with a magical artefact.

I summoned my magic, and blue power glowed around my hand. Plunging my hand into the box just as my mother had done, I called for the face I'd seen last night.

"Clementine Eyesmith," I whispered. "Where are you? Come forth."

Something flung itself into my hand and quickly, I drew it out and pushed it outwards.

"Apologies for the rude summons, my Lady Clementine," I said sincerely.

The elderly half-fae, half-human woman stood there with her arms crossed and a scowl, her sharp blue eyes glaring. She shook a finger at me. "You're lucky you're as good-looking as you are, Drakus. Otherwise, I might've been upset. I was teaching a class."

Lysander and Slade watched on with interest, and Clementine took them in with passing interest, her eyes shifting to their pointed ears and back to me.

"Well, it's a good thing you are a teacher," I said, "because I have a question."

Clementine nodded once. "Out with it, then."

Lysander was sniggering behind me, but I got a terrible feeling that I didn't want to get on the bad side of Clementine Eyesmith. She was a Tyaag like me, after all, and a rejected one at that. Her power would be phenomenal, in theory, even if she *was* elderly.

"You said last night that the Darkmaul Dagger could only be made from the bones of a Tyaag. The last Darkmaul Dagger, the one the Reaper destroyed, whose bones was it made out of?"

"Lily Silverfoot herself."

I nodded. "Of course, my mother hid that from me too. Oh, the irony. Well. It's come to light that I am the Tyaag of our relationship, not the Niyati as we first thought. So how do I do it?"

Clementine's face lit up like a quartz lamp at dusk. "Well, golly, how brilliant! What I would give for a turn of the tables myself! Lucky girl indeed."

"I don't know about that," I said warily. "But this means we do have Tyaag bones after all."

Clementine gave me a wry smile. "As children, beings like us are easier to bind down. But as an adult of full blown power, the Reaper needs an extreme level of force to control. You really must love her—if you'll give up bones for her. It would turn you into something else entirely." She squinted at me in an assessing way. "What exactly *would* you give up for her?"

I said it without hesitation. "I would give her my life."

She tutted at me as if I were a schoolboy. "A life is too easy. What about your legs, hm? What about the ability to walk? To never be able to fight ever again?"

"I'd rather be dead."

"Most would. But are you *most*, Drakus Silverhand?"

My voice lowered an octave. "No. I would give up anything for her."

Slade shifted uncomfortably behind me. Lysander let out a slow exhale.

But Clementine Eyesmith smiled at me. "You've seen what the process did to your mother?"

A dark prickling curl of anger coiled around me. My mother had become dark, selfish, wild. But it had made her into a goddess. Is that what it would do for me? I nodded stiffly. Whatever the cost, I would pay it for my mate and for the continent.

Clementine's eyes glowed with bridled excitement. "You'll need a relative. Do you have one who will help you?"

I made a face as my mind drew to the only full relative I had —my mother. But I was no longer in the business of asking her for anything. She had asked my mate to reject me in the name of power. She understood nothing of what I truly wanted, never actually cared for me. She'd used me as my father had. For power. I was just a tool for her. As for relatives, that only left one person.

I nodded, "I have one in mind."

It looked like Daxian and I, for the first time in our lives, were about to get real brotherly.

## 3 2
## SARAYA

arone, Elya, and I were walking back to my room after a quick break to eat before I tried to go inside myself again, when we heard screams from outside the palace.

My heart fell into my stomach. We took one look at each other and immediately sprinted. Had the Reaper decided to come early? It would be all my fault. We had no protection, only the fae army. The forces from Kaalon had yet to arrive. I led the way, making for the balcony on our third-story floor. If anything was going untoward, we'd be able to see it right away from that vantage point. But when I flung open the glass doors to the balcony and charged outside, it was not an assault that had people screaming.

No, the citizens of Quartz were pointing upward as, high against a periwinkle blue sky flew something massive. It was an incredibly large bird, easily the size of a grown man, its wings spanning many feet on either side of its body.

And it was heading straight for me. My heat leapt.

"Wing-brother!" I exclaimed, waving my arms. It was a great tawny owl and looked like the very same one that visited Drake and me in his tree house. He'd bought me a message straight from Altara, but I'd never thought I'd actually see him in the Human Realm. His kind were definitely a rarity here.

"Dear Goddess!" Elya cried, also waving her arms in the air.

Sarone gripped my shoulder.

"It's alright. I know him," I said. "He's from Ellythia."

"I know," she said. "It's just been so long since I've seen one of our winged cousins. They're rare enough on both islands, but they *never* actually leave the isle."

As we stepped back to allow him space to land, I nodded. "I didn't know that, but he brought me a message from my sister where she's staying at the Jungle School."

Sarone nodded with a slight frown. "That is *very* interesting."

Wing-brother, as Altara had told me to call him, beat his powerful wings to lower himself onto the stone railing of the balcony. Powerful black claws clung securely onto the rail. Pale tones of sable and gold flashed from his feathers under the light of the sun, his amber eyes, keen and bright with intelligence.

As I looked into those eyes, I knew it was the same one from last time. I wished Drake were here to see this, but he was out seeing Daxian.

"Well met, wing-brother!" I said excitedly.

"Good afternoon, Your Highness," he replied in a deep, resonant voice with a slight clicking undertone due to his beak. "I bring news from Princess Altara."

"Is she well?" I asked desperately. "You told her I miss her?"

He nodded regally, "I relayed Your Highness' message exactly, though I apologise we were not able to send word sooner. There were…difficulties at the school."

My blood ran cold. "Is she alright?" I pressed. "My sister?"

He bowed on the railing. "She is well, Your Highness. But she wishes you to urgently know that she is bringing help,

261

although…" his amber eyes darted around the balcony and the empty air behind him, "…I cannot speak any more on it."

"Ah," I said, disappointed and more than a little confused. "What help?" I muttered to Sarone. "Wait, *bringing help*? Tell her to stay there!" I urged the owl. "It's not safe for her here. She *cannot* be here. We are on the verge of war!"

The tawny shifted uncomfortably on the stone, his claws scraping. "I smell it in the air, Your Majesty. The unrest, the blood to come. I understand. But Princess Altara also understands. Please forgive me. I am not permitted to say more."

I sighed, long and slow, trying to calm the panic that was rising up in me. My first and every thought was to protect my sister—as it always had been. We were less than a year apart in age, but it made little difference in my urge to keep her safe. And for so long now, she had been away from it, safe and sound deep in the Ellythian Jungle school. She couldn't come here right when it was most dangerous! What was she thinking? "Please, wing-brother," I pleaded. "You must not allow her to come. It is far too dangerous for anyone!"

"Forgive me," the owl bowed deeply. "I will relay this warning to her, but my allegiance is to the Princess Altara. I follow her orders above all."

I raised my brows as surprise spun through me. Clearly Altara had made an impression on those over the Lotus Sea. I was glad she had his respect, but she hadn't been here in almost a year, she couldn't know about the Reaper's plans. I nodded slowly. "Right, well, this is all I wish for you to tell her then. Altara, The Reaper will be here tomorrow with an army of demons. I do not know what you are planning, but lives will be lost, war is afoot. Do not come here. Your sister, Saraya. Relay it exactly, Wing-Brother."

"Always, Your Highness. Fare well in your war." He bowed

one last time, and I stepped back as he beat his great wings and thrust himself into the air.

As the three of us watched him ascend into the sky, I murmured to them, "What help could she be bringing?" I was dumbfounded by it. "The Ellythian forces?"

Sarone frowned as the owl wheeled around and then flew westwards. "Queen Cheshni would never send the Ellythian forces. Not even for her granddaughters, she swore an oath, as every Ellythian Queen has."

Queen Cheshni.

Hearing my grandmother's name made a dark feeling rise up within me. My mother had never deigned to speak about her, even when begged by both Altara and me. I had one direct blood relative left after all. But my grandmother had never bothered to communicate with us. After my mother's marriage to a Lobrathian, she had wanted to cease all contact, considering her daughter as good as gone.

It had stung my mother. And though she never verbally told me, her eyes had always become glistening and distant whenever we mentioned it.

"What is she like, my grandmother?" I asked.

"Stern. Cold," Sarone sniffed. "Terrifying, really. I never liked going to see her."

I nodded glumly and led the way back inside. It sounded about right, if she'd given up her daughter as practically dead for doing what she was told to do and getting married.

"I never understood it," I said softly. "Why would my grandmother have my mother marry the Lobrathian king and then never talk to her again? She was told to get married!"

Sarone gripped my arm and whirled me around. "Saraya, you don't know?"

I stared at her, my heart pounding. "What do you mean?

Know what? You even told me there was a parade on the day she left! What was the point if she was never going to speak to her again? How could she be angry when she chose it for my mother?"

She looked at me incredulously for a moment before realising that I really did not know what she was talking about. She let out a breath, glancing at Elya. "I thought you knew, that's why…" she ran her hands over her long braid in exasperation, her beautiful face conflicted. She took a deep breath. "Saraya, your mother wasn't *supposed* to get married to your father. She was the Crown Princess of Ellythia—the next queen. But on the day of her coronation, she went to the Jacaranda tree, as all royals do, to hear her prophecy. When she returned, she abdicated the throne."

My brows shot up. This was *not* the story I had been told.

"The Mother Jacaranda told her of a choice," Sarone continued. "And she chose Lobrathia. So instead, her younger sister, Rahana, was pledged for the throne. But out of spite, Queen Cheshni said she would rule until the day she died. She refused that her chosen would decline."

My mother had chosen a foreign land. She'd chosen my father. "But why?" I asked. "Why didn't she want to rule Ellythia?"

"It's not that she didn't want to," said Sarone. "My mother said it was because the prophecy stipulated that either she could be Queen of Ellythia and reign long or she would die young and her *daughters* would be the most powerful Ellythians since Queen Ellythia herself."

I couldn't breathe. I couldn't think. All I could hear was my heart.

My mother had chosen her daughters. Even before I'd been born, she'd chosen *us*. Even knowing she would die at a young age, she chose to be selfless. My eyes stung. And here I was weak, letting my own kingdom be taken by the Reaper tomorrow.

"I suppose she never told you," said Sarone softly, "because it would have been a lot of pressure knowing that from a young age. But we all knew, in Ellythia. The entire household knew and some did not forgive her for her choice."

"And you?" I asked softly, looking between Elya and my cousin. "What do you think of it?"

Sarone's eyes glistened by the light of sun filtering through the open doors of the balcony. She swallowed. "I think she was brave and honourable. Not all parents would do that for their children." She frowned. "I know my mother would have tried to look for me. But…if my child had been taken by demons, I would have stormed down into Havrok's Realm and lit it up. But she didn't." She wiped a stray tear. "Instead *you* came and freed us. If Aunt Yasani had not come here and given birth to you, I would still be down in Havrok's Court. We would all still be trapped. She did the right thing. Every child deserves a mother like yours."

I wiped my eyes and looked at my cousin. "Your mother will be so relieved to see you when you go back to Ellythia." I said thickly. "So happy."

"Oh, I don't know," Sarone sighed, glancing at Elya with a sad smile. "I have half a mind to stay here."

My heart clenched and tears threatened to overwhelm me. I shook myself trying to free the heavy emotions. "But before you make that decision, we have a war to fight. Let's try again," I said. "With the darkness. I need to do this."

Back in my room, I sat on my bed and lay the Temari Blade across my lap.

Sarone sat behind me with a hand on my shoulder, and Elya guarded the door. "Alright," I said. "No stopping this time."

The girls nodded.

I zoomed into my body, but instead of coming in a roundabout way from my insides, I directly headed to my back. Clementine Eyesmith had said to *take the bull by its horns*. I was a midwife. There was nothing about my own body that I should be afraid of.

*Except,* a nasty voice in the back of my mind said, *something corrupted by the hand of Glacine.*

Before I could stop myself, I dove into the darkness.

Between the bands of old tissue, I dove into that well of stifling dark. It was so deep, and with each second of descent, I felt the wall closing in around me, threatening to swallow me whole. Once again, my heart battered against my chest as I fought that sheer terror. Every strike of the whip against my skin fell upon me anew, vicious and biting. My eyes watered, my breath coming in gasps. This wound could very well eat me up. I might never see the light again.

Something shifted in the dark. Something wild and powerful, vast and deep like the ocean. I gritted my teeth and met it at the floor of the pain, my suffering, my grief.

It was as if I felt my mother dying all over again. That raw pain had me by the neck, that grief like a vice around my body.

Before me, she stood.

Hunched in a posture like a wild animal, this woman stared at me. Her skin was the colour of midnight, laced with threads of lightning that glittered like an intricate spiderweb. Her eyes glowed in the dark, no pupils, only electric blue light. Her nails were long and black, as was her wild hair. Her expression was livid and power like nothing I knew emanated from her. The air crackled, my mind spun.

266

But she was bound. Strings of cartilage tightly wound around her throat, her wrists, her ankles.

I had done this, I realised. With each strike of the whip, my response had been to push down, to delve into myself and push my rage away. Glacine had guided me to do it. Her mark was here as well, a dull red glow around the ligaments tethering the creature down.

The woman looked back at me, panting with tethered rage, her chest heaving, the veins on her neck standing to attention. When she spoke, her voice was a bursting volcano in my ears. *Let us be free.*

I broke out into an immediate and violent sweat.

I caged my own power. And Glacine had forced me to do it without knowing. By giving me pain, I pushed it all away to avoid suffering.

This was the power of my mother's family. The power my mother had sacrificed her own reign for.

"Take the sword, Saraya," Sarone urged from what felt like very far away. "Cut her free!"

The woman looked back at me, panting, her hands clenching and unclenching. She nodded eagerly, her mouth twisting into a vicious smile.

*Let us have blood. Let us kill our enemies.*

The raw, violent power that came off her was one of destruction, one of an uncontrollable tornado. I could not let that type of power out. How could I when it promised death and destruction? There was no way I could let it *take over* me. I would have no control. Anything could happen—would I end up like Drake was in *his* bestial form, where he acted only on instinct?

*You and I are the same.* The Kraasputin's slick red face flashed into my mind

*We are the same, you and I.* The Reaper's six eyes looked upon me with a sick knowing. *You destroyed an entire court.*

My power was pure destruction. My mother wouldn't want this. My father wouldn't. My sister would not. What would Drake think of me?

This wasn't me.

The wild woman suddenly lunged for me, and I baulked. Pain sliced through my core, harsh and terrifying. Jerking back, I reeled and fled to the surface, terror lacing every heart beat, shame corrupting every breath. But I needed out—as if I were seeking oxygen after a long time being underwater. I couldn't do this. I couldn't allow it.

I returned to reality with a rattling gasp, my world spinning like a tornado. Elya rushed forward and grabbed my arm to steady me, and I collapsed onto her, wheezing. The Temari Blade clattered to the ground.

"No!" I reached for it and scooped it up, clutching it to my chest. "I can't do this," I breathed. My mother, my poor mother, had told me to get this sword, and here I was, unable to do anything at all. When had I become so weak? I thought. When did I let anything get in my way? She would be so ashamed. Umali would be so ashamed. What type of High Priestess was I? My wound had taken over. It had been best left untouched, safe on my back. I had been fine without delving into it. I had been fine leaving it alone.

Dark coils of grief spun through me, aggressive in the guilt they dealt me.

"It's alright, Saraya." Sarone's voice was infinitely gentle, tirelessly patient. But a note of steel was threaded through it. "Pass me the Temari Blade."

I looked up at my cousin, standing with pity in her eyes as she looked upon me, crouched on the floor. Pain sliced through my hands, and I realised I'd been clutching the blade so tightly that the sheath had cut into my palms. Hastily, I wiped the blood on my pants. Something angry reared up in me as Sarone's green eyes looked down at me, pity dripping from every cell. *Never* in my life had anyone ever looked at me with *pity* in their eyes.

Glacine still held me down by the neck as if I were still a thirteen-year-old girl grieving for her mother, too shocked to act.

Gritting my teeth, I handed the Blade to her. Reverently, she took it with both hands. Together, we left my room, and I followed her to the entrance hall and out the front doors.

Palace staff, maids, and ostlers stopped to stare as Sarone, beautiful, tall, and confident, unsheathed the Temari Blade. She closed her eyes, whispered a prayer and plunged the sword into the earth.

The ground trembled, and into the dusk sky, a great white light shot upwards. Elya grabbed my hand, but Sarone stood strong as she looked up at the beam of light. Incredibly high above us, it spread out in a wide dome, fingers reaching out towards the city and behind the palace grounds. The shield of light encompassed the entire city in a glowing orb before fading away. Remnants of glitter remained in the sky. It was a fine protection.

Sarone looked at me and nodded once. The poison of shame crept through me, sinister and dark, and I forced myself to nod back.

# 33
# DRAKE

I strode back to Daxian's tent with only Fluffy on my shoulder. Opal had returned with Jerali Jones to the palace. Lysander and Slade were not happy about leaving me, but it was too close to the battle, and I needed them with Saraya and the human fighters. Fluffy seemed to understand that something was happening and he refused to leave my side.

My mind still lapsed into its bestial state whenever I was parted from Saraya, but the news that I really was a Tyaag seemed to have stumped my brain into a sort of shock.

What did it mean for my power and me? I had always known I was meant to protect Saraya. Perhaps Daxian was right and that was really an indication of my Tyaag nature. I wanted to be close to Saraya, defend her, allow her to do what she needed to do while I watched her back.

Daxian, Briar, Skelton and Ashwood were waiting for me when I entered his tent.

I explained to them what I wanted to do. Briar gasped loudly and Daxian crossed his arms. "You're joking, right?"

"No. Not joking." I set down the Eyesmith box on the table and opened it. Clementine sprung out of it in her ghostly astral form, waiting for me.

"This is him, is it?" she asked, looking at Daxian's eyepatch with interest, then swiftly bowed. "Professor Eyesmith, Your Majesty, at your service."

Daxian looked upon the strange elderly lady glumly. "I suppose you're going to instruct me on what to do? Why does it need to be a relative?"

"Drakus will do all the work," she said patiently. "But we need a relative to extract the bones. His body will reject someone else reaching into it. His mate would have been even better. Fern the First did it for Lily Silverfoot, according to my research."

"And Saraya would never do it," Daxian nodded. He shrugged off his coat. "What do you have to do?"

"Lie down," Clementine instructed.

I had no qualms about going over to what was clearly Daxian's pallet and laying down in it. My half-brother did not protest as the others and Briar gathered round.

"Which bone will it be?" asked Skelton nervously.

Clementine came forward and rubbed her forearm. "The arm."

I held up my arms. My right, which had my lotus moon mating mark on the back of it was not an option. "It'll have to be left," I murmured. "I'm not giving up my mating mark to Saraya."

"You just need the arm, though, not the hand," Skelton pointed out.

"How's he going to have a hand if he doesn't have an arm?" Daxian scoffed. "Is it just going to float in mid-air, Skel? Let it hang by a tendon and swing it around like a mace?"

Briar smothered a laugh while Skelton reddened. "Drakus is powerful. Maybe he could—"

"Not that powerful," I chuckled humourlessly. "Looks like I'll be Drakus Onehand from now on."

"No," said Daxian in a low voice, coming to kneel by my side. "You'll still be Drakus Voltanius."

I looked up the King of Black Court in surprise. Daxian's one turquoise eye blinked at me back. He had our father's eyes, that specific shade, like the sea on a summer's day. He looked more like our father than his mother. Xenita was all harsh planes and narrowed features, but Wyxian had broader features, softer cheekbones, a proud nose. I wondered how things would be different if Wyxian were still alive.

This far from Saraya, my mind was a jittery horse, jumping from thought to thought, scrambling to maintain focus. I shook myself.

"There are many ways to store magic," Clementine said darkly. "Bone is the most permanent way. Everything of you is stored in there, Drakus Silverhand. You need to imbue within it everything we need to contain a Niyati. That is, all of your Tyaag power, or as much of it as you can manage."

"He can't put all of his power in here," Ashwood said. "It'll kill him."

"We are planning to bind *all* of the Reaper," Clementine said sternly, looking down her nose at the King of Midnight Court. "We need every drop."

I nodded. I didn't actually know if this meant that I wouldn't be able to fight in the coming battle. But if we didn't do this, we didn't have *any* chance at all.

Closing my eyes, I shunted my power into the main bone of my left forearm.

"Just the radius bone, now, not the Ulna," Clementine said lightly.

"Pardon?" I asked.

"There are two bones in your forearm. We want the bigger bone, not the smaller, thinner one."

"Ah, right."

As I pushed my magic into that bone, my arm heated up, and I listened to Briar tentatively quizzing Clementine Eyesmith.

"So the legend said," Briar began. "That when they trapped Oberry the Gruesome, Lily Silverfoot used one dagger and Fern the First used the other. But we only have one bone?"

"The so-called Darkmaul Dagger is actually one knife that is split into two," Clementine explained. "When Drakus retrieves his bone, he'll need to snap it in two."

I shut everyone out and focused on my own body. My monstrous self was excited as to why I was shunting so much of my power into my left arm. Usually, if I were doing that on a minor scale, it would be to prepare to launch an attack, like the massive punches I was giving the fire wraith back at Black Court.

My left arm was growing hotter and hotter. The poison inside my chest—the poison I'd consumed from Saraya's father—was twisting violently, wanting to go down into my arm with the flow as well. I didn't allow it because there was a possibility it would corrupt the process. The poison was not my magic, after all, it was Glacine's.

Being the son of a Goddess as well as a Tyaag, my supply of magic was large, so it took a good half an hour for me to send it all towards that one bone, all the while hearing the others distantly muttering amongst themselves.

It wasn't until a shadow opened up in my consciousness that I gave pause. Fluffy let out a yelp of protest. Abruptly I opened my eyes and realised the pool of magic at my core was smaller than my fist now.

"That's enough, Drake," Daxian warned. I opened my eyes to see Fluffy's round face staring down at me, growling softly.

"Even your shadow-lumzen is saying so," said Ashwood.

"What did you call him?" I murmured.

"He's a shadow-lumzen, isn't he?" the King of Midnight said. "I thought they were extinct. My grandfather was supposedly buried with his pet, the last one. They died on the same day."

"Hmm," Clementine said with disapproval. "I know the Reaper's power, Drakus. This is not quite enough."

"It's almost all of it!" Briar exclaimed. Bless him, he was worried for me. I made a mental note to try and keep him alive through this war.

I looked over at Clementine, her face grim beside Daxian.

As a half-fae, half-monster, my magic was my life force, the thing that kept me alive. To give it away completely meant that I would be giving my life away with it. My arm was pulsing with the amount of raw power in it, the skin glowing a bright and vicious blue. But Clementine was right. I had felt the enormous force that was the Grim Reaper punching against my own shields. That power was phenomenal. The power that bound him then would have to be equally phenomenal.

Giving Clementine a nod, I closed my eyes and shoved the last bit of my power into the bone, leaving the rest of my body cool and prickly. One of the fae swore. Light shone through my eyelids, and Fluffy gave a low whine.

"You'll need to cut it out now," Clementine's voice was far too casual.

"It'll kill him," Daxian murmured.

"Not quite," Clementine said lightly. "Come on, I have other things to do, you know."

Daxian glared at her in a way that would have had anyone cowering.

"Don't look at me like that, young man. I've faced creatures far more ugly than you."

Daxian let out a long suffering exhale and pulled out a dagger from his baldric.

I tapped the inside of my elbow where my curling tree tattoo slinked upwards. "Start there."

Daxian pressed the tip of his dagger to my skin and pressed down.

"Argh!"

"Oh, Gods!" Daxian wrenched the dagger back.

"I'm joking," I laughed. "Go on."

"Are you giving him a bone?" Skelton said. "Or are you taking a bone out? Hurry up, Dax."

Daxian rolled his eyes and sighed. "You're a right bastard for making me do this."

"Pretty sure that *I'm* the one actually having his bones torn out here. Here, give it to me."

Daxian stared at me for a moment before he realised I was serious and offered me the dagger. Swiftly, I shoved the knife at the end of Daxian's incision and sawed my way down, gritting my teeth against the blinding pain. But the monster in me sort of…revelled in that white hot sting. Perhaps I was insane after all. Light shot out of the wound and Briar, in the corner, swore over and over again. Fluffy cried out and jumped onto my hand.

"Someone grab him!" I called. Daxian scooped Fluffy up, and I watched as the creature sunk his teeth into the flesh of Daxian's hand.

"Fuck!" Daxian frowned down at the creature but, to his credit, did not let Fluffy go. Fluffy chomped over and over again, and blood began to spill.

I angled the bloody knife at Fluffy. "Stop!" I said sternly. "Or you'll get kicked out."

Fluffy let out a sad croon but closed his mouth all the same and continued his unhappy growl at me.

I continued sawing through my arm, feeling entirely like the pain would make me go mad. Or was I already mad, sawing at my own arm? I probably looked it.

By the time I got down to my wrist, Skelton had run outside to vomit, Daxian was white and I was covered in sweat, my head pounding and my chest heaving.

"Ah fuck," I said, laying my head back down as blood dripped freely from me. "Is it enough?"

"Well," said Clementine, who, for the entire time I was cutting myself open, looked like she was watching a particularly interesting sport. "His Majesty will need to dig the bone out now. This is where you'll have to concentrate, Drakus." I wondered, not for the first time, exactly what bloody type of school Professor she was. None of the teachers I knew from the Mountain Academy were anything like this, and most of them were vicious warriors.

"Go on, Dax."

Mumbling under his breath, I took Fluffy in my free hand and clutched him firmly to my chest. Daxian dug his dagger into the top of the incision, and I bit back a groan. As he began severing the bone from my upper arm, rivulets of pain swept across me like a fiery storm.

Closing my eyes, I sunk into myself. That shadowy maw at the back of my consciousness jumped into the foreground. Sleepily, I stared at it, wondering at its smoky, coiling outline.

It was the darkness of the unconscious—the darkness of death that awaited me.

The rest of my body felt empty, devoid of the power of life. I knew once Daxian took that one bone out, my power would be gone with it.

From very far away, it sounded as if Clementine was giving Daxian stern instructions. My body was shaking from blood loss, but there was nothing I could do. I had seen Dacre give blood back to Saraya's birthing patients after they haemorrhaged in the Demon Realm and I wondered where that bastard mage was lurking now.

I had just assumed I would recover from this. The monster would take over, and my body would heal. But now, I doubted that assumption. As that shadow loomed closer to me, I wondered whether I actually *wouldn't* recover.

*Tyaag means sacrifice.*

Was this to be my sacrifice then? Was this the way I protected Saraya? To give my life for her? I had no qualms with giving her my life—as far as I was concerned my life *was* completely hers. I just wished that I could see her one last time, could make love to her properly before I went on to the beyond. Daxian had better make sure he gave Saraya the bone and have it done otherwise I'd haunt him for the rest of his damned life—but wait just a fucking minute. With me gone, that left Saraya a widow. That left, Daxian or anyone else to move into my territory—no, I couldn't let that happen. Saraya was *mine*. We were fucking soul-bound.

There was a thump and a crunching sound and someone retched.

Tiny claws were desperately scratching at my face, and I knew it was Fluffy. My hand had let him go, my body now shutting down.

"Now what?" came Daxian's angry voice as if he were in another tent completely. "Is he to die?"

"Now you file the bone," came the reply. "And we wait."

Angrily I turned to look at my surroundings. But I had nowhere to go except that darkness now. Nowhere to turn.

There was no choice here. Gritting my teeth, I squared my shoulders, pictured the love of my life and launched myself into the dark.

# 34
# SARAYA

As dusk turned into night, Opal and I strode out of the palace, jittery and irritable. I'd never met a foe I couldn't match, had never been this frightened of something. I'd been training to defend myself from enemies since I was a toddler, I'd been helping women birth babies since I was twelve. I'd never felt this way. Not when the fae came to take me away from my home, not down in the Demon Kingdom where Havrok shamed me and literally kicked me to the ground in front of his entire Court, not even when we'd come back to Lobrathia and I'd faced our invaders.

The biggest blow was that I had done this to myself.

Down in the damaged tissue, in the strings of ligaments and cartilage, I *felt* Glacine. Not her, actually, but what she made me feel. Immobile, trembling, frightened.

*I am a midwife, and I do not fear the dark.*

Except I did.

I couldn't destroy this foe, so I turned my anger instead upon what I *could* do. I retrieved Silentfoot from the stables, and quietly, Jerali Jones and Blythe followed me. No doubt they'd heard what had happened from Sarone. Before, my shame had been private. Even in the Demon Courts, when I'd bared the scars to strangers for the first time, I had never felt *this* bare. I'd strutted down the aisle to my marriage to Drake with the Goddess Umali as a talisman in my heart.

But how could I bear the talisman of my sacred Goddess in this moment when none should be proud of me? I had done this to myself. There was no Wyxian, there was no Havrok, there was no Reaper, even, to blame. It was just me.

Silentfoot pranced when she saw me. "Hello, my love," I murmured, stroking her muzzle. "We haven't had a chance to go out yet, hey? Well, now's our chance."

Opal happily bounced off my shoulder onto Silentfoot's head, giving her a swift kiss before perching there, ready to go. She was getting bolder, day by day, and I think Fluffy had something to do with it. The black lumzen was a naughty little thing, but he followed Opal everywhere when Drake was nearby. The two of them were still with Daxian, I think. Now, I too would finally would get a chance to lay my eyes on our fae friends.

Needing something to do with our hands, we refused the ostlers' help. Jerali, Blythe, and I saddled and bridled our horses, and we went out of the palace into the dusk.

My plan was to do a lightning shield around the perimeter of the city, including the fae camp and I'd leave a little opening for when the Kaalon forces arrived. I had sent another pigeon to Osring, perhaps a little passive-aggressive, but Adlain had been there with me when the Reaper took us, so he, of all people, should know the need for urgency.

The air was crisp with a background sort of hush. The citizens of Quartz were nervous, though many lifted their hands to wave as we passed. I plastered a smile onto my face and waved back. All the while, electricity was twitching inside of me, ready to burst out and do some real work.

Although the Umali Blade was going to protect us from any astral assault by the Reaper—which would stop me and the babies from getting stolen away out of our bodies again—we still needed physical protection. A lightning shield had worked at Black Court, and I knew it would help us again.

We began on the western side of the city, and as Jerali and Blythe threw down Quartz blocks in front of me, I put up bolts of lightning. White-hot beams plunged into the sky like swords, ready to pierce the clouds.

But the most shocking thing for me was when we reached the fae camp at the southern end of the city. We were met with a sea of black and red tents as fae warriors, both male and female, milled about almost expectantly. It looked like they'd brought everyone they could. Nervously, I watched as Jerali, riding ahead of me, threw the next block of quartz down. I shot up a beam of lightning from it, and when it sparked to life and sizzled in the air, the fae warriors clapped and cheered. Someone even whistled.

They remembered me from Black Court, it seemed. It was just this time, Midnight and Obsidian Courts were fighting alongside us and those warriors looked quite happy to be on our side.

Around their camp we rode, throwing down my lightning shield. When we rounded the back, I spotted three dark figures, tall and broad, watching me. One was rotund, a bun atop his head. They raised their hands.

My heart leapt with happiness. The three princes, and to my great surprise, Briar! Relief poured through me at my old friend being here, in my home town, alive and well. In response, I shot lightning into the air, not for a shield, but in a display of pretty light. The fae warriors ran alongside Silentfoot, clapping and cheering.

Warriors needed to be given hope. Even if I didn't have so much right now myself, I knew that this was important for them to feel like we had a chance. Waving at them as we left the side of their camp, Jerali, Blythe, and I continued all the way around the back of the palace.

But when we returned to the city, lit up like an orb in the night, I was *still* jittery.

So when Jerali made to return to the stables, I paused Silentfoot by the palace gates. "I'm going to see Agatha," I murmured. "You two go back home."

"I'm not leaving you alone," said Jerali. "We'll come and wait for you outside."

My General was not going to budge. Not after the Reaper stole me away so recently. So, silently, I nodded.

Once, I'd walked these dark streets alone, blissfully unaware of Havrok, of the Reaper, even of the fae. How simple life had been back then. It had been just me and my sister, going about our lives. Naturally it had all come to a screeching end.

When we got to Agatha's cottage, my midwife mentor was heading out, snug in her patchwork cardigan, bag in hand and the smell of blue ganja faintly perfuming the air.

"I'm off to a birth," she fixed me with a stern eye. "I'm worried about the shoulders. You're coming with me."

I stared at her for a moment. That last birth I'd attended felt like months ago, back at Black Court with Daxian's mother, Xenita. And it had been a fae birth, no human midwifery skill required.

"Well, are you a midwife, or are you a goat?" Agatha barked. "Let's go."

I suppressed the choke that rose up my throat. Goddess, she

was right. If a woman needed assistance, it was my job to be there. I had always been a midwife first, above all things. Hastily, I dismounted and gave Silentfoot's reins to Jerali, with Opal still riding on the mare's head.

I hastened after Agatha, with Jerali and Blythe following at a slow walk behind us.

"You got too cocky," Agatha grumbled as we walked down the quiet street. Everyone had shut themselves in their houses for the night.

I gaped at her. "Never!" I exclaimed. "I've never been—"

Agatha waved her hand at me. "I saw it written all over you."

I shut up for a moment. Well, I certainly won't be cocky any more. "I have a problem, Agatha," I said.

"*You've* got a problem!" she huffed. "I've got problems. It's Trisha's ninth babe, and she's well past due. Her babies have gotten bigger each time."

"Ah," I said, nodding in memory. "Her last was a close one." I'd attended that birth late one night at Agatha's behest. That babe had been well over eight pounds.

Being a midwife meant you had to cast aside everything else that was going on in your head and focus on the task at hand. So I did that now, thinking of all the risks this birth would have and what we would need to do in the event of one. Trisha was one of those mums who made our work easy. She enjoyed being pregnant and laboured like it was her everyday work. But that was the way of mothers with that many children. This was business for her.

When we entered their small cottage, the youngest of the eight children being wrangled by the elder ones, we found Trisha and her husband, Shaun in their bedroom, rocking together by the side of the bed.

"Oh, good timing, Agatha!" she said happily as we came in. "I'm just so happy those wretches are gone, Your Highness." She grinned at me, her bright, tanned face glistening a little. "Gosh, it was a marvel, wasn't it, Shaun? I don't know what I would've done if he turned out to be a boy and Agatha had to take—" She gasped as another contraction came. She groaned a little, deep in her throat. I hastily scrubbed my hands in the bowl set up on the dresser and unwrapped the stack of towels next to it. Once the contraction passed, the smile returned to Trisha's face, and she turned to look me in the eye. "It was a marvel to see you, Your Highness. To think magic is returned to the Kingdom! I do hope our baby has magic. How exciting for us!"

Her joy was catchy, and soon, I found myself laughing along as she did between, and sometimes during contractions. Whatever the situation, whatever was going on in the wider kingdoms, women still gave birth every day, the tides still turned, the earth still moved around the sun. I had to remember that. This work that I did was bigger than me. Being a midwife had been a constant reminder of that. I guess in between the battles and the fighting, I had just forgotten it.

"No pushing," Agatha warned. "Hold it off as long as you can."

"Fancy telling a birthing woman not to push!" tutted Trisha. "You know as well as I do, the body does its own thing." She smiled at Agatha and cooed, "It'll be fine. I practically sneezed the last one out. Remember, Shaun? You ladies almost didn't get here on time—ouch!" Trisha leant on the side of her bed and gave out a rumbling all-mighty groan. "He's coming!" she gasped before her waters broke all over the towels I'd laid down on the floor. Trisha, having done it many times before, put her own hand between her legs and steadied the baby's head as he came out. Agatha watched closely and then glanced at me and nodded.

When the baby first enters a mother's pelvis, the widest part of her pelvis is sideways, so the baby's shoulders must enter front on.

But a woman's pelvis changes shape—so that by the time the baby needs to exit, the widest part is actually up and down. So once the baby's head is born, he needs to turn so he's looking sideways and his shoulders line up. Usually, the baby's top shoulder then slips under the pubic bone, and out they come.

But shoulders are wide, and sometimes they can get stuck—most often on that pubic bone and sometimes even on the sacrum around the back of the pelvis.

The best way to know if a baby was big was by looking at the size of the head when he came out. For a ninth birth, this head was coming out rather slow. Trisha groaned. "Oh, he's big!" before the baby's head was born in a small gush of fluid. All three of us, Shaun, Agatha, and I, bent down to look at the baby.

"Look, Shaun!" Trisha chuckled. "I've got two heads!"

Shaun could do nothing but laugh and hold his wife's hand. But Agatha glanced at me with a warning in her eye. That was the largest head I'd seen in a while.

"On your hands and knees, Trisha," Agatha ordered. "Quick smart now."

Trishna groaned. "Oh, alright."

Shaun and I hastened to help her, but going on your hands and knees isn't easy when you've got a baby's head sticking out of you. Trisha was a strong woman and knew her way around her own labours. She carefully placed her hands and knees on the bed.

"Knees in," Agatha ordered. "Ankles wide."

"Oh right," Trisha panted. "It opens the outlet—oh here!"

Trisha bit back a squeal as Agatha placed gentle traction on the baby's head. But he would not turn to the side as he was supposed to. Instead, his chin buried itself back inside as if he were trying to get back into her womb.

My heart plummeted. The first sign of shoulder dystocia. We only had minutes to get the baby safely out before he was compromised.

Agatha stepped back as I stepped forward. "Trisha, do I have your permission to check the baby's shoulders with my magic?"

"Yes, yes, of course, Your Highness!"

Usually, getting on your hands and knees worked to drop the shoulder away from the pubic bone, using gravity to make it easier for the baby to pop out. It hadn't worked this time. If I were't here, Agatha would have put her fingers on the baby's shoulders to try and shift them onto a diagonal.

Quickly, I delved inside Trisha's pelvis with my mind. The baby's chunky shoulder was firmly lodged behind the public bone. No matter how hard she pushed, his shoulder was jamming against that bone. It needed to be shifted diagonally.

"His shoulder needs to be moved, Trisha, or it's not going to come out."

"Yes, yes, it feels wrong!" She squeezed her eyes shut and grabbed onto Shuan's hand.

"Okay, next contraction, we'll all work together. Me and you."

"Contraction!' Trisha groaned.

I placed firm hands on the baby's head as I magically pushed the baby's shoulder diagonally. As Trisha pushed, she let out a yelp as the baby's shoulder eased under her pubic bone, followed by his other shoulder underneath. I let out a relieved exhale as slowly the baby emerged, although I had to ease the rest of him out a little more slowly than I normally needed to.

The babe gave a half-hearted squawk as he was born, but Agatha grabbed a towel and gave him a vigorous rub down. I had no doubt that he was over ten pounds. Trisha turned over and clapped, laughing at her husband. "He's a right soldier, Shaun! Look at him! As big as a cob loaf!"

The baby gave a wet, healthy cry and Agatha passed him to Trisha. She grabbed him and lay down on her bed, cooing happily as she set him on her naked chest.

Then two demons in astral form strode through the wall. Skin stretched over lean muscle, tall and grinning savagely with sharp incisors.

I didn't even need to think. I stepped around Agatha and my astral sword appeared in my hand in a flash. I swung angrily at the first, skewering him right above his belly button. The second froze, but he didn't have time to run before I leapt upwards and beheaded him. His eyes were wide as he hit the floor. They had not been expecting me to be there.

Shaun let out a yell, and Trisha clutched her new baby in fright.

Agatha stared at me and then my sword. "They're still coming?"

I was silent, staring at the floor where the dead demons were currently dissolving. This was a breed of demon I had not seen before. They were wiry and emaciated as if they'd been starved, grey stretched skin and bulging round eyes.

"They should not be here," I breathed.

We knew the Reaper had been petitioning demons from other Courts. Here was more evidence. But Sarone had activated the Temari Blade. I had seen the shield spread over the city myself.

That meant it hadn't worked properly. And I thought I knew why. Though Sarone had the blood of Ellythia in her, the sword had not chosen her. The face of the Fae-Ellythian Guardian from

Sky Court was still fresh in my mind. I had agreed to be guardian of the sword.

"I have to go," I said, rapidly washing my hands and then striding to the door. "Congratulations, Trisha. Shaun. Stay inside. Lock the doors. We'll be patrolling all night."

"It's the Emperor of the demons, isn't it?" Shaun said, following me out, rubbing his large hands in determination. "We're going to fight, Your Highness. We all are."

"Thank you, Shaun. The fae are here and I'm sure Kaalon and Waelan are on their way." I took a deep breath and spoke something I did not fully believe. "We'll be okay. I'll see you in the morning."

Rushing outside, Jerali Jones and Blythe jumped off the wall they were leaning against. Opal let out a scared warble.

"What's wrong?" Jerali asked sharply.

"Alert everyone," I said. "And find my Temari initiates. I need to give them all astral swords. Astral demons are back in Quartz."

# 35
# SARAYA

J erali, Blythe, and I mounted our horses and kicked off into a canter back to the palace. The cobblestoned streets of Quartz were silent and dark now that everyone had locked themselves in until the battle began.

As soon we reached the palace, Jerali leapt onto the ground and summoned a runner to find my Ellythian warriors.

Blythe and I stood at the palace entrance while I began the process of summoning each of them an astral sword.

Way back when Arishnie had taught me how to do this at the Mountain Academy, it had taken me months to construct a sword in my mind and then manifest it into reality.

Now, it took me mere moments. I thought of Blythe, her raven hair and blue eyes, and her sword flashed into my hands —a blue and black hilted blade.

Blythe's eyes gleamed as she took her new astral blade just as Slade and Lysander rushed out of the palace in front of my Ellythian warriors.

"Where's Drake and Fluffy?" I asked the fae, closing my eyes briefly to imagine a sword for Sarone.

"Uh..." Lysander shifted uncomfortably. "With Daxian. Why? What's wrong?"

I frowned at him. "For this long? And I just killed two demons in their astral form, different ones— demons from a different court and I think the Temari Blade's protection is patchy."

When I opened my eyes, Sarone was in front of me, clicking her tongue in thought. She accepted a green and purple hilted blade from me and we all turned to look at the Temari Blade, standing sentinel, stuck into the earth in front of the palace. The glowing blade shimmered in the night, and an upside down Umali screamed at us angrily.

"It chose you, Saraya," Sarone said. "I suppose it was bound to happen."

"It's better than nothing," Lysander pointed out as I passed a purple hilted sword to a panting Elya. She took it from me as if it were a newborn baby and I swear a tear fell down her cheek. I supposed this was myth coming true for her. As in the old stories of the first Queen Ellythia.

"I want a patrol in the city through the night," I said as I finished the remaining swords. A bell resounded in the distance.

"Oh no!" Blythe exclaimed. "Already?"

The bell was followed by two short blasts of a horn which indicated 'friend.'

Jerali nodded at me. "I bet it's Kaalon."

"Right," I said, moving back towards Silentfoot, being held by Slade. "Let's go and see."

"Saraya, I'm not sure if that's safe."

"Jerali!" said, looking at my General in shock. "Do you seriously think I'm not going to be in the thick of things?

"It's not normal for the regent to be out on the front lines," said Jerali reasonably.

"Daxian was," I shot back. "Besides, with my lightning, I think we need me out there."

"I'm sorry to say it, General," said Slade. "But I think she's right. We don't know what numbers are coming. We need everyone out there." He turned to me. "I won't leave your side, Saraya."

"Drake will be there," I pointed out as I mounted Silentfoot.

Slade and Lysander cast each other a look.

"*What* is he doing, anyway?" I said irritably. "He needs to be here, not in Daxian's tent."

Jerali cast Lysander a frown and I froze on my saddle. "You're hiding something," I said, surprised. "What is it? What's Drake doing?"

"It's not for us to tell," Jerali said seriously. "He's alright, Saraya. He'll tell you when he gets back, I'm sure."

"Is it serious?" I clutched my reins so tightly that Silentfoot pranced nervously under me and Opal looked between us in alarm. I cast my mind out into the dark to look for him. But he must've been too far, I couldn't feel him.

"Depends what you count as serious," Lysander said, not looking at me.

"Oh! I have no time for this!" I said angrily, wheeling Silentfoot around as the ostlers brought horses forward for the others. Opal clutched on to Silentfoot's head for dear life. "Hemali and Sarone, I want you patrolling the western quadrant of the city, Elya and Uma, the east. Kill any demons you find and make note of their features. Agatha will have already sent word to the midwives on duty. Sarone and Blythe, get a list of labouring women from her. She's at Trisha's house in Miles Street."

My Ellythian warriors and Blythe nodded.

"Let's move out!" I called. This was it, everything was happening now. Would anyone get any sleep tonight?

I trotted Silentfoot out of the palace gates, nodding to the citizen guards we had there. We arrived at the city gates to find the night watch chattering excitedly and pointing to a shifting group, newly arrived.

"General!" cried the Captain of the Guard, running down the battlement stairs, "Your Highness!"

"We see them," Jerali said smoothly, coming up beside me. "What sigil are they flying?"

"Kaalon, Waelan and...'oo's that?"

I spied yellow and black flags flapping in the night. "Traenara," I grinned, wondering if King Omni might have actually come. He enjoyed a good battle but had escaped with his life at the last one in Quartz, according to Daxian.

But a strange sound came to us on the wind, bold and bounding.

"What's that?" Blythe asked.

"Horses?" the captain said.

"No, it's a woman singing," Slade murmured in surprise.

"That's Queen Helene," Lysander said delightedly. "I'd recognise that voice anywhere!"

I looked sideways at my blond friend. He'd only met Helene once or twice, maximum.

"'Sander has a crush," Slade grinned at me. "Can you tell?"

Shaking my head ruefully at a practically glowing Lysander, I trotted out of the gates to meet our allies.

Oddly enough, it was Adlain who met me first, followed close behind by Queen Helene, who looked threatening in full plate armour, and King Omni with General Tarjin close behind him. I couldn't believe my eyes. They'd all actually come to help us, arguments or not!

When we reached each other, we dismounted and Adlain, to my surprise, rushed towards me and pulled me into his arms.

"I'm so glad to see you alive, Saraya," he said, panting, his face sweating. "I'm sorry we've only just arrived. My father has taken a turn in his health. But I told him and everybody what happened, and we knew we had to come. It's just—"

"It's just we had some disagreements," Helene said, coming forward to embrace me.

"Thank you for coming," I said, smiling up at her cherub like face.

"Thank you?" King Omni boomed. He had deep brown skin and was impressive in his height and build. Though he was a king, he was a warrior tried and true. "The fight for the Human Realm is here!" he said in his resonant voice. "We *all* had a responsibility to come."

"If Lobrathia falls, we all fall," I admitted. I was met with murmurs of agreement. "He will be here on the morrow," I said.

"Well, it's a good thing all this lightning is up, guiding our way!" Helene said excitedly, gripping her sword. "It's as good as day out here."

"Good visibility on the battlefield," Jerali Jones added from my side. "Settle the soldiers and come up to the palace. We must talk strategy."

Once we returned to the palace, we held a meeting to talk about the placement of the fae and humans on the field. We would defend the city from the east, as they were likely to attack us from that side—the direction of the quartz quarry. I had no doubt that my shield would only slow the Reaper down. But importantly, it gave us time. We needed to know when they were on their way.

The regents returned to direct their men. I did not like that they'd had a hard few days travel before they got here and were expected to fight, but perhaps we still had some time before they arrived.

After they left, a sort of fell quiet took over the palace. A maid came and gave me a hot chocolate, but I could not bear to drink it. I also couldn't bear to return to my room alone—what with Drake off with Daxian doing Goddess knew what. But I trusted him to be where he was needed the most. Perhaps he needed to help Daxian command the fae, he had been Black Court's elite forces Commander, after all, and Daxian was only a new king. Yes, that was right, Drake was best suited with the fae, and he trusted Jerali was a competent General who would order our human forces well. This was the way of war. He couldn't be by my side the entire time and in truth, I didn't *need* him to hold my hand in battle. I'd been training for this.

The Order of Temari was trained to fight the demons. That was our purpose, our function, our vow.

*We are the sword in the night,*
*The protectors of human potential.*
*The shield against all that is evil*
*I accept this vow.*

And I would defend the city with my life. Come what may.

IT WAS THREE HOURS PAST MIDNIGHT WHEN I AWOKE WITH A START. Sitting bolt upright from my pallet in the entrance hall, I stared at the wall in front of me, my heart pounding.

Someone had brought down my lightning shield around the Quartz quarry. It had gone out with a snap. Urging myself to slowly and calmly rise to my feet, I cast my eye about the hall.

Jerali, talking quietly with Lysander, took one look at my expression and strode towards me.

I swallowed down the lump in my throat and gave them both

a level look. "He's here," I said as calmly as I could. "They'll be through the quarry in minutes."

"Get the men up," Jerali said, turning to Lysander. "Send word to the camps. In an hour, we go to war."

I left Opal on my pallet with firm instructions to stay there. She crooned with wide eyes. We'd fought together before, but I could not risk her on the front lines—which is exactly where I needed to be. She listened with her wide iridescent eyes and I wished that Fluffy was here to keep her company. I made a cocoon out of my blankets, she settled back in, and I stroked her head until her eyelids drooped shut.

When I got to the stables, I frowned at myself. Silentfoot was a mild-mannered mare, she was no warhorse. I couldn't very well be taking her to the front lines.

A clip-clop sounded from behind me, and I turned to find a monster of a horse—no, *zekar*—was trotting towards me. Razor was a beast of a creature and like Drake, definitely made for violence. And it seemed that he knew he was needed. He stopped in front of me, the ostlers muttering from within the stables, and bowed his head.

"Give me a leg up, please," I commanded one of my ostlers. "Looks like Razor and I are going to be partners tonight." It would have to be bareback too, since Razor would not have a bar of a saddle. So be it. Settled on the zekar's back, his muscular weight under me, powerful and confident, I could not help but marvel at the creature Drake had grown up with. Razor was as wild as Drake and it somehow brought my mind back to the wild woman who sat tied inside of me. Drake and I were more alike than I had ever thought. Drake in his bestial form was wild and untethered, fierce and something completely out of this world.

That destructive thing inside of me was the same. I shook

myself and took one last glance at the Temari Blade, stuck in the same spot in the earth.

"Umali give me strength," I whispered.

Razor let out an approving snort.

Very well. We would go into war like the wild creatures we were.

Lysander, Slade, and Jerali quickly mounted their own horses —the ones they brought from Kaalon's military stables, and we rode off into the night, the sound of the city bell resounding in our ears.

*Wake up,* it announced.

We passed a group of women standing outside Madame Yolande's brothel. I brought Razor up short. Before me, standing with swords, adjusting leather armour around their thighs and chests were familiar faces. Madame Yolande, a wiry older woman, turned and saw me watching them. Clutching a sword in hand, she gave me a bow. "Your Majesty."

The other brothel workers turned and realised I was watching them. Chirra, a beautiful raven haired woman I'd helped in her previous birth just before I left Quartz initially, saluted me with her sword. The others behind her did the same.

Her voice was fierce through the night. "We fight, Your Majesty, all of us. For our children. For their futures!"

The backs of my eyes burned as Madame Yolande and the others shouted in agreement.

"Goddess be with you, Your Majesty," Madame Yolande said. The others chorused the same.

I couldn't speak, couldn't breathe. I hated that they had to fight in a war against brutal creatures bred for war. I hated that it had come to this. But my heart glowed with the fierce strength I saw there, in these women who had lived most of their lives fighting.

"Goddess be with us all," I said.

And as we made our way to the gates, the men and women of the city streamed out of their houses, armed with whatever weapons they could find.

"Look," Jerali said, pointing to a group of archers walking up the stairs to the city's battlements. I stared at the line of young women, many with babies strapped to their backs, determinedly clutching newly made bows. The battlement captain was handing out quivers of arrows. "They wanted to fight, Saraya," Jerali said quietly. "So I said this was the best way for them to take part with infants."

I let out a steady exhale as I took these women in, some of them, teenagers.

"Lightning Queen!" someone shouted above us. I looked up to see the line of archers already in position waving at me. A teenage girl had called out. "We'll get 'em, yer Majesty! We'll get these bastards good!"

I grinned up at them, summoned my blade, and shot lightning into the air. The archers stomped their feet and took up a chant.

"Lightning Queen! Lightning Queen! Lightning Queen!"

# 36
## SARAYA

By the time we all reached the eastern field, we only had a short while left before the enemy arrived. It was a controlled sort of chaos, I thought, as King Omni's voice boomed over the Traenaran soldiers and Queen Helene's deep alto rung through the air, a war chant which her soldiers sung back to her as they marched into position.

But the fae. The fae soldiers were silent. They'd done this before, not that long ago and no doubt that nasty battle was still fresh in their minds.

Ashwood's and Daxian's archers quietly made their way to the back lines, where the Quartz archers were. Their mounted soldiers marched into position on either side of the human forces.

Our strategy had been put together by Jerali Jones and Drake, who quickly decided that Naxon was likely to come and support the Reaper with Eclipse Court forces. The battle of Black Court had proven that humans were no match for fae warriors so we needed to be sure we could position our fae warriors right by Naxon's as soon as we determined their position. So we'd broken the fae forces into three and interspersed them with the humans.

I was happy to see Viscount Nightclaw, Briar's father, just as rotund as his son, silently directing the Black Court soldiers alongside his son. Next to them was the Duke Nightsong along with Emery, whom I was delighted to see. They all nodded at me, when I spotted them and I nodded back.

As I followed Jerali right to the middle of our forces and to the very front lines, the air suddenly smelled of smoke and I frowned. It did not take me long to see why. The fae warriors of Black Court were now grasping flaming swords, orange flames licking up into the cold night air.

"Fireswords," Lysander muttered to me on his stallion from my left. "Daxian must have had his mother petition her family in the Court of Flames."

"Trying to make up for the fire wraiths, I suppose," I said darkly. "Where *is* Drake? I can't see him. I don't even know if I sense him out here." Casting my mind out to search for him around the field, I came up against a wall of nothing. "You don't think—"

"He's fine, Saraya," Lysander said so firmly that I looked at him with raised brows. "Trust me, he's doing what he needs to do."

Now *that* unsettled me. But the look on Lysander's face suggested that he wouldn't be telling me any more. And on top of that, I trusted Drake and his warriors to do the right thing. If he had to be away from me, it was for a good reason. I just wish they would tell me. "Well, he's going to be in big bloody trouble," I murmured. "This is ridiculous."

Our scouts arrived first, sweaty and wide-eyed. Jerali had stationed guards to watch the quarry day and night, just in case I missed the shield coming down. Then they could tell us who and what was coming through. What type of assault to expect first up.

They rode through the small gap in my lightning shield and came straight to Jerali and me. They were two young men, panting and clearly shaken, their horses foaming at the mouth.

"A'int seen nothing like it, General," panted one boy pulling his mare to a stop. "Big demons, bred for war! There's flying ones too, they look like lizards, only bigger."

"How many?" Jerali asked calmly. My General was a quiet ocean, vast and sober, but underneath that exterior, a dangerous current roiled. I knew that as soon as battle began, Jerali would explode.

The boys looked at one other. "More than I've ever seen," said the second. "Thousands. And…"

"What is it?" I pressed.

The boy bowed in his seat and glanced nervously at Lysander and Slade. "Apologies, Your Majesty, but there are fae at the front. Flying a red crescent moon standard."

I gritted my teeth and nodded. Eclipse Court. So Naxon, the stupid bastard, had in fact brought his warriors to die. The flying demons were not surprising either—we knew they existed because we'd seen them on the day of the initial invasion on my first wedding day. One had crashed through the palace window, but we'd not seen them again, even down in the demon lands. They must have been bred and trained hidden from us.

Jerali nodded and cantered off to talk to the sergeant of the archers we had around the back lines.

"Head to the city," I nodded to the boys. "You've done well. Go and rest."

"No, Your Majesty," bowed the second again. A fierce fire lit up his eyes. "We are *fighting*."

Their faces were stubborn, their jaws set. Smiling at them, I nodded. "Find what weapons you can, then. And be vigilant."

Jerali had been working on training volunteer civilians. Three days was barely any time to train but they'd been forced by the demons to train for combat for months before that. I'd watched many of the boys in the training arena at the back of the palace and they'd had both stamina and technique. The demons had trained them hard.

Less than fifteen minutes later, a deep warhorn blared in the distance. My heart kicked up into a rapid beat and goosebumps littered my arm. The horses pranced nervously, except for Razor and the other Midnight Court zekar, who stood stock still as predators do.

"Demon horn," Slade said through gritted teeth.

I had instructed my other Temari initiates to remain in the city with their astral swords in hand and physical swords at their hips. Astral demons were still a big threat and there was a chance they'd bring them in numbers too.

But now it was time. It had come to *this*. To defend the Human Realm at the seat of Lobrathia.

I nudged Razor forward, murmuring to him what I wanted to do, but he seemed to know my mind already. We walked out the front of everyone, between the front lines and my lightning shield, still crackling brightly before us.

Shivering with the adrenaline now pouring through my veins, I flashed a sword into my hand, lacing it with lightning, I nodded to Lysander and a small cheer came up from the humans before me. The fae warrior's green magic flowed toward me, magically amplifying my voice. My priestess mark began to burn as power lanced through my arms.

Tonight, I am the Goddess Umali, come to bring death. I

might not have the Temari Blade at my side, but I was still Umali's chosen.

I rode down the line of soldiers, fae and human. Daxian and the three new fae kings eyed me intently. Fern, with his tiny force, no more than twenty males, Ashwood with a much larger group and Daxian with a comparable size. Briar was not present beside his father, for which I was most grateful for. I hoped he was back with the archers somewhere. Queen Helene, surrounded by a contingent of her fiercest warriors, gave me a nod, her eyes glowing just as bright as her armour. King Omni thrust his sword into the air as our eyes met, and Adlain gave me a solemn nod. We had agreed that he would head to the back lines with the archers when battle came. He was a fine shot, like Altara, and as the sole heir to Kaalon, I did not want him to die an early death—which was likely if he stayed out here.

My voice rung out down the line of our combined forces. "Today, we fight, not only for the Human Realm, but for the Fae Realms as well!" Razor cantered down the fae lines. "We are the sword in the night! The protectors of human and fae potential! I took this vow, and I will defend this city with my life!"

The roar of human and fae soldiers alike filled the night air like our own warhorn. Daxian gave me a nod of approval, and I nodded back to him and the other Fae Princes. Fern, Ashwood, and Skelton wore grave faces as they thrust their flaming swords in the air.

They could very well lose their lives tonight. Any one of us could. I suppressed a shiver as I urged my mind to think about strategy instead.

My target was the Reaper. Darkmaul Dagger or not.

The warhorns got louder and louder as each second passed by. And what I thought was the roar of the wind was actually the voices of shrieking demons.

Something slammed into the lightning shield above me, and it crackled and spat as it devoured something stupid enough to have barged right into it.

Several of our men jumped. Razor tossed his head. Jerali returned from the archers and gave me a nod.

Taking a deep breath. I commanded my lightning shield to extinguish. It abruptly let out, leaving us in darkness for a few awful moments while our eyes adjusted. I muttered a prayer as the air became charged. In my core, I knew my magic was finite. I needed to be wise with its use because I was still not more powerful than the Reaper. I needed Drake here. Another Niyati to match our enemy.

Across the field not a hundred paces from us, was a long line of shadow. They looked like phantoms in the night. When my eyes focused on the enemy lines, I frowned at what I saw. Demon warriors stood snarling, holding spears, axes, and jagged swords. Lesser demons were half naked, most holding weapons too. But spread out between those were demon lords who sat atop mounts the likes of which I'd never seen before.

They were twice the size of an ox, just as muscular but grey and vicious-looking with long curved tusks and intelligent, predatory eyes. They snorted aggressively, pawing the ground. Razor huffed in irritation.

"Snargbeasts," Slade barked. "Of course, they bought fucking snargbeasts!"

"Any way you can manifest armour?" Lysander asked me, eyeing the tusks of the monstrous creatures. "That way none of us will be blasted by a lightning shield if we get too close to you."

"Right," I nodded in agreement. I'd not ever done it before, but I *had* thought about it plenty of times. Jerali hated plate armour, but Queen Helene revelled in hers. I'd been thinking about a lighter design, something that would allow movement but still deflect a blow in a melee. Being able to create and adjust such a thing in real-time was a luxury because I made it exactly how I wanted it.

In a flash, I was covered with light plate armour around my shoulders, torso and legs. I made it with gaps around my hips and knees so I could twist, run and jump without restriction.

The demon lords leered at us.

"What are they waiting for?" I muttered, flexing my fingers. Lightning skittered around my arms, keen to be put to work. Under me, Razor took an eager step forward. In the far right of the field I made out the red crescent moon standard. I trusted Daxian and the other fae to make a beeline straight for Naxon.

The Reaper was no where in sight. I glanced up at the sky, expecting to see that green chariot whip around. I had set a lightning trap above us, aimed right for his magic. But I'd done the same at Black Court, so he no doubt would be ready for that.

Lysander opened his mouth to reply to my question, but I raised a hand and aimed it at the first demon lord on the front lines.

There was a flash, and the demon lord toppled over and fell right off his mounts.

I guess the Reaper didn't think I'd be so bold as to be on the front lines. Well, bad luck for them.

The demons took a breath to register what happened before one of their lords gave a cry, and whipped his snargbeast with a roar. The demons took that as permission to surge forward.

So it began.

I kicked Razor into a canter, gripping onto his mane, and he leapt forward eagerly. Lysander and Jerali flanked me, kicking their stallions into a gallop. One of the demons let out a signal of red magic into the air and cries came from high above us as winged demons plunged to attack.

The archery command at the back of our lines was given the order to release, and a shower of arrows shot through the air.

I'd never ridden to war, never ridden a warhorse or fought in a chaos like this. But there was a hunger inside of me that spurred me on and gave me a fire to protect my city. Heat tore through me as I registered exactly how many demons had come to take my kingdom. My heart leapt into my mouth and I let out a fierce cry.

We hit the front lines of the demon army with a savagery I'd never born witness to. My lightning blade flashed, and demons were blown backwards.

Razor kicked and bit at a snargbeast, and I stabbed the demon lord riding it right through the chest, sending him careening out of his saddle.

Demons screamed and shrieked, humans cried out. Next to me, Lysander chopped a vicious seven-foot-tall demon down. On my other side, Jerali Jones was like a tornado, whipping through enemies faster than any of them could see coming.

It was mad, mad chaos, and it made me think of Drake.

*Where was he?*

As demons were cut down, the bodies only created obstacles that I could easily trip over, and I was glad for my flexible armour. I was relentless with my lightning sword, but even my energy was not limitless. On the demons came, new breeds and species I'd not seen before. Tall blue muscular ones, flat-faced canary yellow horrors who bit with their teeth and slashed with their claws. Demon lords with black armour and one with a flaming mace that struck down one of my warriors with a crack to the head.

How many were there? How long would this go on for? The

demons stretched back as far as I could see, and in the dark, it was hard to make out their exact numbers, except to know there were too many. Jerali was at my side, eyes darting around as if the same thing was on the General's mind. Jerali cut down a demon at my back. I beheaded a slimy one just in front.

To my left, Lysander and Slade were chopping a demon lord off his snargbeast.

Far to the right of the field, fae magic flew, green and lethal, striking and killing where it landed. I hoped Naxon was on the receiving end of that.

Blood splattered, someone screamed, steel met steel.

"How many?" I cried to Jerali.

The shouts and shrieks almost drowned my General's voice out, but I heard "too many!" easily enough.

"Saraya, I think you should head inside the palace!" Lysander cut down a flat-headed demon with an enemy axe he'd picked up. "The Reaper is bound to be around here—"

"Where's Drake?" I cried. "If he's here—"

"Leave it, Saraya," Lysander cried, ducking as a flying reptile swooped down for him.

I blasted it with lighting, and it shrieked before skidding to the ground behind us.

"I'm fine!" I cried back angrily. "You guys just—"

Something dark in the sky caught my gaze. I frowned up at it —almost like a dark cloud, although the night sky had been clear moments before.

"Watch out!" Jerali called.

Slade picked up a fallen spear and shot it into the air. It hit something, and it came careening down.

Suddenly the sky was full of shrieks. It wasn't a cloud at all.

The horde of flying demons was shooting down towards us, their sharp beaks leading the way. I threw a shield of lightning above us just in time to have thirty reptile-like demons sizzle noisily into it. The smell of burnt flesh flooded my nose.

Lysander swore.

"We're not prepared for an air attack like this!" Jerali cried. "We don't have enough archers!"

My sister, I thought. My sister was the best archer I knew. Luckily she was not here. Perhaps she'd heeded my warning after all.

From high above us, there came a high pitched cry. I prepared to launch another shield above our forces but the cry was distinctly different. Shapes shifted in the dark, metal glinted. Alarmed, everyone looked upwards.

"Sky Court!" a fae warrior shouted. "It's the fucking Sky Guard!"

Relief poured through me as readily as surprise. The Sky Queens had explicitly said they wouldn't get involved.

Winged fae in armour shouted battle cries and speared the flying demons with crystal blades. A wild scream sang through the air, and I got the vision of navy hair streaming through the sky before a winged demon let out a guttural scream.

*High Queen Leena.*

Then Chalamey Springfoot was zooming towards me on the back of a rainbow-coloured bird. He was wearing armour custom fit to his small body, complete with a tiny helmet of gold, small wings attached to the temples. His purple eyes were set on me.

"Run, Your Highness!" Chalamey screamed, waving his sword. "He's—"

A dark green spark of light shot through the night sky.

Jerali grabbed my arm.

Magical hands grabbed my consciousness—not just my consciousness but my physical body too. I looked around for

help. Lysander, his face bloody, was wildly making his way
towards me.

"What's wrong?" Jerali shouted, cutting down a gangling
blood red demon.

"It's the Reaper!" I shouted back, swiping my lightning blade
in a blast that sent several demons shooting backwards. I shook
my head, trying to fight the sensation. "He's trying to—"

I hurled up my shields, but it was useless. The Reaper
swatted it away like it was made of cotton. He reached for me,
grabbing me again.

Where was my mate?

"No!" I screamed. "DRAKE!"

And then I was flying.

# 3 7
# DRAKE

I n that shadowy darkness of unconsciousness, a light appeared, far too bright and painful on my retinas. I squinted as a figure approached me from a distance.

As it solidified, I recognised turquoise eyes, a strong face encased by a black beard. He wore robes of white, and he looked upon me with an expression I was not used to seeing on his face: concern.

It was Wyxian, the fae who'd given his seed to birth me.

His eyes were serious. "You're here far too early, Drakus," he said simply.

I supposed I should explain. "I had to give my magic up for—"

"I know," he interrupted. "I've been watching." Then, after a moment of silence, "You have to make a decision."

"It doesn't seem like I have much of a choice," I pointed out. "My magic has been pulled out, I'm empty."

"If that were the case, you would be dead already. You might be a monster, Drakus, the son of a Goddess, but you are also my son. A part of my heritage lives in you. A part of you is Dark-cleaver."

A slither of something dark prowled up my spine. "You never claimed me as yours," I reminded him.

He nodded gravely. "And I regret that. I resented your mother for tricking me. She bedded me for the purpose of conceiving you. But that was not your fault."

I stilled. Went so still I thought I would disappear into the ether. "What are you saying?"

"I'm saying you are my son and that the Darkcleaver name is yours. If you want it. If you accept me as your father."

His voice held a cadence of such sincerity that it shocked me, struck me in the gut as if a fire wraith had punched me.

When I didn't reply, he said quietly, "Something in you is keeping you alive. It's not your magic but someone else's."

I felt into my body, but all that remained was Glacine's sickly green, pulsing poison. "I took on a poison to save someone else." It had been made to keep Saraya's father, King Eldon, incapacitated.

"Well, this poison is keeping you alive, but it's also warping your brain. If you accept your Darkcaleaver heritage, you'll open a pathway of magic that belonged to us when we were granted that name. You come from a line of kings, Drakus. And with that comes certain privileges."

"Which is?"

"We cleave through the dark. You'll cut through that which is hurting you."

I nodded slowly. "But once that's done, I'll have no magic. I've given it all away to make the Darkmaul Dagger."

Wyxian smiled. "You are the son of a *Goddess*, Drake. You don't think your body has been regenerating itself even as we've been speaking? The monster in you is a survivor. It won't be defeated by the *simple removal of a bone.*" His eyes glimmered as if he were laughing at my folly. "I forget how young you are, sometimes. You were always so…capable, so sure of yourself."

I'd spent the first decade of my life fantasising about my mysterious fae king father, who would one day save me from my wild life. After I'd met him, I'd spent the next decade trying to *forget* that he was my father. That last time I'd even used that title was the night he'd been murdered. And before that, when he'd made me Commander, I'd seen on his face he intended to use me, but never love me. But now? I looked at him then. Really looked at him. Perhaps there was more of him in me than I had originally thought. Now he was looking at me in a way he never had when he was living. His eyes shone brightly with raw emotion. I thought I'd never see this day, shoving that hope far back into my mind to avoid that pain of rejection. But perhaps it was worth trying it out again. "Thank you… Father."

He smiled at me and my heart leapt into my throat. "I'm your father. It is my responsibility to help you up when you fall."

*You come from a line of kings.*

My father said the words I'd wanted him to say since I was a ten-year-old child, attending his court for the first time.

"Drakus Darkcleaver, you are my son. You have always been my son."

Something in me unravelled. It was a tiny knot, but it had sat in the centre of me since that day I'd been turned away from my father.

Then from so far away it felt like a different universe completely, through time and space, I heard Saraya calling my name. Her voice was laced with fear…and desperation.

Blind rage erupted from my core and suddenly I was pure fire. That storm in my mind that made me insane returned with full force, knocking any humanity within me sideways.

And it brought out that vicious, burning, monster in me. The one who had leapt into the mouth of an ancient fire wraith and killed it with my bare hands.

Immediately, pins and needles began in my feet, as if the life were coming back into them. The sensation rapidly spread upwards. A torrent of magic surged through me and I snarled.

My father smiled.

I woke up with a start. Saraya's screams were louder now, pounding in my ears. Looking down at my forearm, my skin pinched as the jagged wound rapidly knitted itself together. Underneath it, I saw fresh bone solidifying.

Son of a Goddess indeed. Perhaps I'd have to go and thank my mother too. Fluffy began rapidly licking my face and I pushed him gently off me. I cast my eye around. The Darkmaul Dagger was not here. But—

"Drakus?" Clementine Eyesmith's form stared at me in surprise. She stood up from where she'd been sitting cross legged on the floor beside me.

I growled at her as my bestial form took full control of me, my mind a red stormy haze. A state of mind that I had not succumbed to since Saraya had rejected me. I wanted blood. I wanted death. It was a call for blood, a call for breaking bones, and it was a call for the end to the Green Reaper

Clementine smiled as if she knew. She raised her chin. "The Fae King has the dagger. Go to the Reaper and tell him I said hello."

I grabbed Fluffy, looked him dead in the eye, and growled as clearly as my voice would allow me. "Opal. Go."

Fluffy growled in agreement, leapt to the ground and shot out of the tent.

I jumped from Daxian's pallet and, tearing through the tent, I roared my mate's name into the night.

# 38
# SARAYA

When I was pulled into the sky, I knew it was not by the hands of any flying demon nor anyone from Sky Court. The look on Chalamey Springfoot's face when he screamed at me was one of sheer horror.

The battlefield had been outside of the patchy astral projection of the Temari Blade. The Reaper had been able to grab me through my one weakness—the wounds on my back. Invisible, magical claws dug into those old wounds, and I screamed in agony as they were torn open. My hands reflexively filled with lightning, but the burning across my back made it fizzle out before I could even try and launch an attack.

My vision went dark—either from the Reaper or the sheer torrent of pain I was in.

He pulled me through the air, wind and cold assaulting my face and arms. And then I was falling. My stomach leapt into my mouth, and I landed with a crash.

Pain splintered through me, raw and tearing. My skin was scraped across the cold stone. I blinked my eyes open and saw with horror that I was at the top of the palace, sprawled across

313

the stone roofing. Before us lay the city of Quartz, the astral projection of the Temari Blade glittering around it. But there were holes in that shield—holes that were not visible from the ground.

My throat tightened up, and I angrily punched the stone with the bloody fist.

"This way, we can still see the battle," called the Reaper's voice.

I snapped my gaze upwards to see the Reaper in a green chariot flying through the air led by two winged zekar warhorses just as beastly and vicious as Razor. One of them was injured, a long cut across his neck and I looked upon the poor creature with dismay. My lightning traps had not been for him.

Inside the chariot was the Reaper in his handsome, fae form, and by his side was Glacine in full plate armour. They came to a shaky landing, and I had to scramble back to avoid getting trod on by those might zekar hooves. The zekar tossed their heads as the Reaper and Glacine sauntered off the chariot, but it was not at either of them that drew my horrified gaze.

On the top of the chariot were two spikes, and one held the severed head of a man who looked like a younger version of my father—Uncle Ansel. The second spike sat empty and waiting. I turned away, resisting the urge to heave, my heart tearing into two. I clutched my stomach and stumbled as far away from the chariot and these people as I could get, but my legs were jelly after the long fall onto the stone, and I crumpled onto my hands and knees.

"My, my, Saraya," sneered Glacine. "Haven't you made a mess?"

"I've done nothing," I choked "You're—"

"All of this, Saraya," the Reaper said, crouching down in front of me. "Is because you refuse to be my Tyaag." His handsome face surveyed my body. "You would really destroy your entire Kingdom based on principle?"

*That* gave me the burst of energy I needed to heave myself onto feet and stepped away from him. "How dare you come here and act as if you're trying to save us?"

"I am the only ruler of this realm, Saraya," the Reaper said simply, his handsome features twisting into a grin. "And I will destroy anyone who gets in the way of my power. Including you. But I am giving you one last chance." He held a single finger up. "Just one."

I gritted my teeth and manifested my lightning sword. The Reaper sighed. Without moving a further muscle, my entire body went rigid.

"My Ellythian Princess," the Reaper sighed. "I could kill you right now, and not a single person would neither know nor care."

His hold on me was like steel. I wasn't strong enough to beat him. My head was spinning, my heart sitting like a black stone in my chest. Where was Drake?

"Plenty of people care," I gritted out.

"But they could do nothing. Against me, they are just as powerless as you. Even your Drakus. Where is he, anyhow? I assumed he'd be by your side, just waiting for me."

Still unable to move, I just clenched my jaw and glared at him. My mind raced. How the hell was I going to get out of this? We had no Darkmaul Dagger, no Drake, and no Temari Blade. I had no help either—by the looks of it, did anyone even know where I was?

My Ellythian warriors would still be inside the city walls, fighting off any astral demons. They might not have had the time to look up here and see me. Perhaps Lysander, Slade, or Jerali had followed. Even then, it would take them time to get here from the midst of battle. And then what? They couldn't come up against him.

Perhaps I could give off a signal to alert them. Drake would be able to hunt me down immediately, though he probably didn't know I'd been taken

Irritated, I could only wrack my brains for some other solution.

But Glacine, then speaking with a tone I'd never heard her use before, confused me. With a sort of whine, she said, "When will I get my turn?"

The Reaper cast an annoyed look at her. "Soon, my love, soon."

Glacine pursed her lips angrily, and like a petulant child accusing a parent, she whined, "You said as soon as we had her and if she refused, I would get what I want!"

The Reaper stared at me for a moment and I actually thought he looked like he wanted to strike her. Instead, he said quietly, "Then let it be done. You may begin the ritual." Glacine smirked as she got her way, but the Reaper blocked my view of her by striding toward me and roughly grasping my chin in a cold hand. The smell of burnt flesh filled my nose, but even if I wanted to gag I couldn't.

His green swirling eyes penetrated mine, and he spoke with the ferocity of a monster claiming its prey. "I am going to take over Lobrathia," he said. "Then I will take every ounce of Quartz you have and move onto Kaalon. Before you die, I want you to know that your attempt to beat me failed, and failed miserably. The Order of Temari will die with you and your six others. The demons will win, and the fae will serve under me for the rest of their lives."

"You need a Tyaag," I rasped. "That's what you need. And Drake is still alive. You'll never kill him."

"That's where you're wrong!" Glacine snarled, stepping up to me. "I'm going to take your power. I will be a Tyaag and the Reaper and I will rule over this land."

She'd wanted my power. All along, she'd been trying to leech off me, trying to get to it and all I'd done was force my true power deeper and deeper.

"We just need it to come out," Glacine said matter of factly. "And it is clear that force is necessary." She reached into the chariot and brought out a long length of leather.

I stared at her in shock. "You can't be serious, Glacine," I said dumbly.

A vicious, satisfied smile curved her pink lips. "On your knees, Saraya."

The Reaper released me from the magical hold and I stumbled forward at the sudden lack of force. But a magical foot kicked my feet out from under me, and I landed awkwardly on my knees once again, pain shooting up my thighs. My armour disappeared with a tiny puff of wind, the back of my undershirt torn open. The feeling of cold, biting air on my damaged back made a torrent of sheer terror cover me like an icy ocean wave.

The sight of Glacine holding that whip flipped a switch inside of me and at once, I was immobilised.

"Weakness," hissed the Reaper, his handsome face twisting with disgust. "What kind of ruler quakes in fear by the sight of a simple weapon?"

My heart crumbled inside of me. My legs had transformed into stone, my brain moved like sludge.

Suddenly pain tore across my back, the sound of the whip on my flesh temporarily blinding me. The weight of shame made my head hang down of its own accord. My insides were screaming, but my body would not move.

What kind of warrior was I?

Another strike resounded in my ears, and I sagged with defeat.

Another strike, and I was numb.

My people, my poor, poor Kingdom.

Another strike, and I was vaguely aware that someone was trying to knock on the door to my mind.

*No.* If it was the Reaper, I could not let him in. That would be the end of me. No one could see this. No one should know what I really was.

This time, I could *feel* Glacine yanking on my magic through each strike. I could feel the slow flow towards her. I imagined her red quartz necklace glowing with my power.

The strikes were coming quicker now. My mind shut down, steel bars clamping down on my brain. If I allowed that colossal pain into my awareness, it would kill me. It was too potent, too raw. I knew my skin was being torn to shreds. I knew I was actively bleeding. I knew I was losing blood. She was carving up the skin of my back with her whip, making a portrait of my failures, my defeat. How I'd let down everyone. I'd let down Altara, Drake, Jerali, my mother, my father. Uncle Ansel.

That pain was a red wall of fire at the side of my vision.

"It's not working!" Glacine snapped.

"Try a little more," the Reaper said lazily.

Numb. Numb. Numb. It was the only way out. I imagined Drake's face, his smile, the way his face changed when he looked at me. The way his fingers would trace the planes of my body. The way he made love.

"It's not enough." Glacine was panting. The assault on my back paused a moment. "We need a stronger incentive."

*Oh no.*

"Bring them, my Lord."

But I couldn't turn around. I couldn't think, couldn't move

any of the muscles on my body. Because if I did, that relentless agony on my back was going to tear my soul open. I would go insane.

There was a flash behind me and a gurgling sound, followed by a squeaking cry. My heart plummeted into my stomach.

Nothing on heaven or earth could have made me move in that moment except the sound of a crying infant. Slowly, gingerly, I placed my knuckles on the ground and willed my body to turn.

Glacine bounced a baby in her arms. "Who's this now?" she cooed.

I recognised Bluebell's little girl, Destiny, immediately.

I screamed in a voice that I didn't even recognise.

Lightning shot out of me, swirling and violent and struck Glacine. At the same time, I surged forwards, kicking her violently aside and yanking Destiny to safety in my arms. Holding her close, I crouched down as a storm of power erupted from me. Destiny buried her face in my neck, and I squeezed my eyes shut against the onslaught of sheer rage that erupted from my very bones. Every strike of that whip had collected inside of me, and I released it all out now, manifested as white hot lightning.

It swirled around me like a shield, as if it were a tornado made of lightning, and I was in its eye.

Then quite abruptly, something in me shifted and everything went dark and silent.

I found I could breathe again, my chest wall loosening, my throat unclenching. When I opened my eyes, I found myself in that humid, bloody well in the centre of my wounds. Blood dripped sluggishly around me.

Before me, *she* stared at me, her eyes glowing blue-white, her chest heaving, her wrists straining against her bonds of tendons and cartilage.

*Let us go,* she roared. *Let us be free. I will kill our enemies, I will slash their throats and drink their blood. I will tear their hearts open and sing with the sounds of their pain. Release us, and we will tear the world apart, limb by limb.*

I could still feel Destiny whimpering into my neck. I held out my hand and summoned my sword.

Nothing happened.

Alarmed, I looked at my hand, summoned my power and tried to manifest my sword.

Nothing happened.

*She* growled at me. *Do it.*

I shook my head as sick realisation crawled through me, a corpse, dragging itself to the grave. "I can't."

## 39
# DRAKE

E very demon in my path was dead before they even saw me coming. Saraya's scream had sent me into a blind rage. The bestial storm in the corner of my mind had returned full force.

I was only vaguely aware of the fae and humans fighting and dying around me. All I wanted to do was cut a path of death towards my Saraya and destroy the being who had made her scream. But first, I knew I needed something. A weapon I had made out of my own body—and it drew me in like a fish on a hook.

The colours had also returned in full force. I executed the dark colours, snapping necks, cutting throats, pulling out hearts.

Blood splattered my face and flesh collected under my fingernails, but all I did was rage against that feeling of Saraya being taken away from me.

I followed my own scent across the battlefield, flinging someone away, grabbing his sword and cutting something else down. Screams resonated in my ears and it made my heart smile.

Throats gurgled, demons screamed, souls left bodies.

My eyes found it then, like a beacon in the distance.

*My kinsman.* I concentrated to make out the words he was using.

"Drake!" he cried. "Catch!"

Something flashed through the air like a spear, bloody and white. I leapt up and snatched out of the air, at the same time bashing a creature that had flown towards me. The weapon, with the power of my entire being inside of it, vibrated in my hands.

Now, I had to get Saraya.

The energy of the battle was shifting, with the losing side being my mate's people. Vaguely I knew I should care, but I just could not bring myself to. My mate was my life, I could only care about her.

Roaring angrily as a demon tried to stop me, I cut and stabbed, slashing and destroying until I was at the front of the city gate and the battle was behind me. People were shouting for me, but still I moved on. My kinsman was following me, slashing at our enemies as he went.

*My mate.*

*My mate.*

*My mate.*

I waited for the city to open for me, but a shifting in the west caught my attention and I turned that way instead. My ears picked up the sound of many feet—not feet—the legs of beasts, hooves, four-legged creatures on the road to Quartz harbour. I stilled in front of the gate, staring, waiting. My kinsman waited beside me.

"What is it?" he asked.

Friend or foe to my mate?

Would I have to destroy these new entrants to the field?

I turned to look at my kinsman, trying to see through the fire wreathed storm clouds banging inside the folds of my brain. I concentrated on his scent, familiar to me, *almost* but not quite the same. I needed my humanity so I could think properly for my mate. I squeezed my eyes shut and my inner gaze was flooded with the vision of Saraya, those green eyes looking back at me sternly. I remembered a time when she had put her hands on either side of my face to try and get me to focus.

*Come back, Drake*, she would say to me. *Come back to me.*

The fire died down, the rain lessened, the clouds faded just a touch. Just enough so I knew that it was Daxian standing by my side, panting, his eyepatch stained with black demon ichor. I concentrated again on the wild force that was rapidly moving towards us from the harbour road.

The scent on the wind was different. Salt and sand. They'd come from the coast. By ship, I guessed, some of them had swum in. But another scent was under that. Something dark like the quiet parts of the ocean, something wild like the untamed jungles of tropics. Sweet and sour. And Blood. Old blood. *That* had me excited.

I prowled irritably and waited for them, Daxian shifting with adrenaline beside me.

The pounding of feet grew louder and louder, and just as I was ready to start fighting again, I saw them.

Not human, nor fae, nor demon. The magic was mixed— twined together like vines until you couldn't tell which part was which.

Beasts. A horde of gigantic, ferocious beasts. Similar to me in the way they were monstrous but dissimilar in that *I* was still in my own body. These beasts bore two hearts. One animal, one seemingly a variation of the fae. Large incisors dripping with blood, fur matted with demon ichor, vicious snouts, big claws. More monster than animal. Behind them were brown-skinned

Ellythian warriors astride horses in magical armour, wielding glimmering blades.

But one of the newcomers made me pause and the archers on the city battlements began shouting. A light cracked through the darkness, and what I saw shocked me. There was a young woman riding on the back of one of beasts coming towards us.

The snarling beast—kingly in his bearing, dark in his aura, was all muscle and fangs in a black and gold body, came to a stop right in front of me. The rest of the beasts continued past us onto the battlefield.

I couldn't help but stare.

The woman astride the beast looked much like my wife, except she was shorter, her hair straight and much longer than Saraya's. I had seen her only once before in this very palace.

Her beast looked like it wanted to jump forward and eat me. Excitement pumped through my veins.

I cleared my throat and found my voice. This was important. For Saraya, I could will my mind into submission. I needed thought, not instinct here.

"Altara Voltanius?" I asked, noticing the male beast protectively appraising me, I took a step back. I would not like another male coming close to my mate either.

"You are my brother-in-law." Her voice was like music, soft but moving. A smile of realisation spread across her lips. "Drakus Silverhand!"

But something mischievous glinted in her eye... and so did the mating mark she bore on her right hand. I pointed, "Is that—"

"There will be much to discuss later," she said quickly, "because—" light flashed, and in her hands now lay a gigantic bow of heavy solid gold, intricately detailed with lotuses and vines. Daxian inhaled sharply next to me. The smile disappeared from Altara's lips and was replaced by a look of such fierce determination that the monster in me stood to attention. "We have work to do, Drakus Silverhand."

The colours of the two of them—woman and beast—mingled and caressed one another. Her mate growled in approval.

I nodded. "My mate has been taken by the Reaper."

Altara nodded. "Lead the way, brother-in-law—" she hesitated, then gave a swift bow from where she sat. "And, Your Majesty."

Daxian bowed back.

So I did as she asked and bolted into the city, knowing that Altara's almighty beast of a mate was likely to keep up with mine and Daxian's speed. My mate's magic was all over the city, glints of her purple shining from the crevices and cracks. It only made me pine for her more.

We passed Sarone and Elya, who stared at me in shock before running along after us, their astral blades in hand. I frowned at that but realised what it must mean. I could see the shield around the city myself—it had holes in it like the famous Blossom Court cheese. I bolted on, following Saraya's scent.

But we came to a stop at the palace, and I saw immediately where she was.

"Dear Goddess!" Altara exclaimed. "What is that?"

At the top of the palace, a gigantic swirling ball of lightning had erupted. It moved vigorously around a central point, like a tornado.

"It's Saraya's power," I said in a low voice. "She's made a shield. What do you know of her Ellythian powers?"

Her emerald gaze searched mine, trying to understand.

"It's buried in the wounds of her back. Glacine and the Reaper knew it before us."

The beast gave a growl, and Altara looked down as if they were speaking. Their magic moved and pulsed between them.

Quickly, I explained what Sarone had told me about their Ellythian family's power. But Altara was nodding as if she understood that already.

"Can you tune into her?" she asked. "Her mental state must be in protection mode if she's summoned a shield like *that.*"

I looked back at the glowing ball of lightning, feeling Sarone and the other Ellythian warriors finally catch up with us. Reaching outwards, I came up against a wall of Saraya's magical defences. It was tumultuous. She was in pain—great physical and emotional pain.

Rage tore through me, and I stepped forward, my shadow wings eager to burst out of me. But I paused, because there was no way I could get through that lethal swirling electricity. Saraya was a Niyati. She could very well kill me.

And she didn't even know that yet.

Daxian stepped forward and I shook my head at him. He nodded. "I can see through it." He tapped his eye patch in explanation. "She's on her knees, there's a little human baby in her arms. Her eyes are shut. I don't even think she knows what she's doing. The Reaper is trying to get through it."

Altara blanched.

I could scent two-winged zekar on the wind as well as two other scents I was more than familiar with, as well as the baby. The Reaper was up there and so was Glacine.

I clutched the bone in my hand. We needed to spear the Reaper together. I needed her to get out of that lightning vortex.

Reaching out with my mind, I tugged on the mental bond we had and came up against a dense, impenetrable wall. Daxian was right. Saraya felt like she was deep inside herself. Just as she felt when she had delved into her wounds to free her true power.

Perhaps she was doing the same again. But there was a faint clawing there too. I realised she was trying to do what she had spent all of yesterday trying.

She wanted to cut herself free but was struggling.

"She feels stuck," I said, confused. "Why would she be stuck in there?"

Sarone stepped up next to me, squinting up at the swirling ball. "I think she's exhausted her power. That's an incredible amount of magic she's using right now."

At Black Court, she'd burnt herself out, according to what the others had told me. She'd used too much lightning. And here again, she'd spent it all protecting the city and then again fighting. It was burning her up. This wouldn't be happening if her Niyati power was unbound.

"She needs more juice," Altara nodded. "She needs to free herself and release that power. But she needs *more*." She looked at me as if knowing what I was going to say. "But it can't be anyone else's power. It has to be hers."

Altara cast her eye about the city behind us. "It's almost as if Saraya's power is etched all over the city. I'd never noticed that before."

"She's an Ellythian midwife," Elya piped up. "I saw it when we first came in and knew straight away. We put a little of ourselves into each patient we heal. She's saved so many of the city's women that a little of her exists everywhere."

Realisation tore through me like a spear of light. That was why I was seeing her all over the place, it made complete sense.

"Can we draw it out? Give it back to her?" I asked.

Altara's eyes lit up. She raised her hand, and out flashed an arrow. Instead of a sharp tip, it bore a crescent moon on its end. "I have an astral arrow that shoots through space. If I can draw out the magic, I can collect it into the arrow and shoot it into her.

That'll give her the boost she needs to get out of her own wounds."

Elya clapped. "We need to gather the city's women then! All of them!"

"Run door to door," I ordered the Ellythians. "Tell the mothers of the city that their queen needs their help."

"There won't be anyone in the houses," Sarone said wryly. "They're all on the battlements."

Of course they were, I thought. The women of the city take after Saraya.

As the Ellythian warriors sprinted toward the city gate, I bolted to the first person I knew who held sway over the women of the city.

AGATHA SORTED THROUGH THE CROWD OF GATHERING WOMEN. THEY were of all ages, from teenagers to women with silver hair and hunched backs. All of them were armed and more than half had babies on their hip or tied to their backs. They all stared up at the lightning globe of Saraya's protection.

Altara stood up on the back of her mate and whispers broke out immediately.

"Princess Altara!" someone cried.

"Oh, my God, it is! Princess!"

Altara's mate, the beast, let out a low growl which made everyone shut up.

"I'm back to help!" Altara called. "Up there—" she pointed up to Saraya's glowing orb of turning lighting "—Saraya fights a battle with the demon emperor. But she can't do this alone."

As quickly as she could, Altara instructed the women to gather into a large circle.

"Each of you Saraya has *ever* healed or helped with her magic in pregnancy or birth, hold a tiny little part of her power inside of you. I want you to release it now, into this." She held up the crescent moon arrow. "All you have to do is think about her. Think about the time she helped you or your daughter or someone you know. Hold that thought your mind like a prayer. Hold tight and I will gather it. Can you do that?"

"Yes!" a woman cried, pushing her way desperately forward. She was young, still a teenager, but she clutched a babe to her chest as if her life depended on it. There was a wild, red-rimmed look in her eyes. "The Reaper has taken my little girl! I'll do anything to help Saraya kill him!"

"Yeah!" the crowd chimed back. Women nodded, murmuring in assent. So we knew whose baby it was up there.

"Alright then." Altara said, still on the back of her mate, "Hold hands with your neighbour and let's do this."

When the women began holding hands with one another, Daxian and I stepped a little backwards, the fierce eyes of Altara's beastly mate never taking his eyes off us. I gave him a nod, and he nodded back.

Altara then held the astral arrow between both her palms as if in prayer and closed her eyes. And then I felt it. Soft magic began to gather in the air above the crowd of women. To my monstrous eyes it glittered and spun, danced and twirled. But as it gathered, its quality began to change. It evolved into something wilder, darker, fiercer. The women of the city frowned and tensed as they too, felt magic zooming around them. Altara began pulling on it, drawing towards, her gathering into the crescent moon arrow she held between her palms.

The women of the city gave a piece of themselves for her. I saw it as tiny purple points of light, like stars, glittering through the air as they soared towards Altara. The princess gathered it towards the arrow, her magic filling the air with sweet pink sincerity laced with heavy power. Dazed by the colours and the sheer display of love for my mate, it came as a great shock when Altara opened her eyes and summoned her gigantic golden bow. It was already strung, and with what I guess was enormous strength, she hefted it up easily.

She knocked the astral arrow on the golden bow and set her chin. And as she looked up at the ball of lightning that held her sister, a single tear slid down her cheek. To my surprise, she then closed her eyes.

And with perfect form, she loosed the arrow.

The crowd gasped loudly as we all watched the glowing arrow soar, carried on its own magic, towards the top of the palace and slide straight through Saraya's glowing orb. I had never seen this done before. I'd heard about it in old fae stories, where ancient archers could shoot arrows impossible distances. But I never imagined I'd ever get to see something like this in my lifetime.

The two other energies on the palace roof shifted in surprise. I clenched the bone still in my hand.

A sudden idea struck me. "Altara," I said, moving forward. "Do you think you can do that one more time but for someone else?"

# 40
## SARAYA

I was trying to claw my way out of my own body, but the emptiness I was coming up against was telling me that my magic had run out.

My true source of power strained before me, her bonds stretching, cutting deep marks into her wrists, making her bleed. The power emanating from her in sparks of lightning was so strong it made my own breath come in gasps.

My power was running out because of the massive shield I'd put up around us.

Something struck me like a gong, and I was thrown onto my backside. Bluebell's baby was still safe in my arms, but my body felt like it was vibrating from a blast of—

Frowning, I turned my awareness to my body, which felt as if my own magic had been blasted into me. I glittered with hundreds of points of purple light. While they were both foreign and familiar, each one felt slightly different to my magical sight.

Heat tore through me.

At the height of every labour, just before the cervix is fully dilated, comes what we call the transition. It's the dark night that comes before the dawn. The moment when the terror comes.

We don't know why it happens. But something opens in a woman. All her primal fears and her deep rooted anxieties come out in that moment. She wants to hide in a safe corner and never come out. She wants it all to end.

But what she doesn't know in that moment is that she needs the women around her to help get her through. To hold her in their arms, kiss her hair and tell her that she is not alone. That she can do this. That the baby is almost here. That the final hour has come.

Then come the guttural groans of a baby being pushed down into the birth canal. It's terrifying, but midwives know it comes before the light. That's when a woman must trust herself to handle anything that comes.

Power surged through me now, painful and ridden with bursting energy. Moments filled with screams, moans, pain. But it came on the wings of a song. A melody as old as time, the timbre of pain, the baritone of courage and the chorus of pure love and acceptance. My heart filled to bursting.

Amongst it all, I heard Agatha's voice in my ear.

*"What do we tell our women, Saraya? When the pain comes?"* It felt like I *saw* her beady blue eye fixed on me. Accusing, stern.

"Let it come," I whispered, "With the knowledge that it will go."

*"Let it come,"* Agatha said, nodding, *"because we are here with you. We'll face it together."*

I looked at the source of my power, sitting bloodthirsty and nodding eagerly in front of me. Her wild hair swayed as she beckoned me with her chin, her arms crackled with a scattering of bright light.

*"Fall into it,"* Agatha's voice said from the void. *"Let it come. Go into the dark."*

Bluebell's voice, Chirra's sweaty face, Fessima's pale smile, Trisha's joyous laugh, even Glacine's grimace of pain. Every woman I'd ever helped was a part of me. They were all there in my head, spurring me on.

*Look at your pain, Saraya, and there you will find your freedom.*

"I am a midwife," I whispered. "And I am not afraid of the dark."

I opened my eyes and raised my hand. A heavy hilt slammed into it. Alarmed, I found it was the lapis lazuli hilt of the Temari Blade, Umali's face screaming at me. *Go.* She was saying. *Be the tempest. Be the storm.*

Then Drake's face swam into my vision. Not the way he looked at me when we made love, but that burning tornado of ferocity that had been his face when his power had first been unleashed in Havrok's Court. It was violence incarnate and he'd revelled in it. He'd never been afraid of the damage he would cause.

The Reaper was wrong.

I had been wrong.

I had destroyed an entire Fae Court because it had been the right thing to do.

Drake's soft voice rumbled in my ear. *Sacrificing yourself to protect your family is the noblest thing you can do.* And this entire city was my family. The fate of the entire Human Realm sat with me.

Lightning does not yield. But tonight, I would yield to myself. To my own power.

I looked at her, she looked back at me, and we both grinned.

Surrounded by the faces of the women of the city, with the

Temari Blade humming in my hand, I slashed at her bonds of cartilage and blood.

Light flared, lightning sparked, a feral scream resounded in my ears. It hit me with all the force of a raging storm.

Pure, violent, raw energy. My head rang with it, my blood sang with it, and my magic exploded outwards. Something inside my very soul unlocked.

My mind became a haze of red.

For the first time, I knew what Drake went through when he turned bestial.

I wanted blood. And I would have it. But first, I looked at my surroundings, the broken flesh and tissue prison. Allowing my magic to lift me up, lightning prickled under my skin. I looked down and saw that my skin was laced with strands of lightning, crackling and fizzing excitedly.

But I needed to heal myself first.

Bringing myself up through the deep wounds, I knitted them together, piece by piece. The separated lacerations met in the middle and at their seam, light burst forth. One by one, each long wound joined together, flesh was made whole.

When I was done, I looked at the smooth, healed skin of my back and snarled in approval.

Destruction would happen tonight.

I opened my physical eyes.

Still inside that whirling vortex of bright power, I was holding Destiny close to me. Carefully, I set her down and put a layer of protection over her.

Rising to my feet, I raised my hand and lowered my lightning vortex. It went out with a whisper.

The Reaper was standing there, next to Glacine, and they both stared at me in a sort of shock. But the Reaper didn't miss a beat and came forward smoothly, looking upon me as if I were some marvel to behold. As if I had been made anew. The Temari Blade sat satisfyingly heavy in my fist.

"My Lady," he said, offering me a palm, his green swirling eyes sparking with red. "Will you join me?"

There was no heart beating in his chest. There were no lungs expanding with breath. In my core, I could feel that he was surviving purely on magic alone. As Gods do. As I was now doing. We were the same, he and I. He had been right, back in his astral ballroom. But not in the way he thought. I saw it plain as day, and a thought that had been germinating at the back of my mind now burst into full bloom.

The Ellythian-Fae Guardian of the Temari Blade had called me *Niyati*. It didn't register at the time, perhaps I thought she'd made an error. But of course, she was right. I could see it as plain as day in the crackling destructive force that I now was. *I was a Niyati.*

The cry of a bird came from above, and all of a sudden, I felt my mate above me, his energy like a dark swirling cloud. A feral snarl came from the sky, and Drake was falling towards us, his eyes all black and sparkling with silver as he looked upon me. In his hand was a long white bone. I cocked my head to look at power emanating from it and smiled. My mate. My Tyaag.

But the Reaper immediately shot away.

# 41
# DRAKE

As I flew down onto the stone roof of the palace, my black shadow wings dissolving, Altara's mate gave a cry next to me. He'd transformed into a giant sleek black eagle so seamlessly that I hadn't even been able to see the male beneath. More incredibly, Altara had managed to astride him the entire time.

But now, I only had eyes for my mate—

Who looked almost like the Goddess Umali herself. Her skin was laced with rivulets of lighting, coiling around every limb, crackling and bursting with power. Her eyes were lit up with glowing blue light all way around so I could not see any iris. The air vibrated with her power. A Niyati had been unlocked today.

She was the most beautiful thing I had ever seen and it was all I could do to not fall at her feet.

And I smelled the fear of the Reaper as readily as I smelled Glacine's.

I had made a beeline for the Reaper but he'd shot off as soon as he'd seen me.

But Saraya was quicker.

With a force I had not thought possible, my beautiful mate darted after him, snagging him by the neck just as he tried to disappear into the ether. His body was forced to solidify as her lightning-laced fingers lit up his neck and he tensed as if having a seizure. He shook violently before the illusion of his handsome fae self fell away, and his real form began to take over.

Swinging around, he punched her in the jaw. I snarled, and was about to leap on top of him, but when the punch landed, Saraya merely stood still as if he'd hit concrete. A slow smile graced her precious lips as the Reaper's true form manifested— three pairs of eyes set into that disgusting excuse for a face.

I watched, fascinated, as Saraya held the Reaper in her power like some Goddess of old, and he was rendered utterly defence-less. But then she did something that made me smile

She reached for his face and I could see the Reaper's magic trying to push her violently away. But it could not find purchase as the tempest of electric power simply swatted him away. He could not stop her as she reached into his face and viciously dung her fingers in the middle right eye socket.

The Reaper screamed, but I could only hear it with my magical ears. Saraya pulled out the eye and put it in her pocket. Then she pushed him away.

He staggered backwards, hunched over, clutching his face. And then began the fizzing sound of an assault being generated. The Reaper pulled back, and swirling green magic exploded out from his body. Saraya launched herself into the air just as I darted toward her. She surrounded us both with a lightning shield and the poisonous green magic scattered around it, fizzing out into nothing.

I wasted no time, and neither did the others. Seemingly at once, all of us sent out an attack. I struck the Reaper with a whip of pure blue power. Saraya shot out a stream of lightning so powerful I had to scoot backwards in the air, summoning my shadow wings to keep aflight. Saraya's own magic seemed to be keeping her in the air alongside me as she lit up the palace roof with her assault. Altara, now glittering as if her skin and hair were made of diamonds, was shooting arrows made out of fire at the Reaper, the black eagle keeping her position stationary. The two sisters' magics worked together as the Reaper tried to block their attacks.

A tiny movement caught my eye and I was surprised to see Opal and Fluffy creeping along the side of the roof as if they thought they could not be seen. They were heading straight toward the tiny orb of lightning that was Saraya's shield around the baby the Reaper had brought up here.

But one of the zekar from the chariot suddenly launched himself across the roof, stampeding toward the baby and I turned to see Glacine standing with its harness in her hands, smirking. Just as I was about to intervene, a flash of Opal's magic shot out and the baby disappeared under her illusion. At the same time, Fluffy leapt into the air, straight for the zekar's face. The stallion reared up, but Fluffy was as bloodthirsty as I was and gouged out the zekar's eyes with his teeth. Blood spurted as the zekar let out a terrified sound and began stomping, blind around the roof. Suddenly, Fluffy began vibrating and black smoke billowed out from him, snaking into the zekar's nostrils and seemingly down his throat. The zekar stumbled, choking on the black smoke and fell to the ground with a heavy thud.

Mildly surprised at this new power, I looked away, knowing my two lumzen would take care of the infant while Saraya could not.

The Reaper was struggling under the assault of the Voltanius sisters, who were relentless with their magic. Altara's arrows ran endlessly as her eagle soared in circles around the roof and I gathered my magic too, shooting it toward the Reaper in a third assault. The smell of rotting flesh filled the air strongly now, and the Reaper had fallen to his knees, his black cloak billowing around him.

It was then that Altara let out a cry and took out a glimmering arrow made entirely of glowing blue quartz. Saraya ceased her assault and so did I. Immediately, Altara loosed the quartz arrow right for the Reaper and the arrow split into six, striking each eye socket.

"He won't be able to see now!" Altara cried nodding at us. Her eagle let out a cry and the air vibrated painfully around us. The Reaper screamed, clutching his head.

Saraya turned her lightning eyes to me and nodded, shooting down toward the roof.

But I was ready. I shot behind the Reaper and snapped my Tyaag bone into two on my knee. I tossed one of the pieces over the Reaper's head.

My mate grabbed it, baring her teeth at me, and at the same time, we shoved the pieces into his torso.

It was as if all time stood still. No one breathed.

The Reaper shook violently and the scream that tore from him made my eardrums burn.

He crumpled in on himself and the bone dagger sucked him in like a maelstrom of Tyaag magic. Binding, blocking, keeping. I felt the force it through my own body, my magic recognising the familiar power, and I knew at once the Reaper was done.

The glowing bone turned black, and now fused together, fell to the floor with a heavy thud as if it weighed a tonne.

My mate turned to look upon me and I could not help it any longer. I surged towards her and crushed my lips to hers, holding her tightly. I would never let her go, never. Not in all the lifetimes I had on this earth.

A scream from behind us made us tear ourselves away from each other.

On the other side of the roof was Altara.

# 42
# SARAYA

W hen I turned and saw my sister's beautiful face and form standing nearby, my heart stopped in my chest. I made to run towards her but what I saw stopped me in my tracks. Glacine was on her knees with an arrow in her shoulder. From the wound, a familiar blue poison had seeped through her chest and up the sides of her neck.

I looked back at Drake only to see his chest was smooth and clear. No poison ran beneath it. Somehow they'd transferred the magic into an arrow then into Glacine. The poetry of it made my heart sing. Gleefully I turned and went over to my sister. The gigantic black feathered eagle towered protectively behind her while she, beautiful and strong and older than I remembered her, held Glacine on her knees before us.

"Look what I found, Sara!" Altara said fiercely. "Give me the word, and I'll break her neck." She held Glacine's chin in one hand, her other hand around her neck, ready to kill.

The voice that came from me was unfamiliar—deeper and husky with the weight of my new found power. "No," I said.

"She is mine. She has been mine from the start. Let her up. I will fight her properly."

Glacine glared at me as she got to her feet and, panting with pain, moved into a fighting stance. The blue poison was now seeping up the sides of her face and into her temples. Her time was limited.

"Look," I said and turned around to show her my back, newly healed and mark free. "I am free of you now. Whatever you did to me is long gone. After this, none of us will ever remember you."

Her pale skin went paler, her eyes flashing. But her red quartz necklace lit up as if she wanted to use it.

I smiled at her. "There is a special place in hell for those who take advantage of the kindness of others."

Her magic rose out of her hands, red and angry. I let her use it, just to see what would happen. Her attack simply bounced off me, dissolving into nothing. I smiled at her and she glared back at me.

"Now, you pay for what you did to my family," I snarled. "Now you go to hell where you belong. Now, you lose." She never stood a chance. I summoned the Temari Blade and slashed her throat in one clean strike.

Her eyes widened in shock as she clutched her throat, landing with a thud, her blood spilling onto the stone.

I simply stared at her for a moment. This woman who had such a hold on me for so many years was now staring, eyes glazed over, unseeing, her mouth agape, her lifes-blood draining from her.

I looked up at the sky. "Father, Mother, I fulfilled my vow."

My mate came up from behind me, and I was not prepared for the flood of emotion that shook my body. Altara looked up at me with shining emerald eyes, her magic pulsing powerfully around her. Her voice caught, "I love you, Sister, and I am so glad to see you."

"Altara, my heart, we make our parents proud today."

She nodded, a fierce look in her eye. "I know they are both watching."

I turned and scoped out the roof. Opal popped into view as she let her magic fall away. She was sitting in the lap of Destiny, licking her face as Fluffy stood protectively over them, growling at the other zekar still standing harnessed to the Reaper's chariot.

"That creature was covering the baby's eyes during the attack," Altara said in wonder. "And the black one was covering its ears."

My heart warmed as I strode over to them, quickly pulling Destiny into my arms and straightening her clothes and fussing over her. Opal and Fluffy leapt onto my shoulder and just as I was about to turn around, the roof door slammed open and Bluebell stormed out, followed closely by Sarone, Blythe, and Daxian.

"Oh, Tiny!" Bluebell cried.

I hurried over to them and passed a happy Destiny into her mother's arms.

"Thank you!" Bluebell cried, putting her arm around me.

I shook my head. "The Reaper knew exactly how to get to me. I'm so sorry, Bluey."

"No," she said, looking up at me, tears spilling freely down her flushed cheeks. "Don't be sorry. The fault lies only with him."

My mate murmured behind me, "There is still a demon horde to kill."

I straightened. "Go somewhere safe, Bluey." I nodded to Sarone and Blythe who were looking at me as if I'd grown a second head. I glanced down at my hands, and knew I probably looked a little different. I grinned at them and Sarone wiped a tear from her eye. Opal and Fluffy both bounced after Bluebell.

The gigantic vicious eagle behind Altara gave a cry of agreement. Power poured from him, dark and magnificent. Delighted, I watched as Altara manifested that huge golden bow with a flash into her hands. I grinned at my sister before turning to my mate. "Then let us destroy them."

As the others exited the roof down the way they'd come, Altara jumped onto the black eagle with an ease that suggested she had done it many times before. I barely had time to wonder what type of school she had been to, before she shot up into the air and headed for the field.

My mate reached for me, twisting me around to hold me close, pressing his hard body against mine. He whispered against my neck "My mate, my love, my wife. You are the most precious thing my eyes have ever beheld." Tingling desire shot through me as he grabbed my face and kissed me deeply.

I felt the lightning storm in my mind calm a little as our powers twined around each other, like cats, purring in pleasure. His power stroked my insides and I smiled savagely up at him. I pushed him roughly away from me. "Then catch me."

His all-black eyes flashed as I ran to the edge of the roof, the Temari Blade still in hand. With a gut instinct that called for my power, I leaped off the roof, right into the open night air.

Someone below screamed but my power swept me upwards, lifting me on its own electric current. I grinned with glee as my stomach gave a happy tumble.

Behind me, the dark force that was Drake shot for me, grabbing me around the waist, his dark shadow wings erupting outwards. I cried out happily as he flew us over Quartz city. Below us, Blythe, Sarone, and the other Ellythian Warriors cheered. A hundred or more women had gathered before the palace and I knew at once, who had helped me get out of my flesh and blood prison. I saluted them with my sword and they clapped and wept, running with us toward the city gate.

We followed Altara and the eagle onto the battlefield.

Altara immediately began firing glittering arrows, summoning them out of thin air. Queen Leena, her navy wings dressed in armour, gave a whoop as she saw us, Chalamay close behind her.

From this high up in the air, I could see that the battlefield was a bloody mess. The Sky Guard fought tirelessly and new soldiers made of fangs and fur fought on our side along with the Ellythian contingent Altara must have brought. But still, the demons with their sheer numbers were clearly winning.

My power surged angrily as I spotted Lysander and Slade, Jerali Jones and the other humans blood stained and tired. Jerali Jones faced off with an eight foot tall demon of hulking muscle. But my General was grinning, blood all over a glowing face and teeth. Then, leaping up quicker than was possible Jerali lodged the blade right through the eye of the demon and through into its skull. Jerali landed back down on its other side in a crouch, looking up to see the monster fall with a triumphant grin.

Drake made a sound of appreciation deep in his chest and warmth spread through me.

With the Temari Blade in my hands again, the Warrior Midwives reappeared in the night and readily spread across the field, their weapons at the ready.

"Let me go," I commanded my mate as we descended.

Abruptly he dropped me, and with a cry, I unleashed my lightning with its full force. My own magic took over, keeping me in the sky as I picked off demons left right and centre.

Drake grinned savagely at me, landed on the ground and ran loose, allowing his monstrous side to take over completely.

A wild wind whipped up and I raised my arms, letting a sheaf of lightning swirl above us. Wherever there was a demon, my lightning began to strike of its own accord.

Happy with this, I held the Temari Blade in one hand and a lightning blade in the other. Then I descended right in the middle of the enemy lines and began a dance of blood and death.

"The Reaper is dead!" I shouted, swinging the Temari Blade a wide arc. Demons flew through the air, blasted backwards. I swung again and demons flew even further. "The battle is lost, the Reaper is dead!"

My soldiers let out a cheer where they stood, a renewed vigour encouraging them onwards.

Lightning stuck, flesh burned and demons screamed. And none of us stopped until every single demon on the field lay dead or had fled.

Eclipse Court was massacred, their red crescent standards trampled and bloodied by Black Court soldiers.

It was over within the hour.

FIVE HOURS LATER, I SURVEYED THE BLOODY BATTLEFIELD. THOSE OF us with magic healed as many wounded as we could and gave quick deaths to those who were too far gone. We removed every living person from the field as quickly as we could.

Drake and the other fae worked tirelessly alongside the soldiers from Kaalon, Waelan and Traenara, hauling the soldiers from the field and setting up a makeshift infirmary out in the open. Briar and Emery's fathers were experienced in the ways of battle and organised everything with military level efficiency alongside Jerali Jones, General Tarjin and Queen Helene. I'd ordered everyone to kill any wounded demons but to collect any human slaves that had been brought along by the enemy.

I found Briar crying over a pallet in the infirmary section and I raced to him, my heart pounding. Emery's body lay on a pallet, his face corpse white, his body still. I threw myself down by Briar's side and he pulled me into his chest, crushing me and sobbing. The Duke Nightsong came to kneel by us.

"He fought well," Emery's father whispered softly, holding his boy's hand. "He fought so well."

"He did," Briar sobbed.

I nodded, crying into Briar's arms, as the Duke patted me on the back, silently watching over us mourn over his son.

"How did it happen?" I asked, disentangling myself from Briar's arms. "There's no wound?"

"A demon lord blasted a magical attack," the Duke said. "But Emery killed at least fifty demons before…"

I swallowed the lump in my throat as my face crumpled. I knew there would be deaths, how could there not be? But Emery's pale face would be seared in my brain forever. He'd been one of the first fae I'd met at the Mountain Academy, celebrating my wins in combat class, studying and eating meals together. The Duke got to his feet and strode away and a shadow fell over us. Briar and I looked up to see Daxian, grim-faced, staring at Emery. He knelt down next to me and sniffed. Silent tears fell down my face and Briar put his head on my shoulder, clutching Emery's hand.

I sighed, looking around at all the people, humans and fae, working together to heal the injured, console one another and carry the enemy to be bunt at the side of the field. I suddenly remembered that there was still something in my pocket. I reached in and pulled out the squishy, bloody eyeball of the Reaper's that I'd clawed out of him. Briar gave a shout and pulled away from me while Daxian frowned down at the thing in my palm. I shrugged as I looked up at his one eye. "I felt that you were owed an eye and the Reaper had six...." I offered it to him. His eyebrow shot up as he took it from my palm, the corners of his mouth twitching. "My sister shot out all his eye sockets, I can't feel any of his magic in it, so it's safe."

"You're a strange woman, Saraya," Daxian's eye glimmered. "But I'll take this as compensation for all the grief you've given me."

I gaped at him aghast. "What grief?"

He smirked and pocketed the eyeball. "A broken engagement, for one." He stood up and looked down at Emery's body, before bending down to pull the sheet over his face. Taking a deep breath, he said, "But, friends, we must mourn after we've helped the living. Come on Briar, your father needs our help."

AMONG THE ENEMY'S DEAD, I CAME UPON THE BODIES OF HALVEM and Yarnat, Glacine's guards. Someone had killed them, though I'll never know who. I wasn't upset by that. A lot of blood had been shed tonight, and they had deserved their deaths as Glacine did. For my part, I was just happy to have fulfilled my vow to my father.

Sarone had found Marissa and Tenna, Glacines henchwomen, and had them on their knees, bound and gagged for me to judge.

"I found them sneaking inside the city pretending to be Lobrathians," she said irritably. "What do you want done?"

"They'll both live their days in the dungeons," I said mercilessly. "They helped Glacine do the unthinkable in the demonlands. A life sentence is well deserved."

Sarone nodded, yanked them to their feet and took them toward the palace.

Feeling Drake behind me. I turned and he put an arm around my shoulders. I was thoroughly spent and ready for a good meal and sleep. There would be more work to do yet, but we needed a rest for the moment. Jerali Jones, Lysander, Slade, and Daxian were looking weary too.

Turning around to look for Altara, I found her bandaging a soldier's wound, a tall man standing by her. Terribly handsome, muscled, with a small point to his ears. The eagle had disappeared. Then two other males appeared, having strode in from the other side of the field. They were similar in height to Altara's friend and bearing an unmistakable similarity in energy, but not in appearance. They were self-assured, built like warriors.

"Who is that with Altara?" I frowned as I asked Drake.

"A...friend of hers, we can ask about it later." He began tugging me away towards the palace.

"No, but I must know." I tried to pull away, but Drake held me firm.

"He's her mate."

Shock spun through me. I made to stomp over there and ask who exactly who he was. "Her *what*? I demand to know—"

"Give them a moment, my love," Drake cooed at me. "We may spend as much time with them as we like later. I'm sure they have a story to tell us, just as we do."

"I suppose you're right," I said begrudgingly. Looking around at the battle field, we had more important things to do than demand to know a man's entire ancestry. Was he even a man? Goddess! What *had* she been doing at that blasted school?

An Ellythian General walked up to me, wiping blood from her face. Her plated armour shone with a magical light and her eyes swirled a magical blue. "Your Majesty," she said in a deep voice, bowing. "Queen Cheshni sent us."

I found Sarone at my elbow. "General Reeta?" She said in disbelief.

The General's eyes widened, before she bowed again. "My Lady Sarone? Is that...it cannot be!"

"Dear Goddess!" Sarone let out a short laugh as she grabbed the General and embraced her roughly. Embarrassed or in shock, the General could not find her words. "I'm alive," Sarone said. "We were in Havrok's Court until Saraya saved us." The General looked at me with horror.

I gave her an apologetic smile. "Thank you for coming. We did not expect it." I glanced at Sarone who nodded.

The General sighed. "Princess Altara was quite convincing and once the Queen...understood, it only made sense to send us to act quickly."

I shook hands with her before Sarone whisked her away to meet the other Ellythians.

Not half an hour later, back in the palace, I was wolfing down a large piece of bread alongside Blythe when Altara came in with her...*mate.*

She grinned and ran towards me. I opened my arms and she hugged me around the neck.

"Oh, I missed you!" she exclaimed, her green eyes tired but lit up with excitement. "Allow me to formally introduce you too—"

"Is that Dacre Liversblood?" came Lysander's loud voice. We all whirled around to see a rather tattered-looking Obsidian mage standing expectantly behind us by the open window. His pet monkey sat on his shoulder and both looked rather windswept.

"Did you just come in through the window?' I asked, horrified.

"Forgive me, Your Majesty," Dacre bowed deeply, sweeping back his long black robes. The monkey hung on to Dacre's ear for dear life. "I am leaving this world for another. I'm taking up tenure at Morktalis, the dark school of magic. There are provisions of securing dark objects there. If you want to be rid of Reaper forever, truly rid of him, then give the Darkmaul Dagger to me and I will take it for safekeeping. I will never let him out. I will swear it on the Temari Blade."

I studied him for a moment, but his tattooed face was earnest. I cast a look at Drake, who was standing next to Chalamey Springfoot and the two Sky Queens. They all cast each other a look before looking towards the Dean of Mountain Academy.

Chalamey looked sternly upon Dacre for a moment and I swear the old mage paled under the tiny fae's speculation. But Chalamey finally gave a single, stern nod of approval. I glanced at Drake and he brought out the heavy black bone.

"I think it's a good idea, Saraya," he said. "We don't want it lying around here, really. And besides, it's my bone. I'll know if he goes back on his word. He knows I would hunt him down and feed him to our new beastly friends here." He nodded at Altara's new friends. One of them bared his fangs at the mage.

Dacre grimaced but was good natured about the threat.

I took out the Temari Blade for him to swear upon. "The further away from here, the better. But…I'm keeping the Eyesmith box." Clementine Eyesmith was a person I definitely wanted available if we ever ran into magical difficulty in the future.

Dacre Liversblood swore upon the Blade of Temari and bowed as he accepted the dagger.

We watched him leave with it, though I made him use the front door.

The room lightened significantly after his exit, and it was as if a great weight lifted off my shoulders. Beaming, I grabbed Altara once again and swung her around.

The sound of her chiming laughter filled my heart to bursting.

# 43
# SARAYA

My coronation fell on the night of a full moon.

In my room, Altara, Lucy, Tembry, Blythe, Tarangi, and Flora helped me dress. I could not help the tears that came to my eyes as Flora brought out my gown.

It was purple Ellythian silk, made by Flora with the help of the seamstress she had apprenticed under in Kaalon. It was a stunning ballgown, fit for a queen. Opal and Altara gasped as Tarangi and Flora hung it between them.

I grinned at the girls.

The gown had a sweetheart neckline that cinched in at my waist and then flared out grandly. But its most beautiful feature was the fine detail on the skirt: fine jewels representing twinkling stars laced with rivulets of lightning.

"I love it!" I breathed. "Oh, Flora, it's perfect."

Flora was overcome with blubbering, so Blythe quickly grabbed her side of the dress and they helped me put it on.

Tembry had always been the best with my hair. She helped me style it, so it was half up, half curling down my back. With elbow-length white silk gloves and the Temari Blade strapped to my hip, I was complete.

The girls all stepped back when there came a knock at the door.

Altara opened the door and stepped back with a smirk at me. Drake stood there, resplendent in a fine blue and silver embroidered vest, black shirt and pants. My heart leapt as it always did when I laid my eyes upon him and my magic stood to attention, wanting to be closer to him, recognising him as mine. I strode up, and he took my hands in his.

His hazel eyes glimmered in the yellow quartz-light. "You are the most precious and wonderful thing in my life, Saraya Volatanius."

I placed my hand on his offered arm and grinned up at him, "I love you, Drakus Silverhand."

"Let us make you a queen."

Grinning ear to ear, we walked down to the throne room. Nerves bubbled in me, though I couldn't even begin to fathom that—I had been through worse, much worse than a coronation. But today was important because for the first time in living memory, I would be the first female monarch of Lobrathia.

Everyone headed to the throne room ahead of me to get into position. Blythe held in her arms both Opal and Fluffy— who was in the habit of licking Opal, who then squealed in delight at the tickle. Shaking my head and smiling, Drake escorted me to the throne room. Outside, through the open doors of the palace, half the city was gathered, awaiting the moment I would emerge as their queen.

I waved as we passed them, and a mighty cheer arose. Drake disentangled himself from me and bowed low.

"I guess this is the last time I get to call you 'Princess,'" he murmured, bushing his lips over the back of my hand.

I sniffed. "I suppose it is, although you know you can call me whatever you like."

He straightened, glancing at the two fae soldiers by the closed doors. "I'll be watching, my love."

"I know."

Drake disappeared around to the side entrance while I waited for my call, taking a shaky breath.

"Deep breaths, Your Majesty," one of the fae warriors said shyly. I recognised him as one of Drake's warriors— Captain Callan.

I smiled at him. "I will take that advice. Thank you, Captain."

Remembering the first time I'd ever laid eyes upon the fae when Daxian and his family had first come to Quartz for my engagement, I chuckled to myself. I had thought I was leaving Lobrathia forever to rule a distant foreign land with an unknown Fae King. Now, a fae was coming to live here, married to me, as I ruled Lobrathia.

A series of trumpets sounded, and outside, the crowd roared. I controlled my expression and straightened my spine just as the doors were pulled open.

The throne room was packed.

At its end stood Agatha, looking beautiful in a glittering new gown of silver.

Ordinarily, the High Priest of the Father's temple coronated the king. But that wasn't right for me at all. I wanted Agatha to coronate me. It felt only right that one of the eldest women in the city should anoint me as its ruler. A woman who had helped birth not only me but so many of the people of Quartz. Now she would be here for the birth of me as a queen.

I walked down the brand new crimson carpet. It had been sent from Ellythia, made from the finest no-stain material. The hall had been repainted and the glass windows at the back repaired from when they'd been smashed in by the invading demons. Decorations of purple flowers and pink lotuses lined the walls and red carpet, and it smelled like my mother as I walked towards my midwife mentor. I smiled at Briar and his father standing proudly together, and Emery's father, Duke Nightsong, with his mourning band around both biceps. He gave me a small smile and I returned it.

Jerali Jones stood next to Agatha, my General in a new ceremonial uniform of navy blue and silver, complete with a sword. Altara stood next to Drake, along with my honorary Order of Temari initiates—Sarone, her eyes burning with pride, Elya, Hemali, and Uma. Altara's mate stood nearby along with the delegates of the foreign nations. Daxian, Queen Helena, Adlain, soon to be coronated and King Omni. The other rulers rarely came to a coronation, but that, it seemed, like so many other things, was to change.

As I came to stand before Agatha, Altara brought forward a purple velvet cushion upon which my official crown rested. It had been specially made for me with rare iridescent quartz hidden deep in our quartz reserves. Lysander had taken them to Sky Court where fae jewellers shaped a band of diamond moons upon which the shards of quartz rested. It was studded with diamonds and sparkled brilliantly under the throne room chandelier.

It was then that all the lights in the hall went out. Immediately I stood and whirled around.

A cold wind struck the hall, and people gasped. The warriors put their hands on their swords. Jerali Jones came protectively to my side. Then the very air became charged with an enormous static power and everyone fell silent as time seemed to stop.

A figure appeared silhouetted at the throne room entrance. By her walk, by the cadence of the very air, I knew who it was.

A few of the Ellythians began to weep.

The Goddess Umali walked in as if straight from a Godly battle field. She was haloed in her own blue-violet light, her midnight skin was bare, long black hair was wild, a long garland of skulls graced her neck, and she held a bloody, jagged sword.

The Ellythians fell to their knees first, followed by everyone else except me. I was frozen in place by some magic, tears springing from my eyes. Umali's bright eyes held mine as she sauntered towards me. Her magic caressed mine, pressing on me with sheer, terrible power. The wild magic in me responded with delight, dancing around me, swirling upwards.

When her voice reached my ears, it was as if the ocean were crashing right here, in this room.

*A queen is to be born today. And Umali's chosen must be ordained by Umali. Tell me, Saraya, Princess of Lobrathia, do you know rage?*

Umali stood before me, resplendent in her light, terrible in her form. And though I wanted to, I could not sink to my knees. My High Priestess mark burned on my forehead.

"I do," I said, my voice surprisingly stable. "I've known it all my life. I've known it to destroy my enemies and free the people of my Kingdom and the Human and Fae Realms.

When Umali smiled, her red lips parted to reveal her bone white incisors. My heart shuddered in my chest. She whispered only for me. *You have served well. Kneel before your teacher.*

Between one breath and the next, Umali disappeared. I whirled around to see her standing beside Agatha, who'd gone as white as a sheet, her gnarled hands trembling, just a little.

I dropped to my knees, my gown flaring around me. Above, I felt Agatha shakily take the crown from the pillow Altara held.

No one else made a sound, frozen by fear or awe. Agatha held the crown in the air.

*Speak your vow.*

I took a deep breath and entered myself. These were, possibly the most important words I would ever say in my life. I spoke so everyone would hear. "I vow to serve the Kingdom of Lobrathia, its people, its land as a just and wise ruler. I bear no bias. I pledge my life for my Kingdom. I live to serve the people of Lobrathia as not only one of their midwives but as their fair and just monarch."

In that voice like thunder and rain, like a tempest storm, Umali spoke again. *Then I announce you as Her Royal Highness Saraya Yasani Voltanius, Queen of Lobrathia, High Priestess of the Order of Temari, bearer of the Temari Blade and Umali's Chosen.*

I bade my tears to stay behind my eyes as Agatha rested my crown atop my head.

*May you reign long, fair and justly.*

My exhale was long and terribly slow.

Magic rushed through me, filling my veins, binding me to the throne. Binding me to my oath.

*There is another vow in your heart, Queen Saraya Voltanius.*

I looked up at her and gulped. "Yes, Goddess, thank you."

She bowed her head in approval and I turned to look at Drake. Perhaps in response to the Goddess' violent magic, my mate's eyes had turned black again, but this time, they sparkled with bright purple lights.

Agatha and Altara stood back and Drake stepped forward. Even before a full blooded Goddess, Drake's power made him seem huge. Darkness swirled behind those eyes and his magic reached out for mine. We stood, side by side before Umali.

I unsheathed the Temari Blade from my hips, and holding it horizontally in my palms, I swore. "Drakus Darkcleaver Volta-nius." The corners of Drake's lips quirked up wards but he regarded me seriously when he realised what I intended. "Son of Wyxian Darkcleaver. Son of the Black Widow, Lily Silverfoot, the first Queen of the Fae." A few people gasped as this was new information to most fae and humans. "I claim you as my mate, from this day forward until the end of the time. I vow to love you, to protect you, to honour you, to stand by your side forevermore. And I swear it on my mother's name, on my father's name, the Blade of Temari, and on the Goddess Umali."

Drake's eyes glistened as he looked upon me. He had already made his vow long ago, in Havrok's Court. Declared his love for me many times. But he held his hands out for the Blade and accepted it reverently.

"Saraya Yasani Voltanius, I will serve you as your husband, as your protector. I will love you with every fibre of my being. I will trust you, honour you, and if you ever forget how perfect you are, I will be there to remind you each and every time. In this life, and every life that comes until the end of time."

I bit back tears as the blade disappeared from Drake's hands and appeared in Umali's. We turned to face her and she stepped towards Drake. I stepped back as Drake sunk onto his knees looking up at Umali in awe, his handsome face serious.

Umali's voice, as if recognising Drake's magic, took on a hint of fiery sharpness. *I appoint you, the Fireborn Drakus Darkcleaver Voltanius, King-Consort of Lobrathia. May you serve this Kingdom well.*

Drake bowed his head as Umali touched each one of his shoulders with the Temari Blade. Out of nowhere, lightning struck Drake's head—to his credit, he did not flinch—and his crown appeared on his dark hair. Black Quartz set with silver moons, a mirror of my own.

With a flash, the Temari Blade was gone and reappeared back in its golden sheathe at my hip.

Then Umali looked at me dead in the eye, a crackle of lightning fluttered over her face and she smiled.

*Long live the Queen.*

Between one breath and the next, she was gone, and the lights came back on.

Everyone seemed to take a collective breath of relief. The weight of the presence of a Goddess is never an easy one to bear.

I turned around and found Drake standing by my side. "Long live the queen!" he shouted.

The entire hall let out a resounding "Long live the queen!"

I grinned in relief at everyone and Drake took me by the hand, leading me out of the throne room and onto the palace steps where the people of Quartz awaited. The crowd let up a cheer when they saw us and when Drake swept me into his strong arms and kissed me, the cheer became a roar.

THAT NIGHT, DRAKE, MY ORDER OF TEMARI INITIATES, AND I WENT outside the palace with the Temari Blade. Outside, Arishnie awaited me with Epelthi, Silent Tara, and the hundred-odd warrior midwife ghosts. I presented her my sword, holding back tears.

"We did it," I said to my warrior mentor.

She grinned at me and bowed low. "I'm so proud of you, Saraya. I knew all along you were capable of this."

I nodded as I tried to compose myself. "The Blade will go back to Ellythia, with Altara, where it belongs."

"You make a wise and worthy queen already," Arishnie said in a choked-up voice. "Who would have thought? A Midwife-Queen at the seat of Quartz?"

The ghosts let up a quiet cheer and I grinned at them. "We

cannot thank you enough. Thank you for showing up in the middle of the night in a fae camp a year ago."

Arishnie laughed.

"I wish I could hug you." I held back my tears. "And I'm glad I could do the Order proud."

Arishnie could only nod.

"Go," I sniffed and looked out at them all. "Be at rest now. You've served long and well even in death. You deserve peace. We'll take care of it from here."

Armour glinted in the moonlight as the Warrior Midwives bowed low, and I couldn't help it, I curtseyed back.

When I rose backup, they had faded away into the night, leaving nothing behind.

Sarone and Elya were crying and hugging Blythe, who'd also burst into tears. Uma and Hemali were breathing shakily, looking up at the full moon.

When we went back inside, to my surprise, Xenita Darkcleaver was waiting with Daxian, still wearing his eyepatch. She was holding her babe in her arms, now two months old and gurgling happily in her mother's arms. I walked over to them, unsure of what to say.

"We came to get the Blessing of the High Priestess of the Order of Temari," Wyxian's widow said seriously. "If you'll give it."

I had not yet been asked for such a thing. Taken aback, I laughed and nodded. "Of course, what did you end up naming her?"

Xenita smiled. "Lotus. In honour of the woman who saved her life. And our entire Court."

The smile fell off my face as I was taken by surprise. My throat closed up as the unexpected emotion overwhelmed me. Drake took my hand and squeezed it.

Fighting tears, I laid my hand upon the baby's tiny head. "Well, sweet Lotus Darkcleaver, may you live a long and happy life and serve your people well. Just as your eldest brother has."

Drake put an arm proudly around me as his half-brother gave me a grin.

# EPILOGUE: SARAYA

The Blossom Court sun shone comfortingly on my face and the sweet smell of magical flowers tickled my nose. The Valley of the Jacarandas bloomed bright and brilliant shades of purple and violet. The massive thousands of years old trees standing proud and sentinel as the summer wind whispered through their leaves.

I grinned at Drake as he came to stand next to me in front of the giant golden gates that would allow us inside. We'd journeyed here with a full guard, Lysander and Slade flanking us. Behind them stood Altara, in a brilliant pink gown, waiting patiently for her turn.

It was time for Mother Jacaranda to give me my post coronation prophecy.

We all wore full regalia including my quartz crown. I wore my favourite purple gown, more of an ode to the Mother Jacaranda this time, complete with a sash of electric blue Ellythian silk, embroidered with the Voltanius lightning crest.

The magnificent gilded gates, which had stood for thousands of years, depicted the first king and queen of the fae, bordered by grand trees. I eyed Drake knowingly as the magical gates swung silently open of their own accord.

Swallowing my nerves away, I clasped my hands in front me and swept through onto an ancient path of stone. Massive Jacaranda trees in a full forever-violet bloom stood as a guard of honour either side of the path. Ancient forces fizzled through the air and my magic soared out of me, meeting it happily in a merry waltz. My heart pounded as I beheld the Mother Jacaranda, waiting, queen of all trees at the end of the path. She was huge, easily the biggest tree I'd ever seen and the sight of her took my breath away. I craned my neck to see the top of her broad branches, spanning like wings outwards, dressed with those impossible violet leaves.

The wind seemed to sigh around me and her sweet scent filled my nose. Then a voice like deep earth and summer wind rumbled through my very bones. *"Who approaches?"*

I took a deep breath as I came to stand in front of her. In a deep curtsey, I said "It is I. Saraya Yasani Voltanius, Umali Chosen, High Priestess of the Order of Temari, Queen of Lobrathia."

*"Come forward, child of lotus and lightning,"* breezed that old voice like rustling branches. *"Let me see on the far winds what comes. What omens travel through time and space."*

Goosebumps erupted all over me as I struggled to steady my breathing. What verdict awaited me? Would it be about my children? About Drake? About the Reaper?

The Mother Jacaranda tree shivered her mighty boughs, the purple blooms dancing and catching the light of the warm sun. I clasped my hands nervously as she deliberated.

Finally, she sighed and in that voice of summer and ancient things, she said, *"You and your mate will stand tall on the helm of Lobrathia and your combined powers will benefit not only this realm, but other realms."* She sighed contentedly, as if she had waited centuries to breathe the words. *"You and your mate will reign long and well, my Queen."*

THE END

OF

THE WARRIOR MIDWIFE TRILOGY

# EPILOGUE: DRAKE

It was dusk, in the middle of spring in Quartz when Saraya met me in the forest outside of the city walls. She wore a deep green dress the colour of her eyes and a playful smile on her lips. The fae diamond necklace and drop earrings I'd given her as a coronation gift sparkled under the light of the half moon. As always, the moment she came into my view I found myself breathless and in awe that this woman was my wife. That she was a Queen and just as importantly, that she was all mine.

I swept a dramatic bow under the sticky trees, "My Queen."

She chuckled and gave me a swift curtsey before looking around with raised brows. "And what are we conspiring about tonight, my King-Consort?"

I quickly placed a finger to my lips, casting wide eyes around us. "Be careful, they're listening." And before she could reply I grabbed her around the waist and pulled her in towards my chest. Bringing out my shadow-wings I leapt up into the cool air and straight upwards into the trees above. Landing softly onto a wooden platform high above the forest floor, my wife's eyes went impossibly wide.

*"You didn't!"* she said in a hushed voice.

I buried my nose into her neck and inhaled her comforting sweet cinnamon scent. "I did."

But she pushed me away and strode around the new treehouse I'd built with my bare hands over the past week. It was a smaller version of my house in the Black Grove, but it was cozy, with smooth wood panels, a sloping roof and most importantly, a very large comfortable bed complete with velvet blankets and soft pillows. It was open on one end, with a perfect view of the western aspect of the city, perfect for sunset viewing.

And I planned to watch many sunsets here with my mate. Saraya strode to the railing I'd built against the open section, looking at her city as the quartz lights lit up in response to the growing dark.

"Oh Drake," she whispered, a hand over her heart.

Warmth blossomed through me at her approval. I came up behind her, wrapping my arms around her stomach and pulling her close. She leaned her head back on my shoulder and looked back at me. "This is so perfect," she breathed.

I stroked her cheek with a knuckle. "I needed a means of getting you away from everyone, where it was just us, but not so far that we would be away from the children."

Her lips quirked up at the mention of who I'd been calling the 'children', namely Fluffy and Opal, who pined after Saraya if they were away from her for too long.

"Jerali will have a fit if we're out too long," she said pointedly.

"Oh Lobrathia's General is fully aware that you've been kidnapped by me for the night. I had to make sure everyone was aware. I don't want to find a knife angled at my throat in the middle of the night." I chuckled at the thought.

"Oh Drake."

The way she drawled my name made the monster in me peek at her and I felt my eyes clouding into that all-black.

Her voice was low and seductive. "The only person capable of putting a knife at your throat without you knowing is *me*."

My entire body hardened with desire. I growled as I held her tight and leaned down to bite her neck lightly, her breasts heaving as she gasped. "I'm going to fuck you over this rail, sweet wife, and I want to hear you call my name as we look over your city."

She let out a sigh and I rapidly undid the fine ties at the front of her dress, sucking on her neck, tasting her soft skin.

Gods, this woman was like no other. She made my entire body light up like Quartz at night, bringing out a possessiveness and raging lust that I'd never thought possible. Her dress slipped to the floor and I almost moaned when I saw the delicate lace underwear cupping her beautiful round behind.

She cast me a playful look over her shoulder and made to turn around but I grabbed those luscious hips and fell to my knees. I nudged her legs outwards and growled deep in my chest as I buried my face right into her ass. She made a surprised sound of pleasure as I licked and sucked at her precious core, her moisture encouraging me on, the monster in me taking over. When I licked my fingers and found her clitoris she gasped my name and I grinned against her wet heat, my tongue working my way around her delicious, delicate folds. The sound of her pleasure was like drug to me, and heat speared through my cock as it jerked in anticipation.

She pressed herself back into my face and I moaned my agreement, lapping up the feeling of her innermost folds. I squeezed her beautiful rear and jumped to my feet.

My voice was little more than a rasp as I murmured against

her neck and unlaced my pants. "I need to be inside you, my mate."

"Oh, yes," she gasped, arching her back, pressing herself impatiently against me. "I need you to come inside me."

By all the Gods, I couldn't dream of a more perfect woman. I tore off my shirt and kicked off my pants, running my hand over the smooth brown skin of her back. My mate was strength incarnate and I couldn't help but kiss her shoulder blades in reverence. She healed herself and in many ways, healed me too. I fisted my cock in one hand, sliding the crown along her wet sex. She mumbled in pleasure, leaned back towards me.

I captured her lips with mine, shoving my tongue deep in her throat, wanting more. I just couldn't not get enough of her, the way those soft lips parted for me was heaven, her tongue seeking pleasure from my mouth. I shoved my hard length into her and she moaned.

"Mine," the monster in me growled against her neck. "Tell me you're mine."

She moaned back at me as I sunk myself in all the way to the hilt, stretching her out slowly, just the way she liked it. I'd studied her every breath, her every moan, her every curve in these last few weeks, and each time, I discovered something new that I loved about her. I squeezed her breasts, rubbing my thumbs over her taut nipples as I thrust into her.

"I'm yours," she gasped, shuddering with pleasure. "Only yours."

The monster rumbled in deep approval and began to thrust in long stokes, savouring every inch of its mate.

The city was lit up now, all the quartz lights twinkling in their many colours. I jerked inside of her, grumbling with my own pleasure and she cried out, gripping onto the rail. Hurriedly she covered her mouth and looked back at me in alarm.

I grinned savagely and kissed her cheek, still moving inside of her. "I put a shield around," I said gruffly. "No one will see or hear us."

"Oh, thank the Goddess!" she moaned as I thrust into her roughly, reaching down to circle her sweet clit. I pounded inside of her, my skin slapping against hers in a way that made her cry out and buck against me. I wanted more of her than my hands would allow, so my magic leapt around her, stroking her skin of her neck, her shoulders, her thighs. She shivered in pleasure, her magic joining in the dance, pulling closer, making me grind against her, the deep rooted parts of our souls seeking each other out, wanting their own union. Tingles swept up my core and and I felt it happen in my mate's body too.

She cried out as she had her release, her inner muscles clenching and unclenching around my cock as I joined her in oblivion, roaring her name as my vision blacked out with the enormity of the pleasure. I held her tight and shuddered as I emptied myself into her.

She sobbed my name, gripping onto the railing and I held her tight against me, murmuring sweet words into her hair. "I love you, sweet Saraya."

She leaned back into me, placing her hands over mine as her High Priestess mark burned brightly. "Mmm, I can't imagine doing any of this without, you Drake."

It made my monstrous heart swell to the size of the moon.

Afterwards, as she lay in my arms and I fed her the strawberries and fresh cream I'd brought along, she licked my fingers clean and said. "How many children should we have?"

I froze. As still as a block of ice, only my insides were heating up. Children. Me, a father? A stupid smile spread across my face and I squeezed her tight. My mate wanted my children. I imagined a miniature version of Saraya, running around the palace with a practice sword, chasing Opal and Fluffy. I could get a zekar foal for her to learn to ride, Jerali Jones would start teaching her sword play straight away, and I would teach her hand to hand combat. Excitement buzzed within me, like a hoard of bees racing under my skin.

"Any number, anytime." I said immediately. "Anytime. Just tell me when and I'll fill you up twelve times a day."

She chuckled. "Not yet. I'm not quite ready. We still have a lot of work to do in the city with the refugees and figuring out how to raise these half demon children and infants from Havrok's Court. But maybe in a couple of years. I'd like a few I think."

A few of the women from Havrok's Court had been pregnant when they arrived in Kaalon. Most of them had moved to Quartz to be closer to Saraya's help after the battle. Many of them had terminated their pregnancies with Saraya's help, as the physical risk to them was too big. But a small few had wanted to keep their pregnancies, so we now had the task of protecting them in birth and then raising the children.

If anyone knew about having a rough childhood, it was me.

Once, the prospect of the future had felt like a barren wasteland to me. It had stretched out, unrelenting and torturous.

But now? Now, this feeling in my chest had me wanting to leap out of this tree house and fly around the city with joy. With Saraya by my side, I knew we would both be happy. And with children? With the ability to create a place of safety where not only our children, but the children of the city could grow under careful and loving care?

Not in the whole universe could I imagine anything better.

Thank you for coming on Saraya and Drake's journey with me. I really hope you enjoyed this finale.

Thankfully it's not *quite* over yet.

Join me for Altara's story in: The Archer Princess (Book #1 of The Archer Princess Trilogy). Order your copy at your favourite bookstore, or my website at www.ektaabali.com/shop.

For updates on Altara's story, sign up to the email newsletter at:

www.ektaabali.com/warriormidwife

Signing up to my mailing list means that you get first peek at everything I produce, including book covers, new releases, exclusive excerpts and bonus material that I don't post anywhere else.

# ACKNOWLEDGMENTS

This trilogy was a whirlwind! From start to finish we did it in less than six months. My thanks is not only for this entire book, but for the whole series.

Thanks to my mum, for her help in packing pre-orders, her support when I was tearing my hair out, for her shoulder to cry on.

Thank you Rachna, constantly cheering me on and being a source of wisdom and advice.

To Sheree, my hype woman, for bullying people into reading my books and for everything else you do for me! I don't even have the words to explain how thankful I am to you.

To Carly, for her extraordinary level of talent with these covers. Honestly I couldn't have asked for better. Readers display these books on their shelves because of you!

To my copyeditor, Maryssa for this series. Despite challenges you always pull through and give me wonderful feedback.

Once again, a massive thank you to my fae-eyed proofreaders: Sheree, Breanna, Amy, Siobhan and Beth. You guys are all amazing and I owe each of you a tremendous level of thanks.

To my readers, thank you for coming with me on this ride and for supporting a small Aussie indie author like me.

# ALSO BY E.P. BALI

**NA Fantasy**

**The Ellythian Princesses:**

*#1 The Warrior Midwife*

*#2 The Warrior Priestess*

*#3 The Warrior Queen*

*#1 The Archer Princess*

*#2 The Archer Witch*

*#3 The Archer Queen*

**YA Fantasy**

**The Travellers:**

*#1 The Chrysalis Key*

*#2 The Allure of Power*

*#3 The Wings of Darkness*

**Middle Grade Fantasy**

**The Pacific Princesses:**

*#1 The Unicorn Princess*

*#2 The Fae Princess*

*#3 The Mermaid Princess*

*#4 The Tale of the Three Princesses*

Lightning Source UK Ltd.
Milton Keynes UK
UKHW041830010922
408208UK00009B/163/J